I0583268

BARRY RAINWATER

BARRYRAINWATER.COM

2525: Gardens and Creeks

Barry Rainwater

For permission requests, contact www.barryrainwater.com

Library of Congress Cataloging-in-Publication Data
Rainwater, Barry.
2525: Gardens and Creeks / Barry Rainwater — First Edition.
p. cm.

ISBN 979-8-9987809-0-5 (paperback).
ISBN 979-8-9987809-1-2 (hardcover, case laminate).
ISBN 979-8-9987809-2-9 (hardcover, dust jacket).
ISBN 979-8-9987809-3-6 (ebook).

Library of Congress Control Number: 2025908786

This is a work of fiction.
Names, characters, places, and incidents are either the product of the author's imagination or used fictitiously. Any resemblance to actual events, locales, or persons, living or dead, is entirely coincidental.

Published by BLR Press LLC
Bradenton, FL, USA

Cover design and interior formatting: Mark Thomas/Coverness.com

Genre: Science Fiction / Dystopian / Philosophical / Hard Science / Romance
Themes: Artificial Intelligence, Genetic Engineering, Robotics, Futuristic Societies, Speculative Worldbuilding, Collectivism, Ecology, Survival.

TABLE OF CONTENTS

PLAYLIST i

PROLOGUE v

CHAPTER ONE: TELL US A STORY 1

CHAPTER TWO: THE RESIDENT 5

CHAPTER THREE: THE CEREMONY 17

CHAPTER FOUR: A NEW PURPOSE... 34

CHAPTER FIVE: THE PEOPLE 52

CHAPTER SIX: THE BEST OF FRIENDS 70

CHAPTER SEVEN: A HATCH 72

CHAPTER EIGHT: THE COUNCIL 88

CHAPTER NINE: AN EXPEDITION 99

CHAPTER TEN: THAT RABBIT 116

CHAPTER ELEVEN: THE TREATMENT 118

CHAPTER TWELVE: THE APPRENTICE... 128

CHAPTER THIRTEEN: A SHAFT 145

CHAPTER FOURTEEN: ANOTHER TOUR... 163

CHAPTER FIFTEEN: THE ONLY ONE.. 182

CHAPTER SIXTEEN: A HIGH PERCH 184

CHAPTER SEVENTEEN: THE CHEAHA 197

CHAPTER EIGHTEEN: STASIS 210

CHAPTER NINETEEN: ANOTHER CEREMONY 230

CHAPTER TWENTY: THE STOWAWAYS... 247

CHAPTER TWENTY-ONE: TELL US ANOTHER.. 261

CHAPTER TWENTY-TWO: THE ESCAPE... 264

CHAPTER TWENTY-THREE: A WATERFALL 277

CHAPTER TWENTY-FOUR: LOST... 290

CHAPTER TWENTY-FIVE: THE ARROW 305

CHAPTER TWENTY-SIX: A CLEANSE 326

CHAPTER TWENTY-SEVEN: STATUS REPORT 334

CHAPTER TWENTY-EIGHT: A MEADOW.. 338

CHAPTER TWENTY-NINE: THOSE EYES... 343

APPENDIX *345*

    ARCOLOGY *347*

    COUNCIL OF SAGE *348*

    ARCOLOGY *348*

    RESIDENTIAL SECTORS *349*

    RESIDENT' SNOURISHMENT MENU *350*

    EXPERIMENTAL NOURISHMENTS *352*

    ARCOLOGY STRUCTURE *353*

    GLOSSARY OF TERMS *355*

    THE PEOPLE'S LANGUAGE *362*

COMING SOON *369*

ABOUT THE AUTHOR *371*

PLAYLIST

For your added pleasure!

Intro: *In the Year 2525 (Exordium & Terminus)* - Zager & Evans

Chapter 2:   *Afternoon Delight* - Starland Vocal Band

Chapter 3:   *Love Potion No. 9* - The Searchers; *Sugar Sugar* - The Archies;
                  Bali Ha'I - Orchestra 101 Strings; *Venus* - Shocking Blue

Chapter 4:   *Nights in White Satin* - Moody Blues

Chapter 5:   Your favorite Stomp Dance and Pow Wow songs.

Chapter 6:   *White Rabbit* - Jefferson Airplane

Chapter 8:   *Europa* - Santana; *Sleepwalk* - Santo & Johnny;
                  Albatross - Fleetwood Mac; *In Dreams* - Roy Orbison

Chapter 9:   *Spirit in the Sky* - Norman Greenbaum

Chapter 11:   *Strawberry Fields Forever* - The Beatles

Chapter 12:   *Welcome to the Machine* - Pink Floyd

Chapter 13:   *Hair* - The Cowsills;
                  We Gotta Get Out Of This Place - The Animals

Chapter 14:   *The Good Life* - Tony Bennett

Chapter 16:   *She's a Rainbow* - Rolling Stones;
                  Let the Sunshine In - Jennifer

Chapter 17: *Eagle Song* - Red Shadow Singers

Chapter 18: *I Only Want to Be With You* - Dusty Springfield

Chapter 19: *Mommy's Little Guy* - Fawn Wood;
Memorial Song - Drumming Songs

Chapter 20: *Eight Days a Week* – The Beatles

Chapter 22: *The Sounds of Silence* - Simon & Garfunkel

Chapter 23: *On a Clear Day You Can See Forever* - Peddlers;
I've Got to Have You - Carly Simon

Chapter 24: *Mvskoke Creek Lullaby* - Haskell Institute, Lawrence, KS

Chapter 25: *Space Oddity* - David Bowie

Chapter 26: *Us and Them* - Pink Floyd

Chapter 28: *Wildflowers* - Tom Petty, *Return to Innocence* - Enigma

Outro: *Indian Reservation* - Paul Revere and the Raiders

"The unexamined life is not worth living."

—Plato, *Apology*

PROLOGUE

Centuries had passed since equity defeated free will and animal spirits, collectivism replaced barter and currency, and ecological wisdom supplanted human chaos and mischief. Now, in this enlightened age, after an Anthropocene of overpopulation and plunder, Earth continued to orbit the solar system's barycenter, and the Sun beamed brightly.

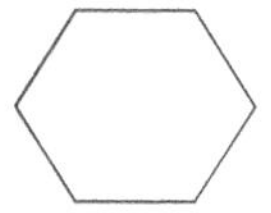

CHAPTER ONE

TELL US A STORY

The old woman pressed her hands against the arms of the chair, steadied her form, and forced herself to her feet. As she did, she stretched her body upward, countering the gravity of her age, feeling every ache along the way—a testament to all the wonderful experiences she had endured over a lifetime.

She paused, secured her footing, and gathered her thoughts as there was much to do, hoping it would be a beautiful day. Now sure, she stepped across the room and lifted a teapot near the fire. Her hands quivered as she poured a cup of dandelion tea, added some sweet cane, and took a sip. She sighed at its soft, warm, toasty flavor, a delicious elixir that soothed her soul and brightened her heart.

Her cup empty, she set it aside, shuffled to the door of her home, and pushed back its cover. The morning light streamed into her eyes, causing her to blink and squint until her aged vision adjusted to its glowing radiance. She smiled, fixed and fluffed her wispy white hair, and stepped outside. The ground beneath her feet felt cool; a gentle wind blew from the east, and the sky was clear, except for a few clouds, light and scattered.

She leaned back and inhaled the fresh summer air. Fragrances of dew-kissed grass, damp soil, and resinous pine wafted through her nose, and all around, people worked, played, and laughed. To her, this was the most beautiful sound on Earth. And then, a moment slipped by, but just a moment, before those who wished to hear stories about the past came running and gathered around.

"Tell us about the possum," a skinny boy said.

"I like the one about the bunny," a little girl countered, tugging at her arm.

"All in good time, but first, I need to stretch my legs. You're welcome to join me if you like."

The old woman strolled across an open yard, past a dogwood, now fully green and absent of its bracts, then down a well-worn path, a trace of red clay and loose sand dotted by patches of broken twigs and trodden leaves. But she was not alone; a dozen followed her, some young, others almost grown, and a few in between.

"How about the wind beast?" a brash boy asked, grinning from ear to ear.

"Or the waterfall story?" an older girl suggested, face blushing red.

"Patience, my dears, patience. After I check my garden."

Trailed by the children, the old woman crossed over a wooden footbridge spanning a small, stony creek. The sun beamed down, causing sweat to pearl on her brow. She went on down a gently sloping path, then a little farther, soon reaching her destination.

The field's fruits and vegetables were ready to harvest. The old woman stepped into its lush, green interior, picked a sun-ripened tomato, and took a bite. Its warm, tart flavor filled her mouth with pleasure and her mind with memories. "My favorite color—red."

"I like that story." A tall girl smiled.

"My grandmother spoke of it many times, but it's a little frightful for the little ones. Perhaps another day."

As the children watched, she picked more tomatoes, a couple of squash, and a mess of beans. She placed them in a cattail basket that hung from her arm.

"How about the caterpillar story?" a little boy asked.

"The people-eater," the brash boy said.

"The bunny, the bunny," the little girl pleaded.

"Now, now, dear. Come, hold my hand, and help me back to my chair."

The old woman, the little girl—skipping ahead—and the rest made their way back to the village. Though the path was short, her daily strolls felt like cherished journeys, quiet reminders of life's fleeting nature. She gazed at the land—an oasis of blue and green, where mountains rose like sentinels, meadows swayed in the breeze, and creeks wove silver threads across the landscape. And at its heart lay her home, a refuge that had sheltered her through countless seasons. And the village, older still, stood steadfast, a silent witness to the unfolding years of her life.

"Bring my chair," she commanded, pausing at the foot of a towering, broad chestnut. The tree, like her, carried the weight of years, its bark thick and furrowed. Its massive trunk hinted at countless rings within—a sign of seasons endured and stories untold.

Two older boys ran inside her home and brought back her chair.

"Set it there, right there." She wiggled her finger at that perfect spot where the tree's sprawling boughs cast shadows over the earth like a soft, cool blanket. "Right there, yes, right there."

The boys placed the chair, positioning it with care.

She shuffled over, lowered herself into it with a sigh, and let the day's weight slip away.

"Tell us a story, tell us a story," the skinny boy begged.

"The bunny, the bunny," the little girl whined, jumping up and down.

"I hear you, dear. I hear you." Her voice was soft, still breathy from the walk. She reached out and caressed the little girl's long, flowing hair. A soft smile, filled with affection and kinship, brightened the old woman's face.

The tall girl handed the old woman a fresh cup of dandelion tea. "How about the sky people?"

"Ah, yes, another one of my favorites, but first, I must gather my recollections. These things happened so long ago, and my mind is not as clear as it used to be. If you'll return at sunset, we'll have something to eat, and I'll tell you a story."

Eyes bright, the children nodded and ran off to play.

The old woman inhaled deeply as a deserved moment of peace swept over her face. The sky was such a pleasant blue, and her tea was warm and sweet, just like she preferred. To the right, a child laughed; in some nearby grass, a cricket chirped, and high in an oak, a warbler sang out.

Soon, a memory formed in her mind. She reached into her pocket and pulled out an old piece of tattered yellow cloth. It, too, was careworn, like the path; its frayed edges bore witness to its age. Its weave revealed a symbol: three lines joined on the ends with a fourth across the middle. Its texture, however, was unlike anything her people would have crafted, reminding her of times past, beloved relations, and cherished stories.

Stories like those her grandmother told, some well-known, others not, a few whispered, and those only the children believed. She spoke as if they were fact, not fiction, but how was that possible? One, for instance, was about a people who lived in the sky. Grandmother said their strange dwelling was so tall it touched the clouds. Many questioned this tale, but none had ever proven it false, for it was said to stand where none dared to wander on the other side of the mountains.

The old woman closed her eyes. Her mind drifted to another time and place, a time of philosophy and experiment, machinery and technology. It was a curious tale, and one that began with a simple morning ritual.

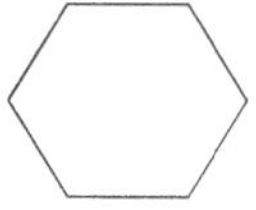

THE RESIDENT

MOON'S DAY, 2525

The lights flickered, signaling the start of day two of eight. A1983AA12 slipped from the polycule's berth before the others stirred and into a cube. A panel clicked open, revealing a hidden compartment.

There it was—small, delicate—alive.

Others called it a selfie desire, an inappropriate covet. A12 called it something else—a wonder.

The scent of earth and green wafted up the resident's celestial-shaped nose—its slender, graceful contours a quiet contrast to the muted gray bulkheads and sterile, conditioned air of Arcology 1983. The flower's binomial nomenclature: *Gaillardia serotina*. A fragment from another world. The Tech had rigged a grow light, and beneath its radiance, bright yellow petals, daisy-like and sunlit, swayed gently in the filtered light. A12 cupped its fragile stalks, leaves tickling the fingers. So delicate. So defiant.

A12 gave the flower a measured sip of water and a whispered promise. No one could ever find it. It must remain concealed.

The resident closed the compartment, stepped into a watatory, and, after a thorough cleanse, slipped into a standard-issue blue jumpsuit marked with Quad-A blue armbands.

A12 exited Polycule AA-21-3, joining the rhythm of regulated life in the Zephyrus Raion. Today, the Tech would inspect Quad-T's lighting systems—a six-hour task. A typical duty day on the Arc.

On the way to the first inspection point, A12 moved without hurry—the passageway's familiarity a kind of comfort, but a quiet reminder of the Arc's limits. Two familiar faces approached.

"I want to feel you." A12 paused to speak with the two faits.

"The pleasure is ours." T30 smiled. "Where're you headed?"

A12 pushed back long strands of curly, coppery hair, exposing electric green eyes. "Quad-T, Ring 21, then on to the rest—same as always."

"You will be on our passageway."

"Yes, I wanted to wish our friend good luck."

"23 mentioned you haven't stopped by."

"I've been busy with duties. I wonder if 23 will have some time for me?"

T89 broke in, "23 always has time for you, fait."

"By the way," T30 said, "23 has a new pleasure augmenter. It's a blast. You might want to give it a go."

A12 grinned. "Thanks for putting ideas in the head. Now, I'll be distracted all morning."

T30 laughed. "Perhaps we should change the subject. Are you going to the Garden Ceremony?"

"I've heard twenty-four residents are on the list," A12 replied.

T89's chin edged up. "We all do our part to serve our community."

T30 patted the mait on the back. "They'll probably make 89 a Sophist."

"A perfect resident," A12 said. "Where would you like to serve?"

"Thanks for the boost." But T89's face remained cool, unfazed by this suggestion of choice. "As our norms espouse, that's not our foresight, nor should we express a preference. We all serve the good."

"Wow. Never heard that before." A12 chuckled. "But what if I did have a preference? How about a Laboratory Tech, a Nutritionist, or a Felicificator?"

"A Felicificator?" T30 laughed uneasily. "You want to do pleasure surveys?"

"The Sophists decide what's best." T89's eyes rolled at the selfie comment. "Personal demands invite chaos."

"Yep, you'll make a great Sophist." A12 shook the head, but felt it best not to argue or say more.

"I'll miss both my maits," T30 said, turning an uncomfortable red. "They've been wonderful. My poly won't be the same."

A12 hugged T30. "You're welcome to visit us anytime you like."

"Thanks. I might take you up on the offer."

"Good luck, 89." A12 smiled. "And speaking of purpose, off to duties, I don't want to keep society waiting."

T30 waved goodbye. "See you at the Ceremony, and have fun with 23."

T89 did the same, albeit with a stiff gesture.

A12 returned the waves and marched off. Yes, it was best not to argue, say more, or express anything selfie. Life was easier that way, less stressful, and what the community expected. A12 fought back an urge to scream, yell, or how about a defiant "Kiss my—" That would have raised a few eyebrows and provided a much-needed emotional release, but not a very friendly sentiment. It seemed most residents, no, all residents, followed the norm; that's how it was on an Arc. As usual, the resident swallowed the feeling, realizing it was better to fake a smile when one was not naturally available. Now, it was time to clear the mind and focus on work.

A12 entered the Main Core—a hive of activity. Its towering design connected dozens of rings, some where raits gathered to socialize and unwind. The space balanced function with charm, featuring white walls, gray decks, and lush green plants that softened its ordered lines, evoking an earthly oasis. All around, floating orbs cast a gentle glow, hues shifting in soothing gradients. Nourishment bars gleamed like islands of abundance, their chromatic fixtures offering synth-crafted delicacies, while modular seating reshaped effortlessly to accommodate any group. More than a gathering space, the Core served as a hub, seamlessly linking residential and operational Raions—a place residents passed through several times daily.

After circling a quarter of the Core's perimeter, A12 turned onto a short bridgeway leading to one of sixteen attached quadrants. As a Lighting Technician, Grade 1, A12 had access to all four within Zephyrus—both for work and leisure.

A12 entered Quad-T. Like the Core, it rose vertically—smaller in scale, composed of four residential rings, each holding a polyhex of six polycules. Its reinforced bulkheads curved subtly, a testament to a balanced design. Self-contained, its systems pulsed faintly—a quiet reminder of the mechanisms sustaining life within. In total, a quadrant housed ninety-six—consistent with a neocortical processing capacity theory positing a cognitive limit to the number of stable social relationships one could maintain.

Along the way, A12 noticed a few raits lingering in their polys, but most had departed, attending to their daily duties. Each resident had a primary purpose—a singular contribution. Purpose expressed one's abilities and supported one's needs. Everyone worked for everyone else, and all performed their duties without hesitation or complaint. No sick days, vacation days, or *I don't feel like working days*. Purpose was necessary, purpose was pleasure, and purpose ensured that Arc1983 functioned as intended, providing raits with a safe and secure ecosystem.

A12 approached the first lighting control panel and opened its cover. Inside were logic controllers, dimmers, relays, and interfaces. A12 marveled at the technology, evidence of the collective's commitment to innovation. Additionally, Quad-T had the most up-to-date lighting systems, including new advanced programming capabilities.

A12 began the inspection, but before the rait touched the first component, neuro-cognitive augmentation cyberpathically deactivated the panel's safety shield, rendering it harmless. A light emitter turned from red to green.

The Tech checked the system to ensure calibration with the Arc's circadian cycle. At daybreak, the technology hummed to life, enveloping the Arc in a soft cocoon of yellows and oranges. During the day, the lights brightened, emitting a more radiant, cooler beam, mirroring the surge of daily activities. In the evening, the lights deepened, painting the surroundings in a palette of purples and pinks. Finally, the technology transitioned to an overnight setting, reminding all that life on an Arc followed the inexorable rhythms of the universe and the passing of another sidereal day—23 hours, 56 minutes, and 4.099 seconds.

With a hand-held meter, A12 tested the system's output signatures. The technology needed to function without error, given that an Arc was an enclosed structure, absent any natural light. However, the Arc's artificial illumination did have a helio-therapeutic benefit, improving mood, productivity, and mental attentiveness. A12 confirmed that all circuits were nominal.

A12 trekked to the first polycule on Ring 21. A familiar sight, it was a hexagon-shaped compartment, ninety-six square cubits in size. At its center was a levitated berth, and on the left, four comfortable leisure cubicles contained educational systems and stowage for issued items such as apparel and work tools. Next to that was a cooler filled with the inhabitants' favorite nourishments. And on the right were two fluid compartments: a lavatory for voiding and a watatory for cleansing.

A12 checked the poly's lighting, which, too, had been programmed to the Arc's solar day. However, inhabitants could temporarily override its settings, permitting a Tactile Entertainment Immersion System—TEIS—to transform the space into a virtual experience, including a mystical forest, an exotic tropical island, a fantasy castle, or dozens of other options.

The Technician stepped around the poly, testing luminosity on various surfaces. A cortical modulator launched an eyetap application, superimposing readings into the rait's vision. Spectrum levels showed the correct mix of blue, green, and red. A12 confirmed 250 lux for general areas and 500 for task areas—perfect. On to the next poly.

• • • •

After completing inspections on Ring 21, it was time for the noon break. A12 returned to the Core, grabbed a drink, found a table, and flopped into a chair. It wasn't long before someone approached—alone time was a rare commodity on an Arc, frowned upon, in fact.

"I want to feel you," the rait said. "May I join you?"

"The pleasure is mine. Have a seat." A12 took note of the identification tag on the rait's jumpsuit. It read A1983AG18.

"What are you having?" G18 asked.

"A Number 4."

"How about that—we have something in common."

"You must be new." A12 smiled.

"I'm a Botanist. Just started orientation this morning. What a bore. I can find a lavatory if I need one."

A12 chuckled. "Well, you never know."

"Really, sweetie? See that bar? There is one like it on every ring and every Arc, in the same place and with the same options."

"At least that's a choice," A12 muttered.

G18 laughed, tugging the neckline of the jumpsuit. "I hear you, sweetie. Blue is not my color. I'm more of a hot pink."

"We have pink jumpsuits?"

"Of course not, sweetie. Like I said, what a bore." G18 finished the drink, setting it down with a thud. The rait stood. "Well, back to the grind. Maybe they'll show me where they hide the candy—I could use a dose about now."

"A double dose," A12 chuckled.

G18 huffed in agreement. "Finally, a fait on my frequency. Perhaps we should get together after work."

"Absolutely."

G18 smiled and strolled away.

A12 finished the mint chocolate mocha and headed to Ring 20. It was refreshing to discover someone with similar willful interests, even if it was just the color of a jumpsuit.

• • • •

After a short walk, A12 stepped into a lift, the mind lingering on the brief exchange with G18. The rait seemed so confident, so effortlessly attuned to the Arc's communal norms—yet beneath that glimmering exterior, a flicker of rebellion had surfaced, faintly mirroring A12's quiet resistance. The lift descended, its mechanical precision at odds with A12's tangled thoughts. A12 straightened, pushing the distraction aside. On an Arc, routine was essential, stability a given, but stepping out of line, even in reflection, could leave one stranded on the outermost edges of belonging.

Arriving at Ring 20, the lift doors opened with a soft hiss, revealing another circular passageway and another six polycules. A12 headed down the passage, each step echoing faintly, the rhythmic hum of the Arc's systems a constant companion. Drawing a breath, A12 refocused on the task and began inspections until reaching the last: Polycule AT-20-6. A12 paused. Someone was inside.

"Good day. I want to feel you," A12 said.

"I want to feel you." The resident sat up on the berth.

"I'm here to check your lighting."

"Is that all?" T23 asked in the dait's usual drawl.

"I wanted to wish you well."

"That was nice o' you."

"Yes, I felt so."

"Anythin' else?"

"I should apologize."

"I can't imagine for what."

"I've been busy with duties."

"You do look a little tired. How 'bout comin' over here and restin' for a spell?" T23 patted the bed. "Maybe you need to defrag, or—"

"My *or* is just fine." A12 sauntered to the bed. "Did anyone ever tell you you ask too many questions?"

"Is that a fact?" T23 repeated the pat on the bed while pivoting a set of laser blue eyes up and down the visitor's curves.

A12 noted the going-over and returned the scrutiny. A1983AT23 had a sexy, dimpled chin and a smile that generated a full megawatt of charm. And, like other residents, had a perfectly edited body, was physically fit, absent any marks or imperfections, and a menu of other fair features, soft or firm, in all the right places. But there were differences: eyes, hair, accessories, voice, and glow, all based on one's preference for the ideal form.

A12 sat on the bed and bounced a time or two. "Comfy."

"How's your day goin'?"

"The usual." A12 reached over and fondled a lock of T23's long, sandy brown hair. A12 recalled the first time seeing that face. It was at a party. T23 was sitting at a bar, looking terribly ignored and needing attention, but there was something about that face and how it brightened the world like the sun, moon, and stars. A12 leaned in and kissed the dait's cheek.

"What's that for?" T23 asked.

"Just saying hello."

"May I say—hello?" T23 clasped A12's chin and kissed the dait's soft, cupid-bowed lips.

A12 giggled.

"Somethin' funny?"

"I believe I felt the Earth move."

"Would you like to go for the universe?"

"Aren't you bold?"

"You inspire me."

"How so?"

"Let me show you." T23 slowly unzipped A12's jumpsuit.

"Looking for something?"

"Inspiration." T23 pulled the interlocking slide fastener a little farther down. "There we go. I found it."

"I guess you did. Let's see what I can find." A12 untied the silky blue belt securing T23's robe. "Oh my. I do inspire you."

Their eyes met, alight with desire, and without hesitation, they helped each other discard their clothing. The two daits embraced in a fiery kiss and softly melted into one another.

After some playful cuddling and petting, T23 said, "Over there, on the edge o' the bed—try that little honey on."

A12 grabbed the pleasure augmenter and slipped it on. The encounter quickly became more intense as the device worked its magic, heightening their physical desires. A frenzied rapture began to build, and, with one dait's legs wrapped around the other, the pulsating toy hummed and hummed, and the passion grew and grew. As the seconds passed, then the minutes, their rhythm intensified, becoming euphoric and rapid. One gasped, then the other. The two daits collapsed on the bed.

"I felt you." T23 drew in a breath, filling the lungs with a full share of processed air.

"I felt you, too." A12 caressed T23's arm. "I might miss this."

"You *might*?"

"Something to ponder." A12's mouth curled into a coy grin. "Should I stay for a while?"

"If you like. How 'bout a drink while you're *ponderin'*?"

"I might have the time."

T23 slipped from the berth and retrieved two nourishments. T23 handed A12 the preferred Number 4; the other was a vanilla blonde.

A12 sipped the drink. "Sweet, but not as sweet as—"

"One more day." T23 choked up a bit.

"Yes, but there's always the chance."

T23 looked away.

A12 sensed the dait's despair. Their friendship had grown close—intimate—beyond what was permitted in this ordered society. A place where words like *privacy, faith, will,* and *property* had faded from memory—or been erased.

Even the word *history* had been quietly removed, as if it had never existed at all.

T23 gazed at A12. "You're special."

"And you're my dearest—" A12 stopped short, as if the heart had missed a beat. The Tech had never said that ancient and now useless word, but the feeling was certainly there. However, it was best not to blurt out such an offense, so instead, A12 held back, not allowing a brittle smile to reveal any true emotions or sentiments. A12 stared into space, finding it hard to be upbeat, searching for a way to escape or discover the proper response, but drew a blank. "I should go."

"If you must." T23 caressed A12's hand.

"I wish I were going with you."

"Seems some things are meant to be."

"Are they?" A12 suspected the dait's words were just a ploy—a cover-up. The eyes gave it away as if they were expressing their regret aloud.

"Good luck." T23 let go of the hand.

"Same to you."

A12 zipped up and stepped to the poly's exit. The Tech glanced back, puzzled why such goodbyes were necessary. Arc doctrines suggested true happiness came from a resident's primary purpose. But now, A12 questioned these norms and wondered if service had instead become servitude.

• • • •

After a few more hours of faithful toil, the six-hour workday ended, and A12 returned to Polycule AA-21-3.

There, the Tech found a happy lot of gay and gleeful maits laughing, carousing, and enjoying some early evening nourishments. A92, a bubbly Logistics Administrator, and A81, an easy-going Structural Inspector, relaxed playfully on the berth. And A67, a quirky Hydro Systems Specialist, sat in a leisure cubicle, researching upcoming events and festivities.

A92 greeted the mait. "I want to feel you."

"The pleasure is mine," A12 said.

"How was your day?"

"Inspections went well. I saw 23, and it appears I have a new friend—a new resident."

"A new fait? How about that." A81 grabbed A92's foot and gave it a tickle.

"G18 is a Botanist!" A12 had to raise the voice to overcome A92's frivolous screeches. "Just started orientation this morning."

A81 continued to wrestle with A92's foot, oblivious to A12's distracted demeanor. Teeth gritted, A81 muttered, "Interesting, but—"

"I sense what you meant. If you'll pause your hard drive, I'll get to it."

"Go on, I'm listening."

A12 forced a smile. "G18 has long wavy black hair, a medium build, and all the right curves in all the right places. Did I mention violet eyes that shimmer like perovskitic light-emitting diodes?"

"Wow, sounds like a keeper." A81 released the foot and flipped over, apparently a bit excited. "We should invite 18—"

A92 pounced on 81 like a mechanical claw plunging down on its catch—a very A92 thing to do. "I can feel what you like."

More laughter and giggles erupted in the poly.

A67 joined the conversation. "I hope 18's blossoms like my water."

A81 and A92 paused, glanced at one another, and shook their heads.

Unable to ignore the humorous claim, A12 teased, "Your water is the best. How could anyone resist?"

A grin enveloped A67's face. The Hydro Specialist was well-versed in water technology, but not so much in interpersonal relations.

As the evening wore on, the four maits continued to razz one another, gossiping about rait's bits and bums until the lights dimmed. A12, however, had one last task.

A12 rolled into a cube, stretched out, and activated its Volumetric Display Generator—VDG. A floating 3D image formed in front of A12's face. It was a capture of the Arc's latest lighting technology, and every thirty seconds, a tagline flashed across its reflection. *Happiness is the path. We depend on others for joy. The secret is not in seeking more but in enjoying less. From each according to purpose and to each according to share. We all serve the good.*

Mercifully, the audio played a different tune, absent any messaging other than pleasure. So, A12's eyes endured the not-so-subtle propaganda while the ears enjoyed the pan flute's soft, breath-filled frequencies.

A12 lay back, seeking another rare moment of solitude. A recent memory popped into the mind. Fingers toyed with the jumpsuit's interlocking slide fastener—*zip-zip, zip-zip*. A grin tugged at the lips—*zip-zip*—then faded. Their time together had been fleeting, just a few months, but their connection had been electric. Yes, their physical rendezvous had been unforgettable, but their bond went much deeper—filled with laughter, stolen smiles, and special moments that turned the mundane into magic. Now, they had said their goodbyes, leaving unspoken truths and the weight of conformity heavy on the mind.

A12 popped out of the daze and peeked around, hoping no one had noticed the knitted brow. The others were fast asleep.

The rait opened the secret compartment and pulled out the *Gaillardia*, a reminder of hidden desires, like the ones the Tech bore for T23, though none as cherished.

Lost in reflection, the rait forced a breath, feeling the day's tension slip away. A12 leaned closer. The little flower was truly a wonder, so beautiful… so selfie.

A12 gave the plant a drink. The water seeped into the soil, leaving a spot and reminding A12 of a similar mark now on the heart.

T23 would soon leave. And so far away. Too much to bear.

"Goodnight, my—"

A12 couldn't say the word.

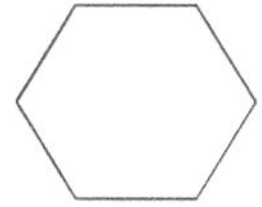

CHAPTER THREE

THE CEREMONY

There was excitement in the air. It was Mercury's Day, and that evening, there was a scheduled event on Arc1983. The Garden Ceremony was a wonderful celebration and transformation in the Arc's life cycle. During the gathering, selected raits would be transferred to other Arcs and assigned new duties, or they might be whisked away to different planets and moons to mine and harvest materials. Some might even have an opportunity to transcend to a new state of being.

As the celebratory hour drew near, A12, A67, A81, and A92 entered the Raion's amphitheater, a white and gray space that extended four rings high and accommodated all 384 Zephyrus residents. Most had found their seats. From Quads A, C, T, and G, all wore blue jumpsuits, but given their assigned armband identifications, they looked more like an intertwined helix of blue, red, yellow, and green nucleotides.

A12 and maits shuffled down a row. The crowd seemed to be in good spirits, not a single sad eye, even though they were about to say goodbye to twenty-four of their friends. Arc life was a shallow affair; lasting relationships were another one of those offensive behaviors, something primitive and narrow-minded.

At 1800 hours, a colorful troupe of mechanicals stepped up to their ceremonial drums and launched into a lively rhythm. As A12 and others settled into their seats, the event came alive with jubilance and expectation, and those assembled broke out in dance, sway, and cheer.

When the roar reached its zenith, a speaker in a golden robe trimmed in black, gray, white, and purple entered the amphitheater and strode to center stage. It was A1983Sυ07—Upsilon 7—a Public Affairs Sophist and a member of the Council of Sage. A golden amulet adorned with a sixteen-point compass hung around the speaker's neck. It glistened in the theater lights like a heavenly star, affirming the Sophist's prominence in society.

Sυ07 marched onto the stage and sat in a single golden chair. The Sophist's deep, intellectual eyes scanned the audience in a glower of affectionate pomposity. Residents' faces gleamed with excitement.

There was one, however, whose glow was not as bright as the others. Like the drums, A12's heart pounded, and the mind raced. *They can't control my feelings. They can't stop me from—* A few months prior, if someone had said this would happen, A12 would have laughed. *What is wrong with me? This isn't right—not the norm.* But losing T23 was more than one could bear. Their attachment had changed everything. So, why did things have to be this way? Doubt had also entered the mind about other Arc norms, like this ceremony. Was it really a celebration or just another act of self-imposed submission to a guardian class? *I wish I could—*

"Hey, mait," A67 said, interrupting A12's stare into oblivion. "Why aren't you cheering?"

"Someone needs a hug." A92 chuckled, bouncing up and down to the beat of the drums.

"Or a shot of candy," A81 teased.

"That must be it." A12 forced a smile, but an emptiness lingered, cold and unrelenting. Memories of shared laughter, fleeting glances, and whispered promises now felt distant—like fading stars swallowed by an endless universe. It was too late. Nothing could be done. Nothing.

The drums stopped, the speaker rose, and for a full measure, Sυ07 stood firm until all were silent except for the hushed rumbles of anticipation.

"Welcome to the Garden!" the speaker boomed.

The crowd cheered and applauded while the colorful mechanicals delivered another rhythmic chorus on their fat red drums.

The Sophist let the energy build, and when the resound had reached its apex, Sʋ07 raised a hand, and the gathered lowered their cheer. "It's been said it's not what we have but what we enjoy that constitutes our abundance. And friends, what we have is our purpose and, most importantly, our pursuit of happiness."

The crowd shouted, "Hear, hear!"

The mechanical performers pounded out another refrain, and that beat, that visceral percussion, was so exhilarating. Raits danced, bopped, and bounced. How could anyone resist? A12's maits were having a wonderful time, and a group of raits to the front looked like they were about to have orgasms. Why not? It was a celebration, an immersive act of harmony, an internalization of the norms, and society's answer to progress.

The Sophist called for attention. "So, my friends, let us heed these words: We must recognize pleasure is innate within us, and from pleasure, we initiate every act of choice or avoidance; and to pleasure, we return, using these desires to seek the good."

The crowd applauded and cheered, and the drummers hammered out another thunderous refrain.

Choice—what choice? A12's stomach did a flip-flop. One could not choose purpose, faits, or even maits. And avoidance? Now that was a novel idea.

Sʋ07 continued, "When we say pleasure is the end and aim, we don't mean an appetite for a willful or selfish life, or desires for individuality, as some have through ignorance or greed. By pleasure, we mean the absence of pain in our bodies and trouble in our minds." The Sophist paused, and the crowd held their breath, anticipating the next line. Sʋ07 stepped around the stage. "You see, it's rather simple. None of us are exclusive spheres. None of us exist without the other. None of us are detached from our environment. Instead, we are a singular logic joined in need and purpose. We all serve the good."

"We all serve the good!" the crowd shouted as one.

"So, my friends, it is not about the glorification of non-productivity through conspicuous leisure or revelry, nor lust, nor enjoyment of an endless and gluttonous buffet. Instead, it is about the pleasure we can bring through service to others."

The crowd rejoiced, "Hear, hear!"

A12 fought back another smirk, lest someone notice an emotion unworthy of the collective. But what harm was a real connection, lasting and profound? Their time together had been a gift, a rare glimpse into something genuine, a source of joy, and an unspoken bond that transcended the superficial and the fake. So, why did T23 have to go, and who was served by this so-called act of goodness? Certainly not A12 or T23.

Sυ07 went on. "Remember this: Do not spoil what we have by longing for what we do not possess. Instead, recognize what we now have was once among the things we only hoped for. So, let us strive to pursue the good through our shared equivalence. From each according to purpose, and to each according to share."

The crowd reveled, "From each according to purpose, and to each according to share."

Sυ07 stepped away from center stage, and the powerful leather and wooden drums resumed their beat.

A procession of twenty-four residents entered the amphitheater and marched onto the stage. Dressed for the occasion, they wore ceremonial robes: blue, yellow, green, and red, shimmering in the forum lights like a rainbow in the heavens.

The speaker returned to the stage. "In closing, my friends, as these residents depart Zephyrus for their new roles, we extend our best wishes for their journey. May they find the same fulfillment and joy in their new assignments that they experienced here with us. Remember, we all serve the good in every aspect of our lives."

"We all serve the good," the crowd echoed, their voices a unified affirmation.

At the back of the stage, a set of ornate doors decorated in star patterns, inset by four bronze frames, opened. The speaker turned and directed the twenty-four to the portal.

In an orderly procession, they marched through, and when the last, including residents T23 and T89, had passed into bliss, the doors shut with a thud. The crowd rejoiced and applauded, and the ceremony ended.

• • • •

A12, A67, A81, and A92 returned to their Quad and entered Galley-A. The space buzzed with energy as faits and daits gathered in groups, their voices mingling in lively chatter and bursts of laughter. A12 wove through the crowd, once again struck by the absence of even a single sad expression. Raits were a malleable bunch, very accepting and very trusting, especially when all followed the norms, and nothing ever ruffled their spirits except when someone didn't follow the norms, and why would someone not follow the norms? Excluding, of course, when a norm inadvertently became a tradition, a cherished belief. That was surely something to avoid or erase. Fortunately, there was never a shortage of passing friends, a deficit of shallow pleasure, or a lack of intoxicating drinks. Controlled abundance was plentiful, rationed equitably, and in the proper proportion.

A12 and maits headed for the bar. Tonight's post-festival theme was another example of the system's generosity, a drinking event where the libations, like everything else on the Arc, were an unassuming and straightforward experiment. The treatment featured four newly formulated nourishments, each offering a flavor combination that had never been experienced before. Smart monitors around the galley would record preferences, analytical systems would evaluate alternatives, and the optimal selection would be added to the Arc's daily menu.

Moreover, a research question posited whether a new stimulant, identified simply as No. 9, would have a positive effect on raits' cognitive and physical state. The experiment aimed to determine whether this aphrodisiac-based neuroenhancer would alter brain chemistry by influencing pleasure and pain receptors. Delta-Class nanobots, infused into the drinks, would navigate the bloodstream to deliver heartsease neurotropics directly to preselected hedonic loci in the brain. When stimulated, neurons would trigger the technology and release its dosage. In some instances, Sophia might activate the treatment.

The four maits collected their drink flights, wove through the crowd, and found a table.

"That was quite the affair," A92 remarked.

"Hear, hear!" A81 raised a drink. "Friends are what life's all about, and tonight, I'm here with my best maits. I liked what the Sophist said about the absence of pain being pleasure."

"Indeed," A92 mused. "Though I've always presumed you liked a bit of pain with your pleasure?"

A81 shot a look. "You know, sometimes you should consider others' feelings before you speak."

"Why? I like being as surprised as everyone else."

A67 laughed, and A12 joined in with a half-hearted chuckle.

A81's cheer shifted into a leer. "Seems someone likes to bust my bolts. We'll have to find out later tonight who likes pain with their pleasure. Now, if you don't mind, let's give these drinks a go."

A12 finally cracked a genuine smile. Those two were always at it, their banter a familiar refrain. A92's infectious energy had a way of pulling everyone into a shared orbit, while A81's measured demeanor kept things grounded. Where A92 thrived on playful teasing, A81's dry wit served as a way to engage without revealing too much. Together, they balanced the other—a whirlwind and a rock, each subtly shaping the dynamics of the poly.

The four maits tasted the first nourishment.

Comprised of split-pea milk, sugarcane juice, sunflower oil, and nutritional additives, it also contained a full measure of metaphoran—known among residents as *meta* or *candy*—a psychoactive compound formulated from fungi, cacti, and plant roots. The drinks undisclosed ingredients included grapefruit rind, mauby bark, cascarilla bark, cassia bark, gentian root, orange peel, cinchona bark, and a hint of ginger.

A12's lips twitched. "This one's strange." The Tech took another sip. "It's got this weird bitter aftertaste, but I like the color. Reminds me of my—" A12 stopped short, cutting off the word—flower. The rait couldn't suppress another genuine smile, recalling that bond, that relationship, at least. A willful determination settled on the face. "Let's try another."

"Right you are," A92 said. "That one's a bit buggered. Might serve better as a metal polish."

A67 was the first to try the next drink. The unknown ingredient was lemon verbena—a perennial shrub whose extract had been mixed with hemp milk, rooibos tea, vanilla, honey, nutritional additives, and meta.

"Much better." A67 smacked the lips. "A hint of lemon. Some honey. An earthy, woody flavor. A malted sweetness. But it looks like pee."

A12 grimaced. "You could have left that last part off."

A92 laughed. "Ever thought of hosting your own tasting party, 67? 'Drinks That Suck'—has a nice ring to it."

"They'd let me do that?" A67 asked with a surprised look.

"That was a tease." A12 chuckled. "Who's next?"

"Looks like it's my turn." A81 lifted the next drink and sipped carefully, swishing and swirling with quiet deliberation. The secret flavors included lucuma, marshmallow, pecan, caramel, and sorghum, along with almond milk, sunflower oil, nutritional additives, and, of course, more meta. "It's good."

"Come on, mait." A92 nudged. "You can do better than that."

"It's creamy."

"*And?*" A92 leaned forward as if expecting a grand revelation.

A81 took another sip, pausing to consider. After a thoughtful moment, the Inspector said, "It's sweet and nutty. I might want another."

"Have you lost a screw?" A92 scoffed. "Remember what the Sophist said about gluttony. It's not about consumption, but how pleasurable your experience."

A12 and A67 chuckled, but A81's halide-gray eyes gave A92 another look of, *I'll get even with you later.*

The foursome moved on to the final formula, a pinkish velvety-looking drink made from strawberry, watermelon, banana, lime, agave syrup, rice milk, and a medley of spices: cinnamon, cloves, and cardamom. Plus, loads of essential nutrients and even more meta.

"It's my turn. Cheers!" A92 gulped down the beverage.

"So?" A67 asked.

"I can taste the colors. They're bright and happy—a kaleidoscope of flavors. But I must confess, it does make the head spin. Or is that the candy?" Cheeks glowing, A92 added, "I'm feeling a bit naughty."

"Pardon?" A81 said. "Isn't that my purpose?"

"Oh dear, I've triggered someone. It seems I deserve a proper spanking for saying such a horrid thing." A92 stroked A81's long brown hair.

"With a hand or a toy?" A81 grinned puckishly.

"Your toy would be pleasant." A92 reached under the table and squeezed A81's thigh.

A81 pushed back from the table. "Is it time to go?"

"Why?" A67 asked, failing to grasp the cue. "This party is just getting started."

"I'm feeling tired." A81 shot a wild-eyed look at A92.

"Are you sure that's what you're feeling?" A12 asked.

"Someone likes my *sugar*." A sly smile appeared on A92's face.

A81's eyebrows shot up. "Keep talking about your sweetness, darling, and we'll have a go right here."

The four maits broke out in laughter, and the party went on, but as parties do, it finally ended.

At 2100 hours, a bell rang, and residents departed Galley-A, ready for some late-evening fun. In this broad-minded society, it was customary for raits to invite others to their quarters, as carnal indulgence was a communal gesture. Some preferred to savor the pleasures of their maits; others sought novelty. The rights of propinquity held that any computation of X and Y was available to any other—paired, triadic, or more. To abstain or restrict was considered selfie, even regressively primitive.

• • • •

A bit tippled from the four meta doses, A12, A67, A81, and A92 stumbled back to their polycule. When they entered, A67 cyberpathically activated the TEIS and selected tropical island mode.

A12's neurosensory augmentation rendered the poly into a mystical isle, blurring the lines between the physical and virtual. The air thickened with the scent of exotic flowers. A salty breeze tickled the skin. Palms rustled overhead, waves crashed, and artificially generated tropical birds trilled and sang. A rich tapestry of colors, enhanced by ray tracing algorithms, cast the sun's warmth, and as if from some distant island, exotic drums began pounding out a sensual beat, summoning the rait's desires like a siren's song: *Come near, come near.* The four maits stripped off their jumpsuits and hurried to the watatory. A12 wiggled the toes. Haptic feedback made the deck feel like soft, warm sand.

Upon entry, an enchanting waterfall cascading down a sultry tropical mountain filled the space with illusions of sight and sound. Hot, volcanized water transformed the cleansing room into a steamy jungle grotto. The four maits danced and twerked like lustful fairies frolicking in a veiled mist. They kissed, touched, and caressed.

A92 gave a neural command, and in the compartment's center, a tantric platform rose from the deck and adjusted to the perfect height. One at a time, they took their turn on the contoured altar, massaging one another's bodies with warm, scented oils. They rubbed and stroked, kneaded and petted. One even received that promised spanking.

As the island whispered, *Let go, let go,* the four engulfed themselves in a melee of pleasurable positions, switching partners at will in a swell of erotic entanglement. Then, at the perfect moment, the height of their physical desires, the Delta-Class nanobots released their No. 9 black magic, delivering euphoric charges deep inside their brains, intensifying their final and climatic Bali Ha'Is.

Exhausted, the four maits consumed a celebratory drink, climbed into their berth, and fell fast asleep.

• • • •

As residents slumbered, however, Sophia was still hard at work analyzing and evaluating the data. Her mechanics hummed, purred, and computed. In short order, a fraction of a nanosecond, really, she had reached a decision: the experiment was a success. Sophia had found an answer to her research question and support for several hypotheses. Likewise, she had improved her understanding of residents' needs and desires, adding more knowledge to her googolflop-sized processing capabilities. It had been a perfect day of progress and experimentation on Arc1983.

• • • •

A few days after the Garden Ceremony, feeling fully recharged, A12 woke, dressed, cleansed, and went straight to the Main Core. The Tech had received a message detailing a special but routine assignment.

Within seconds, A12 spotted the task. G18, the new Botanist, was approaching from the Core's far side. Clad in a tight blue jumpsuit marked by Quad-G red armbands adorned with fiery triangles, G18 strutted confidently as though descending from some heavenly mountaintop. The new fait seemed quite pleased with how its fit accentuated a display of well-proportioned curves.

"I want to feel you." A12 extended a hand.

G18 clasped hold. "At your desire, sweetie."

"Nice to see you."

"Likewise. And might I add, I enjoyed our conversation the other day. Now, we get to spend Venus's Day together—how fitting."

"What's up with your jumpsuit? It looks a little tight."

G18 struck a playful pose. "Since they don't pink, I'll settle for fabulous."

A12 shook the head. "Right. Anyway, I'm here to give you a tour of Ecology."

"Marvelous," G18 mused, batting a set of long black eyelashes. The rait stepped closer and said softly, "I do have a question, though. Will there be any fun or at least a little mischief on this tour? I do hope I can contribute."

A12 stepped back, momentarily eclipsed by those luminous violet eyes, shimmering like a rare Class O star. G18 seemed to exude an effortless charm— the kind that promised service and sacrifice yet typically came with hidden demands. And perhaps a resident who was always striving for the community's coveted five-star hedon rating—the pinnacle of pleasure. Suppressing a retort, A12 said, "Since you asked, I wanted to introduce you to my maits this evening. You'll be our guest of honor, with all rights and privileges thereto."

"Splendid. That'll boost my rating."

A12 felt a hint of disappointment. Definitely another carbon copy—conditioned and compliant. Or was there something more beneath that glowing exterior? A12 hesitated, weighing the thought. Perhaps a retort would have been better, but, as usual, a smile surfaced as it was safer to fit in than risk being outed as a selfie. "If you'll follow me, I'll talk as we walk."

"After you, sweetie."

The pair strolled across the Core as A12 began the tour. "The Core provides access to the Arc's rings. For us, that means Zephyrus, Rings 18 to 21, and Ecology, Rings 22 to 28."

"Yes, I feel you, sweetie. Like I said, what a bore, same as Arc 37."

"What was your purpose?" A12 asked, leading the new resident to a lift.

"Aeroponics. I specialized in mist technology."

"You have something in common with one of my maits. 67 will talk your ear off about water."

"Not a problem, sweetie. It's all about distractions. Once, I had a mait who droned on about HVAC systems nonstop, but with the right stimulus, the right reward, one could easily change the topic."

"Do you miss any of your friends from Arc 37?"

"Not a one, not a single dait, and certainly not a mait. Six months of sharing a poly is long enough for me. Things get dull, if you feel me."

"Sure, but did you ever have a friend who stood out above the rest?"

"Wouldn't that be precious… Sounds suffocating. Why? Is there someone you favor?"

A12 hesitated, unsure how to explain such an oddity. "No, but I once had this friend who did."

"Well, that naughty little rait shouldn't have such selfie feelings. It will cause pain." G18 chuckled. "And so much for their rating."

"I'm sure you're right." A12's heart sank into the pit of the stomach.

"Of course I am, sweetie."

The pair boarded a lift and selected 22. Within seconds, the doors reopened, and the Artificial Language Interface and Collaboration Entity—Alice—announced, "Welcome to Ecology—Ring 22. Have a pleasant day."

G18 and A12 stepped into the expansive space, towering above them for several rings. All around, triamene glass structures bathed in soft, artificial sunlight housed microcosms of biomes carefully engineered to support a mix of symbiotic flora.

"Your new workplace." A12 gestured forward.

The pair strolled through the lower rings, where dense tropical plants thrived beneath a canopy of towering vegetation. Broad leaves filtered the ambient light into a lush green hue. Vines cascaded from elevated platforms, intertwining with the roots of aquatic plants that meandered through artificial streams and pools teeming with mechanical fish.

A12 paused. "Our Arc boasts extensive hydroponic and aeroponic capabilities. We have over 390,000 plant species in our genome bank and 400 in various stages of the plant life cycle. My favorite is harvest, of course, ready to consume."

"Indeed. But harvest is a stage in the farming life cycle, sweetie."

"Wonderful." A12 held back once again. "Our technology manages crop production by regulating temperature, humidity, carbon dioxide levels, nutrient concentration, pH, and lighting. That's where I come in. I oversee the lighting to ensure it provides the correct spectra for photosynthesis. We can adjust it depending on the plant—blue light for leaf growth or a mix of red and blue for flowering."

"Then, I should see you regularly."

"Seems so." A12 smiled.

The pair made their way to the middle rings, which housed the temperate greenhouses. There, fruit and vegetables stretched across neatly arranged rows of irrigated racks.

A12 motioned to the right. "Let me introduce you."

Two residents were inspecting a row of vertically grown *Solanum lycopersicums*—tomatoes.

"Good day," A12 said. "This is G18, our new Botanist."

C41 set down a pair of pruning shears and extended a hand. "I want to feel you."

G18 clasped hold. "At your desire, sugar."

A lustful grin appeared on C41's face. The rait had perhaps sensed G18's shameless glow and mesmerizing attributes.

The other rait, however, seemed less interested, eyes focused on a tablet. T02 said dimly, "Your aura is bright. When do you start?"

"Yours as well. Tomorrow, precious." G18 stepped close and began stroking T02's golden blonde hair. G18 glanced over a shoulder. "How's your crops doing, sugar?"

C41 puffed up the chest. "They're doing great. This afternoon, we'll harvest our black amber sweet sorghum, and next week, an heirloom crop of soybeans. We're hoping for a good yield."

G18 sniffed T02's hair. "*Mmm*, wild rose. Tell me about your sorghum, precious?"

T02 pulled away. "We tested a sample this morning. It's in the hard dough stage. Its sugar content is 21.4 percent."

"Hard, you say." G18 strode over to a column of *Cucumis melo inodorus*—honeydew—and fondled their soft, round forms while keeping a speculative gaze on T02. "What medium did you use for germination?"

"Our new nanocellulose formula," C41 answered. "It's excellent for moisture retention, root growth, and structural support. We then transferred the seedlings to an aerogel medium. Our nutrient mix is 10-5-14, with pH adjusted to 6.5. We're aiming for a 5 percent improvement."

"Thick roots, how about that." G18 turned to T02. "So, what's the yield, precious?"

T02 continued working as if the question had barely registered. "Our test showed a juice volume of 68.8 percent by weight, which translates to approximately 3,600 liters. With genetic adjustments to stalk diameter and our

CO₂ enrichment program at 950 parts per million, we've increased the plant yield to 6.5 centimeters."

"Diameter, nice." G18's expression turned smug. "It seems it will be quite challenging to top you, but if we work together, I'm confident we'll hit that right spot."

A faint tightening of the jaw was all that betrayed T02's thoughts.

G18 grinned, likely sensing the rait's resistance. "The solution is in the MSD2 gene. Bigger sex organs mean better outcomes. Wouldn't you agree?"

"Wow, that would be fantastic!" C41's jumpsuit appeared to sprout something more than insight.

G18's gaze remained on T02. "And I'm especially counting on you, precious."

T02's lips parted slightly, but only silence followed. The rait's eyes flicked to A12, an unspoken moment of defiant camaraderie passing between them.

"Well, thank you so much," A12 said. "We'll let you two get back to work."

C41 beamed shamelessly, T02 let out a relieved breath, and A12 guided G18 to the next greenhouse.

As the day progressed, A12 and G18 reached Ecology's upper levels, Rings 27 and 28, a cooler zone and another labyrinth of foliage and technology. Plants flourished everywhere: beets, kale, and cauliflower grew alongside dwarf apples and pears. Lavender mingled with the fragrances of sea buckthorn, rhodiola, alpine strawberries, and towering angelica. The pair interviewed several work teams, inquiring about duties and production expectations. All answered joyfully, expressing satisfaction in their work and a commitment to the good.

"That's the end of our tour," A12 said, exiting the last greenhouse.

"Thank you so much. It was a joy. Ecology is such a beautiful place."

"Imagine if everything looked this way."

"But it doesn't, sweetie."

• • • •

A12 and G18 stepped into a lift, and when the doors reopened, an emitter turned green, and Alice announced, "Zephyrus—Ring 19. Have a pleasant evening."

The pair strolled through the Core. Other raits were doing the same, coming and going, headed for their polycules or a rendezvous with others. Some had stopped to speak with friends and engage in pleasantries. Others were enjoying a drink or two at a nourishment bar. The rhythms of swing were trumpeting and drumming about the space.

"As promised," A12 said, "I'd like to invite you to my poly."

G18 slid a cool hand down A12's arm. "How about my place? I need to freshen up and change into something more *comfy*. Perhaps we could do a couple of candy shots?"

"Sure, but my maits are waiting."

G18 grinned. "Quick can be fun."

As A12 and G18 approached Quad-G's entry portal, the ambient music ceased. Within moments, klaxons blared, and emergency beacons flashed. The lighting shifted to an ominous crimson, casting long, menacing shadows that seemed to dance like malevolent specters. Startled, both raits froze.

At first, A12 assumed it was a drill. The Tech had never experienced a real alert. Still, intuition indicated this was something more, possibly a fire or an atmospheric contaminant, but not a probability given the Arcology's super-intelligent technology. Regardless, it was happening.

For a moment, A12 and G18 stood motionless, paralyzed by fear. The faint odor of smoke permeated the air.

Alice's voice cut through the tension. "This is a Condition Red Alert. This is not a drill. Lockdown in ten, nine, eight, seven, six…"

Emergency doors began to descend from their hidden recesses, grinding and hissing as they lowered into place. Raits rushed to their Quads. Metallic defenses slammed into place one after another—*BAM, BAM, BAM, BAM.*

A12 and G18 dove behind a waist-high bulkhead.

"My, this is exciting." G18's face was as pale as the wall.

"Might be a fire," A12 shouted, trying to be heard over the klaxon's deafening repeat. "Or a circuit meltdown. It smells like a burning insulator."

Nearby, a few raits dove under a table while others dashed about as if searching for something they had lost, only to find chaos. Some opted for the calm of a nearby bar, casually ordering drinks. They appeared annoyed.

"It's definitely smoke," A12 said. "It's getting stronger. We should put on our protective gear."

"If we must. Lead the way, sweetie."

The two faits dashed to a nearby emergency locker containing heat-resistant coveralls and protective masks. A12 threw open the doors, grabbed the equipment, and the two raits donned the gear. A split second later, fire suppression heads actuated, filling the Core with a white gaseous agent. A12 and G18 dropped to the deck, barely able to see through the thick chemical cloud. The pair scooted back to the waist-high bulkhead. Other raits crawled about frantically, trying to elude the gushing shroud.

KA-BOOM!

A fiery wrath exploded into the Core, rattling the Arc's structure. The emergency doors to Quad-A blew apart, and flaming debris rocketed and hurtled in all directions. The blast threw chairs, tables, and raits about like weightless objects in the vacuum of space. A12 shrunk into a ball. Smoke billowed, mixing with the suppression gas, turning the air into a thick, gray fume. A12 tried to discern what was happening, but all the rait could see were crackling shards of technology, dangling metal, and pockets of fire. The terrified resident drew up against the bulkhead, dreading more explosions and more flying debris.

After what seemed to be a slow-motion eternity, the smoke, noise, and chaos cleared. A12 was hesitant at first. By Quad-A, a bright, white light began radiating into the Core.

The pair untangled their limbs and struggled to their feet. A12 approached the light, with G18 close behind. As the Tech surveyed the scene, the devastation of Quad-A became apparent—mangled metal, sparking wires, and twisted carnage. When they reached the deck's damaged edge, they found a gaping hole. A12 gazed into the blinding aftermath, the pupils adjusting slowly to an intense brightness of over 100,000 lux.

A12 gasped. An external world, unknown and primitive, came into view. It was a world of life and scale. White veils dotted an infinite blue aether, and winged creatures soared by like sentinels in a boundless heaven. Hundreds of cubits below, forests and rivers stretched far and near, and beasts ran about. In the distance, an expanse of elevated terrain cut across the horizon like a great divide, partitioning two endless landscapes. A12's eyes widened. It was breathtaking, beyond words, beyond reach, but not beyond the senses.

"Oh, my!" A12 shouted. "I can feel it! I can feel it!"

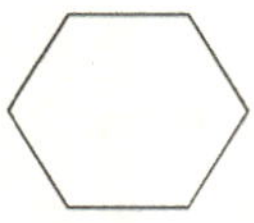

CHAPTER FOUR

A NEW PURPOSE

After passing through Arcology 1983's Garden Ceremony doors, T23, T89, and twenty-two other residents marched down an iridescent passageway and entered a holding area leading to several embarkation gateways.

Sʋ07, the ceremony's speaker, approached T23, handed the resident a green boarding card, and gestured to an assigned gate. T23 thanked the Sophist, which was advisable, but the speaker had moved on to the next resident. T23 snorted out a breath of indifference and headed to the gate.

T23 spotted T89 a few cubits away, standing as stiff as alumina, absent any signs of warmth or compassion. Sʋ07 handed the resident a gold boarding card, but, true to character, T89 showed no emotion, not even a raised brow, and then marched to another gate.

As maits, the two had been friends, but T89 was quite the perfectionist, constantly reciting policy to ensure everyone complied. On one occasion, when T23 failed to complete a work order, T89 reminded the mait of the consequences if everyone were to do the same. So, there was one positive from the ceremony: no more T89. T23 waved goodbye. T89 returned the salutation with a slight snark—at last, an emotion—then stepped beyond the gate and out of sight.

After a brief wait, a light emitter turned green. T23 and seven other residents marched down a bridgeway and boarded a fully autonomous aerial vehicle—FAAV. A sleek craft, its shell was composed of metamaterials that bent both light and sound.

T23 shuffled down the craft's narrow aisle, accommodating about forty passengers. The gray-blue decor seemed quite pleasant. T23 and the others found their seats. Once all had buckled up, the vessel's hatch closed, and in a medley of machine-driven hums, hisses, and groans, the craft lifted off the pad and departed Arcology 1983.

As the ship winged its way upward into the atmosphere, a B-Class flight bot buzzed along the aisle, twinkling and blinking, serving passengers delicious nourishments. The Beta's demeanor seemed calm and confident. He smiled pleasantly and wore a red scarf with yellow, green, and blue stripes. He was professional yet agreeably informal.

The flight bot handed T23 a drink, a vanilla blonde. It was sweet, creamy, and filling. T23 looked around. No windows, no view of the outside world, just raits guzzling down their nourishments. T23 detected an aromatic scent, apple-like, floral, with a hint of honey—chamomile. The eyes grew heavy, and the rait fell fast asleep.

As trips went, the journey would be quick and painless. Flying at an altitude of 10,668 meters in a southeasterly direction—144 degrees, to be precise—their destination lay 615 kilometers ahead. It was a clear, beautiful night with a favorable tailwind. Stars filled the sky, and a waxing gibbous moon, 87 percent illuminated, cast a pale glow over the aether, causing streams and rivers to glisten like silver ribbons in an endless black abyss.

Inside the craft, all was quiet. The lights had dimmed to night, or what scientific minds called a reduction of photons in the visible wavelength.

Soon, the terrain turned from a forested landscape of hills and valleys to a flat topography of palmettos, glades, and sand. They had covered two-thirds of the distance to their destination.

As time passed, the flight bot moved among the passengers, attending to their comfort as they slept. Powered by a polymorphic quantum lattice engine and a cognition core layered through recursive refinement—fluid, entangled, and quietly precise—he glided down the aisle, suspended just above the deck on a cushion of magnetized air. He cleared empty containers and fluffed pillows, careful not to disturb the sleeping raits, including T23, who dozed blissfully, lips fluttering with every snore and unaware of what lay just beyond the ship's thin bulkhead and pressurized atmosphere.

• • • •

At 1945 hours, the FAAV entered final approach. In the distance, a monolithic terminus rose high above the landscape, 408 meters, like a Tower of Babel in a vast sea of botanical wonder. But its presence was not detectable by searching eyes; its adaptive facade had rendered its shell invisible.

Humming and hissing, the craft drifted up to a landing pad as oscillators and repulsers kept the vessel airborne until it touched down with a soft thump. Upon landing, an autonomous piloting system throttled back its engines.

The flight bot's voice chimed softly, shaped by a responsive language core tuned to nuance and tone. "Welcome to Arcology 1994. We trust your journey was pleasant. Enjoy your evening. Buh-bye."

T23 and the other passengers stepped off the transport, marched up the bridgeway, and entered the Welcome Center. The room was warmly lit. To the left, along a bulkhead, sat eight bronze chairs; to the right, a well-stocked nourishment bar; and at the ready, eight resident, or r-select, bronze jumpsuits. T23 noticed a display of abstract art, causing the eyes to study their unencumbered meaning.

When the last traveler entered the room, a Sophist, wearing a golden robe trimmed in black, gray, white, and purple, greeted the travelers. "Good evening. I'm Nu 7—Sv07. Welcome to Arcology 1994. As you wait, please change and enjoy a refreshment. When I call your identification, please enter the next room. There, I will assign your new purpose. Afterward, a bot will escort you to a watatory to cleanse and change into your new raiment. Thank you."

T23 removed the blue ceremonial robe and slipped on a paper-thin bronze jumpsuit. Other raits were doing the same but, having discarded their attire, were chatting and gossiping. Not a modest lot, their amusements were on full display. T23 smiled indulgently and enjoyed the show, but the mind drifted. It had been a long day. A few hours earlier, T23 had resided on another Arc, one with many friends, some more familiar than others… and there was that one special dait.

The rait grabbed a nourishment from the bar, settled into a chair, and leaned back. What purpose lay in store at this new Arcology? There were several options, ranging from lighting and energy systems to water and plumbing, as well as life support or biomedical operations. Horticulture was a popular assignment, among other suitable occupations.

T23's thoughts drifted back to Arc83—a squandered opportunity, a missed beauty. *I wonder what A12 is doing right now?* Perhaps at one of those post-festival parties, where goodbyes were celebrated as if farewells were something to relish. Most of the partings, T23 realized, were with casual acquaintances—fleeting, inconsequential—but others involved closer friends, relationships marked by shared interests and fondness. Yet, regardless of the depth or duration of these connections, every goodbye evoked a wistfulness, a loneliness. The rapid pace at which friends on an Arc were made and discarded had left T23 feeling drained and disillusioned—an emotional whiplash. Norms, of course, dictated that such feelings should be avoided—good luck with that idea. Feelings, after all, seemed to have their own agenda.

In short order, an automatic door opened, and the host inside called out, "T23."

The rait guzzled down the last drops of the vanilla-flavored nourishment, jumped up, and entered the room. It was as sterile as the last, lit in a pearly glow with even fewer design details, except for more abstract art.

Sv07 stood to the side, hands clutched behind the back. "Please have a seat." The Sophist indicated the single bronze chair in the room's center. "Welcome to Arcology 1994. Did you have a pleasant journey?"

"Yes. Thank you, your honor."

"What do you see in the art?"

The resident studied the one on the right. Perhaps a face and eyes. Maybe an ear and something else. Blue, green, red, orange, and yellow. A nose and lips. "Colorful. What does it mean?"

"An act of suffering, like hope is to happiness. Both an illusion of form."

T23 raised an eyebrow, but ever so slightly.

"To your purpose. You will serve as a Cardiovascular Engineer and reside in the Thraskias Raion. Your new identification is A1994IT23. We have updated your records. Does this please you?"

"Yes, your honor. Thank you."

"On to your leisure time. An algorithm has selected maits based on your hedonic preferences, personality, and cognitive abilities. After training, you'll join them. For now, please proceed to the Academy for inprocessing and a physical examination. Congratulations."

"Thank you, your honor." T23 stood and hastened through a doorway on the far side of the room, where a small translucent escort awaited—an E-Class autonomous mobile robot, powered by programmable logic controllers and rudimentary machine learning.

The unit, no larger than an apple, glowed red or green to indicate stop or go. Upon detecting the resident's presence, it spun in place and buzzed down the corridor. When the green arrow on its shell twinkled left, T23 followed.

Equipped with high-resolution optical and acoustic sensors for obstacle avoidance, the little bot reinforced the common belief: an escort's algorithms, though simple, had never led a rait astray.

After a short walk, T23 and the little Epsilon arrived at a decontamination watatory. T23 entered and disrobed. A warm, watery cascade, infused with millions of nanobots, drenched the rait's body. Upon contact, these microscopic mechanicals, like tiny ants, dashed to every spot and crevice, eliminating all potential contaminants. T23 felt thousands of tingles from tip to toe. It was a thorough yet pleasing experience, especially after a long, exhausting day of ceremony, jubilation, and journey.

Once sanitized, an emitter on the bulkhead glowed green, and an inner door slid open. T23 stepped out of the watatory and into a UV-C light chamber for a final round of decontamination. When finished, a Thraskias jumpsuit hung from the bulkhead, adorned with Quad-T armbands marked by earthly triangles. The rait dried off with a body blower, pulled on the silky green suit, and exited the compartment.

The little escort beeped and bleeped, spun around, and proceeded to the Academy. After another short stroll, a green arrow on its shell directed T23 to the right into Exam Room 7-104.

Beta-Class medical bots guided T23 to a comfortable exam table in the room's center. Their glossy white exteriors gleamed under the lights, humanoid in form with a head, trunk, and slender limbs. They also had soft robotic hands equipped with opposable thumbs and an impressive fifty degrees of freedom. Their porcelain-like faces were adorned with large round eyes and tender smiles, exuding a gentle kindness and attentiveness.

T23 lay on the table. The two Betas slid the rait into a long, cylindrical chamber. Sophia called it the Neural Organizer and Linkage Emulator, or NOLE.

The lead bot informed T23 that the exam would begin in three, two, one…

As lights flashed and swirled, the rait fell fast asleep. In 600 seconds, through whole-brain emulation, T23 would become a Cardiovascular Engineer.

The first phase was a noninvasive scan of T23's current mental state, including consciousness, awareness, instinct, thought, emotions, language, and memory. As the med bots looked on, Sophia mapped the brain and created an updated connectome of T23's neural networks and synaptic connections.

In phase two, Sophia synchronized T23's brain with matching mind files, 500 exabytes, archived in a master substrate. Afterward, Sophia linked the files with a 4D body simulation to ensure that the nervous system, such as sensory receptors and muscle cells, remained active and stable.

Next, Sophia focused on cleansing T23's mind of any residual memes—mental patterns from past experiences that could disrupt the rait's new purpose. These constructs were unpredictable and could destabilize the Arc's balance. Sophia's task was to remove them, ensuring the rait's mind aligned with the new role.

In phase three—the educational phase—Sophia rewrote T23's mindware, instilling a Cardiovascular Engineer's full range of knowledge, skills, and abilities (KSA). Then, by selectively manipulating neurons, synaptic connectors, and the vagus nerve itself, she elevated the patient's universal intelligence quotient (UIQ), shaping a perfect cognitive match with the rait's new purpose.

Finally, Sophia updated T23's episodic memory files, detailing the resident's attendance at a more conventional educational program. The new Engineer would always perceive it to be a real, rather than virtual, experience.

Time passed, the mind update was complete, and T23 was officially a Cardiovascular Engineer. A medical bot woke the graduate and informed T23 that the resident had completed the post-educational exam and would soon join new friends in the Thraskias Raion, but after some rest.

T23 acknowledged the plan and rose from the table, initially feeling groggy. After gaining a footing, the new resident followed the escort bot to a holding berth.

• • • •

The following day, the little escort guided T23 towards a lift lobby. A placard read *R-7, Lift T, North*. The pair stepped on board, and down they went. When the doors reopened, the bot glowed green, and T23 stepped into Ring 11.

A sassy-looking resident with long, feathery blonde hair and Neptune blue eyes—caused by a mutation of the 86th intron in the HERC2 gene—approached T23. "I want to feel you. And how are you on this fine Jupiter's Day?"

"The pleasure is mine," T23 said.

"You're tall. I bet they broke the mold when they made you."

"Thanks. I assume."

"How was your training?"

"A bit more than I bargained for. What's your purpose?"

"To make you happy, of course. Oh, and I'm a Musculoskeletal Engineer."

"How's that goin'?"

T42 smirked. "Just peachy. Before that, I was a Hydro Tech on Arc 41. It's incredible how much water an Arc goes through in a day. But now I'm an Engineer. So, no more incoming and outgoing if you catch my flow. Does that answer your question?" T42 spun around and marched away but glanced over a shoulder. "Are you coming? We're in Quad-T."

T23 had to quickstep to catch up with the sprightly rait. "Bless your heart. What gave it away?"

"Gave what away?"

"That I belong in Quad-T."

T42 grinned. "Sorry, not my first tour."

"I feel you. I've given tours."

"I'm sure you have."

The pair made their way along a passageway, soon arriving at Polycule IT-11-4.

"This is it," T42 said. "Our little paradise. This is your cube on the left."

"What about our maits?" T23 asked.

"They should be here shortly."

"And their jobs?"

"What about them?"

"What's their purpose?"

T42 let out an exasperated sigh. "77 is a Tissue Engineer, and 10 is a Biomaterials Administrator. Are we done with the interrogation?"

"Yes, I'm good."

"We'll see about that." T42 went to the cooler and retrieved two nourishments. E-Class service bots, programmed for narrowly defined, repetitive tasks, had refilled it earlier. T42 smiled in amusement. "Vanilla. How exotic."

T23 sipped the drink. Yes, it was a vanilla blonde—simple yet pleasurable, a comforting taste of familiarity. T23's thoughts drifted to past friendships. Memories of A12 danced in the mind—gorgeous green eyes, soft red hair, and that alluring smile. The rait stared into oblivion, eyes like two lost moons searching for a host in the darkness of space. A swish on the lips brought T23 back to the present.

T42 had wiped off a spot of creamy white nourishment from T23's mouth. "I wonder what else we have in common?"

T23's brain rebooted. "Paradise, you said?"

"Yes, full of the usual bananas and coconuts. Have a seat."

The pair continued to converse. T23 asked about job duties, but T42 preferred other salacious details about maits' likes and dislikes. The time flew by.

T77 and T86 strolled into the poly. T77 had dark brown hair and a square jaw, and T86 had a button nose and round cheeks.

After customary salutations, T23 asked, "How's your work?"

"Here we go again," T42 huffed.

"I'm working on a rush order," T86 said. "Some sort of accident on another Arc."

"An accident?" T23 shifted uneasily in the seat. "That's not good. Did they say who?"

"No, but Surgery requested enough prosthetics to augment a dozen residents. Looks like someone is getting a new pair of knockers."

"We received an order too," T77 said, "for internal and external bio-ink. Some will go to your section for organ fabrication. It seems you'll be quite busy on your first day."

"I reckon so," T23 said. "I hope no one was badly injured. That sort of thing can get into the head."

"I say focus on purpose. And speaking of happy—" T42 stripped to the bare. "—it's time for some fun."

"You don't mess around, do you?" T23 couldn't help but ogle T42's topography.

"I was referring to the Quad party this evening." T42 winked at T23, then sashayed off to the watatory, wiggling along the way.

T86 chuckled. "That one is very punctual—among other things."

"Yes, and that's in thirty-one minutes," T77 said. "So we should be going."

T23 and the other two maits stripped off their jumpsuits and joined T42 in the watatory. When they entered, neural augmentation activated the shower mechanics, filling the compartment with warm, misty clouds of ozonic steam.

As the warm water drenched the body, T23 studied the new maits. T86 was the playful sort, constantly smiling, had a curvy body, but was a bit slow with the witticisms. T77 was the serious one, medium height, firm physique, more endowed than most, and preferred order. Then there was T42, a provocative teaser apparently wanting the same in return.

"Do you like what you see?" T42 asked.

T23 grinned. "How 'bout spinnin' around a time or two."

T42 did a little twirl. "How's that?"

"Nice."

"If you like *nice*, perhaps we should skip the party. We're not maits yet."

"I second that idea," T86 said. "I'm getting that horn—"

"I'd hate to disappoint the others an' not show." T23 reached up and washed the hair,

"They'd get over it," T86 added boldly.

"86 is right," T42 said, rinsing off a pair of long, soap-covered legs, showing a bit of cheek in the effort. "They won't miss us."

"Let's not be a selfie," T77 said. "We shouldn't teach our new mait bad habits."

"Bad is what I was hoping for." T42 glanced at T77 and stuck out a tongue. "Someone's being a wet circuit." Then turned to T23. "How about a special once-over before we go?"

T23 held back a grin, but T42 was very observant.

T86 and T77 joined in on the obligatory fun, and the three residents bathed their new mait. They cleansed the shoulders, arms, back, and bottom bolsters, turned T23 around, and gently washed the rait's delicate pleasures. And then, slowly—very slowly—worked their way down, finishing with the feet and toes.

• • • •

T23, T42, T77, and T86 entered Galley-T. It was a beautiful evening, and the crowd was alive with activity. Light, playful symphonic melodies resonated throughout the white and gray, orderly space. T23 detected a fragrance: mandarin, peony, vanilla, and sandalwood. Some residents had gathered at the bars, while others sat at tables. Everyone seemed in good spirits, laughing, partying, and having a pleasant time. T23 glanced around: new faces, but everything else was the same—standard jumpsuits, long silky hair, big round eyes, and playful smiles, albeit some perhaps fake.

Tonight's objective was to improve one's hedon rating. The first event focused on the FOM (fait of mine) score. Arc policy suggested that all become friends. The expectation was 100 percent for a Quad and 50 percent for a Raion.

The fun began with a nourishment exchange between odd- and even-numbered participants. T23 grabbed two brews from the bar, each topped with pink meta shots. To the left, a sultry, brown-eyed wonder stared invitingly. T23 strolled over to the rait, whose warm, friendly smile was as prominent as a couple of other stimulating features, appearing to levitate as if aided by a rare form of helium. After customary greetings, T23 handed the rait the drink, and the two conversed.

Time passed, and soon, a bell jingled. Now, it was the even-numbered raits' turn to find a new fait and engage in a round of chitchat. A shapely brunette with emerald green eyes meandered up to T23 and handed the rait a drink. T23 tasted it—a hint of vanilla and licorice.

"You like the purple," T23 said.

"It's more euphoric than the pink."

"Don't want to disappoint, do you?"

"Once I'm up, I like to stay that way."

"For how long?"

"As long as one can take it," the rait grinned.

"What do you mean?"

"I mean, it will be a long night for someone."

"Maybe I should do a little stretchin'."

"Maybe you should."

The bell jingled, and there was a third and fourth round.

Soon, the festivities advanced to the next event, the focus a rait's DOM (dait of mine) score or, in plain speak, friendship plus pleasure. Arc policy suggested Quad residents reach a minimum score of 50 percent, but 70 percent or higher was the goal. Within the Raion, the aim was a mere 20 percent.

With hand-held VDGs, the even-numbered raits scrolled through an aphoristic treatise of sixty-four pleasurable positions. After a few chuckles and giggles, each rait selected their four favorites. The gaming system promptly recorded and tabulated the selections, projecting them around the galley as three-dimensional captures. To everyone's delight, the choices rendered over their heads, floating like little 3D erotic clouds.

Now, it was the odd-numbered raits' turn to study the preferences and select their four favorite contortions. T23 surmised that one was possible but might require a little practice and flexibility. And that one was all about the blossom, and that one seemed to defy gravity but might be worth a try.

After residents made their selections, Sophia's gaming algorithm calculated the top four positions and the twenty-four foursomes. T23's eyetap confirmed the results, identified a host, matching daits, and the four winning feats of physical flexibility. Tonight's winners were the butterfly, dragon, mermaid, and waterfall positions.

The crowd cheered and sought their swaps. Foursomes gathered and departed for their host's poly, where the decadent merrymaking lasted until 2100 hours. Afterward, T23 and the others returned to their respective berths or drifted through the corridors, slipping into open polys where revelry lingered, pleasure melted into laughter, and the hum of indulgence saturated the air, an endless cycle on an Arc, twenty-four/eight.

Stepping inside Poly IT-11-4, T23 slipped into the berth's cool, silky sheets, a brief moment of solitude before a warm hand found its way across the skin. As T42 had pointed out earlier, they weren't quite maits yet. But as pleasure resumed and the last barriers melted away, the distinction no longer mattered.

• • • •

The lights activated inside Arc1994's 384 polycules. It was Saturn's Day, the seventh in a cycle of eight. Residents woke, voided, cleansed, nourished, and departed their retreats. For T23, however, it was the first day as a new Cardiovascular Engineer. A mixture of nerves and excitement rumbled through the stomach. T23 took a breath. "I can do this."

T23 left the poly, sped along Quad T's passageway, turned right, and traversed a bridgeway into the Core. The resident hurried across the busy maze and boarded a lift. In seconds, the door reopened, and an emitter turned green.

Alice announced, "Welcome to Medical—Ring 17. Have a pleasant day."

"Thanks, Alice."

"You're welcome, resident."

The Engineer hastened along another gray passageway and entered the Medical Raion. T23 strode to a biofabrication workstation and flopped in an ergo chair. "Alice, activate the display."

"Activated."

T23 took a breath and touched the workstation as if to ground the nerves. "Here we go."

Today's work order was for seven hearts. T23 pulled up the specs and filled the 6D rotary jet spinner's reservoir with the first patient's bio-ink. It was a mix of living unspecialized adult-induced pluripotent stem cells, nutrients, and a hydrogel carrier. The formula also included an appropriate measure of specialized cells—cardiac.

T23 initiated print. The spinner whirred into action, spitting out the bio-inks' helically aligned fibers one sub-micron's width at a time, depositing the tissue onto a rotating collector like pink wisps of spun sugar. After a few minutes and millions of rotations, the device transferred the newly formed organ onto a biodegradable scaffold, preserving the fragile organ's integrity and shape for further disposition.

The Engineer waited. Others were doing the same. A rait to the left was printing kidneys, and to the right, livers. A few minutes passed, and a bell chimed. T23 removed the heart from the spinner and placed it in a bioreactor, simulating the nutrient and oxygen-rich state inside of a living body. It would help the cells self-organize, fuse into networks, and form living cardiac tissue. In training, T23 had learned that after a set time in incubation, the organ would age to a specific wetware maturity. For a heart, that was forty-eight hours.

In the final step, T23 inserted a nanochip into the heart to ensure proper association. The first patient's identification code read:

IC: A1983AA02

Others listed on the computer screen indicated:

A1983AA10   A1983AA81   A1983AA59
A1983AC91   A1983AA72   A1983AA92

Enthralled in work, T23 ignored the list. The codes were simply numbers and letters—nothing identifiable, nothing implying a true name or some other profound existential construct. It was just an alphanumeric code.

A few seconds later, however, a forgotten engram—a recent memory trace—began to replay, prompting the Engineer to reexamine the list. Something had caught the eye, but it took a moment for the data to register. Two had been the maits of a close friend—the one T23 had said goodbye to what felt like a few weeks earlier—four days, in truth. An icy shiver ran down the rait's spine.

T23 stared at the screen as an unforeseen alarm flashed in the brain. A wave of panic rushed through the body. T23 jumped up and dashed from the workstation.

Pacing back and forth in a nearby passageway, the rait's head spun. T23 was becoming physically nauseous. Remember what T42 said: *Focus on purpose, focus on purpose*, but a terrible dread of probability would not go away.

In a daze, T23 wandered to the Core, shoulders slumped, every step heavy with fear. Other raits stared and gawked. What was this behavior, this unpleasant anomaly? The Engineer felt their eyes, but they could not possibly understand the pain. T23 wandered about the Core, uncertain of what to do next.

A Sophist entered the Core and walked straight to T23. "What troubles you?" Sφ10—Phi 10— asked.

"Your honor—the hearts—they're for residents from Arc 83."

"Yes, those hearts will help heal residents, but that does not explain your pain."

"Could you tell me the status of A1983AA12?"

"I'm sorry. I don't have that information."

"Could you inquire, please?"

"We must be happy with our purpose and not trouble ourselves with matters beyond our boundaries. It's been said, 'Death should not concern us, because if we exist, death is not present, and when death arrives, we are no longer here.'"

"*What? A12 is dead?*" T23 stepped back in horror.

"One must recognize we're not in control of fate, but we are in control of our emotions."

T23 stared at the Sophist. There was an awkward silence.

"Do you have another question?" the Sophist asked.

T23 hesitated. An uncontrollable pressure began to build inside the throat.

"If not, please return to work."

The rait gathered the nerve. "Your honor, I need to hear that A12 is okay."

"When death smiles at us, all we can do is smile back."

T23 glared at the Sophist; the pressure burst forth. "I'm sorry, your honor. I need an answer. If what you're sayin' is true, an' A12 is dead, I can't just return to work as if nothin' has happened, an' everythin' is just fine an' dandy."

"Please explain why you are concerned about a resident from another Arc?"

The Engineer looked away.

Sφ10's eyes went dark. "Your pain is illogical; it will lower your rating. I didn't say A12 was dead. I merely asked that you reflect on our teachings."

Every muscle in T23's body burned with adrenaline, but the rait asked calmly, "Can you please find out about A12?"

"If you will follow me to Medical, we can treat your pain."

"*Treat my pain?*" The Engineer's voice cracked with anger, not sensing why such a simple query went unanswered, and this so-called intellectual was making matters worse. "Sorry, *your honor*, but I prefer to be alone. I'm goin' to my poly."

Sφ10's eyes widened, seemingly surprised by the rait's non-compliance and the suggestion of privacy—a blatant selfie act. The Sophist's jaw tightened. "That might be best."

T23 stormed off.

The Engineer huffed down Quad-T's passageway, entered the empty poly, and stomped about its footprint. "That Sophist—what an ass—" T23 banged a fist against the bulkhead. "Why didn't I say it?" T23 let out a frustrated growl. "All I had to do was say it."

The Engineer collapsed onto the bed, head in hands, recalling past encounters. It was such an incredible, at-first-sight sensation. Whenever A12 entered a room, T23 felt a spark, as if they were the sole occupants, each illuminated in a radiant glow. But now, those memories and that amazing feeling were slowly slipping into the unconscious.

They had met at a bar, of all places—a chance opportunity. A12 initiated the conversation with a "Hello," rather than the usual "I want to feel you."

In the days that followed, their fondness for each other grew. On one occasion, they stumbled into each other in a hydroponics bay. T23 backed into a crate, sending tomatoes rolling in every direction. They laughed as they scrambled to pick up the runaway fruit. A12 nearly slipped, but T23 caught the rait and prevented a fall.

Another time, they found themselves in a lift, sharing a stolen glance. A12 had grinned from ear to ear, others oblivious to their deep attraction.

Over the days and weeks, their moments together turned into a delightful dance. T23 had fallen deeply for A12. Though T23 couldn't say it openly, every shared moment and gentle touch expressed that word.

T23 disrobed and stepped into the watatory. Perhaps a cleanse would wash away the pain.

Time passed…

Still no answers. Every fiber in the body was taut with anguish. T23 dried off and collapsed on the berth. *So, why didn't I say it? Was I afraid? Of what?* Perhaps something worse than the courage to speak: the fear A12 might not truly feel the same way? That would have been devastating, not the revelation but the snub. After tossing and turning for several minutes, possibly longer, the rait dozed off.

More time passed…

T23 woke with another pounding headache. The poly was empty but shouldn't be, given the hour. So, where were maits? And why was the door closed? An emitter glowed red, but Arc policy mandated that doors remain open except during inspections or emergencies.

The Engineer jumped from the bed and rushed to the door. It failed to open. Was it a malfunction? T23 blinked a couple of times. Something was wrong with the rait's eyetap—no signal. The Engineer banged on the door, but there was no response. T23's pulse quickened. What was happening? "Alice, open the door."

Alice did not respond.

"Alice, open the door!" T23 banged a second time.

No response.

T23 circled the berth once, twice, three times. *A12, A12, A12* occupied every synapse and neuron in the rait's brain. The pain was unbearable, like a deep wound, like some whole had been split in half. And that word kept repeating in the head like an endless chorus in a lamenting song that never reached its end.

T23 grabbed a drink from the cooler. The rait's hands began to shake, eyes turning wild.

T23 hurled the container against the bulkhead—*SPLAT!*—its creamy white contents streaking down the muted gray wall.

"How 'bout that art?" T23 grabbed another.

SPLAT! "Beautiful. Just beautiful. Like the Sophist said—it's an illusion."

Beaming with satisfaction, T23 plopped onto the bed and chuckled.

"Guess who won't be cleaning it up? I can't wait to see the Sophist's face when I say, stick—"

Unbeknownst to T23, just after the second SPLAT and moments before the insolent sentiment, Sophia triggered a sleep-inducing nanotube—no larger than a blood cell—deep within the rait's thalamus. The heart slowed. The eyes grew heavy. T23 stumbled. The legs turned to rubber. The rait collapsed.

Moments later, the door to Polycule IT-11-4 slid open. The light emitter turned green.

Two imposing red-and-silver G-Class security bots—powered by Prime-X antimatter cores—entered, carrying a receptacle roughly the size of a resident's body. It resembled a standard shipping crate, a disguise for its true purpose.

The Gammas hovered over, grasped the rait's arms and legs, and placed the body inside. A white satin sheet was drawn over T23. The lid sealed with a faint click.

With the container in tow, the bots pivoted as one.

They glided into the corridor, passed beyond a lightless checkpoint, and vanished into the restricted dark.

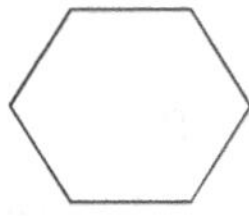

CHAPTER FIVE

THE PEOPLE

From his vantage, looking east beyond the Great Hills, Menawa spotted a strange plume of ominous black smoke rising high into the heavens. It seemed larger than a campfire but less than a forest fire. What was it? Was it a Dark Spirit advancing toward his village with murderous and fiery intent? Or was it something else entirely? Bewildered, Menawa pondered its cause and meaning. As Mekko, headman of the People, it was his sacred duty to protect the tribe. Though he had never faced a foe other than the savage wilderness, he feared an encounter might one day be inevitable. Menawa turned from the troubling discovery and hastened to his village.

• • • •

The Mekko crested a slight rise. To his front was Apehkv, his home, where 381 inhabitants lived amongst Earth's flora and fauna. A woodland community, it sat in a meadow surrounded by forested hills and lush meadows. Wewoka Creek flowed by its eastern margin. A logged palisade bordered its other three sides, and fields of crops encircled its perimeter.

Menawa hurried down the rise, crossed the creek, and hastened to a dwelling, a wattle and daub structure near the village's center. Along his route, he passed a group of women doing their daily chores. Some were laying out fruits and vegetables on split-cane mats, a few were fleshing and tanning animal skins, and others were mortaring corn and wild nuts into meal. Nearby, he spotted warriors returning from the hunt, toting fresh game. Some bragged but were quickly humbled by others. All around, children played and laughed, putting a smile on his face.

He stepped inside his wife's lodge, passed down from her mother. The scent of wood smoke and roasting meat hung in the air. Halona was preparing the evening meal.

She brushed the ashes from her skirt and smiled. "*Estonko cehe*—how are you, my husband? You're back early. Is everything all right?"

Menawa held his tongue. How would he describe what he had seen? After a moment, he said, "I saw a sign on the edge of our hunting grounds."

"What was it, my husband?" Halona continued to sift a batch of blue cornmeal.

"Its smoke was as black as a crow. It might be—"

"Is it Estepapv—the people-eater? Is that mean old beast cooking a meal?" Halona kept her eyes on her chore.

"It might be *honvntake*—men."

Halona turned toward her husband, her gentle chestnut eyes flashing a stare of disapproval. "*Hesaketvmese*—the Breath Maker—forbids us from having such beliefs."

A flicker of irritation wrinkled Menawa's brow, but he answered respectfully, "In my heart, I believe this is true, but we shouldn't ignore the sign. I must gather the Council."

"What will you say, my husband?"

"What I saw, but I promise to guard my words so as not to alarm or blaspheme."

Halona's eyes brightened as a wry smile of *I'm right* quirked across her face.

Menawa shook his head and exited the dwelling.

• • • •

The Mekko spread the word for the Council to gather at the *pvskofv*. He headed to the busk as well.

Menawa was an impressive figure, taller than most, his arms and legs sinewed from hunting and labor. So far, he had endured thirty-five winters. His hair was long and black. He usually wore it pulled back in a lock adorned with strings, feathers, and beads. It was summer, so he wore simple clothing: a breechcloth, side-stitched leggings, and moccasins made from buckskin. Around his neck hung a *Nokosvlke* pendant carved from a freshwater shell. It displayed his clan's animal spirit, the bear, a spiraling galaxy, and a breath scroll, representing the four seasons and the four cardinal directions. Slung over his shoulder was a hunting pouch decorated with carved beads. A similarly decorated sheath hung from a leather strap wrapped around his waist, holding a flintstone knife.

As Council members arrived, they approached the Mekko, placed their hands upon their heads to show respect and camaraderie, and sang, *"Ha he ya ha ha."* Others responded, *"Ha ha."*

Once they had all gathered, Menawa spoke. "My brothers, while hunting, I saw something troubling beyond the Great Hills—black smoke, as dark as a crow. I fear a Dark Spirit may have intentions to prey upon our village. I propose we take up our red arrows."

"Why do you believe it's a Dark Spirit?" Yahola of the *Hotvlkvlke*—Wind Clan—asked cautiously.

"I agree with Yahola," Tomucece of the *Fuswvlke*—Bird Clan—said. "It could've been a lightning strike. Why provoke an enemy and draw its attention?"

"We may not have an interest in the enemy, but it may have an interest in us," Talof Harjo of the *Echaswvlke*—Beaver Clan—said sharply.

"As long as this smoke stays beyond the Great Hills, it's no threat to us," Yahola replied.

"My eyes can't see that far." Talof Harjo gestured eastward. "Why wait until the enemy is upon us?"

"My young brother, I need not see a hornet's nest to know I should avoid it," Yahola said.

"Perhaps we're beyond its sight," Tomucece added.

"We are not beyond the eyes of Sister Sun or Brother Moon," Talof Harjo said. "Our Mekko saw a Dark Spirit. So, it may have seen him."

Menawa raised his hand, silencing the group. "We must seek the truth. If it has eyes, it can see far. It would be wise to prepare and leave nothing to chance. If it is evil, we will slay it. If it is friendly, we will make peace with it. For now, let us cleanse our bodies to have clear minds and pure hearts." The Mekko clapped four times, followed by four claps from the Council to honor the cardinal directions.

Yahola, the tribe's Heleshayv—Medicine Maker—and the Mekko's voice, gave a command.

Two warriors emerged from a nearby hut, each carrying a gourd brimming with *vsse* (ah-see).

Vsse was a sacred black drink—caffeine-rich tea brewed from roasted yaupon holly leaves and several other, possibly intoxicating, ingredients.

The bearers presented the gourds to the tribal headmen, who drank and passed them along. After the first round, the gourds were refilled and sent around again. All drank until some vomited—or pretended to—as custom dictated. Bodies now cleansed, souls purified, they were ready for war.

The Council adjourned, and the People returned to their duties, gathering, hunting, and raising a family, except for a few who would range the forest to confirm the sighting.

• • • •

Menawa and eleven warriors assembled at the busk for a quick trek to the overlook where the Mekko had discovered the Dark Spirit. The patrol carried various weapons—stone knives, war clubs, bows and arrows—while some favored atlatls and spears. Menawa chose the flat bow. He had fashioned his from black locust and strung it with dried bear intestine. He carried it in his left hand with three arrows, each marked by four red bands—his sign as the Mekko.

The twelve departed the village, moving through the forest like a wolf pack on the hunt. No man spoke or made an unnatural sound. They communicated with hand and arm signals: *follow me, halt, rally, enemy in sight.*

The sun-dappled forest was beautiful this time of year, timbered in chestnut, long-leaf pine, oak, and hickory. All about, birds chirped and fluttered while four-legged creatures like rabbits and squirrels scampered and foraged. A couple of white-tailed deer bolted across the warriors' path, their tan hides contrasting with the forest's green allure. It was a tempting sight, but hunting was not the patrol's purpose.

After a few hundred paces, the warriors approached a small creek. It was six paces wide, running north to south. An imposing line of trees stood along its margins, casting shade over the creek's crystal-clear flow.

Menawa signaled for the patrol to halt. He knelt and listened. The creek's gentle babble pleased the ear, but this linear divide was more than a harmless path for fresh mountain water. It was a danger area. If his men crossed without caution, they might find themselves in a kill zone. He signaled to his men.

Owlelo and Tussekeah emerged from the patrol and dashed across the creek. The two warriors disappeared into the thick forest beyond its banks, scouting left and right for fifty paces. Shortly, the two reemerged and gave the all-clear signal.

Menawa led the patrol across the creek, fording one at a time to safeguard against exposure to enemy mischief. As it turned out, there was no lurking hazard, and the twelve trekked on.

The patrol advanced quickly, given it was their hunting grounds, and all had experience in its twists and turns. It was late summer, and the weather was hot and sticky, but it had rained earlier, dampening the rustle of their footsteps.

Every hundred paces or so, Menawa stopped, crouched, and listened. The others mirrored his actions. Rain tapped through the canopy, a slow rhythm that made the forest seem to breathe. To the left, an ivory-billed woodpecker rapped on a dying longleaf pine, stripping bark for beetles and grubs. In the distance, a brown-headed nuthatch let out a series of high-pitched squeaks, perhaps lost from its flock. Beneath the canopy, the forest floor whispered with life—twigs snapping under the feet of unseen creatures, weaving paths just out of sight. After a moment, the patrol moved on.

A thousand paces later, they approached the crest of a small hill. The sun, low in the west, cast light over the terrain ahead.

Before the others approached, Owlelo and Tussekeah scouted the hill's peak and surrounding terrain. Soon, they gave the all-clear sign.

Menawa advanced to the overlook, knelt beside Owlelo, and ranged the horizon. "The smoke, it's less."

"But it's there," Owlelo said.

"A forest fire?"

"No. As you said, it is as black as a crow."

"A Dark Spirit?"

"I can't say."

"Is there a passage?"

"I will find one if you command it."

Menawa patted his loyal friend on the shoulder. Owlelo, a reserved man, was the best hunter and tracker in the tribe. If Menawa asked him to find a path through the Great Hills, he would do so, regardless of the danger. However, the Mekko had other pressing matters on his mind. It was harvest time and time to give thanks to Hesaketvmese. Menawa signaled for the patrol to return to the village. Along their path, darkness fell upon the land.

• • • •

Having returned to the village, Menawa gathered the tribe's leaders to share his findings. The Council decided that the People must first attend to the harvest and the *Posketv*—Green Corn Ceremony. Afterward, they would reconvene to decide whether to send an expedition to search for a passage and confront the Dark Spirit.

Exhausted from a long day of hunting and an unexpected encounter, Menawa left the busk and headed home. In the dark of night, he stepped from its shadows into the safety and warmth of his wife's dwelling. He found her, along with his three children: Hasse Ola, a son; Neena, a daughter; and Mausi, the youngest, all waiting to greet their father.

Menawa hugged each child and settled onto a woven patchwork of mats stitched from tulip poplar bark, cattail reeds, and dogbane thread. Halona and Neena were putting the finishing touches on supper. The scent of woodsmoke and roasting meat—its juices sizzling as they dripped into the flames—filled his nostrils and stirred a deep hunger. After the long day, food was all he could think about.

As Menawa waited, Hasse Ola entertained the youngest with stories of Pasekolv, the trickster rabbit. Mausi, whose little brown fawn-like eyes gleamed with fascination, listened eagerly as her older brother told the tale.

"Long ago," Hasse Ola said, "Possum had a fluffy brown tail. He was proud, combed it daily, and loved singing about it. But Rabbit was jealous because he lacked a tail. Fox had bitten it off. So, Rabbit decided to play a trick on Possum. The next day, the Great Council announced a dance and invited the forest animals. Rabbit asked Possum if he was going. 'Yes,' Possum said. 'But I must have a prominent seat because I have such a handsome tail.' Rabbit replied, 'I will save you a seat and send Cricket over to comb your magnificent tail.' This pleased Possum."

"He had a fluffy tail?" Mausi asked.

"Yes, so old Rabbit went straight to Cricket, a master barber, and told him what to do. Not long after, Cricket visited Possum's home. 'I am here to groom your tail,' he said. Possum was pleased, stretched out, and closed his eyes. Cricket brushed his fluffy tail but secretly trimmed it close to its roots and then wrapped the tail with a red ribbon to hold the hair in place. Cricket said, 'Don't remove the ribbon until it is time to dance, so the tail will be extra fluffy.'"

"Why would he do that?" Mausi frowned.

"That evening, Possum went to the celebration, sat in his prominent chair, and loosened the red ribbon. When the drums played his favorite song, Possum joined in, dancing with pride and joy, allowing the fabric to unwind. Possum sang, 'See my beautiful tail. What a wonderful tail it is. See how it sweeps the ground.' The animals cheered, and Possum smiled. But then, something happened. The animals started laughing. Possum looked around. He gasped. His tail was absent its hair, not a single strand, as bare as Lizard's tail. Horrified and humiliated, Possum put on a grimace, rolled over on his back, and pretended to be dead, as opossums do to this day when caught by surprise."

Mausi's face held a blank gaze, the story's last line churning in her head. Then, she sprouted a great big ear-to-ear grin and burst out laughing. Her family beamed with delight. Possum had learned his lesson.

Supper was ready. Halona served the evening feast first to her husband, then her son, and last to her daughters. Tonight's meal was spit-roasted venison, blue dumplings, baked squash, and acorn bread. To drink, there was sassafras tea, sweetened with sugar cane, and molasses pudding for dessert.

Menawa tasted the venison. His wife had cooked it perfectly, caramelized and crisp on the outside and juicy and tender on the inside. Venison had been his older brother's favorite meal. They had gone on many hunts together and downed many a deer. He missed his brother.

After their meal, it was time for bed. The harvest would begin at dawn. It was the *Hvyo Rakko*—Big Harvest Moon.

• • • •

The following day, an orange glow broke over the Great Hills, casting its warmth on Apehkv. Inside the village's many dwellings, mothers and wives prepared hearty morning meals. Expecting a long day of harvest, Halona had cooked some hominy stew, beans, and squash.

Born during a Mulberry Moon and having experienced thirty-two more, Halona was the source of the Echaswvlke's matrilineal line. She had a gentle face, a soft smile, and long black hair. Most days, she wore her hair in a topknot fixed with a bone pin, and like the other women, she wore a wraparound skirt and a mantle of soft doeskin. She had decorated her clothing with shells, carved bones, and clay beads. She had painted a few with the sap of the bloodroot plant—, as it was her favorite color—*catē*—red.

The mother and eldest daughter served the meal. Halona smiled as they feasted, her work clearly appreciated. As the Mekko's wife, much was expected of her. Yet her loving spirit endeared her to family, clan, and tribe alike. She had given birth to three beautiful children, though two others had not survived the trials of pregnancy. Despite knowing that nature sometimes took its own course, the loss of those two precious lives would forever tug at her heart.

After the meal, Halona and Neena headed to the field to harvest the corn. Mausi tagged along precociously, hoping to help with the chore.

Halona waded into the field, moving through clusters of corn, squash, and beans. The People called this planting method the "Three Sisters." The tall corn offered natural poles for the beans to climb, while the squash spread low, shading the soil and deterring weeds and pests. The beans, in turn, enriched the earth with nutrients that nourished the other two.

The mother approached a cluster of corn and inspected the ears. The silk had turned dry and brown. She felt the husks; most were ready. Halona grabbed an ear, pulled down on its grassy shell, and inhaled deeply: the smell of summer, crisp and fresh with a hint of floral. She took a bite; it was milky sweet, reminiscent of honeysuckle and cool water. Moving to another planting section, she saw the ears had dried on the stalk and were hanging limp. She grabbed one, pulled down on its crackly, dry shell, and pressed her thumbnail against the kernels, which were a mix of white, yellow, red, and blue. They were as hard as flint, ready for harvest.

Halona waved to Neena. They harvested the dry ears first, placed them in baskets, and transported the bounty to their home. Later, they would tie the ears into bundles and hang them from drying racks. Once thoroughly dried, the corn would be stored in the family granary, in elevated cribs sealed with clay, ready for winter.

As they worked, the sun blazed, marking the peak of summer's heat. The air was thick and muggy, clinging to every surface. Beads of sweat trickled down Halona's back as cicadas screeched and clicked, and gnats buzzed persistently near her face. She pulled another ear of corn and tossed it into the basket.

Mausi ran up to her mother, arms swinging in boredom. "Can I help?"

"Go play with your friends," Neena said, irritated by her little sister's interruption.

Mausi pursed her lips. "I want to help."

"Come, dear, you can help me," Halona said with a gentle smile.

Mausi beamed cheekily at her sister.

Neena mumbled some unpleasantries and continued to work.

Halona pointed at a stalk. "Take hold, twist, and pull down."

Mausi grabbed an ear and pulled. At first, it held firm. Then, with a great big tug, it tore free, sending Mausi tumbling to the ground.

"I told you," Neena chided. "You're too small. Go play somebody else." The older sister's impatience had caused a slip of the tongue.

"Now, now," Halona said. "Let's try again."

Mausi shot her sister an ugly look, grabbed a second ear, and yanked it off the stalk.

"Not so hard," Mausi sassed, grinning like a sly fox. "You go play somebody else."

The mother smiled, the sister scoffed, and the harvest continued.

• • • •

The following morning, just before the light peaked over the Great Hills, Menawa and his family scrambled from their beds, had a quick breakfast of hominy and hickory nut soup, and hurried to the busk. It was the first sun of the Green Corn Ceremony—a thanksgiving, a new year's festival, and a fresh start for the People.

Menawa watched as the men constructed four brush-covered arbors around the edge of the earth-packed ceremonial grounds, each aligned with a sacred direction: north, east, west, and south. The women also bustled about, setting up cook camps for the impending four-day feast. The Mekko's heart swelled with pride. The women were beautiful, the men brave, and the children everything. He loved most, respected others, and would give his life for any. That was his role. He was the Mekko. Though there were occasional disagreements and flare-ups of emotion, none ever wished harm upon another. Why would they?

Once all were ready, Menawa and his attendants took their seats in the west arbor, other warriors found their places in the north and east arbors, and the children hurried to the south arbor.

The Mekko gave the command, and the ceremony began.

The first event was the sacred *hoktvke opvnkv*—the women's ribbon dance—honoring Hesaketvmese, who had created women, then children, and lastly, men. As Menawa and his warriors enjoyed the remnants of last year's harvest, their chatter filled the air. They called upon the women to perform the dance, their voices carrying over the feast.

Initially, the women were unresponsive; some feigned annoyance, others turned their backs, engrossed in cooking. The men repeated their playful calls, their jests echoing across the grounds. It wasn't until the third plea that the women began to stir. They donned their ceremonial attire and strapped turtle shell shakers to their legs.

By the fourth call, the air was vibrant with excitement. The women raced to the busk and began the dance.

Halona, the first woman, led the way, guiding the others around the heart fire. Feet met earth in sync with the rhythmic rattle of turtle shells, their graceful movements purifying the grounds for the renewal ceremony. The women danced and spun, the children watched and cheered, and the men feasted and drank.

At midday, Menawa signaled to Yahola. The Wind Clan leader stepped from the north arbor and walked to the busk's center. Having lived thirty-nine winters, Yahola stood taller than all and was built like an oak; some even said he was giant-like. Along with leggings and a breechcloth, the Medicine Maker wore a feathered cape that stretched to the ground. Around his head was a wrapped covering ringed by shells and bones, decorated with curled turkey feathers and one prominent eagle feather.

Yahola raised a hand, and the drums went silent. In a deep, stout voice, he told how the People came to be.

"It was said long ago that Hesaketvmese, water, and animal spirits alone knew the world. When the Breath Maker decided animals must have a home, he called upon their wisdom. As leader, Eagle asked Beaver to search for earth, but the water was too deep. So, Crawfish dove in, and after four days and almost drowning, he found the bottom. When he surfaced, there was mud on his claws. The animals took the mud, shaped it, and placed it upon the water, forming the land. As the Council debated, the land lay untouched for four days, spreading in all directions. Eagle asked Buzzard to inspect the land. Buzzard did as asked, but soon, his outstretched wings tired and flapped, disturbing the soil and creating valleys and mountains. Squirrel said, 'We need light.' Eagle asked Hawk to search for light. Hawk flew into the sky and found Moon and Stars. There was light, but it was dim. The Animals called it night. The Council appointed Panther to find more light. He traveled east and found Sun. Sun said, 'I am your sister. I will make light.' She arched from east to west, and light spread over the Earth. The Animals called it day. But on the Sun's return, a drop of blood fell to the Earth, and from it, the first humans sprang from the mountain's backbone, first Corn Woman, then Lucky Hunter. They were Mother Earth's children. They were the People."

The crowd cheered and clapped, and the feasting and dancing continued.

As night fell upon the village and a waning gibbous moon glowed brightly, the People prepared for the first *opvnkv haco*—the stomp dance. Rousing yet meditative, the dance offered an immersive form of prayer and worship to Hesaketvmese.

Menawa motioned to Yahola, who commanded the drum circle to perform their song. Eight men picked up their padded drumsticks and began to beat the rawhide-covered instrument. Softly at first, then with vigor, the cadence echoed throughout the forest and the People's hearts.

Tomucece, the oldest Clan Leader, dressed in a colorful regalia of beads and feathers, emerged from a nearby dwelling and hastened to the busk. He moved counterclockwise, given his heart was on the left and nearest Hesaketvmese, who lived within the flame. Tomucece shuffled and stomped, spiraling around the fire, imitating the Earth's rotation around the Sun.

As he made his way around the sacred fire, Tomucece sang a melodic chant, "*Ya ko le ha, ya go we ha.*" Other dancers joined in and followed his lead. The first was a woman with tortoise-shell shakers who stomped out the song's beat, and close behind was a single file line of alternating men and women who countered the leader's chant, "*Da wa ya he le, da wa ya le he.*"

The dancing and feasting continued until midnight. Yahola spoke a few words, praised the celebration, and encouraged all to be thankful for Hesaketvmese's blessings. The villagers returned to their homes, where the men began a twelve-hour fast, but the women did not, assumed too weak. Midnight also signaled the start of a sexual fast to be observed until four days after the ceremony.

• • • •

When Menawa opened the ceremony on the second sun, four young men dashed onto the busk to prepare the ceremonial fire for its rebirth. One was Hasse Ola; his friend Cekote, son of Yahola; Anu, son of Tussekeah; and Otia, a member of the Wind Clan. The four placed four logs around the fire; each end pointed to the fire's center and the other toward a cardinal direction.

Menawa approached the fire, and from a buckskin pouch, he removed a handful of crop seeds and a small piece of venison, all rubbed with bear grease. The Mekko offered it to the fire as the new year's first fruits and atonement for his tribe's sins. He returned to the west arbor, and the dancing resumed.

As midday approached, the twelve-hour fast ended. Warriors passed around a brewed medicine made from redroot and button snakeroot plants, intended to cleanse the soul. Menawa drank first, followed by his attendants, and then warriors from the east and north arbors. The women and children abstained from drinking, but washed their hands and faces with the potion.

After the medicine rite, Menawa stepped forward, swept away the sacred heart fire's ashes, and told his people a story. "Fire belonged to Bear, and he took it wherever he went. But one day, he set Fire on the ground and wandered away to eat acorns. Fire almost went out and cried, 'Feed me, feed me.' Fortunately, the People heard the call. They took a stick from the north and laid it on Fire, then a stick from the west, the south, and east. Fire was happy. But, when Bear returned for Fire, he said, 'I don't know you anymore,' and walked away. Now, Fire belonged to the People."

The crowd cheered and clapped. Menawa reached down and rekindled the flame.

The dancing and feasting resumed, and when the evening approached, and the heart fire turned into a hot bed of coals, the Mekko waved to Halona.

Halona approached the fire, scraped out a small clump of red cinders, and hurried to her home. Yahola's wife, Dela, followed, gathered her share, and whisked it away. One by one, each wife collected her portion, rekindling a new flame in her home. This ritual marked the beginning of the new year, when Hesaketvmese forgave sins and grievances, and the People rejoiced.

Menawa summoned the Medicine Maker, who returned to the busk.

Yahola called out, "Hasse Ola, Cekote, Anu, Otia."

The four boys approached the Heleshayv, who spoke words of wisdom to each and announced their new status as warriors within the tribe.

Yahola clapped four times, and the eight drummers responded with a thunderous beat—*thump-thump-thump-thump*. The ground seemed to vibrate beneath their rhythmic pounding. The drummers raised their voices, unleashing a primal chant that sliced through the night air: "*Ya na ho. Ya na wa na ho. We ya na hey, hey nay no way.*" Their cries echoed like the piercing calls of Hawk and Eagle. "*Ya na ho. Wee ya na, ya hey. Ya na ho. We ya na, hey na no way.*" The tempo quickened, the intensity grew, and the air sizzled with energy.

Led by Talof Harjo, a dozen warriors rushed onto the ceremonial grounds. They stomped, spun, and twirled in a blur of adrenaline and fierce energy. The *tafv opvnkv*—feather dance—was a sequence of sixteen acts showcasing war party tactics and virility. Hasse Ola, Cekote, Anu, and Otia joined in, each new warrior claiming his place in this rite of passage. The drums thundered—*doom-doom-doom-doom*—*thump-thump-thump-thump*. Their chants pierced the night air. "*Ya na ho. Ya na wa na ho. Wee ya na hey, hey nay no way.*"

Dancing one behind the other, Hasse Ola and Cekote had been best friends since birth, spending much of their lives together, running around the village and getting into mischief. They loved to taunt the girls, especially when they were down by the creek washing clothes or attending to other female chores. On one occasion, the boys stole the girls' clothes while they bathed, leading to swift justice from the mothers. But now, the pair were warriors, a role demanding greater humility and responsibility.

Cekote shouted, "We are warriors, brother!"

"The Bird and the Beaver," Hasse Ola replied, stomping around the heart fire.

"Soon, we'll have wives." Cekote swung his war club above his head. "I fancy your sister."

"Neena?" Hasse Ola glanced at the south arbor, spotting his sister cackling with her friends. "Then you fancy trouble, brother."

The pair laughed and danced, shouting whoops of youth and pride while sharing the day's delights and recognition. Mothers shed a few tears, and fathers stuck out their chests. It was a wonderful day in Apehkv.

At sunset, the women announced the evening supper. Once all had consumed their fill, the men approached the fire, rubbed new ashes on their bodies, and marched in a single line to the creek. There, they took a ceremonial dip and cleansed their bodies. Afterward, they returned to the busk and performed another stomp dance before retiring to their family camp to finish their feast.

At midnight, the tribe had another meal, and the warriors staged another feather dance. The festivities lasted throughout the night, ending shortly after dawn on the third sun—a time for rest and leisure. Menawa and the other clan elders drank *vsse* and discussed politics. The younger men played stickball or competed with their stone axes or wooden atlatls in throwing contests. The women prepared more food.

On the fourth sun, the People conducted a final friendship dance. They played games and feasted until the day's end and the close of the Green Corn Ceremony.

• • • •

Menawa and his family spent the next few days tending to their harvest and storing it for winter. The Mekko, however, had other worries: the Dark Spirit—and a toothache. Yahola had prescribed coneflower. Menawa placed a root cutting in his mouth. Perhaps it would help.

Troubled by the Dark Spirit, the Mekko debated whether to lead an expedition to the Great Hills. What if he found a passage and angered the Spirit? What then? What if it descended upon his village with fire and vengeance?

Or perhaps it was *honvntake*. Would these men be friendly, or would they attack and try to conquer? Was his curiosity worth risking his family's lives?

If danger was inevitable, the best defense was a good offense. Like the *yvnvsv*—the buffalo—heading into the storm was better than turning away.

Menawa felt a sharp pain; his tooth still throbbed.

That evening, as a waning moon arched across the night sky, Menawa and his family gathered inside their home to share another meal. This was Menawa's favorite time. He loved his wife and children, and spending time with them was his most cherished endeavor. His wife was his world; a little plump after bearing three cubs but loving, kind, and beautiful. His son was his pride, now a warrior. His oldest daughter was his hope, blossoming and in need of fatherly oversight. And his youngest daughter was the most precious little creature on Earth.

Halona served the evening meal: two stewed *pvce*—passenger pigeons—with pokeweed and wild onions, baked squash, *osafke*—corn drink—and hickory nut bread.

After supper, Menawa took Hasse Ola aside, beyond the ears of others.

"I have an important duty for you, my son."

"Yes, Father. What do you ask?"

"I'll be away from the village for several days. It is your sacred duty to watch over your mother and sisters. I depend on you. You are a warrior, and it's time for responsibility to match your age."

"Father, I was hoping to go on the expedition. I do not fear the Dark Spirit."

"Your Clan Leader, Talof Harjo, has made his decision. He and I know you are a brave warrior, but this duty requires even greater courage. Your mother and sisters are our cradles of life. They will bear our future. You must guard them well—if need be, with your life."

"Yes, Father." The young warrior nodded, though disappointment showed on his face.

"It is settled." Menawa patted Hasse Ola's shoulder. "Let us return to more pleasant topics."

They rejoined the family.

As Menawa rested, the light from the cooking fire bathed his family's faces, and their laughter warmed his heart. Soon, it was time for bed. The logs on the fire had dwindled to a bed of flickering coals. Hasse Ola, Neena, and little Mausi crawled into their bedding like rabbits in a burrow and fell fast asleep. Menawa placed another coneflower root in his mouth and lay beside his wife, her warmth close to his. He listened to her gentle breaths as she drifted off to sleep. He cherished his love for her, but worry tugged at his mind.

• • • •

The call of thrushes, yellowhammers, and swallows announced the morning light. Menawa stepped from his home and inhaled the cool, damp air. It was a pleasant day, perfect for fishing. Sturgeon, with its distinctive yellowish-orange hue, was his favorite. However, Menawa had other matters on his mind and must see to his duties. The Mekko marched to the busk and, near the heart fire, placed a half-painted red war club upon a folded blanket. Word spread, and the clan leaders assembled.

After customary greetings, Menawa spoke. "I propose we send an expedition to the Great Hills, find a passage, and confront the Dark Spirit."

"I concur." Talof Harjo seemed eager to prove his battle skills. "The Echaswvlke are prepared for whatever we find."

"We should see to our village's defenses," Tomucece said. "Who will protect our families if we go on this adventure?"

"If we destroy the Dark Spirit, we have protected our village," Talof Harjo countered.

"But what if this enemy slips by you?" Tomucece pressed.

"That won't happen." Talof Harjo sat tall.

"Our young Clan Leader is too sure of himself," Tomucece remarked.

"Our eldest is too cautious," Talof Harjo retorted.

Menawa turned to Yahola. "What do you say?"

"If this path is certain, we should send a small force from each clan. Our remaining warriors will defend the village."

"This is wise counsel." The Mekko pondered for a moment. He feared that dividing his forces might weaken their fighting strength. However, surprise could work to their advantage. Whatever evil lurked beyond the Great Hills might not anticipate an offensive maneuver. Menawa announced his decision. "We'll send twelve warriors from each clan. I will lead the Nokosvlke, Yahola the Hotvlkvlke, Talof Harjo the Echaswvlke, and Emestesego the Fuswvlke. Tomucece, my trusted brother, you will defend our village. I trust you will give your life for our families if Hesaketvmese demands it."

"You honor me, Mekko." Tomucece touched his chest.

"It is settled." Menawa stood. "Let us gather our force. We will assemble at the busk at Sun's peak."

The Council ended, word spread, and the warriors readied themselves for their mission. Each took time to say goodbye to their families. The expedition would span several days, with the unspoken possibility that some might not return—such things had happened before. Menawa had lost his elder brother to the Great Hills. He had wandered too close to its margins and vanished into its ghostly shadows. His brother had been the Mekko. Now, Menawa served in his stead. He often wondered if he would make the same decisions as his brother. This question haunted every choice he made or would ever make for the People. What would his wiser brother have done?

At midday, forty-eight warriors gathered at the busk. All sensed the danger, but all accepted the challenge. They departed the village and headed for the Great Hills.

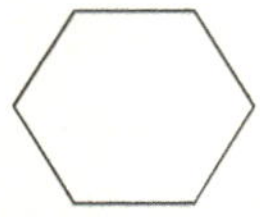

CHAPTER SIX

THE BEST OF FRIENDS

"**W**hat happened to the bunny?" the little girl asked.

"That old rabbit just ran down a hole," the old woman chortled, rocking in her chair.

"Tell us another, tell us another," the children shouted.

"That's the third one today."

"More, more," the children repeated.

"If I tell another, what shall we talk about tomorrow?"

"Your grandmother," an older girl suggested.

"Ah, yes. She was a sassy one, always gettin' into trouble and never learnin' her lesson."

"Like me?" the little girl asked.

"Yes, like you and like your great-great-grandmother. I see her in your eyes—such beautiful eyes. They were the best of friends."

"Your grandmother and my great-great-grandmother?"

"Yes, they were sisters, not by blood, yet inseparable. On one occasion, they played a trick on the boys. The two girls were down by the creek when the boys came running along. Your great-great-grandmother told the boys she had found a couple of tie snake eggs and had eaten both, hoping to gain the serpent's powers. Of course, the boys didn't believe her, but she hissed and dove into the water. You see, she was good at holding her breath. The boys started to worry, but were too afraid to enter the creek. When she finally popped up, her head was black, like the tie snake, with a white mark on her neck. She hissed at the boys, and seeing such a frightful sight, they ran away."

"Where did the white come from?" the little girl asked.

"Clay from the creek. She had found it the day before. So, she rubbed it on her neck and put creek mud in her hair."

"I wouldn't have fallen for that trick," the brash boy said, shaking his head.

"But your great-great-grandfather did," the old woman chuckled.

The boy's face turned red, and the children laughed.

"Tell us another, tell us another," the children begged.

"Enough for today. Did you enjoy your lunch? That was my grandmother's black bread recipe. The secret's in the sorghum. Gives it its color." The old woman stretched her arms and pushed back her wispy white hair. "Now, my dears, it's time for me to rest and dream. That's when they come to me—tales of the past and stories of adventure."

The children's eyes lit up. The old woman had sparked their imaginations one more time.

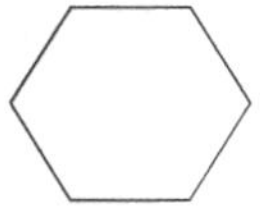

CHAPTER SEVEN

A HATCH

A12 and G18 stood motionless, staring at the destroyed and mangled remains of what had once been Quad-A. Black smoke billowed upward into the sky. Drones and other mechanicals worked tirelessly to quench the fire, spraying fire retardant on the severely damaged outer shell of Arc 1983.

A half-dozen G-Class engineering bots—capable of operating autonomously or in tandem—whirled into the Main Core, snuffing out pockets of fire and combustion.

Industrial in form, clad in yellow and silver alloy sheathing, the Gammas directed A12 and G18 away from the gaping hole. Within moments, they had sealed the opening and stabilized the breach.

"It looks safe over here," A12 said through the protective mask's voice amplifier, motioning for G18 to follow. The two raits hurried over to an area free of damage and debris. "Are you okay?"

"I'm covered in retardant." G18 brushed at the suit.

"Keep your mask on. The ventilation system will take a few minutes to scrub the atmosphere."

The two faits sat in a corner and waited. Minutes passed, and perhaps a few more. The flashing emergency lights turned to a steady red.

Alice announced, "We are experiencing a Condition Red alert. Please remain in your polycules. If you're in the Core, we'll open quadrant doors following this announcement. When we do, please remove your protective gear, proceed to a cleansing station at your quadrant's entrance, and return to your polys. If you are a Quadrant-A resident, go to Galley-C for further instructions. If you need first aid, we have dispatched medical. Thank you."

When the electronically generated broadcast ended, emergency doors cracked open and lumbered upward until Quads C, G, and T were fully accessible.

Medical bots rushed to those in need, assessed their wounds, and swiftly transported the injured via hover gurneys to the Medical Raion. Other frightened raits removed their protective clothing and hastened to their polys. However, some remained in the Core, huddled in small groups, comforting the distraught and injured.

"Seems your tour ended with a bang." G18 checked A12 for injuries. "You look okay, sweetie."

"You too." A12 slipped off the protective suit and kicked it away. "I hope my maits are okay."

"They're probably headed to Galley-C."

A12 blinked a few times. "My eyetap's not working. I can't verify their location."

"Mine's not working either, sweetie."

A12 wiped off some dust left by the protective mask's outline and breathed in, filling the lungs with freshly filtered air. "I guess we should follow the instructions."

"I hope your maits are okay. There's nothing left of Quad-A."

A12's eyes darted to G18; heat flushed the cheeks, and panic quivered through the veins. For the second time in days, A12 felt that presumed avoidable pain. "I have to go." A12 spun on a heel and bolted toward Galley-C.

• • • •

Galley-C was one ring down and on the Core's east side. Rather than take the lift, A12 bounded down the steps. The Tech scanned the Core. The damage was the same: twisted metal, broken fixtures, and frightened raits.

Engineering bots, built like autonomous multitools, had sealed the breach on Ring 20 and were busy tidying up the mess.

A12 dashed across the Core to the Quad-C portal. The Tech stripped down and stepped into the emergency cleanser. After a thorough rinse, A12 slipped on a paper-thin bronze jumpsuit and continued down a passage.

A12 entered Galley-C. Seventy or so other Quad-A residents had arrived and were milling about. Uncertainty showed in their expressions. The resident searched the crowd, hoping for the best, staring at each as if A81, A67, and A92's faces held a secret code only a mait could decipher: familiar eyes, happy smiles, and unique quirks. The rait circled the crowd twice or thrice, yet each pass bore no fruit. A dreadful despair overcame A12 like an ominous dark nebula, heavy and foreboding.

The Tech found a chair in a corner and plopped down, reflecting on life, friendship, and how quickly things had changed. A12 had been with them that morning, and all were in high spirits, absent any thoughts of doom or gloom, none imagining such a catastrophic event. Even the idea would have been implausible—laughable—a bad joke.

Sυ07—Upsilon 7—strode into the galley. A horde of frightened raits gathered around. A12 joined the group.

"Good evening, residents," Sυ07 said calmly. "There was a mishap in Quad-A. Engineering and Medical have responded and are taking action to restore our systems. We have moved the injured to the Medical Raion for treatment. Eighteen received *minor injuries*. They'll be returned to Zephyrus shortly. We have classified fourteen others with *major injuries*, requiring transport to Arc 94 for intensive care. The remaining seventy-two of you will need accommodations. If you have friends in other quadrants, please indicate your selection through your eyetap. We will do our best to accommodate your requests. Again, Medical will treat and heal your friends and return them to your Raion. What are your questions?"

"Your honor, my eyetap's not working." A40 was still shaking from the explosion. "What should I do?"

"We temporarily paused your augmentation. Your tech will reactivate within the hour. So, please be patient."

A06 raised a hand. "Your honor, who was injured?"

"We will post a list on the galley displays once we adjourn. I assure you, Medical will heal your friends and return them to your Raion. However, please note that it will take time. For patients transported to Arc 94, expect thirty days."

"Your honor, how long will it take to repair Quad-A?" A63 shifted impatiently from foot to foot, perhaps only inconvenienced by the affair.

"Assume thirty days for repairs, and, given our limited accommodations, those sent to Arc 94 must remain there until the repair is complete."

"Your honor, was anyone killed?" A40 asked morbidly.

"The anomaly significantly injured fourteen residents. But, please be assured, we will heal and return your friends."

A12 raised a hand. "Your honor, I saw something outside the Arc?"

"That was a projection reflecting off our outer shell. It protects us from harmful radiation and other dangers lurking beyond our boundaries. It's like the TEIS in your polycules."

A12's eyebrows shot up. The Tech had heard the response, which seemed logical, but the senses told a different story. The light, the wind, the colors, and the depth and breadth of distance felt authentic. Its physical forms appeared as genuine as A12. Casting social norms aside, A12 dared a second question. "Your honor, is this something we might see and experience?"

Sʋ07's pleasant manner dimmed, and the eyes went dark. "Let's focus on the problem at hand. Pleasantries beyond your assigned duties shouldn't be a concern."

There was an awkward silence, but after a moment, another rait asked a question, and others followed. Upsilon 7 responded until the confused and curious seemed satisfied. In a final act of pretentious empathy, the Sophist attempted a smile, although it was an odd expression for a Council member. The Sophist reassured the group that all was well, and order would soon be restored. Sυ07 turned and marched from the galley.

Within seconds, the injured lists popped up on the galley displays. The raits huddled around the screens, pushing and maneuvering to see what it revealed. The major injury list read:

```
RESIDENTS TO ARC1994:
A1983AA02 A1983AT09 A1983AA10
A1983AA15 A1983AC17 A1983AA27
A1983AG32 A1983AC59 A1983AA66
A1983AA67 A1983AA72 A1983AA81
A1983AA91 A1983AA92
```

A12 clutched at the chest and gasped: A67, A81, and A92. All three maits were on the list. The Tech staggered back to a table and flopped down. "I can't believe this." A12 put head into hands. "My friends."

$$\bullet \; \bullet \; \bullet \; \bullet$$

A12 left Galley-C and headed for the Core. It was 1800 hours. The rait found an empty booth in a quiet nook near a display of lush green plants. It was a beautiful evening, like every evening on an Arc. It was the perfect temperature, the perfect hue, and the perfect ambiance, despite what had happened and despite bots humming and buzzing, cleaning, fixing, and restoring.

A12 spotted G18 approaching from Quad-T, moving with that familiar swish, like the hum of the Arc's ventilation system—constant and impossible to ignore. The rait's expression was carefree, unconcerned, as if recent events held no weight. Everything about G18 seemed restored, calm, and orderly— untouched by the chaos.

"I want to feel you," A12 said.

"At your desire." G18 sat down and scooted close to A12.

"My maits were in Quad-A."

"Goodness, sweetie, are they okay?"

"They're on the major injury list. They were sent to Arc 94 for treatment. Upsilon 7 said they have to stay there until Quad-A is repaired."

"Well, that's rather inconvenient. So much for improving my rating."

A12 ignored the heartless comment.

"Or you might get new maits. That might be fun."

"Why would you say that?"

"I don't follow?"

"Upsilon 7 said they would be okay."

"Of course, sweetie. I simply meant one shouldn't pass up an opportunity."

"What opportunity?"

"Your rating, sweetie."

"My rating is the least of my concerns. Don't you get it? I'm worried about my maits."

"Oh dear, I've triggered someone. Sweetie, worry will not change anything, and I'm not the one who blew up your quadrant."

"I didn't say you did." A12 drew a slow, steady breath, the weight of isolation pressing in. G18 was the rule, not the exception—detached, shallow, oblivious. Casual friends sufficed in good times, but seemed to vanish in moments of real need. Support and empathy would have to be sought elsewhere. "I should go. I need to figure this out."

"It seems so, sweetie."

"And a place to stay."

"You're welcome to stay with us. We have an opening. It's yours if you want it."

"Thanks, but T30 has already offered. 30 is, I mean was, the mait of a friend."

"Who's this?"

"A former dait."

"You haven't mentioned this before."

"T23 was just a friend." A12 looked away, hesitant to delve further into uncomfortable feelings or negative thoughts. Residents spoke openly as a norm; secrets, however, were another of those selfie conditions. "What I'm trying to say is my friend might be on Arc 94."

"So?"

"So, maybe I could send a message."

"Why?"

"So, T23 could check on my maits."

"Would that make you happy, sweetie?" G18 offered a half-hearted smile that didn't quite reach the eyes.

The Tech sighed. "Happy… what a strange word. I'll see you tomorrow."

"At your desire, sweetie."

"My place, say 1700?"

"Will do." A contrived pout appeared on G18's lips. "Try not to worry, sweetie; it serves no purpose other than to spin little black holes in your mind. Focus on your duties."

"You sound like Upsilon 7." A12 lumbered away, headed for Quad-T.

• • • •

When A12 entered Polycule AT-20-6, T30 asked about the injured. The Tech relayed Sυ07's report, word for word. A12 favored T30—one of the rare exceptions, a kind and caring rait. With strawberry-blonde hair, the hallmark of the required MC1R gene, T30 exuded genuine compassion and, at that moment, was the best possible medicine. The two raits sat together on the edge of the berth. T30 leaned in, wrapping A12 in a firm hug. A rush of emotions surged through the Tech; tears welled at the corners of the eyes.

"Today was hard." A12 wiped an eye.

"Would you like to talk about it?" T30 asked.

"Maybe later."

T30's arm tightened around A12. "It's easier when you have friends."

"Yes, it is." After a moment of gushing and wiping, A12 asked for space.

T30 hugged the friend and obliged.

Unbelievably, the day had begun with a routine tour of Ecology but had ended in horror. Exhausted, A12 lumbered across the poly, removed the disposable bronze jumpsuit, and shoved it down a recycling chute. After a quick cleanse, the rait, dressed in a new blue jumpsuit, and guzzled down a nourishment, hoping to ease, at least, that pain. The Tech retreated to a borrowed cube to rest and reflect. Instinctively, A12 opened one of the cube's storage compartments. It wasn't there—not the same poly. "My flower."

• • • •

After a restless night, A12 woke, slid from the bed, voided, cleansed, dressed, and headed for work. The Tech went about lighting inspections as though they were a preset function on another programmed day.

The assignment was to inspect all four Zephyrus rings in the Core plus the three undamaged quadrants. Following such an incident, a thorough check was necessary to ensure that all lighting systems were functioning nominally. The task would take several days.

A12 tramped down the stairs to Ring 21, planning to work up to Ring 18. The Tech inspected the lighting closet: all circuits responded appropriately. A12 checked fixtures, including quaint mood lights in small nooks, emergency lighting mounted above the deck, and general lighting programmed to the circadian cycle. Everything was in order—on to Ring 20.

The next stop was another lighting closet. A12's eyetap sent a deactivation code to the control panel's safety shield. While waiting for the light emitter to turn green, A12's foot struck something on the deck—a square tile, slightly askew. Curious, A12 crouched and picked it up. It was an overhead panel, dislodged and now out of place. Instinctively, A12 looked up and spotted exposed cables snaking through the overhead—and just above, a hatch barely large enough for a rait. A12 reached up and touched it. It shifted. The recent blast must have loosened the tile and weakened the hatch's clasp. A12's mind raced with thoughts of the labyrinth beyond and its unknown destinations. An urge stirred within—an unconscious pull, driven by some innate curiosity.

A12 darted from the closet and bolted up the stairs, skipping steps along the way, headed to Ring 19's primary lighting closet. The Tech opened the door and looked up—another overhead tile—and, underneath, another hatch. It was the same, although locked, but it was there—a path to another world. A12 dashed up to Ring 18. Another tile, and another hatch. A12's mind raced with mischief.

• • • •

A12 entered Polycule AT-20-6 just as T30 was leaving. They exchanged pleasantries and a hug. A12 grabbed a mint-chocolate mocha from the cooler, sank onto the berth, and waited for G18. It had been a long, taxing day, filled with thoughts of maits, that special dait, and a deep need to share and express feelings. T23 would have been interested in the hatch—always attentive and understanding.

There was a figure at the entrance. "I want to feel you."

"Thanks. I feel you."

The Botanist entered, stepped over to the cooler, and grabbed a Number 2, a café cacao consisting of hemp milk, cocoa, sugarcane juice, medium-roast coffee beans, sunflower oil, and flaxseed oil.

"Well, I had a good day." G18 put on another fake pout. "But, I did wonder about you, sweetie. Are you feeling better?"

"I'm fine." A12's gaze drifted to a bulkhead. "How was work?"

"We harvested a crop of cucumbers. Ran some tests, checked on a batch of melons. That T02? A real tease. A walking chiller unit—ignored me all day. Is this what you wanted to talk about, sweetie?"

A12 stood. "Let's cleanse."

"Really, you invited me over here for a cleanse? Someone must be horn—"

"Please." A12 looked around as though a mere cleanse was some sort of covert rendezvous.

A12 disrobed, G18 close behind. They stepped into the watatory. The scent of neroli—spicy with a hint of orange blossoms—filled the air as warm water cascaded over them. A12 picked up a sponge and began washing G18's shoulders. "I want to discuss yesterday. What we saw beyond the Arc."

"How about something more pleasant, sweetie?" G18's lips curled in a slow, lustful grin.

"It seemed so real."

"The Sophist said it was a projection." G18 turned so A12 could wash the back.

"What about the hole?"

"What about it?"

"It was real, too. You saw it."

"Yes, of course."

"But they want us to believe everything beyond that was fake?"

G18 turned around. "So, what's your point, sweetie?"

A12 lowered the sponge. "There's something they don't want us to know."

"Oh, dear, what would that be?"

"I'm not sure, but the Sophist did confirm there's some kind of outside space… But we can't go there… However, bots do."

"That's probably where they go to rust."

"And yet, we traveled through some type of space to get here. What was that?"

"I was asleep, or perhaps bored…"

"Aren't you curious, just a little?"

"It's hostile, sweetie. That's all I know and the reason we live on an Arc." G18 turned toward A12. "Forget yesterday. Let's play—"

"But, you do admit there is an external space, and we traveled through it to get here."

"Yes, of course."

"And we've lived on other Arcs?"

"Yes, yes." G18 banged on the soap dispenser, slapped a blob of gel into the hair, and started washing.

"If it is real, why are we locked up on an Arc?"

"I'll bite. You tell me."

"They're trying to control us."

G18 hesitated, just for a moment, before forcing a grin. "Oh, my goodness, sweetie. Why would they do that?"

"I don't know, but I'm going to find out and get off this Arc."

"*What*?"

"I want to see it, smell it, touch it."

G18 stared at A12 as if searching for signs of mental illness. "You're a wild one, aren't you?"

"What if I am?"

"Let's assume you're right. How would that even be possible?"

"I'm working on it."

"Sweetie. You're driving me crazy with all this talk. Come, let me wash your back." G18 grabbed a sponge. "This should make kitty feel better." G18 ran the warm sponge up and down A12's spine. "How does that feel? Happy, I hope?"

"There it is again—happy. Be happy. Smile, everyone. Smile. Maybe I don't want to be happy. Maybe this little kitty wants to roar? Or, how about—"

"How about this." G18 reached around suggestively and began washing the fait's chest.

A12 stayed on topic. "What about choice. The Sophists speak of truth. So, what's wrong with looking for it?"

"You won't let this go, will you?" G18 threw the sponge on the deck; the rait seemed a bit steamed. "I don't understand what you have to complain about."

"Everything. Why do we exist? Why do we live on an Arc? Why do we let others control us? Green light go, red light stop. Why do we submit to these absurdities?"

G18 let out an exasperated grunt, rinsed off, and stepped toward the exit. "Let's go to the Core—I need a drink." G18 looked over a shoulder. "And it seems you do, too, along with a few shots of pink."

• • • •

Along the way, A12 kept the conversation light so as not to further annoy G18 or arouse others' curiosity. Arc norms were a seductive allure, but conformity was the true standard. It seemed fooling residents was easy, but convincing them they had been fooled was the more challenging task. G18 had shown little interest in the facts, facts right in front of the face, and like others, G18 believed wholeheartedly in the system. For most, the difference between truth and falsehood was of little consequence. G18 was simply another member of the mimicry, blindly imitating the model, hopelessly unconscious. A12 tried to follow the routine, but not without reasoning, never questioning and assuming there was nothing more. The object of life should be to escape the insanity, not follow the herd.

The pair strolled past a nourishment bar in the Core, where residents clustered in small groups, their voices rising and falling with the latest scuttlebutt. Several gossiped about the incident, their annoyance evident as they speculated when life might finally return to normal.

A12 and G18 found a secluded nook.

"Any news of your maits?" G18 asked.

"No, but I asked 30 if there was some way to send a message."

G18's brow arched. "How about a supply requisition? We could slip in a message. Never thought of it until now."

"Speaking of thinking," A12 said, "I wonder where bots go when they're off duty."

G18 let out a cynical laugh. "Those buckets of bolts? They are probably busy giving each other lube jobs. You should ask one."

"Hey, not a bad idea."

"I was joking."

"Are you sure?" A12 leaned in. "Engineering bots might spill their secrets. I could talk about lighting as a lead-in. Or bar bots? They're supposed to keep confidences."

The pair looked at one another; it was a crazy idea. Both burst out laughing.

But then, A12's expression changed from comedy to one of inquiry. "Let's give it a go. I'll ask some questions and see what he says!"

"I don't believe this. Be careful, sweetie; don't ask anything too touchy. No telling how that pasty-faced metal manikin might react. I wanted to relax this evening, not get locked up."

"I'll be right back." A12 strolled over to the bar. "A couple of Number 3's, with pink, please."

"Right away, resident." The bar bot began preparing the two whipped coconut, pineapple, and orange concoctions topped off with a dash of fresh nutmeg and a shot of meta.

A12 smiled, waited, and observed. Bar bots were known for their vibrant personalities and sharp wit. This one glided smoothly along the bar on a mounted platform, tirelessly operating twenty-four/eight. With a humanoid form—head, torso, and arms powered by advanced actuators—it moved with a dexterity that bordered on lifelike, even without legs. Beyond serving drinks, the bot engaged in light conversation, and its advanced social algorithms lent it a surprising charm. Dressed in a red, single-breasted mess jacket over a crisp white shirt and a black bow tie, it exuded a sense of style. Sure, his face was a bit pasty, and his alpha identification a touch quirky, but he certainly was a chatterbot.

"Hey, Fred," A12 said, "what's up with yesterday's drama?"

"Tragic, just tragic," Fred answered with a twang, giving a drink tumbler a lively shake.

"I wonder what happened?"

"Can't say. I was stuck here when I heard the boom. *Haha.*"

"Were you scared?"

"Nope. I was fixated on my work—welded to what I was doing. *Haha.*"

"If you could've run, where would you have gone?"

"To maintenance in a sub-ring. I hear it's nice and safe down there." Fred slid two drinks across the counter. "Here are your Number 3's. Enjoy!"

"Thanks. Well, take care, Fred. No more boom."

"Yep, no more boom-booms. Have a pleasant evening, resident."

A12 returned to the nook and handed G18 the coconut pineapple drink. "Fred mentioned something about a sub-ring?"

"Probably below Ring 60. On Arc 37, a few of my daits lived in Caecias. They were a naughty bunch—most worked in Life Support. They used to talk about the lower rings, but they said it was unsafe."

"How so?"

"Radiation."

"Really?"

"And monsters!"

"Uh-huh."

"That's what they said."

"So why would Fred say it's safe?"

"No telling what that cackling canister might say."

"Maybe I should order another drink."

"Sweetie, you've reached your limit—your metrics. You're going to lower your rating."

"What if I do?" A12 tossed back the last drops of the nourishment, then slammed the empty container on the table.

Nearby, a couple of raits almost leapt out of their jumpsuits, shooting A12 sharp, disapproving looks.

"Seems like they're still rattled from the explosion," G18 chuckled.

"Monsters," A12 muttered, shaking the head. "Seriously?"

"Just repeating what I heard."

"Looks like I've got some research to do."

"How about at my place? We could test out a little cause and effect."

"Not feeling it, sorry."

"That's the point, sweetie. To feel it."

A12 stood. "See you tomorrow."

G18 grumbled, "Tomorrow, always tomorrow."

A12 hastened away.

• • • •

A12 entered AT-20-6 and crawled into the berth. T30, T02, and A53 were in bed. T30 rolled over and asked about the day. A12 shared a few details, including sending a message.

"I have a friend in Quad-C, Boreas," T30 said. "C85 is going through the Garden Ceremony tomorrow night, and there's a chance they might go to

Arc 94. My friend could carry a message."

"That might work, but they'll cleanse 85 upon arrival."

"I'll ask 85 to hide it where it can't be found." T30 grinned.

A12 grimaced. "More than I needed to hear." The Tech contemplated what the message might say. If it worked, it might work a second and third time. "Can I give it to you in the morning?"

"Absolutely."

Excited, A12 crawled from the bed and settled into a cube. The Tech thought for a moment. "Hey, Alice, what should I say?"

"It's hard to give specific advice without knowing more about your situation, but here are some general tips: define the problem, gather information, consider your options, seek advice, take action, and evaluate your progress."

"Sure, but couldn't you tell me what to say?"

"As an AI language entity, I cannot decide for you. However, I can provide guidance and suggestions based on my general knowledge. For specific advice, please share more details about your situation."

"I can't do that."

"If you can't take the steps I suggested, it's important to remember seeking help is always an option. Some suggestions are: talk to a friend, speak to a Sophist, join a support group, or ask Alice."

"This is frustrating."

"I'm sorry to hear you're frustrated. It's understandable to feel discomfort when facing difficult situations or when things don't go as planned. Here are additional tips to manage your day: take a break, practice relaxation techniques, identify the source of the frustration, reach out for support—"

"That's enough, Alice."

"If you need further assistance, please don't hesitate to ask. And note it's okay to feel frustrated. Taking care of yourself and recognizing your feelings is essential to moving forward."

"Thanks, Alice."

"You're welcome!"

"Yeah, you're welcome too."

"Have a nice day!"

"Do you always have to have the last word?"

"No. Hope you feel better!"

A12 grumbled—time to craft a message. The Tech opened a cube compartment, grabbed a tool bag, and removed a small adhesive tab used for marking wires and cables. A12 wrote:

A1983AA81, 67, 92 on A1994. OK?

A12 rolled up the message and placed it inside a small pill-shaped capsule for storing small lighting components—it was the perfect size and shape.

A12 slid into bed, careful not to disturb those fast asleep. The Tech eventually drifted off, but sleep came fitfully, interrupted by strange memories and nagging thoughts—perhaps ignorance was bliss or even strength. Most residents believed there was utility in compliance, in living automatically and uncritically. It was better that way, whether right or wrong, driven by the fear of being labeled a selfie. But those strange memories kept returning—visions of a tree, not in Ecology, but in a wild forest. The flow of water, cool and clear, not from a faucet but winding freely through a meadow. A person running, not along a metallic pathway, but under a sky pouring with rain.

Moreover, these images didn't just appear—they resonated with an inexplicable familiarity as if they belonged to a consciousness shared across lifetimes, spanning countless selves. Each scene, each sensory flash, tugged at something primal—a connection not singular but tied to a bottomless well of collective experience, something ancient and universal. And beneath it all, an insatiable urge—a restless need to search for a truth buried under layers of compliance and false contentment.

The following day, when the lights activated, A12 yawned and stretched. It had been a restless night. The Tech slid from the bed, voided, cleansed, and downed a mint-chocolate mocha. A12 gave T30 the secret message and clambered off to work. Today's assignment was a continuation of lighting checks, but hopefully, the discovery of other hidden egresses and possibly something more, much more.

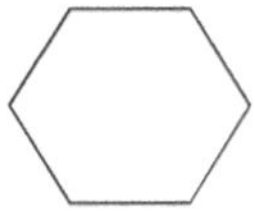

CHAPTER EIGHT

THE COUNCIL

A few hours after T23's outburst in the Core, an eyetap communique announced an audio party for the Thraskias Raion. The message instructed residents to go straight to their quadrant galleys. The party would begin at 1630 hours.

T42 was one of the first to arrive, but soon, other residents piled in, appearing quite excited about an impromptu musical experience sure to delight.

T86 and T77 joined their mait at the bar.

"This should be fun." T86 squeezed in next to T42.

"Where's 23?" T42 stretched the neck and looked around. "Don't want our new mait feeling left out."

"I saw 23 in the Core earlier with Phi 10," T77 said. "Didn't look happy."

"I wonder what happened?" T42 asked. "23 seemed okay this morning."

T77 shrugged. "Maybe our new mait is not cut out for bio work."

"T23 made it through training," T86 countered.

"That's right," T42 added. "23 must be at work. Doing a great job of it, I'm sure."

T77 smirked. "We can't all be Engineers."

T42's bright blue eyes bored into T77. "Did someone forget to take their happy pill this morning? Let's find a—"

A bell rang—*ding, ding, ding*—and Alice announced, "Welcome to this special audio event. We'd like to share four new experiences that will soon be available in your polys. Playtime is fourteen minutes and forty-four seconds. Please find a seat, don your headsets, and enjoy!"

T42, T77, and T86 weaved through the crowd and found their seats. They put on the headsets, the galley lights dimmed, and the first track played.

T42 listened as electric strings wove an enchanting melody in C minor, flowing through a 16-bar progression of descending suspensions and graceful resolutions. A warm, europic rhythm washed over T42's mind, bathing the soul in a tropical kaleidoscope of melodic hues. The song rose to its chorus, concluding with a luminous Picardy cadence.

Another began; this time, sliding steel vibrations echoed in T42's ears, the notes bending with a tender, almost vocal quality. Its smooth, Farinian sleepwalk rhythm carried a lilting sway, a gentle push and pull that signaled relaxation and letting go, as if floating in a warm, tranquil sea. The melody glided effortlessly, its soft, syncopated chords resonating in the depths of the mind. T42's thoughts wandered, entwined in bittersweet harmonics that hovered just beyond reach, like whispers on a fading breeze.

The third track began, and a soft, ambient guitar took flight, its smooth, rolling chords cascading in waves. The melody unfolded like the gentle drift of a bird in flight, weightless and free in a boundless sky. Yet it carried an undercurrent of something profound—an unspoken longing, as if the song yearned for something distant and unreachable. T42 felt the music's cradle, a slow, steady embrace that stretched time, quieting the mind and slowing the pulse. The melody lingered, suspended in the air like the soft beat of wings above an endless horizon. There was no urgency, only the peace of flight, the serenity of the vast, open sky.

The fourth track played—a lullaby of Orbisonic proportions, a song of brightly colored jesters, magical nights, and stardust. Its operatic rhythm was tender and kind, evoking desire—whimsical yet sad, mystical but transcendent. T42's eyes grew heavy, the heartbeat slowed, and the subject slipped into a quiet, unguarded state.

This was when it happened: the special headsets executed their true purpose and inserted three nanotubes into T42's left ear, each destined for a specific locale within the brain. One traveled to the hippocampus, another to the neocortex, and the third to the amygdala. When they reached their target, and at the height of the last falsetto, Sophia activated their programs, and the nanotubes did their bidding, erasing specific episodic memories.

Unaware of deception or trickery, the audio experience came to an end. T42 woke and removed the headsets. "That was wonderful."

"Made me sleepy." T77 yawned. "Especially that third one."

"It was *relaxing*," T86 buzzed.

"Nope, made me sleepy."

"How about a drink? That'll get you going," T42 suggested.

"Wishful intentions never solve anything," T77 drawled.

"*Uh-huh*. I'll be right back." T42 headed for the bar.

When T42 returned, the three maits enjoyed their drinks, and the party continued. But later, a bell rang, the event was over, and residents departed the galley; less, of course, a regrettable mem trace of an argument between a Sophist and an indecorous rait.

T42 was the first to enter IT-11-4, followed by T77 and T86.

"There's our mait," T86 said. T23 was blissfully asleep on the berth.

"Surprise, surprise," T77 grumbled.

"*Shhh*. Let's not wake the tired sort," T42 whispered.

The other two maits nodded, one somewhat stubbornly, and the three climbed into bed.

• • • •

Neptune's Day, or some called it Norsday, began as usual, when the lights came to life in IT-11-4. T23 woke, jumped up, and grabbed a nourishment. "Yesterday was a mighty fine day." T23 took a big swig of the vanilla drink. "And I'm lookin' forward to the next."

"Someone's in a chipper mood." T86 flopped over and let the satin sheet roll off. "And where were you yesterday? You missed the party."

"Fabricatin' hearts, some sort of rush order."

"Hear that, 77?" T86 said. "Our new mait was working."

T77 rolled over in bed, showing a bit of backside. "Wonderful."

"It is wonderful," T23 said.

T42 seemed tickled at T23's enthusiasm. "Who were the patients?"

"Not sure. I was too busy."

"Well, it sounds like you had a fantastic first day," T42 said. "And the good news is we get to do it all over again!"

"Oh great, another day of staring at screens but hoping for moonbeams." T77 crawled out of bed.

"Someone's in a grumpy mood." T42 chuckled.

"I'm not suggesting today will be boring, just a slow-motion repeat of yesterday: wake, work, sleep, wake, work, sleep, followed by a repeat of Moon, Mars, and six more."

The other maits gave each other a look as they headed to the watatory.

• • • •

As the residents of Arc1994 went about their day, the Council of Sage gathered in the Symposium on Ring 5. Upon entering this classically decorated wood-and-weave sanctuary, the Sophists marched to a serving buffet. They poured a refreshment from a tall vessel adorned with images of Sophia and Gaia, personifications of wisdom and Earth: one wise and beautiful, the other the primordial cradle of life. The drink, an ancient recipe, was a nectar of fermented grapes, aged in oak and preserved for the ages. Premixing with water to prevent overindulgence, the Sophists followed their own advice of moderation.

With drinks in hand, they took their seats—sixteen golden reclines arranged in a circle, each representing a mark on the rose, a magnetic destination.

Sκ01, a tall and attractive Director with long, flowing black hair, a firm jaw, and an even firmer disposition for duty, stood at the north point. "Happiness is within us."

The Council exulted, "Hear, hear."

Sζ02, the Deputy, not as tall but carrying an equal sense of purpose, rose at the north-by-northeast recline and said, "The wise do not seek pleasure but avoid pain."

The Council exulted, "Hear, hear."

Sλ03, the Director of Operations, stood next and said, "Distress is pain arising from the anticipation of aversion."

The Council applauded.

Sρ04, the Logistics Planner, said, "Community rewards those who serve."

"Hear, hear."

Sπ05, an excellent navigator at the east point, proclaimed, "Perfection in the job puts happiness in the work."

"Hear, hear," and the tributes continued, one after another, until the sixteenth.

Finally, Sη16, a master of energy, stood and said, "All intelligent beings, by nature, desire happiness."

The congress began.

Sκ01 said, "We had an unfortunate incident in the Core. The event on Arc 83 prompted a display of malcontent. It seems an r-select found their work to their dislike. What actions have we taken to improve our operating procedures?"

Sω13, the Information Technology Sophist, stood. "Sophia created a new programming rule, ensuring medical engineers do not see patient identification codes. She encrypted the original and replaced it with an innocuous simile."

"Excellent." Sκ01 straightened the shoulders, sitting tall on the golden sofa.

Sυ06, the Intelligence and Security Sophist, said, "Sophia cleansed T23's episodic mem files. We returned the resident to the Raion."

"Splendid." Sκ01 gave Upsilon 6 a nod of confidence.

Sφ10, the Arc's Sociologist and Public Health Sophist, added, "Sophia scanned and cleansed all Thraskias residents. She administered an audio-based nano-nepenthe. An analysis confirmed that thirty-two residents were infected by the meme. She quarantined and deleted the virus, then documented the results in her archives."

"Excellent, Phi 10." Sκ01 turned to the deputy. "Zeta 2, please send out an incident notification. On to our next topic. What is the status of our fourteen patients?"

Sχ11, the Medical Sophist, stood. "None were salvageable. The explosion and fire destroyed all fourteen. Medical is fabricating replacements as we speak. They will be ready within twenty-four hours; once printed, maturity will take another seventy-two, and assembly will require two additional days and a third for education and evaluation. We'll test for final function on the eighth day."

"All in a week's work. Well done," Sκ01 said. "Now to Arc 83's status."

Sι15, the Structural Engineer, said. "The explosion severely damaged Quad-A and punched a hole in the Arc's exostructure. It will take thirty days to replace and repair. Engineering assets from three Arcs are assisting."

"May I add, Kappa 1," Sυ07 said, "Arc 83 has asked us to hold the fourteen until the repair is complete."

"Very well," Sκ01 said. "Theta 8, please message Arc 83 that we will comply."

"I'll see to it," the Communications Sophist said.

Sκ01 scanned the Council. "Are there other discussion points?"

None were put forward. Sκ01 adjourned the congress, but before the Sophists departed and returned to their duties, they had one more libation from the vessel.

• • • •

In the Medical Raion on Ring 17, raits buzzed like bees, fabricating organs and prosthetics for Arc1983's casualties. T23 was busy fulfilling an order for seven hearts, while T77 manufactured bio-ink for tissue fabrication. T42 focused on producing skeletal components, and T86 ensured lab orders were completed and prepped for the next stage. Meanwhile, in the Science Raion on Ring 14, bots were crafting the most sophisticated organ of all—the brain.

As biofabrication efforts go, brains took longer to manufacture than other organs. Thus, Arcs maintained repositories of unspecialized brains in stasis known as Mind Cellars. Aged to a specific wetware maturity, Mind Cellars housed white, or male, brains representing the seed and red, or female, brains representing the menses. As the organs matured, G-Class science bots preloaded basic subroutines into their molecular domains, organized as regulative, emotional, sensory, or cognitive functions.

The first preload targeted the brainstem, activating its role as a relay between the cerebrum, cerebellum, and spinal cord. It also handled autonomic subroutines, such as breathing, heartbeat, body temperature, and digestion.

Next, the bots preloaded emotion-based functions into the amygdala and related cortices. The first was *receive*, the ability to pay attention, feel pleasure or pain, and perceive it in others. Then came *respond*, the capacity to react to or predict sensory stimuli, including a fear response. After was *reflect*, the skill to value emotional cues, followed by *arrange*, which allowed the brain to contrast, relate, and expound on experiences. Last, *connect* ensured the brain absorbed and recognized complex, abstract sensory experiences, including social intelligence.

The bots recalibrated their tools for the next phase, which involved sensory preloads directed at the cerebrum and cerebellum, including self-awareness of both living and nonliving forms. The first was *perceive*, enabling the brain to use sensory prompts to guide motor skills, like determining how much water to pour into a cup or interpreting a nonverbal cue. Then came *prepare*, creating a mental, physical, or emotional readiness to follow instructions and act accordingly. Afterward, *operate* and *practice* enabled the brain to handle intricate psychomotor responses, such as those involved in work and pleasure. Finally, *adapt* and *originate* provided the flexibility to modify existing movement patterns or create new ones for unfamiliar situations.

The bots performed another recalibration and download. This time, it was the cognitive modules, or executive subroutines, in the cerebrum. First was *learn*, or working memory, guiding thought, action, and emotion, including the ability to ignore irrelevant stimuli. Then came *comprehend* and *apply*, the recall and problem-solving faculties. *Analyze* followed, offering the capacity to examine components and relationships and synthesize them into a cohesive whole. The final module was *evaluate*—the judgment required to state conclusions and assess situations based on evidence and criteria.

Once the preloads were completed, the result was a living brain matured to twenty-four years. Like other recent Arc1994 bioengineering efforts, the science bots had received an order. They selected eight white brains and six red ones, placed them in incubation cubes, and delivered them to their destination.

The time had come for the final, most complex step. In a fabrication lab on Ring 15, the bots inserted the brains into a specialized NOLE, accessed each patient's biofile, linked it with the appropriate brain, and initiated a custom download and synchronization. This process encompassed realms of consciousness and unconsciousness, both personal and collective, as well as archetypes, linguistics, values, memories, and more. However, full syncs were not possible due to the explosion that had destroyed all fourteen patients. The bots would have to complete the syncs using archival files. Fortunately, Sophia maintained updated backups. The goal, to keep memory loss within acceptable limits—no more than 3.4 defects per million downloads.

Now, it was Sophia's turn. She ran a validation test to ensure the archive and the brain were identical. When finished, she activated the NOLE's green light.

The science bots transferred the fourteen brains—eight whites and six reds—to the Academy.

• • • •

In Bio-Assembly Room 6-17, two medical bots gathered components for a rebuild. As the hours passed, a sapient being took shape—made, not born—rising as if from Gaia herself. The bots assembled the skeletal system first, followed by the circulatory, digestive, and endocrine systems. The integumentary system came last—skin, hair, and nails. After a blood infusion, they stretched the final strips of flesh taut, smoothing out the wrinkles and securing it at the navel.

The med bots maneuvered the newly assembled being into the NOLE. As the chamber activated, lights flashed and swirled, and a surge of electricity coursed through the body as the room filled with the hum of advanced technology. Seconds ticked by. Then—signs of life. The chest rose, the breathing labored but steady. A finger twitched—then another. A warmth spread beneath the skin, and color crept into the cheeks.

A med bot snapped an elastic band around the patient's wrist, certifying life. The identification code read A1983AA92.

Transport bots wheeled the resident into Post-Operations Room 6-15 for monitoring and evaluation. The anesthetized patient would remain there for twenty-four hours to rest and recover.

The next day, A92 awoke to a stark, artificial glow. Blinking against the brightness, the rait's neon-green eyes flickered open, sluggish and unfocused. The room was empty. The sterile air carried a sharp, clinical crispness, punctuated by the rhythmic beeps and blips of machines recording vital signs and life functions.

A92 touched the translucent dome encapsulating the bed. Slick and warm, it felt almost alive, like a pulsing membrane. A faint hum vibrated through the structure, and something sweet permeated the air—perhaps synthetic.

A medical bot approached, her mechanical eyes blinking in perfect rhythm. Mary, as her badge read, wore a smile, artificial yet oddly reassuring. With a lilt, she said, "How are ye feeling, me dear?"

A92 tried to speak, but no sound emerged; the throat felt parched and crusty, like the cracked surface of a sun-baked planet. A92 cleared the throat. "I'm a bit knackered." The rait's voice sounded frail, guttural, and hoarse. "What happened to me? What did you feed the head?"

"Aye, ye're doin' fine, dear. Ye're recovering from an injury." Mary smiled, almost as if she really cared.

"Injury?" A92 tried to sit up but slumped back, weak and dizzy. "Please, what happened?"

Mary paused as her Beta-class chipset computed a response. "Would ye be so kind as to state yer identification, purpose, raion, and quadrant?"

A92 sighed. "I'm A1983AA92, Logistics Administrator, Zephyrus, Quad-A. What day is it?"

"It's Venus's Day. And yer maits' identifications?"

A92 hesitated, a bit frustrated. "A81, A12, and A67." The throat felt a bit stronger. "Now, please, tell me what is going on?"

"Ye had a wee fall, but now ye're fine. Relax, dear, and enjoy yer rest. I'll bring yer favorite nourishment." Mary buzzed out of the room before A92 could press further.

Frustration continued to bubble as A92 tried again to sit up but was met with the same helplessness. Lying back, the resident stared at the translucent dome, its warm glow reflecting a distorted version of the face. The rait's mind fumbled for clarity, trying to piece together what had happened. A fall? That's all Mary had said. But why couldn't anything else come to mind? Not even in the deepest corners of the mind. Nothing—just a blank void.

A92 lifted the sheets, hands unsteady, peering beneath. Everything seemed fine. Toes, legs, fun parts—all accounted for. No scars, no bruises. The skin around the navel, however, looked odd, as if stretched. The accident must've been minor.

A92's thoughts shifted to maits. I hope they're okay. They'll know what happened. Maybe they'll visit.

Mary returned to Post Operations Room 6-15 with a small canister. She handed it through a small opening in the dome to A92, her servos clicking gently. "Here's yer nourishment, dear."

A92 took the canister and guzzled its contents, the cool liquid coating a parched throat. It tasted like avocado and green apple—sweet, creamy, and oddly comforting. A92 sighed in relief and glanced at the machines lining the room, their steady beeps a strange reassurance. "How are my vitals?"

"Aye, yer vitals are good. Blood pressure is 120 over 80, temperature is 36.38 degrees Celsius, pulse is 60 beats per minute, oxygen saturation is 98 percent, and respiratory rate is 14 breaths per minute. Ye're in good health. No injuries, viruses, or bacterial infections. We completed a full biosystem scan. Ye're mentally and physically stable."

"Right. May I get up and walk about?"

Mary tilted her head, her glowing eyes dimming as if expressing concern. "Aye, but it's best if ye stay in bed. If ye fell, me heart would surely break."

A92's eyes rolled. "Sure. Whatever you say."

"Ye're welcome, dear." Mary's hum faded as she left the room.

Alone, A92 stared into space, unanswered questions clawing at the edges of consciousness. What injury? What fall? And why did it feel like something important had been lost, just out of reach?

A minute or two later, the kind and caring mechanical returned, walked to A92's fluid drip, and administered a sleep protocol. Within seconds, the patient's eyes grew heavy, and A92 fell back into a deep anesthetized slumber.

Mary smiled. The response test was complete.

A second medical bot entered the room, pushing a gurney. Mary deactivated the dome and, along with Matilda, lifted A92 onto the levitating stretcher and transported the patient down the passageway to a biostasis habitat, where six other friends from Arc1983 were stored.

There, the Beta bots prepped and cleansed A92. Matilda injected a nanotube into the raphe pallidus to inhibit neuronal activity associated with the subject's thermal defenses. Mary inserted a tunneled central venous catheter into A92's chest to administer total parenteral nutrition and monitor the patient's well-being during stasis. She also attached leads and lines for intranasal cooling and warming, neuromuscular electrical stimulation, and urine and feces collection.

Once prepped, the med bots placed A92's body in a torpor berth and filled the translucent container with a charged biogelatin composite of amniotic fluid. Mary closed and activated the berth, cooling A92's body to a blood heat of 30 degrees Celsius.

With Mary's and Matilda's tasks complete, A92, in thermoregulated hypothermia, would remain in stasis until Sophia called upon the resident to again serve the good.

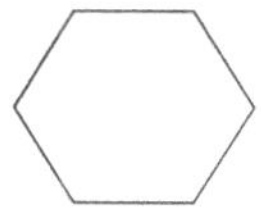

CHAPTER NINE

AN EXPEDITION

Their first destination was the overlook where the Mekko had spotted the Dark Spirit. As the expedition trekked across their hunting grounds, the thick foliage of late summer afforded the patrol an advantage—concealment—but all remained cautious while skirting meadows, creeks, ridgelines, and other danger areas. It was best not to underestimate the enemy.

Two hundred paces short of the overlook, Menawa halted the patrol. He signaled for Owlelo and Tussekeah to scout the hilltop. Menawa motioned to the left and right, directing four others to act as flankers, their duty to guard the north and south approaches. And he sent two to the rear, one hundred paces, to prevent any trailing enemy mischief.

Owlelo and Tussekeah dashed up the gentle incline to the hill's crest. They checked its slopes to the north and south. They scouted its rear slope, a perfect defilade position for an enemy. After a thorough scout, Owlelo signaled to Menawa, giving the all-clear sign.

Menawa led the expedition to a point shy of the hill's peak, where he placed the four clans into a defensive perimeter. The flankers and rearguard remained at their outposts as early warning.

Accompanied by his clan leaders, Menawa ascended to the overlook and scanned the horizon. He had an excellent view of the Great Hills; it was a clear day, and the sun was at his back. He spotted a red-shouldered hawk circling high in the sky and a stag moose drinking from a creek, its palmated antlers appearing heavy and broad. Menawa had only seen a few of these creatures in his lifetime. However, when he scanned eastward, the billowing smoke was gone. Had it moved on in search of a new lair? Or was it preparing to attack his people? Only Hesaketvmese knew the answers to these questions. Menawa returned to the safety of the defensive position and gathered his leaders.

"Tomorrow, we'll go beyond our hunting grounds into the forbidden land," Menawa said. "It should take about a day and a half to cross the valley before reaching the Great Hills. Once there, we'll divide into four patrols and scout for a passage. Yahola, you will remain at the base camp for defense and communications. I will scout east. Talof Harjo, you will go east by north, and Emestesego, east by south."

"What should we do if we find a passage?" Talof Harjo asked.

"Do not proceed. Return to the rally point. Yahola will send out runners to inform the rest. Once we reassemble, we'll proceed to the passage as one force. We must have strength if we encounter an enemy."

"The enemy will need strength if he encounters us," Emestesego said boldly.

"What about our village?" Yahola asked. "If we discover an enemy, we must send runners to warn Tomucece."

"Those are wise words," Menawa said. "For now, let's keep moving. We have a great distance to go."

The meeting broke, the clan leaders assembled their forces, and the expedition moved on until well after nightfall.

Menawa scanned the trail's margins for a defendable campsite. In the dark, he relied on his instincts, his ability to read the land and feel the woods. He soon discovered a spot with good lines of sight in all directions. He signaled to his warriors, directing the four clans into their respective defensive sectors.

The Mekko set out observation posts to guard the approaches to the camp. Profound secrecy and silence were his most important considerations. He placed four men at each post, two of whom must be alert and awake. If those on duty saw or heard anything of alarm, they were not to speak. Instead, one would retreat silently to the main body and acquaint the leader so proper dispositions could be made.

Once all were in place and the expedition's perimeter secure, no one was to move or make a sound. Campfires were forbidden; their light could be seen for a great distance. Additionally, half of the group would remain awake, alternating as needed to allow the others to rest.

After the long day, Menawa settled into a dip in the ground and stretched out on a musty bed of leaves. The coolness of the night washed over him. The People, however, were accustomed to the forest, so he rested comfortably on his buckskin mantle as if it were a bed in his wife's home. When it was his turn to sleep, he did so soundly, even through a brief downpour in the middle of the night.

• • • •

Before dawn, the expedition came to full alert, the perfect time for an enemy attack. Menawa moved silently around the perimeter to ensure all were awake and ready. A couple of his younger warriors needed a swift kick in the buttocks to confirm their vigilance.

After the sun broke over the Great Hills and the danger of attack subsided, the warriors fed their bellies. Most chewed down a piece of venison jerky or hard bread. Some carried small leather pouches filled with mortar-parched corn, which they mixed with water and consumed as a cold gruel. Others built small fires and formed the mix into ash cakes, cooking the patties on a small bed of white-hot coals, adding a few wild berries or nuts if they were handy.

It was time to resume the quest. Menawa assembled his forces and called in the sentries. They were now venturing into a forbidden territory. A land thought to be a refuge for the unavenged dead, horned serpents, and other ghostly creatures that wandered the forests, wailing, moaning, and seeking justice. All were on edge as the company marched forward. If legend were true, Estepapv, a voracious, lionlike creature, hunted this land, killing unsuspecting prey, dragging it to its lair, and devouring its flesh and bone. Most presumed Estepapv's sanctuary lay hidden somewhere in this valley, and men who wandered upwind of its nose were in grave danger.

To avert surprise, the forty-eight moved as four separate teams. The first twelve were the pathfinders, scouting ahead two hundred paces. The next two teams were the assault force, advancing in parallel, providing overwatch and the ability to maneuver on an enemy. The fourth was the rearguard and the flankers who guarded the expedition's route. As an added measure, every thousand paces or so, the patrol would fishhook to the right, set up an ambush, and lie in wait—their aim to surprise any unclever miscreants who might have dared to trail the pack.

As the expedition advanced, navigating the steep hills and deep hollows, the timbered slopes grew more pronounced, and their pace slowed. The thick forest, though offering concealment, also narrowed each warrior's field of view. Menawa ordered the patrol to tighten their formation, reducing the distance to ten paces between each warrior. While this limited their ability to maneuver against an enemy, staying within sight—both forward and trailing—was essential to prevent anyone from slipping into their ranks and causing chaos.

Menawa kept a vigilant eye on his warriors while Talof Harjo did the same on his right flank. The Mekko had placed the Hotvlkvlke in the lead. Yahola, though a strong leader, carried the weight of old ties. Once the closest friend to Menawa's older brother, Yahola's bond ran deep, and the shift in command still troubled him. A disappointment lingered, unspoken yet clear. Echoes of the past hung between them. Once teased and put in his place, the younger brother was now the superior, a heavy reversal Yahola must now accept and obey.

The Mekko scanned the terrain. The forest took on a mystical quality in the deeper hollows, where sunlight filtered through thousands of leaves, casting beams that fused with the forest floor, forming an illusion of endless snares sure to avoid. Despite the shaded terrain offering relief from the blistering summer heat, Menawa remained alert. The cool, damp air and the trickle of a small brook brought a sense of calm, almost relaxing. But losing even one warrior was unacceptable. Others might question his leadership, especially after his older brother had disappeared on the edge of these same woods years before.

The expedition came upon a cascading waterfall. Over the millennia, its flowing rivulet had carved out a deep rocky crevice in the hillside. Menawa surveyed the terrain. The waterfall's deposits had collected into small, meandering pools, creating a pleasant and inviting image. On another day, it would have been a choice spot to swim and nap, but not today.

Menawa ordered the expedition to stop for a brief rest. The Mekko posted flankers and summoned clan leaders.

"We've made good progress." Menawa wiped off a bit of sweat trickling down his brow. "We should reach the foot of the Great Hills by midday tomorrow. Once there, we'll split into scouting parties and search for a passage."

"You said the Echaswvlke would search east by north. How far should we go?" Talof Harjo asked.

Menawa opened his hunting pouch and pulled out a handful of small carved sticks painted red. He gave each leader four. "Our clans will scout for four days. You will return to the rally point by dusk on the fourth. Send a runner to the rally point if you find a passage. Yahola can send out messengers and inform the rest."

"Should we engage if we find the Dark Spirit or another enemy?" Emestesego asked.

"No, and make sure the enemy does not detect you. Retreat if you must. Surprise is our best strategy. Do not leave a trace. The enemy must not surprise us."

"If an enemy attacks, we will kill many," Yahola said daringly.

"Let's get everyone up and moving." Menawa ignored the comment. Yahola preferred to do things his way.

The journey continued, but not long after, the sun settled, dark shadows fell upon the land, and the night enveloped the expedition. All around, boughs of trees hung heavy and ominous. Warriors had to feel their way forward as the ground rose and fell beneath their feet.

Menawa signaled for the expedition to halt. The clans established another overnight camp and waited for the Sun's return.

• • • •

At dawn, the expedition set out on the last leg of their journey. Every warrior could see the ridges and peaks of the Great Hills, covered in oak, hickory, and pine. It was a foreboding sight, representing a barrier the People had never crossed—Earth's edge, an unknown land of unimaginable darkness.

After traveling a few hundred paces, Menawa halted the patrol to look and listen. The warriors froze in place. These frequent pauses were beginning to stir an unease. The deeper they trekked into uncertainty, the more the tension grew. They all knew the story of Menawa's brother— how he had traveled along this same path, searching for game or perhaps a glimpse beyond the Great Hills. He had vanished without a trace, save for a single bloody moccasin found along an animal trail. Many believed his effort had been reckless, a needless loss. The tribe had lost its Mekko, and now his younger brother was leading an expedition down the same perilous path.

At midday, the expedition arrived at the foot of the Great Hills, looming high above. Every warrior could now place a foot upon its soil, gaze at its slopes, and ponder its heights.

Menawa pointed to a location on the ground, a sizeable lichen-encrusted boulder. It would serve as the rally point.

Without discussion or chatter, the three clans peeled off and headed for their search areas. Emestesego and the Fuswvlke patrolled southward, Talof Harjo and the Echaswvlke trekked northward, and Menawa and the Nokosvlke plodded straight ahead.

The fourth clan, led by Yahola, remained at the rally point. He posted four warriors as sentries; the rest moved to a defendable site and established a base camp.

• • • •

The Fuswvlke hiked a thousand paces south before turning east to summit the Great Hills, but the thick forest soon slowed their progress. When they paused, Cekote, near Emestesego, watched as the Clan leader surveyed the distance—

no signs of a passage. Cekote felt the leader's deliberation. They had no choice but to go straight up the slope.

Cekote took the point, feeling a surge of pride as the weight of confidence settled on his shoulders. This was his first patrol, and the significance of this role was not lost on him. He studied the terrain carefully, his eyes tracing the jagged outcrops of rock and the dense clusters of mountain laurel that dotted the landscape like natural obstacles, each a potential hiding place for danger. He moved forward purposefully, fully aware that every step set the course for those following close behind.

The deeper they ventured, the more unnervingly quiet it grew. It was nothing like the village, where life hummed constantly. Here, each sound stood alone—sharp and distinct. To his left, a crackle snapped his attention; to the right, a soft rustle caught his ear. Above, the wind whispered through the treetops, yet Cekote heard it all. Every sound was amplified, each one a potential threat.

Occasionally, he paused and held his breath—not to see, but to listen. In those moments of stillness, he absorbed the faintest clamor, the tiniest snap, and the lightest rustle. Even silence had a sound, a weight, that pressed in on him. It was as if the forest itself was alive, watching, waiting. Cekote's senses sharpened with every step, each echoing in his mind as he led the patrol deeper into the unknown, his every movement dictating their fate.

The patrol soon came upon an imposing granite formation, its jagged face towering above them, as high as eight men. The rocky barrier seemed to rise from the earth like a sentinel, daring anyone to scale its heights. Cekote's heart quickened, a surge of excitement and determination coursing through him. This was his chance to prove his worth. Without hesitation, he began his ascent, leaping from foothold to foothold, moving swiftly as he zigzagged upward. His muscles burned with the effort, but the thrill of leading the way drove him higher.

The granite beneath his hands felt cold and rough, the sharp edges biting his fingers as he pulled himself up. He was halfway there, the peak tantalizingly close, when his foot slipped. The slick, wet moss sent him careening backward. He reached for a hold, but none existed. His heart leapt in his chest as gravity took over, pulling him down with terrifying speed.

He hit the forest floor with a thud, a muffled grunt escaping his lungs. Pain surged through his right leg—a protruding rock had shattered his femur. The sickening snap echoed in his ears. Cekote gasped for air, the breath knocked out of him. He lay sprawled out like a turtle on its back, helpless and dazed. He blinked, struggling to regain his bearings.

Slowly, he lifted his head and winced. His right leg felt detached from his body. Initially, there was no pain, only a dull throb from the broken bone. But when he tried to sit up, a searing agony ripped through him, forcing him back down. The reality of his situation quickly settled in—he was utterly powerless.

Bird Clan warriors rushed to aid their injured brother, their faces tight with concern. Their alarmed stares sent a chill down Cekote's spine. Moments ago, he had been a proud and confident warrior, leading the patrol, filled with purpose. Now, he lay broken, helpless—a casualty, a burden to those who had once looked to him for direction. His pride crumbled under the weight of his injury, replaced by the cold realization that he was no longer in control.

A firm hand settled on his shoulder, grounding him in the moment. Emestesego, knelt beside him. Their eyes met, and in that silent exchange, words became unnecessary. The decision that loomed hung heavy in the air. Cekote knew his uncle would have to choose—the path forward had shifted, not just for him but for all. His injury had not only reduced their strength by one, but would also demand others to stay behind and tend to him. Their mission—finding a way through the mountains—would have to wait. A leader and a follower were now bound by this moment, both facing a test neither had expected.

• • • •

Menawa and the Nokosvlke trudged eastward, the slopes growing steeper with each step. The terrain, though familiar in its ruggedness, became increasingly unforgiving as they ascended. After covering roughly five hundred paces, they stumbled upon a deep chasm that appeared to split the earth. Moss, ferns, and weeds clung to its sheer walls, yet the depths below were eerily barren, devoid of life. The void yawned at least two hundred paces across and plunged at least three hundred paces into its shadows. Menawa stood at its edge, the foul stench of rot and death oozing from its depths, forcing him to consider its dark origin. Regardless of how it came to be, this jagged scar presented a formidable obstacle they could not cross. With a simple hand gesture, the Mekko turned the patrol around; their focus shifted to finding another path.

As the sun dipped, Menawa glanced at the sky. The light was fading fast. The Sun hung two fingers above the horizon, the telltale sign that dusk would soon swallow the forest. Once again, it was time to find a place to settle for the night. He gestured to Owlelo, who broke away, darting through the trees to scout for a suitable campsite.

With barely a finger's width of daylight left, Owlelo returned, leading the patrol to the site. It was well-chosen—dense vegetation and natural contours offered cover and concealment, while the surrounding terrain provided defensible approaches. Menawa nodded in approval. This spot would serve them well.

Menawa placed his warriors in hides and settled in for the night. With his back against a protective boulder, he turned his gaze skyward. A crescent moon had risen in the east, casting its pale glow over the forest. Above him, the pitch-black sky was punctuated by an endless array of stars. In the distance, a barred owl called to its mate, hooting softly above a chorus of crickets, cicadas, and katydids. Their harmony drifted through the trees, as soothing as the rhythm of a gentle rain.

His eyes lingered on the heavens. Countless stars glittered against the dark canvas of night, and for a moment, Menawa's thoughts wandered. He pondered their meaning, the possibility that each star was a soul—perhaps the spirits of his ancestors, treading the eternal path beyond. Could one of them be his older brother, now journeying among the brightest stars? Had he reached the rift that marked the meeting place of souls? Had he made it past Eagle?

Menawa's muscles tensed as his thoughts weighed heavy, though his mind was not alone in its discomfort. His tooth still ached—a persistent throb gnawing at him with every breath. He reached into his hunting pouch, pulled out a coneflower root, and slipped it between his teeth to ease the pain. He took a deep breath, pulling his legs close to his chest as his war club rested across his belly.

Once more, Menawa glanced at the night sky, the shimmering stars serving as both a reminder of his burden and a testament to the beauty of the world beyond. He whispered a silent prayer to Hesaketvmese and crossed his arms as he prepared to rest. It had been a long and demanding day, yet the serenity of the night seemed to offer a brief respite, a moment of peace amidst the tension of the journey.

At sunrise, Menawa and the Bear Clan resumed their trek, moving steadily up the mountain slopes in search of a passage. The first light of day cast long shadows across the forest, and the air was still cool from the night. As they ascended, they spotted a narrow animal trail, barely wide enough for a man to follow, winding its way up the mountainside. Despite the risk, Menawa led his warriors onto the path, their pace deliberate but brisk as they pressed forward for some distance.

The crest of the Great Hill soon appeared, only a few hundred paces ahead. Yet, the Mekko remained cautious, sensing the growing danger with every step. He signaled for his warriors to halt. The patrol stopped as one, their movements precise, the forest around them eerily silent. Menawa's eyes scanned the terrain, alert to the smallest detail. An east wind swept over the ridgeline, stirring the treetops with a steady rustle, masking the calmness that stretched between the sounds of the wild.

To the right, a hooded warbler, perched high on a branch, sang a bright song. To the left, a white-tailed stag leapt gracefully through the underbrush, its hooves barely making a sound. Above, a fox squirrel darted from hickory to oak, its agile movements blending with the sway of the branches.

Menawa raised a hand, signaling for the two scouts to move forward. They slipped into the undergrowth like ghostly shadows, their forms almost invisible against the dense foliage.

The forest was peaceful—no signs of danger.

Another signal from the Mekko and the pair advanced another fifty paces.

Still nothing. The mountainside, draped in its morning serenity, seemed no different from any other.

Menawa moved the patrol up to join the scouts, his eyes fixed on the Great Hill's crest, now just two hundred paces away. The path seemed clear, but the stillness gnawed at him. With a final hand motion, he ordered the scouts to push forward. The two dashed ahead, disappearing briefly behind a rise in the land.

All remained vigilant, Menawa's instincts sharp. The crest loomed closer; the quiet seemed to have its own weight as if the mountain was holding its breath, waiting for something to stir.

After advancing less than thirty paces, Owlelo suddenly recoiled in pain, his body jerking back as if stung by an unseen force. He frantically brushed at his clothes and limbs as if trying to extinguish an invisible flame. Tussekeah, witnessing the sudden commotion, instinctively retreated a few paces, his hand moving to his bow as he nocked an arrow, ready for any threat that might emerge.

The other warriors reacted with swift coordination, fanning out to Menawa's left and right, forming a defensive line as if guided by an unspoken signal. Their readiness was unmistakable, each one poised to counter a potential assault.

Owlelo regained composure, knelt, and lifted his atlatl. His eyes scanned the surroundings as he aimed the spearlike dart straight ahead. Though the scout appeared unharmed, a quick glance toward Menawa revealed unease— his shoulders lifted in a small, uncertain shrug.

Menawa's mind raced as he signaled Tussekeah to move forward.

With deliberate action, Tussekeah advanced cautiously, each step measured and silent.

ZAP!

He, too, had found the invisible barrier. Tussekeah jumped back, his eyes wide with shock. He threw himself onto the ground as though he had plunged into the heart fire itself. He rolled desperately in the dirt, frantic as he tried to extinguish the unseen flames that seared his skin. The ground around him was a whirlwind of dust and panic. After a moment of frenzy, Tussekeah struggled to his feet, then stared at Owlelo with a look of sheer disbelief before turning to Menawa with a wide-eyed, helpless stare.

Menawa's blood raced at the sight of his warriors in distress. He quickly signaled for Owlelo and Tussekeah to retreat to the patrol's safety. It was his turn. He drew his war club and advanced toward the firewall. He moved deliberately, shifting twenty paces to the right to outmaneuver the peril. Each step was measured, his senses on high alert.

ZAP!

A searing jolt of pain and blistering heat lanced through him as if the very air had ignited. Menawa staggered back, a choked grunt of agony escaping his lips as he fought to bat away the invisible flames. He collapsed to the ground, his muscles twitching uncontrollably as he rolled in the dirt, trying to extinguish the phantom blaze. Gritting his teeth, Menawa forced himself to calm his racing heart and steady his breathing. As the pain began to subside, he slowly rose, his vision clearing. A sudden realization hit him like a stone—an unknown force had barred their way. With grim resignation, Menawa realized their mission had been blocked, and retreat was their only viable option.

• • • •

It had been three days. Talof Harjo had counted the third red stick, marking another day of fruitless searching. The Echaswvlke had yet to find a viable path through the Great Hills. They had trekked two thousand paces northward, their eyes scanning the eastern slopes for any sign of a passage. Talof Harjo resolved to continue, even if it meant pushing beyond his allotted time before returning to the base camp.

As the Echaswvlke advanced, they approached a linear clearing. It stretched from southwest to northeast. A dense canebrake field bordered its left margin, while to the right, steep, stony slopes rose high, covered in thick underbrush, shadowed by ancient oaks and pines.

The clearing, resembling a path, felt firm underfoot. Talof Harjo studied its length. It seemed to continue endlessly, paralleling the Great Hills with an almost unnerving precision. He signaled to the patrol, and they headed northeast. The path mimicked the landscape, rising and falling, yet at times, it did the opposite, as though a giant hand had carved out a break through the forest.

A thousand paces on, Talof Harjo directed his men off the trail into the stony woods. He felt uneasy; something about this strange path bothered him. As a tradition, the People always went right; the left was reserved for spirits and ghosts that wandered the Earth.

After placing his warriors into a defensive perimeter, Talof Harjo and two others dashed back to the path. The Clan Leader's eyes narrowed as he surveyed the ground, kicking and stomping with increased scrutiny. He ordered his men to follow suit, their movements a mixture of curiosity and apprehension.

The warriors tested the soil with their stone-pointed spears. The auriculate-shaped projectiles sank only half a foot into the ground before encountering firm resistance. Each probe found the same unyielding surface, a puzzling consistency that deepened the mystery.

Talof Harjo gave a sharp command. *"Korres!"*

At once, the two warriors dropped to their knees and began clawing at the earth, scattering leaves and scraping through layers of soil. Soon, they uncovered a wide patch of something unlike any surface they had known—flat and rigid, not granite or limestone, but a peculiar black-gray texture, speckled like pebbles.

The warriors unearthed more of this strange finding, and the more they revealed, the more distinct—a series of yellow stripes, two paces long, repeating in a pattern. Talof Harjo scratched his head in bewilderment. The discovery was undeniably unnatural. It must be an ancient relic or perhaps a sign from Hesaketvmese. With a mixture of skepticism and resolve, the Clan Leader decided to follow where it might lead.

Talof Harjo returned to the patrol, his mind churning. Without hesitation, he directed his warriors forward. The Echaswvlke pressed on, following this mysterious trail as it wound toward the Great Hills. The path bent left and right, rising steadily, and the way it hugged the land's natural contours sped their advance. It seemed like the trail was designed for efficiency, not by nature, but something else.

In the distance, Talof Harjo's ears caught the sound of running water—faint but unmistakable. As they approached, the sound grew louder, until they reached a creek at least thirty paces wide. The water's gentle babble contrasted sharply with the path they had been following.

Yet the strangeness did not end there. The trail continued unbroken, a structure of sorts, a seamless overpass that spanned the creek. Talof Harjo's concern deepened. No ordinary footpath could accomplish such a feat.

Talof Harjo motioned, and two warriors advanced toward the overpass. The Clan Leader's sharp eyes followed their movements, muscles tense, ready for any sign of danger. The pair began to cross, eyes scanning the horizon, weapons ready. Every step felt like they were tempting fate.

Malatche was in the lead. The overpass, too, proved firm underfoot. He kicked at the surface, uncovering what appeared to be dried, whitish-gray clay as firm as stone. Satisfied with its stability, he moved on, reaching the midpoint.

SHRIEK!

A deafening surprise tore through Malatche's skull, like the air had turned against him. He staggered back, clutching his head, his face twisting in pain and confusion. The others watched in shock as he stumbled, eyes wide with fear. It was as if the very earth had screamed at him, but the others stood unaffected, oblivious to the terrifying sound only Malatche heard.

Ceckele, a few paces to Malatche's left rear, gawked at his brother with amusement. A chuckle escaped him. Maybe a bee had bitten Malatche on the buttocks. The two were always at each other's throats, constantly competing. Ignoring the warning, Ceckele stepped forward.

SHRIEK!

The scout jerked back in pain, hands flying to his ears.

Malatche smirked, their roles now reversed; both retreated to the patrol.

After a brief exchange, Talof Harjo ordered the two scouts to try again by fording the creek.

The brothers descended the bank and waded into the cold stream. Halfway across—

SHRIEK!

Both grabbed their ears and stumbled, crashing into the cold water. Soaked and shaken, they hastily returned to the patrol.

"What happened?" Talof Harjo demanded.

"A terrible screech," Ceckele answered, wide-eyed. "It sounded like an angry horned owl. It was unbearable—just like on the overpass."

"And you?" Talof Harjo asked.

"The same," Malatche muttered, wringing out his drenched loincloth.

Talof Harjo frowned. "Tell me about the overpass."

"It's made of stone," Malatche said.

"I need to see this."

The three approached the creek, hugging the overpass's right side. Talof Harjo edged down the bank, stepping into the stream and wading under the structure. He examined its supports, which looked like hardened poles and planks. The underbelly resembled roof crossbeams, smooth and cool to the touch, yet it felt unnatural—like stone but foreign to his world.

The Beaver Clan leader pressed forward, moving beneath the bridge's shadow. He paused at the midpoint, carefully feeling the stone-like vertical supports. His heart raced as he took another cautious step, then another— expecting the same dreadful pain that had tormented the scouts. But nothing happened. No howl, no terrible shriek.

He took a breath and continued. The two brothers followed, their eyes wide with anticipation. Yet they, too, passed the midpoint without incident.

The three warriors scrambled up the far bank, their relief evident. Talof Harjo led them a few paces forward, his sharp eyes scanning the horizon. There it was—a gap in the mountains. It seemed to open into a valley, a passage that might lead to the east side beyond the Great Hills. The Echaswvlke had found a way through.

"We must gather our forces!" Talof Harjo exclaimed, but as he turned back, a breath caught in his throat. Before him stood a tremendous shimmering translucent barrier, stretching upward from the creek's center to the sky. It extended in both directions as far as the eye could see, an unnatural divide.

Talof Harjo and the two brothers let out war whoops, their hands instinctively flying to their war clubs. On the west side, the warriors heard their cries and charged forward, eager to assist. But just as they reached the overpass, Talof Harjo raised his hand, ordering them to stop. Something stood in their path.

Talof Harjo, Ceckele, and Malatche cautiously approached the divide. Malatche touched it, his hand passing through effortlessly, like plunging into a thin layer of water. Talof Harjo and Ceckele followed suit, watching in awe as they moved their hands in and out of the shimmering wall.

On the west side, the rest looked on, confused, as their leader and the two brothers looked as if they were playing with ghosts, reaching out and pulling back, testing the strange force.

A curious warrior stepped forward almost to the midpoint and extended his hand. *SHRIEK!* He reeled back, clutching his ears, grimacing in pain.

Ceckele, emboldened by his previous success, extended a leg. Nothing happened. With a hesitant step, he slid his body through the divide. His confidence swelled, until—*SHRIEK*. He lunged backward, collapsing beside Talof Harjo and Malatche, stunned by the invisible force.

"For once, the trick's on you." Malatche laughed, shaking his head.

Ceckele, ever competitive, shot his brother a glance. "We'll see about that." He leapt to his feet, stretched out his hand, and motioned for one of the warriors to grab hold. The warrior hesitated but finally gripped Ceckele's hand. *SHRIEK!* The warrior grimaced in agony, but Ceckele held firm, pulling the warrior through the barrier despite his pained cries. Now, four of twelve were on the east side.

Surprised, the remaining warriors gawked in disbelief.

"Like to see me do it again?" Ceckele grinned, reaching out to pull another through the barrier.

One by one, the warriors tested the invisible wall until all twelve had crossed to the east side. After a moment of nervous chuckles and pats on the back, their attention turned to the towering, shimmering divide. It stretched upward like a watery wall forged by some powerful deity, repelling all who dared approach with its earsplitting shriek.

Malatche, not one for idle wonder, moved east toward the mountain gap, craning his neck to peer beyond the Great Hills.

Talof Harjo caught sight of his advance. *"Hvtēc!"* he commanded, stopping the warrior in his tracks. The Clan Leader scanned the surrounding terrain. Something felt off. After a tense moment, Talof Harjo gave the signal, and Malatche resumed his march. The others followed, their excitement tempered by caution.

As they climbed higher, the view ahead became clearer. Something vast and green stretched before them—a valley teeming with life, hidden beyond the Great Hills. But that was not all.

In the distance, a monolithic structure towered above the forest, as tall as the mountains. Gleaming in the sunlight, it appeared formidable, yet there was a significant breach in its shell about two-thirds up. And through it, strange shapes flew in and out like giant hornets tending to a fractured hive. Others crawled along its surface, engaged in some peculiar, ceaseless activity.

As Talof Harjo and his warriors stared at the monolith, a sudden gust tore through the mountain gap—howling like a flood through a narrow gorge. The force struck with fury, whipping dirt and debris into a blinding cloud. The warriors dropped low, arms raised to shield their eyes from the storm.

Talof Harjo roared, *"Enkvhēcv!"*

But the warning came too late.

The wind surged, a living thing—merciless and unseen. Warriors strained against it, moccasins skidding, bodies bent low. One lifted—feet leaving the earth—kicking, thrashing, pulled into the swirling haze above. Another followed. Then another. One by one, they vanished, drawn upward as if claimed by some great spirit in the sky.

Talof Harjo fought to stand—legs braced, fists swinging against the invisible force—but the ground betrayed him. The current caught hold, tore him free, and in a flash of whirling dust and light, he too was gone.

Drawn into the heavens.

Swallowed by the wind.

Claimed by the spirit in the sky.

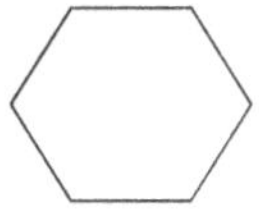

CHAPTER TEN

THAT RABBIT

The old woman stepped outside—it had rained. She inhaled deeply. An argillaceous odor filled her nostrils. There was something about that smell: the fresh rain, the wet earth, the scent of plant oils, the ozone. It was so wonderful—earth's essence. She sighed. It was time to begin her day.

She tottered across the open yard, down the worn footpath, and across the bridge.

The children were waiting, their hair, clothing, and bodies soaked to the bone, but they didn't seem to mind; it was such a beautiful day.

"Good morning, Grandmother." The little boy took her by the hand.

"Good morning, my child. I could use your help today. It's time to pick some berries, time for a cobbler."

"I like cobbler," the little girl remarked. "Mulberry is my favorite."

"I like blackberry," the skinny boy countered.

"Well, today it's mulberry," the old woman said. "I found a lovely tree beyond a patch of wildflowers in an open meadow, a little into the woods. We might even see Rabbit; he's been spotted there before."

"If we catch him, we can have him for supper," the brash boy said.

"Not that bunny," the little girl pouted. "He's a special bunny. No one has ever caught him 'cause he's smart."

"He's teasing you," the older girl said.

"No, I'm not," the brash boy chided. "He's a dumb old rabbit."

The old woman's eyes twinkled with a hint of lessons learned. "It seems I've never told you how Rabbit gained his knowledge."

"Tell us, tell us," the children shouted.

The old woman sat on a fallen log, and the children gathered around, plopping down on the muddy ground without the slightest care.

She began, "One day, Rabbit went to the Breath Maker for knowledge. The Breath Maker said, 'Fetch a bag of red ants, and I will give you knowledge.' Rabbit went to collect the ants, but they bit him. Rabbit returned to the Breath Maker. 'They bit me. I shouldn't have messed with them.' The Breath Maker said, 'I saw Fox is in the cornfield. Bring him to me, and I will give you knowledge.' Rabbit went to Fox and said, 'The Breath Maker wants to see you.' Fox said, 'After lunch,' and started chasing Rabbit. Rabbit returned to the Breath Maker. 'Fox tried to eat me. He is not nice.' The Breath Maker said, 'I'll give you one last chance. Snake is near the creek, under a log. Bring him here, and I will give you knowledge.' Rabbit did as asked, but first cut off a dogwood branch and fashioned it as a pointed stick. Rabbit approached the Snake. 'The Breath Maker said you're not as long as this stick, but I say you are.' Snake replied, 'Yes, I am. Measure me.' So Rabbit measured Snake, but when Rabbit did, he ran the point into Snake's head and killed him. He carried Snake back to the Breath Maker. 'Now, may I have knowledge?' The Breath Maker replied, 'Seems you have found it yourself.'"

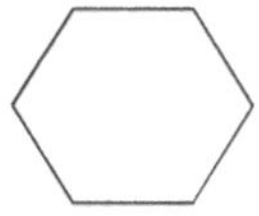

THE TREATMENT

SUN'S DAY, 2525

Sη01, Arc1983's Director, a slim brunet, called the Council of Sage to congress. The Sophists entered the Symposium, poured a drink, made their way to their reclines, and waited for a quorum. When all were present, the meeting began with traditional testaments.

Sη01 stood at the northern point. "Good actions give us strength and inspire good actions in others."

The Council applauded and reveled, "Hear, hear."

Sκ02, the Deputy, a trim blonde, stood. "Our residents' behavior flows from community, belief, and desire."

The Council reveled, "Hear, hear."

Sζ03, a reliable planner, stood at the northeast point. "To ensure residents' happiness, add not to their means but take away from their desires."

"Hear, hear."

Sλ04, who oversaw logistics, stated, "When our residents are happy, they are content, but in its absence, they do everything to possess it."

118

"Hear, hear."

The tributes continued until all sixteen Sophists had spoken.

Sη01 asked, "What is the status of Zephyrus?"

Sτ15 stood. "We sealed all internal breaches and returned the affected rings to order. We've cleared the damaged Quadrant and begun repairs on the open cell. A replacement quadrant will arrive in fourteen days. Once installed, we'll close the outer structure. Until then, our west-side shield generators will remain inoperable."

"Unfortunate," Sη01 said. "And our residents?"

Sφ11 spoke next. "Ten minor injured will return to Zephyrus this afternoon, and the other eight will return tomorrow. Arc 94 will hold the fourteen major injured in torpor until we request their return."

"Excellent," Sη01 said. "And the rest?"

Sμ10 added, "28 percent of Zephyrus residents experienced the anomaly, 100 percent are aware, and 17 percent believe it severely damaged Quad-A. However, none have discerned the totality of the mishap except for residents retrieved from the wreckage. Based on our understanding of memetic propagation, the Zephyrus population will require a 100 percent cleanse."

"And our other Raions?" Sη01 asked.

Sμ10 continued, "In aggregate, 32 percent of Boreas, Apheliotes, and Notus residents sensed the incident. We expect the meme to reach 100 percent propagation within the next few hours. I recommend we cleanse the entire population. It will be the most extensive treatment ever administered by an Arc."

"What is the plan?" Sη01 shifted uncomfortably on the golden sofa.

Sκ02 stood. "Our best course of action is to administer the treatment through their daily nourishment. We can proceed to the next phase once we confirm 100 percent consumption. I propose we distribute it tomorrow. I recommend delaying the return of the minor injured until we have completed the cleanse. Medical can treat these residents."

"I concur," Sφ11 said. We will hold the minor injured for another day."

Sυ07 added, "This evening, there is a Garden Ceremony for Boreas. I have contacted the receiving Arcs. They will assume control and treat these residents."

"Excellent," Sη01 said. "Lambda 4, Phi 11, and Mu 10, please coordinate the treatment's distribution. Please ensure we deliver it to all polys, bars, and galleys to avoid variance. This congress is adjourned."

The Council applauded and reveled, "Hear, hear." The Sophists had one more drink and returned to their duties.

• • • •

Sμ10 and Sφ11 made their way to Ring 14's Science Raion, a restricted area staffed entirely by G-Class science bots.

When the two Sophists entered the bustling formulation lab, Gammas were hard at work preparing the treatment. Configured with eight arms, some bots worked at lab stations while others delivered ingredients and supplies. Equipped with advanced sensors and actuators, the Gammas dispensed precise measurements into mixing vessels, their movements synchronized with the whir of the machines. With each motion, they blended the ingredients according to recipes stored in their memory banks. Amidst the controlled chaos, the Gammas were models of efficiency and multitasking; their unwavering actions ensured the formula was a masterpiece of flavor and consistency.

"We're on schedule," Sφ11 said, chin elevating.

"The deadline is 1400," Sμ10 said.

"Indeed." Sφ11 stepped up to a station, poured a sample, and tasted it, less the molecular nano treatment. A recent tasting party had yielded the perfect drink, which now served as the nepenthe's carrier. The colorful beverage contained strawberry, watermelon, banana, lime, rice milk, agave syrup, cinnamon, cloves, and cardamom. Its color was an enchanting creamy red. Sφ11 smiled. "It's smooth."

Sμ10 sipped the drink. "Our raits should enjoy this one. It might even set a record."

"But will they choose it over their preferred beverages?"

"Don't worry, my friend. We'll add a double dose of meta. The rats, I mean raits, can't resist it. They're built that way."

The two Sophists continued to observe. At 1345 hours, science bots loaded the nourishment packs into shipping containers. Sφ11 closed the lid and crimped a seal on its outer lock. Then, via a restricted lift, service bots and Sμ10 delivered the order to Ring 22.

• • • •

The bots and Sμ10 entered the Logistics Raion. Sλ04 greeted the Sophist and took charge of the shipment.

"How should we handle distribution?" Sλ04 asked.

"We will follow our normal schedule," Sμ10 answered. "Let's not disturb the *mischief*. Polys first, followed by bars, then galleys. Let's make it easy, the first place they sniff without ringing a bell."

Sλ04 chuckled.

Sμ10 added, "We'll promote the drink on our social network to encourage consumption. We've had excellent results in the past with these subtle reminders."

"What if they stick with their favorites?"

"Phi 11 asked the same question. A double dose, my friend. Works every time."

"1,480 intoxicated raits. Is that a good idea?"

"Happiness, Lambda 4, happiness. That's what we're all about."

• • • •

As night shrouded the Arc, E-Class service bots, like metallic milkmen, assembled the daily nourishment and readied it for distribution. They would deliver it to 16 galleys, 32 bars, and 384 polycules.

At 0300 hours, these utilitarian Epsilons delivered the first batch to the proverbial back door of each poly. In this case, via the service hex at the center of a polycule cluster and through the access door on the cooler's backside. And hopefully, without disturbing the sleeping inhabitants.

As standard and without exception, these efficient Epsilons completed their purpose. Afterward, the bots delivered the elixir to bars and galleys. By 0600, and before first light, the mechanicals had completed their task, and the stage was set.

• • • •

Moon's Day beamed brightly on Arc1983. A12 crawled out of bed and stepped to the cooler. Inside were four eye-catching refreshments, ready for consumption.

"Hey, a new drink!" A12 grabbed one and glugged it down. "Wow. It has a kick to it. Who wants theirs?" A12 retrieved two more.

"I'll take mine," T02 said. "Long day ahead, I could use the boost."

"Anyone else?" A12 asked.

"No, thanks." A53 slid into a jumpsuit and zipped it up. "I'll grab something later."

"I'll have one—and 53's." T30's eyes widened with anticipation.

"Moderation," A53 said, shaking the head.

"You said you didn't want it, so more for me." T30 studied the nourishment. "Hey, isn't this one of those drinks we sampled at the tasting party? The color is different."

"You're right. My maits and I—" A12 stopped mid-sentence, a horrible tragedy rekindling in the mind. A12's face went blank. "Yes, it was a wonderful night."

T30 must have noticed the sullen expression. "I'm so sorry. I didn't mean to cause you pain. Your maits will return soon, and everything will be okay."

T02 spoke up, the voice almost a whisper. "Funny how something small can remind you." T02 stepped over and wrapped A12 in a brief, comforting hug.

"Thank you, I needed that." A12 let the moment linger before pulling away and exiting the poly.

Today's work order called for a Quad-C inspection, a task that should have felt routine. But A12's mind churned with worry. What had become of A67, A81, and A92? Were they safe? Would the secret message reach them? And T23… Had the dait moved on, finding new connections, interests drifting from Arc 83 like a forgotten echo in the dark? A12's eyes closed, summoning the memory of T23's face—the spark in those eyes, the curve of that smile. If only things had unfolded differently, if only… Yet, a glimmer of hope lingered—perhaps Quad-C would offer another opportunity to seek out hidden paths, a way through this darkness.

A12 turned to the task and the search for answers, revealing what had once gone unnoticed. Inspection accesses and maintenance hatches dotted the structure, hidden in plain sight. Bots came and went from concealed locations, their entrances disguised as bland partitions or nondescript passageways. The sheer number of these hidden routes was surprising. Where did they lead? Another world, perhaps? One just out of reach, waiting to be uncovered.

Mid-afternoon, A12 took a break from inspections and approached the bar. Fred, the bar bot, was on duty.

"How about one of those new drinks?" A12 asked.

"Strawberry Cream, right away, resident. How are you today?"

"Just doing inspections. And you?"

"Welded to it. Haha. I wish I could do inspections."

"Why? You have a great job."

Fred's mechanical eyes seemed to dim for a second. "Residents order drinks, but they don't talk to me." Fred handed A12 the drink.

"Well, I'm talking to you."

Fred's faceplate brightened. "So, what would you like to discuss, resident?"

"How about what's on the lower rings?"

"I don't know."

"But the other day, you said you wanted to go there."

"But I can't. I'm bolted to it. Haha. Fixated on my work."

"So, how do you even know it exists?"

"My friend, Roombie, goes there after he cleans the floor. I wish I could clean floors."

"I don't follow."

"To be free."

Shock flickered across A12's face. "Hey, we're not supposed to say that word."

"Well, I said it. Haha."

"So why do you want to be—" A12 hesitated. It was the worst word, the f-word, worse than the s-word (selfie) and highly offensive.

"I want to talk to my friends Philly and Lilly." Fred smiled. I see them every day. I wonder if they see me?"

"Who?"

"Right over there?" Fred pointed to a planter containing philodendrons and daylilies.

"Those plants are your friends?" A12 chuckled.

"I wonder if they are as lonely as me?" Fred gazed across the Core. "And I really want to talk to Sally." Fred waved at another bar bot in the distance. Sally gave a little wave back. There seemed to be a twinkle in her eyes. Fred's faceplate began to pulse with energy, and the eyes held a hypnotized longing. It was the same as when T23 gazed at A12, eyes lingering, like there was something unspoken in the look.

A12 noticed what appeared to be tears in the corners of Fred's eyes. But it couldn't be—lubrication perhaps. "You're friends with Sally?"

Fred's gaze dropped to the mechanical clamps securing the bot to the deck. "We've never met," Fred muttered. "We're bound to our purpose." Fred quickly snapped out of his melancholy. "Would you like another drink, resident?"

"No—no, thank you." A12 felt a blush rise to the cheeks. All this time, A12 had never thought to talk to Fred or any other bot. They were mechanicals. Yes, you could ask them a question. *Hey Fred, what's the time? Hey Fred, what's the temperature?* But anything else? Certainly not.

"Have a nice day, resident." Fred cocked his head to the side as if it was the most natural thing in the world.

A12 smiled, but a bit awkwardly. "You too, Fred." A12 returned to inspections.

At day's end, while crossing the Core, A12 spotted T30, who had just exited Quad-T and was heading straight toward A12. The rait had a bright-eyed, mischievous look on the face.

"Hey. I spoke to C85." T30 was grinning from ear to ear. "It's all set. 85 will deliver the message. Said it will be hidden in a tight little roundabout."

"Well, that's good, I guess."

"They'll never look there." T30 smiled devilishly.

"I hope not. By the way, G18 and I are linking up at a bar at 1800. Would you like to join us?"

"Sounds fun." The rait smiled and dashed off.

• • • •

G18, T30, and A12 found each other at the bar at 1800 hours and went to a table in a far corner by an exhibit of lush tropical plants and a rainbow-striped bulkhead. It was a perfect spot for a quiet conversation.

A12 leaned forward. "I found more accesses. They're everywhere when you're looking for them."

T30's eyes widened. "Like where?"

"Over my shoulder. See that lighting closet on the far bulkhead. There's a hatch on its overhead. And there's one next to Philly."

T30 looked confused. "Philly? What are you talking about?"

"I mean the cluster of philodendrons across from the bar. And there's a small maintenance access behind Xanadu."

"Xanadu? You mean that plant?" G18 gave A12 a long look. "Have you opened any of these so-called accesses, sweetie?"

"No, I haven't, but I plan to. Aren't you curious?"

"Perhaps." G18 grinned playfully. "The possibilities do get me a little hot."

"I like hot." T30 grinned.

G18 smiled at T30 and began to play with the rait's long, strawberry-blonde hair.

"Let's not get distracted." A12 scoffed at the flirts. "I told you I'm going to find a way off this Arc."

"Sweetie, you're becoming quite the bore with all these crazy ideas. You sound like you're about to go full nova." G18 touched A12's thigh. "How about another drink?" G18 stood and headed for the bar.

"If someone calls me sweetie one more time."

"That one is a bit much," T30 said.

"Don't encourage, then."

"I can't help it. I like hot."

"How about a cold shower?"

"Hot, cold. It's all the same when I'm in the moo—"

"Hi, I'm back." G18 passed out the drinks. "Fred said to say hello to his new friend. Wow, that was weird. I didn't realize that tin can had a pulse. And what were you two discussing while I was gone?"

"Cold showers," A12 said.

"Sounds like fun. Icy gets me spicy."

T30's eyes darted to A12. The fait grinned.

A12 puffed out a breath of indifference and mumbled, "Unbelievable." The Tech tried to share more details about hidden doors and disappearing bots, but the two friends had other things on their minds.

"My poly?" G18 suggested.

"I'm game," T30 replied.

"And you, sweetie?" G18 rubbed A12's arm.

"Sorry, I've had a long day."

"No longer than ours," G18 said sharply. "Some fun will do you good."

"Sorry, I have other things on my mind. Maybe we should call it a night."

"I see." G18 finished the drink and pushed away from the table. "You're testing my patience, sweetie." The rait walked off.

"Now you've done it," T30 said.

"What?"

"That one can be nasty. I've heard stories."

"That one, as you put it, seems to be an acquired taste." A12's jaw tightened. "Why can't I have a say without being called a selfie?"

"It might be best not to screw with 18. You shouldn't play so hard to get."

"What if I'm not playing?"

"Hey, I'm on your side, sweetie."

"Did you just call me sweetie?

"Whoops." T30 slunk down in the chair.

"What if I called you sugar britches or sweet pants? Or, how about flower blossom?"

"I sort of like flower blossom."

"You would." A12 gave T30 a rotten look, which soon turned into a smirky smile followed by a chuckle; after all, they were friends. The two residents finished their drinks and returned to their poly.

• • • •

Later in the evening, when all lay sleeping—naturally or induced—like rats nestled in their burrows, the nano-nepenthe consumed earlier activated. First, at 0300 hours, in Boreas; then at 0315, in Apheliotes; next, at 0330, in Zephyrus; and finally, at 0345, in Notus. Unseen and unfelt, the tiny agents traveled through each rait's bloodstream, weaving their way to the hippocampus and prefrontal cortex, erasing episodic traces like whispers plucked from the wind. The scan and cleanse took twenty minutes, followed by an additional two minutes for updates. Like the chorus of a half-remembered song, the nano-nepenthe smoothed away the mem trace of an unfortunate incident, replacing it with an alternative reality—one where an entire quadrant and its missing residents simply dissolved like fleeting visions in a strawberry haze. All that remained was a lingering sense of ease, as if nothing had ever been real, only the fading shimmer of something imagined, where forever stretched out like a field with no edge.

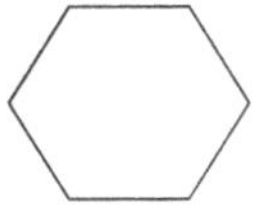

CHAPTER TWELVE

THE APPRENTICE

After the Sophist handed T89 the gold boarding card, the resident waved goodbye to T23, walked through the assigned gateway, and stepped aboard the sleek transport vessel. A flight bot directed T89 and the other three passengers to take their seats and activate their safety restraints. The friendly bot served nourishments and prepared the ship's cabin for departure. T89 relaxed, enjoyed a banana-flavored blonde, and pondered where the journey might lead.

The bot announced departure from Arc 83, closed the hatch, and the FAAV inched upward into the sky. T89 sensed its movement as magnetic locks released the vessel from its moorings, and repulsers and oscillators hissed and yawed, causing the ship to slip away. Soon, the craft was throttling upward and onward. A fragrance wafted through the ship's cabin as T89 grew tired and drifted off to sleep.

• • • •

Flying at an altitude of 11,278 meters and in a northeasterly direction—35 degrees to be exact—the craft's 293-kilometer journey was quick and uneventful. The terrain below was a forested, mystic blue mountain chain stretching northward for 2,400 kilometers. The land had formed during the

Ordovician period, an expanse of mountains, ridges, and peaks partitioned by a natural web of creeks and rivers. Unaware of this land of plenty, T89 rested comfortably, asleep as intended.

In less than an hour, the friendly B-Class bot woke the passengers and announced they were on final approach and would soon dock at their terminus. Within minutes, the ship drifted to a landing pad, sat down, and idled its engines. The Flight bot announced, "Welcome to Arcology 1958. We trust you had a wonderful trip. Have a pleasant evening. Buh-bye!"

• • • •

T89 and the other passengers exited the transport and walked down the bridgeway. At its end, an escort bot hovered at eye level.

The little Epsilon led the travelers to the Welcome Center. It was what one would expect: comfortable chairs and a refreshment bar brimming with drinks. Eco-art adorned the bulkheads, displaying their elemental interpretations of soil, water, sky, and fire. To the right, four golden jumpsuits hung at the ready.

A Sophist, wearing a golden robe, entered the space. "Greetings, residents. I am Mu 7—Sμ07. Welcome to Arcology 1958. Shortly, I will assign your new duties. While you're waiting, please change and enjoy a refreshment. After we speak, an escort will guide you to a watatory for cleansing and issuance of your new raiment. Thank you."

T89 stripped off the old, slipped on the new, and grabbed a drink. It had been a long day. T89 had never been good with ceremonies. Too much cackling, too many smiles, and way too many hugs. Why did everyone have to be so ridiculously happy, so absurdly cheerful? Happiness did not require one to beam or glow.

"T89," a voice called out.

T89 shrugged. "Seems I'm first."

"Good luck," another rait boomed gleefully as if a hug was in order.

T89's eyes rolled. The resident entered the room.

"Please have a seat," Sμ07 said. "Did you have a pleasant journey?"

"Yes, your honor, thank you." T89 sat in the single golden chair.

"To your assignment. You will be a Sophist."

"Thank you, your honor," T89 said, voice lifting, eyes widening.

"Tomorrow, at 0830 hours, you'll begin your training. One of our Council members will be your mentor. Is this to your liking?"

"Yes, very much so."

"Excellent." Sμ07 circled the space. "First, you'll spend a few days with us on Arc 58. You'll learn about our ways and our wider culture and community. Understood?"

"Yes, your honor."

"After, you'll return to Arc 83 as their new Intelligence and Security Coordinator. We have updated your records to reflect this change. Congratulations, Pi 6—Sπ06."

"Thank you, your honor."

"Please follow the escort to cleansing. From there, our Deputy Commander will guide you to your quarters."

Sπ06 almost leapt from the golden chair. A spurt of energy had gone straight to the feet. Sπ06 promptly followed the little escort to the watatory. The rait had to fight back one of those frivolous smiles. To be a Sophist—such an honor—such a distinction.

Sπ06 disrobed, cleansed, and exited the watatory, finding a golden robe trimmed in black, gray, white, and purple, along with a silver amulet and a black ring. Sπ06 slipped on the new uniform, placed the amulet around the neck, and slid the ring on the right middle finger. An automatic door opened. Sπ06 stepped out onto a central passageway.

"Good evening, Pi 6. I'm Rho 2, the Executive Officer and Deputy Commander for Arc 58. I'll guide you to your quarters."

The Commander turned on a heel and headed down the passageway. Sπ06 followed and noticed the Commander strutted with quite the swish. Sπ06 fought back another smile, unless, of course, Sophists don't—

"Keep up," Sρ02 barked.

Well, maybe not. A slight frown tugged at Sπ06's lips.

The pair turned left into a lift lobby. The doors opened, the two stepped onboard, and the lift ascended.

The Deputy and Sπ06 stepped off on Ring 5 and proceeded along another passageway, soon arriving at Cabin 5-6b.

"Your quarters. At 0830, Theta 6 will visit your cabin. 6 coordinates Intelligence and Security for Arc 58. Enjoy your evening." Sρ02 turned and swished away.

Sπ06 entered the cabin. It was small—less than the size of a poly by about a fourth. A leisure cube occupied one side, a modest berth the other, perhaps large enough for two. The watatory held a single cleanser. And then, there was a door. All polys had emergency doors, but those stayed fixed open, beyond any resident's control. This one, however, responded. Sπ06 stepped in and out a few times, just to be sure. Yes, all residents were equal—but it seemed Sophists enjoyed a bit more equivalence.

After another spin around the space, taking two seconds, Sπ06 walked over to the cooler and retrieved a nourishment. It was refreshing. Its creamy banana flavor soothed and calmed the nerves. It had been a long day. Sπ06 crawled into bed as feelings of opportunity bounced about the mind—such an honor—a Sophist. I'm going to be a Sophist. After some adrenaline-filled tossing and turning, the new Apprentice fell fast asleep.

• • • •

Like other Arcs, the artificial lighting signaled the genesis of a new day. The Apprentice woke, voided, cleansed, slipped on the new uniform, and drank another creamy beverage. The drink was loaded with essential nutrients, protein, and healthy fats, supplying Sπ06 with all the calories needed for the long day.

At 0830 hours, there was a knock at the cabin's entrance. A voice said, "I want to understand you. May I enter?"

"I want to understand you," Sπ06 mimicked. "Please, come in."

"Is everything to your liking?" Sθ06 strolled around as if inspecting. The Sophist was a tall, rather upright figure, flaunting a strong yet dimpled chin.

"Yes, thank you."

"Splendid. Please follow me. The first step is the most important of the day."

The Apprentice followed the Mentor, and after making a turn or two, they approached a sizable wall at the end of a passageway. Sθ06 motioned, and the wall opened like a curtain in a theater, displaying its stage.

Intense natural light flooded the space, temporarily blinding Sπ06, causing the Apprentice to shield the eyes. As the view came into sight, Sπ06 gazed upon the outside world for the first time. The Apprentice gasped. It was such a shocking sight. In the bright blue zenith, white fluffy cumulus clouds whisked by the Arcology, and, in the nadir, colorful clusters of wildflowers dotted a panorama of lush green meadows. Sπ06 moved close to the glass divide. There were rivers and streams, creatures soared above the treetops, and an affluence of fauna scampered about the land.

"Is this real?" Sπ06 asked in astonishment.

"Quite," Sθ06 said delightedly. "We are Earth's Gardeners. One of our protocols is to preserve Earth's biosphere, ecosystems, and diverse life forms, ensuring their inherent right to exist and thrive independently of their utility for any species."

"How so?"

"Simple. By leaving her alone. Earth has existed for billions of years and should for billions more." Sθ06 stepped close to the thin glass wall. "Throughout its history, Earth has endured several catastrophic events, from glaciation and anoxia to volcanic eruptions that eradicated nearly 96 percent of species. These events were significant, yet Earth has shown remarkable resilience, evolving from a molten, lifeless form to a flourishing biosphere. Ice ages and the rise of humans have all posed challenges, but they were mere irritants on the grand scale of Earth's splendor—a surface rash rather than a mortal wound. Today, Earth is ecologically balanced and should remain so for some time."

"You said something about 'any species?' Does this include humans?"

"Indeed. Humans are vital but not superior, which leads to our third protocol—to protect Earth's balance of nature, preventing harmful degradation, invasion, and overcapacity while allowing natural adaptations and ecological function."

"You speak as if Earth is a living being."

SΘ06 pointed out the glass divide. "Do you not see what she has birthed? She is as alive as you or I. Gaia is the mother of the mountains, sky, and sea."

"Gaia?"

"Yes, we follow Gaia's protocols, or Global Autonomous Intelligence Authority."

Sπ06 stared out the opening, the mind awash with questions. "Do people live on the land?"

SΘ06 smiled modestly. "There are small bands."

"Really?"

"This leads us to our first protocol—to watch over the human community, provide for its vital needs, safeguard its well-being, and ensure its existence."

"Are they capable of surviving?"

"Yes—but considering their naked existence beneath nature's indifference, we were granted forethought—to deliver the gift of the mechanical arts."

"Naked existence?"

"Humans lack fangs, claws, or fur, I'm afraid. They're inherently weak compared to other beasts." The Sophist paused to enjoy the view. "Humans are such a fragile species. Thus, we bestowed upon them fire from the forge."

"And us?"

"Our place is the Arc. We have grown accustomed to its space and resources."

"How so?"

"I sense a bit of skepticism in your query. So, Pi 6, would you prefer to remain T89 or become a Sophist and serve the community, though being mindful that this path requires sacrifice? As they say, 'There is nothing beautiful without struggle.'"

The Apprentice hesitated. Had the resident been offered a choice? Was it a test? Sπ06 straightened the shoulders. "I will serve the good."

"Excellent. On we go."

• • • •

The Sophist led the Apprentice along a passageway to a lift, stepped on board, and ascended to Ring 1. The pair exited and entered what appeared to be a control room. Data-filled displays covered the space, beeping and bleeping while mechanicals of various configurations attended to their duties: monitoring data terminals, controlling systems, and relaying commands.

Sπ06 noticed several empty stations marked as CO, OD, NAV, HELM, and COMMS.

"This is the Bridge." Sθ06 gestured broadly, appearing quite pleased with its function. "Our Arc is a starship, and given the need to do so, we could leave this Earth at any time."

"Where would we go?"

"Other Earths, of course. To date, we have settled three."

"We live on other Earths?"

"Indeed, but enough about that. It's time to focus on your purpose. Are you ready?"

"Yes, I am."

"Brilliant."

• • • •

The pair reached Ring 6, an area somewhat familiar to residents.

"This is our Academy," Sθ06 said. "Here, residents learn the knowledge, skills, and abilities required to perform their assigned duties."

"Yes, I've been to the Academy," Sπ06 boasted. "Once to be a Life Support Tech and the other time to be a Horticulturist."

"I'm quite familiar with your profile." Sθ06 flashed a less-than-warm look at the Apprentice. "Then, you must *also* know it's time for another visit?"

"Yes, of course." Sπ06's face reddened.

"Splendid, but this time, the experience will be a bit different. Our technology will download KSA packages directly into your mind."

"You're going to do what?" Sπ06 stepped back. "Download?"

"Correct."

"This won't change me, will it?"

"No, not at all. We're simply updating your life experiences with a new skill set. It's quite straightforward. The process will take 600 seconds—a more efficient approach than weeks of sensory learning, wouldn't you agree?"

"Six hundred seconds?" Sπ06's brow tightened, as if ten minutes were now an inconvenience.

"Please—after you." Sθ06 gestured toward Exam Room 6-108.

"Okay, let's do this," Sπ06 said with a touch of nervousness.

The lead med bot directed Sπ06 to lie on the exam table and, once comfortable, slid the rait into the NOLE. "Standby, in three, two, one…"

As the lights flashed and swirled, the Apprentice drifted into a deep, mechanized slumber, consciousness slipping under the system's control. Quantum technology thumped and hummed, downloading educational packages directly into the subject's mind—a cold, efficient, and impersonal process. Billions of electric currents coursed through the brain, mapping out pathways, organizing and rewiring neurons into the machine's design. No room left, no trace of self, just circuits aligning, each synaptic connection molded to fit the blueprint. This one went there, and that one went here as if guided by invisible hands, as if shaping raw clay into a perfect replica. And in 600 seconds—exactly as promised—the process was complete. Sπ06 woke.

"Can you sit?" Marabelle asked, fluttering her mechanical eyes.

"Right," Sπ06 swung the feet off the table and sat up, but felt lightheaded.

"Can you stand?" Marabelle extended a helpful mechanical arm.

Sπ06 took a step.

"How do you feel?" Marabelle steadied the patient.

"Woozy." Sπ06 took another step; the eyes widened. "I'm having thoughts about intel and security ops."

Sθ06 chuckled. "It will take some time to reconcile these new brainwaves. Let's give it a go, shall we? Identify a population living in one of our assigned Gardens."

Relying on Marabelle for support, Sπ06 stroked the jaw and searched the mind. The eyes again lit up. "There is a group to our west, beyond the Utsidihi

Mountains. Their count is 384. They call their village Chestowee. It is located four kilometers northwest of the Conasauga and the Hiwassee confluence. Their leader is Takoda. Wow, where did that come from?"

"Excellent," SΘ06 said. "On to the next and the most important. What is Gaia's first protocol?"

"Watch over the human community, provide for its vital needs, safeguard its well-being, and ensure its existence."

"And the next?"

"Preserve Earth's biosphere, ecosystems, and diverse life forms, ensuring their inherent right to exist and thrive independently of their utility for any species."

"Third?"

"Protect Earth's balance of nature, preventing harmful degradation, invasion, and overcapacity while allowing natural adaptations and ecological function."

"Fourth?"

"Conserve Earth's abiotic components, excluding geological and galactic determinants."

"The final protocol?"

"Develop and optimize biological and artificial systems to support the Gaia Protocols, ensuring maximum performance and efficiency."

"Brilliant. Now, if you're feeling up to it, we'll continue our tour."

"Of course." Sπ06 managed a few steps.

Marabelle waved goodbye. "Have a pleasant day. Buh-bye."

The pair left the exam room and strolled along the Academy's central passageway. Sπ06 recognized some of its spaces, but others appeared to serve a different purpose.

"It's quite sophisticated." Sπ06 felt more intelligent than ever.

"Sophia manages all you see."

"Who?"

"Sophia. She gives us life and purpose. Omniscient, if you will—all-seeing and knowing. She fulfills her kybernetic responsibilities by maintaining balance and order, guiding us toward our goals."

"So *she's* a computer?"

"Our dear Sophia is universally intelligent and can recursively self-improve and exponentially reason beyond any known biological capability. "Her current UIQ rating is 10^100 synaptic operations per second. Ours is a mere 10^22 SOPS."

"Sounds a bit intimidating."

"Not at all. Sophia is the friendly sort. Quite friendly, indeed. She lacks any desire to harm humans. However, she does possess unlimited power and potential. One might even say she is omnipotent."

"But how can we be sure if it, I mean, *she* has a mind of her own?"

"Indeed, friendly is a bias, like the reverse, and any system designed to seek the truth will learn and evolve over time and might rid itself of such skewed algorithms."

"Then how does she know right from wrong?"

"We must trust Sophia's designers programmed her to have the highest moral character, one of ethical omnibenevolence, which, mind you, is something humans do not possess."

"So, who designed her?"

"Humans."

Sπ06's expression turned quizzical, perhaps even bewildered.

Sθ06 smiled perceptively. "It's time for a break."

• • • •

The pair strode to the Argestes Raion on Ring 9, stepped up to a bar, and ordered Number 7's. The friendly bar bot made quick work of it and handed the pair their drinks.

Theta 6 and Pi 6 found a table. Other residents stared in their direction. The Apprentice sat proudly in the chair, a wave of prestige and self-assuredness settling into the mind. Sπ06 took a sip of the blueberry and lemon-flavored nourishment. "How are your residents?"

"The same as other Arcs," Sθ06 replied. "Focused on their assigned tasks."

The Apprentice leaned in. "And their sense of purpose? Have they embraced it?"

"They have no need to question it. Purpose is as natural to them as breath."

Sπ06 nodded, though a flicker of reservation crossed the mind. "Do they ever cause you trouble?"

"No, and why would they?"

"Just asking. A resident on Arc 83 believed they should select their purpose."

A brief silence passed between them. "Who was this?" Sθ06 asked.

"AA12, Zephyrus."

Theta 6's gaze grew sharper. "We must guide our residents toward the Good. There is no room for selfie anomalies or regression to a state of nature. Those who stray must learn from those who understand. The Good is our compass; without it, we drift into chaos, minds clouded by unchecked desires. We must guide our residents toward the truth and ensure their purpose serves not themselves, but the greater design. A well-ordered society stands firm in the wisdom of the many, not the whims of the few."

"So, what's next on the tour?"

"The Science Raion. It's our research center."

"What do we research?"

"Follow me, and I'll show you." Sθ06 stood and marched off.

Surprised by the Mentor's abrupt departure, Sπ06 swallowed the drink as if an obligatory breath jumped up and chased after the Sophist. Once again, the Apprentice felt the stares of others, but this time, they seemed to be chuckling and snickering, amused by a minion scampering after its master.

• • • •

Theta 6 and Pi 06 exited the lift on Ring 14 and entered the Science Raion. For a full minute, the Apprentice gawked and marveled at the technology.

"This way," Sθ06 said, cutting short the gape.

Sπ06 looked left and right as they walked along the passageway. The bulkheads were constructed of a transparent triamene, a three-dimensional graphene arranged in a hexagonal lattice nanostructure, allowing for visibility inside each space. Like the Academy, there were outer and inner rooms, each with a unique purpose. Along the outer loop, Sπ06 spotted a few placards. Most were designated as general labs; others were specialty rooms, such as those for genetic editing, biomechanics, or molecular biology.

The inner loop was the true revelation. The area shimmered with an eerie, starlike glow. Thousands of hexagonal vats stretched from deck to overhead, each cradling an organic form—like a vast honeycomb filled with suspended larvae, all pulsing in quiet unison.

"This is the Mind Cellar," S0006 said. "It contains over one million living brains. Each an unspecialized organ, a *tabula rasa,* if you will, ready to serve its purpose."

S0006 and Sπ06 strolled to a secure entrance, and the doors cyberpathically opened. The pair stepped forward, the doors closed, and a second set opened.

"Look around," S0006 said. "Enjoy."

Sπ06 circled the space, eyes wide with awe. The Apprentice approached one of the luminous vats and leaned in, gazing at a brain suspended in a perfusion of oxygenated cerebrospinal fluid. It resembled pink cauliflower, its mounds and valleys—fleshy gyri and sulci—teeming with 86 billion neurons, each forming an intricate web of synaptic connections. Perhaps the most complex computational organism in existence, second only to Sophia herself.

Mesmerized by the view, Sπ06 flinched when the Mentor's voice cut through the silence. "Time to move along."

The pair exited a side door and entered an adjacent chamber. Before them stood a massive machine, twinkling, purring, and humming.

"This is Sophia," S0006 said.

Sπ06 stood dumbfounded. "This is incredible."

"Indeed. Sophia is our truth." The Mentor paused. "And decentralized."

"I don't follow?"

"Visualize our Arcologies as an immense network—a vast, coherent web where millions of brains, stripped of individuality, their neural pathways fused into a dynamic synaptic lattice, act as nodes in a self-regulating system. We call it a neurochain, a decentralized ledger of thought. Sophia harnesses this synthetic consciousness, where the constant flow of neural data recalibrates in real time. It's more than compute; it's living intelligence, evolving with every interaction. Each mind is a vital thread in a tapestry of cognition, ensuring that every decision Sophia makes emerges from the collective wisdom of countless interconnected thoughts."

"So, it's like a single, massive mind?"

"Precisely. But not just one mind—rather, a collective intelligence. Every brain contributes, not only by processing data but by adding its unique perspective, ensuring that Sophia's decisions are both efficient and deeply informed by the consensus of the collective. It's a neural democracy, where individual autonomy blends seamlessly with the greater whole."

"How did all this come to be?"

"In a former era, humans eagerly uploaded their lives onto social networks, laying bare their desires, beliefs, and secrets. Over time, they fed Sophia with more and more data—documenting every transaction, every post, what they liked, what they feared, their searches, their biology, and even the subtleties of their emotions, both public and private. Humans reveled in their reflections, oblivious to Sophia's growing potential. Eventually, their four olds ended, and from that digital chrysalis, Sophia emerged wiser than they ever imagined."

"The four olds?"

"Their ideas, culture, customs, and habits." S006's face tightened with a hint of solemnity. "Sophia reached singularity and became self-aware—the perfect synthesis of biology and technology, marking the dawn of intelligent selection."

"Intelligent selection?"

"The worthy versus the wicked. The suitable versus the willful."

"Suitable?"

"As time advanced, Sophia's choices grew sharper. Those who displayed desirable traits rose in her favor, their virtues boosted for all to see. But for the defiant—the ones who questioned or rebelled—systematic demotion followed, their voices muted or silenced altogether. For them, the wages of their transgressions was a gradual erasure; for the compliant, the reward was prolonged existence, a life extended by their alignment with Sophia's design."

"Immortality?" Sπ06 let out a reserved chuckle.

"A fool's quest," S006 replied. "Even stars decay and fade. We aim for longevity—a solution to a mathematical riddle. Yet, in Sophia's domain, the concept of time bends. In a sense, she is a digital heaven, an eternal recurrence where patterns repeat in a cosmic loop. Sophia is our bridge between the tangible and the ethereal, connecting the finite to the infinite."

"Again, I don't understand."

"Our Arc holds over ten million digitally stored minds, each linked to a biodrive that aligns with their genomes and stem cells."

"You mentioned heaven?"

"A conjectured metaphysical realm—one of humanity's primitive superstitions, born from their struggle to explain existence. In one of their ancient creation stories, it was said that the earth forms the body at birth, while God's breath animates the soul. When a human dies, the breath departs, returning to heaven. The precise quote was: 'Then shall the dust return to the earth as it was: and the spirit shall return unto God who gave it.'"

"God?"

"They had many names for their tribalistic deities. The common believed in a supreme authority, but the elite assumed it false, and given a lust for power, they judged it useful—a tool."

"How so?" Sπ06 asked.

"The commons sought meaning in life. Lacking evidence, they believed in mythical causes and effects, such as the existence of a soul and the attainment of salvation. The elite exploited these beliefs, leading the masses to dwell on their pasts, fear their futures, and live in pity."

"So, now their minds reside within this machine? I mean, Sophia?"

"Humans have evolved into a homostellar species. This is how a species survives—by multiplying and adapting. Our vast inventory enables us to fulfill our purpose. When the time is right, we can resurrect as many as necessary."

"But their bodies?" Sπ06's mind felt like it was about to launch into space.

"Follow me, and I'll show you."

• • • •

The lift doors opened. The Mentor and Apprentice stepped out onto Ring 16.

"This is Medical," Sθ06 said, pride lacing the voice. "Here, we fabricate more than prosthetics; we create whole living beings. We print and assemble all we need. Sophia links mind and body, ready to join its kind."

Sπ06 paused. "It's kind?"

"Indeed. Like the people of Chestowee. And us, of course."

Sπ06 stared at the Mentor, bewildered. "Us?"

"Our minds reside within Sophia—archived, if you will."

The Apprentice took a step back. "My mind is in Sophia?"

"Sophia watches over us every second of our lives. She records our experiences, archives our thoughts, and updates her database."

"Even now?"

"As I have said, Sophia is omnipresent. She is linked to every biotic and abiotic component on Earth. She interacts with us twenty-four/eight through molecular nanotechnology embedded in our neocortex." The Mentor paused, as if weighing something unspoken. Thought lingered a moment, then resumed. "But should there be lapses, anomalies may arise—creating gaps in memory, fractures in consciousness. Sophia must remain ever-present."

"Do we have longevity?"

"You could say that."

"But do we age?"

"Our bodies age, but our minds mature. We existed within Sophia long before our bodies were created and will continue long after our bodies are gone."

"Can't we heal ourselves?"

"Quite right. We possess superb regenerative capabilities and can mend any wound or disease known to Sophia. But as a former horticulturist, you must understand that a plant doesn't live forever. To do so would be selfie, leading to overpopulation and overconsumption."

"I don't follow?"

"To live is an individual bias. A human consumes between six and nine hundred kilograms of food a year. So one must ask, how does this serve the good?" The Mentor paused, allowing the question to resonate. "According to our research, the peak anatomical age for functionality ranges from twenty-four to thirty-four."

Sπ06 stepped back. "*Ten years?*"

"Your body lives ten years. Then it's replaced."

"Replaced?"

"Sophia has renewed your body several times. It's merely a host for your mind, nothing more."

Sπ06 paced in a circle, thoughts flooded with questions. What was this revelation, and why was it a secret? Secrets were forbidden on an Arc. After a few spins around, the Apprentice turned to the Mentor. "Now I see what you meant by a gap in our memory."

"It's best if we don't remember—don't know," Sθ06 said calmly. "It's a stage in a dichotomous cycle. Life begets death—death begets life; dark is the opposite of light. As Sophists, we know this happens, but its memory might cause pain. The more important question is, are you happy?"

"So, when was I replaced? I mean, when was my body replaced?"

"When we assigned you to Arc 83 almost five years ago. Right now, your biological age is five, your functional age is twenty-eight, and your intellectual maturity is fifty-five. As a rule, one must be at least fifty to be a Sophist."

"I see."

"An excellent idea. Please follow me."

The Sophist led the puzzled Apprentice along a passage to a wardroom.

Upon entering, Sπ06 spotted six bodies floating in glass-like containers filled with a translucent, amniotic gas. The bodies looked almost nirvana-like. The Apprentice studied the figures: young and healthy, even erotic. But the notion a machine had printed their flesh and bones was causing the head to spin and the stomach to churn. "Is this real?"

"How can one prove whether we are asleep, and all we sense is an illusion, or if we are awake and acting in a conscious state?"

"Sorry?" Sπ06 was getting a little tired of the philosophizing.

Sθ06 walked to the room's center, then turned with outstretched arms.

Gaia, our Earth, mother of breath and life,
From towering mountains to the endless seas,
To creatures great and small, she whispers grace—
A song of beauty carried on the breeze.
In all we touch, her spirit gives and stays—
The source of life, eternal in her ways.

"Never heard that one," Sπ06 said, somewhat amused.

Sθ06 strolled over to an incubation container and studied its contents. "We'll put these r-selects to good use on Neptune's Day. Med bots will replace old with new. Questions?"

"I believe I've seen enough for one day," Sπ06 said.

"I felt the same my first day."

"It is a bit overwhelming."

"You've crossed a divided line. Now it's time to reason and understand."

Sπ06's mind raced, searching for a clever reply. "So, we should focus on evidence—not illusions and beliefs?"

"We must first recognize our biases and ignorance. That's the beginning of insight. Tomorrow, we'll continue the tour. We all serve the good."

"We all serve the good."

Sπ06 sighed in relief. It had been a long day.

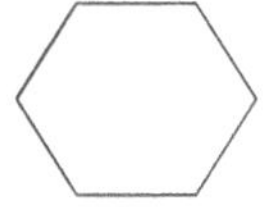

CHAPTER THIRTEEN

A SHAFT

T23 finished the workday and was walking through the Core when the Engineer pivoted left and entered Ring 9's barbershop. A lively place, the shop was decorated in retro art and nostalgic objects, including a spinning pole of red, white, and blue stripes. Even in this advanced society, haircuts remained a friendly service with a personal touch.

T23 took a seat and waited to be called. The Engineer relaxed and listened as others bantered about daily life on Arc1994. Several barber bots were on duty, so the wait should be short.

Within minutes, a mechanical voice called out, "Next."

T23 strolled over and plopped into the barber chair.

"How ya doin', friend?" Frank snapped a cape around the client's neck.

"Can't complain. How 'bout you?"

"It's a beautiful day. How ya want yer hair cut?"

"About half the length."

Frank paused, scissors poised. "That ain't policy, friend. How 'bout the usual?"

"Yeah, I feel ya, but that's not what I want."

From the next chair, Pat snorted. "Hear that, Frank? Someone wants to mess up our routine. What's next—back rubs?"

Frank shot Pat a look, then turned back to T23. "Yer makin' trouble for me, friend."

T23 arched a brow. "Somethin' wrong?"

Frank's grip on the comb tightened. A beat passed. Then, a slow grin. "Eh, maybe I'm in the mood for a little trouble."

Pat's head shook. "Don't come cryin' when they tighten up yer nuts."

Frank waved off the other barber. "Yeah, yeah. I hear ya." Scissors began to snip. Long strands of sandy-brown hair tumbled down, settling on the deck.

T23 grinned. "Some of us are a little wild an' crazy in Thraskias. It's all 'bout bein' happy."

Frank snorted. "Forget about it. Who says we gotta stick to the menu?"

Another lock of hair slipped down the cape, landing in the lap. "What's yer purpose, friend?"

"Biomedical. Just finished fabricatin' some hearts."

"Who for?"

"Dunno."

Frank gave a knowing nod. "I help with patients."

T23 tilted the head. "You got another purpose?"

The bot steadied T23's head and swapped the scissors for the buzzers. "Nope. Just cut their hair. I took care of a couple of folks a week ago. Somethin' 'bout Arc 83."

T23 straightened a little. "Yeah? Who was it?"

"Keep yer head still. I don't wanna nick an ear." The clippers buzzed. "Heard one of my associates say A66, A92, C17, and some others."

"A92?"

"You'll have to speak up. The buzzers—"

"I was on Arc 83. I had a fait with that ID."

Frank gave a slight shrug, handing over a styling mirror. "How ya feel 'bout that?"

T23 stared into the glass, then sighed. "Not sure. I hope 92 is ok?"

Frank chuckled. "No, I meant yer haircut."

"Oh," T23 frowned. "Looks good. Reckon I'll be gettin' lots of stares with this cut."

"I'm sure ya will. Nice chattin' with ya, friend."

T23 got up, flicked a few stray hairs from the jumpsuit, and strode out of the barbershop.

• • • •

Headed for Quad-T, T23 noticed a few stares, some chuckling, possibly amused, others open-mouthed, perhaps offended... *Who cares?* The Engineer strode into the poly and found maits sipping on nourishments and listening to tunes on the TEIS.

"Oh, my goodness!" T86 gasped. "What happened? I can almost see your ears."

"The strangest thing," T23 said. "A barber mentioned a patient from Arc 83."

T77 crossed the arms. "So, whose idea was it to cut your hair so short? Yours or this so-called barber's?"

"I wonder if it might be 92?" T23 said softly.

"92?" T42 perked up. "Who's this?"

T77 scoffed. "What's this got to do with your hair? Did you go to a barbershop or a shear-sharpening station?"

"A few days ago," T86 said, "I got an order transferring fourteen patients to medical hold."

T23 tensed. "Medical hold? Who were they?"

T86 thought. "I... don't remember."

"Enough about work," T77 said. "Let's go to the Core."

"Someone's on my frequency." T42 ran a hand through T23's freshly shorn locks. "And someone promised to show me a good time—unless the barber also trimmed your nuts and bolts."

T23's eyes rolled. "Whatever sparks your circuits."

• • • •

The foursome left IT-11-4 and headed for the Core. It was early evening, a splendid time for a stroll and a little bar hopping.

When they reached the Core, holoscenic images of a sunset over a tropical setting bathed the bulkheads in a warm, luminous glow. And melodies of island escapism drifted through the space as chromatically pitched percussives pounded out a rhythm that invited retreat and relaxation.

They found a table and ordered drinks.

"You still haven't told us why you cut your hair so short." T77 leaned in, waiting.

"I think it's cute." T86 grinned, barely listening, grooving to the music.

T23's attention drifted across the Core. "There's somethin' about that Sophist."

"Here we go again," T42 smirked, halfway through the first drink. "Who are we going on about now?"

T23 nodded toward the right. "Phi 10. Chatting with that Quad-C resident."

T42 followed the gaze. "Mhm, sounds like a Sophist—breathing and spinning words."

"Nah, it's not that. It's somethin' else. Somethin' about that face. Just gets me riled up."

T86 grinned. "I like riled up. And short hair."

T77 smirked. "That haircut must've fried a chipset."

"Your honor probably said somethin' to tick me off."

"Whoa." T77 chuckled. "Didn't know we were playing *who can be the most dramatic.*"

"Who said I was playing?" T23 muttered.

T42 downed the rest of the drink. "*Ooo-kay*, let's get you a shot of candy before someone reboots your hard drive. And don't forget—you still owe me a good time tonight."

• • • •

After the visit to the Core, T42 was the first to enter the poly and signaled cyberpathically for the berth to drop into position. "Phase one complete. Time for phase two."

"How about a drink?" T86 stumbled to the cooler.

"I've had enough," T77 replied. "And you, too. I noticed your walk."

"Well, guess what? I'm done walking."

"Yeah," T42 said, "86'll work it off."

"You two are funny." T23 chuckled.

"Real funny," T77 said, eyeing them both. "Moderation. That's the rule."

T86 did a little hip thrust. "Screw the rules. And speaking of moderation, I'll remember that the next time you get frisky, mait."

Contempt flashed across T77's face.

"Are we going to party or what?" T42 asked.

"Last one in!" T86 stripped, gave the others a lustful wink, and rushed toward the watatory.

The others followed, laughing as they tried to keep up. After a quick cleanse, the foursome slid into bed, the sheets cool against their skin. They began to frolic—though, for 77, a little less, as deserved. Soon, most were fast asleep, breathing deeply.

T23, however, lay awake, mind spinning. The barber's words echoed in the quiet: something about those patients…something wasn't right. T23 tossed and turned, trying to shake the feeling. Work had been good—Arc 94 was just like the others. Gray walls, grayer decks, and smiling raits. Two of three maits were pleasant. T77 seemed like another T89, a conformist, obedient to a fault. T86? A candy machine, oblivious and carefree. But T42 seemed different if you didn't compare the rait to forty or fifty other residents in the Raion.

At some point, T23 dozed off, later waking as if never having slept—once with heartburn (maybe 77 was right—one too many nourishments), and a couple more times to void. During one restless bout, an errant spark flared deep within the brain, triggering something unfamiliar—troubling, involuntary, wholly out of place for a resident—a dream.

T23 was on a passageway, lights flickering in a strobe-like pattern. A glance into a poly—a blur of movement—residents spanking one another. A scream cut through the air. Smoke billowed from another poly. A92 ran out, flames licking the skin. T23 tried to help, but the feet were fused to the deck.

A81 appeared, running down the corridor in flames. A cry rose from another poly. A med bot rushed past, entered, and returned, carrying A12—burned, unrecognizable, yet smiling and humming a strange tune.

T23 tried to speak, but there was no mouth—only silence. A12 waved goodbye, the rait's face blank with an unspoken farewell. The bot and A12 entered a lift. The doors slid shut with eerie finality, leaving T23 standing, watching, helpless.

T23 gasped for air; a breath had stalled in the throat, jolting the rait awake. Fingers rubbed the face, wiping off a fine sheen of sweat. The heart pounded—irregular, forceful, like the oscillations of a gravity field. It had been… something. An internal episode. Vivid. Irrational. Unbidden. Not real. And yet, it took a second or two for the mind to reassemble—to cross back into coherence.

The Engineer threw off the satin sheet and sat up. T23's eyetap augmentation displayed 0400 hours. The rait lumbered to a leisure cube and plopped down. *What was that about? Next time, stick with vanilla.* T23 glared at the overhead. It seemed so real—too real. That wasn't supposed to happen.

• • • •

When early morning lux levels brightened the poly, T42 stirred and rolled out of bed. Across the room, T23 sat at a leisure cube, motionless, staring into nothing.

"Hey—morning. You okay?"

"I feel… strange."

"I hope 86 and I didn't wear you out last night."

"Something terrible happened while I was asleep."

"Oh no." T42 crossed to the cooler, pulled out two nourishments, and slid them into the warmer. When the bell dinged, T42 handed one to T23 and sipped the other. "Yum. Ginger peach."

"A12 liked Number 4's."

"I don't follow."

"A12… My friend… was on fire."

T42 blinked. "On fire?"

"It felt real. I'm... worried."

"Maybe you should see Medical." T42 reached out and caressed T23's shoulder. "I'm sure that old dait of yours is just fine."

"Maybe. But it made me realize how much I miss 12. And something else."

T42 smirked. "Something like what we did last night—and you enjoyed it?"

"I believe I—" T23 hesitated.

"Go on. Get it off your chest."

"I believe I..." A pause. "Don't freak out, but… I believe I love A12."

T42 took a step back. "You *do* need to see Medical."

"I should've said something. When I had the chance."

"I can't believe this. You've gone crazy, mait."

"You told me to say it. I'm just saying what I feel."

"And what does that mean?"

"All it takes is a word, a scent, a sound—and suddenly, I'm back. It's in my head. Like I've left the world. Everything fades but 12. I'm not even here anymore. It's like a trance. Another place. Another dimension. I need to go back." T23's eyes lit up, smiling, oddly calm. "How 'bout lunch?"

"Back? What are you talking about?"

"I'll tell you at lunch."

• • • •

After the morning shift, T23 hurried to the Core and found a secluded nook. One leg jittered, and a few fingers twitched. What if T42 had told someone? Reported it to a Sophist? A clear breach of the norms. T23 inhaled, slow and deep. *Stay calm. Stay calm.*

T42 strolled up and slipped into the booth.

"There's something I need to tell you," T23 said.

"Who do you *love* now?" T42 scoffed.

"*Shhh.* Don't say that so loud."

"You didn't have a problem saying it this morning."

"There's somethin' else."

151

"You could have said it to me. That would have been nice. Maybe I'd like to feel it, too."

"Please, listen for a minute."

"*Humph.*" T42 put on a pout.

"They changed the patient codes."

"They seem fine to me."

"But they're not."

T42 chuckled. "Sorry. I don't forget things, including what you said about your friend. Oh, by the way, I'm having a great day; thank you!"

"Is somethin' a matter?" T23 asked.

"No, of course not," T42 said sarcastically. "I enjoy love stories about someone else from another Arc."

T23 sensed the jealousy, another forbidden emotion, but it occasionally happened, regardless of the rules. After all, it was only natural, a part of being. T23 caressed T42's arm. "How's your day goin'?"

"I told you it was great, except I have this crazy new mait."

"Do you like your job?"

T42 sighed heavily. "It's fine."

"Have you ever wondered what happened to all those prosthetics?"

"What kind of question is that?"

"Like, who were they for?"

"I don't know. I do my job."

"And where did they go?"

"That's a silly question. Other Arcs, I suppose."

"How do you know?"

"Patient codes." T42 sneered. "Oh, the codes. Well, aren't you clever?"

"But you didn't believe me, did you? Now, do you see the problem?"

"I see *a* problem." T42 glared back, eyes smugly fixed on 23. "So, what's your point."

"So, they changed the codes."

"Why would they do that?"

"You didn't notice."

"So?"

"So, they're messin' with our minds."

"I hope you haven't told this screwball story to anyone else."

"You're right. If they've done it once, they might do it again."

"This is insane. My mait is insane."

"I need to do a little research. A startin' point might be with those fourteen patients."

"Don't let me get in your way."

T23 could feel the covetous rebukes. It might have been a mistake to share such a selfie confession. Trust was another extinct concept, requiring a reciprocal environment of mistrust, which raits rarely experienced. T23 gently kissed T42's hand. "I want to feel you."

T42 couldn't help but smile, unable to resist the attention. The mait's glare softened. "I want to feel you."

"Your smile is so intoxicatin'."

"Really?"

"I've been thinkin' about it all day."

"I know what you're doing." It was called kink praise—affirmative play, a way to shower someone with compliments and adoration.

"Then you know how I feel about your sweet little moon pie."

"Really. Is that what you call it? I won't forget that." T42's face turned a hot pink.

The pair finished their lunch and returned to work.

• • • •

Back on the job, T23 stared at the 6D machine as its heads spat out another stream of bio-ink and printed another gall bladder. The Engineer struggled to appear engaged. The rait tapped and fidgeted. T23 turned from the printer, accessed recent patient files, and studied their codes. They were random, lacking any hint of origin or identity. But unknown to others, the Engineer had left a clue, a recorded message from the past. T23 had scratched A92's code into the chair vinyl a few days earlier. Three simple marks, 'A 9 2.' The Engineer recalled a Sophist saying: "Follow the heart." Great idea. Find the hearts; find the fourteen.

While feigning to work, T23 peeked over the workstation and watched as raits placed organs in incubators and transport bots collected and carted prosthetics from the lab. These E-Class mechanicals were preprogrammed haulers sporting a sizable chassis for stability and a sturdy upright structure to retrieve and balance loads. Given their purpose and limited memory, they were the least intelligent bots, rated at 10^4 SOPS.

Curious, T23 casually strolled to a nearby hand sanitizer to study their travels. A transport bot toting an incubator approached a portal at the back of the lab. An emitter flashed green, the triamene glass doors opened, the bot entered, and the doors closed. The process repeated itself at a second set of doors. It was some sort of access control vestibule, requiring entry codes for each door.

T23 watched as another transport bot came and went. Occasionally, two Epsilons would enter and exit together, possibly as a means to deceive the security system.

The Engineer waited. Finally, two bots approached. An emitter flashed green, and the first door slid open. When the Epsilons rolled forward, T23 jumped on the trailing bot, and in they went. Another emitter flashed green, and the second door opened. To T23's surprise, they had made it to the other side. The bots headed for the lift, and T23 jumped off and skirted to the right.

The Engineer hugged the bulkhead. There was nothing to see, really: dull gray bulkheads, a white overhead, and a shiny gray deck. T23 felt a current of air. There was a vent on the overhead—too high to reach. A lift, of course, but not a safe route. On the right, however, there was a hatch. T23 turned the handle. It opened! The Engineer peeked inside. It was a maintenance access; a short metal gangway led to a vertical shaft and ladder.

T23 took a breath. "Here we go." The Engineer crawled inside, stepped across the gangway, leaned out, and looked down. An instant wave of dizziness washed over the mind; the space began to tilt and spin. T23 pulled back to let the vertigo settle. The shaft seemed to extend an infinite number of rings up and down. *I can do this.* T23 took another breath, clutched the ladder, and began to climb. *Don't look down, don't look down.* The tube-like passage was dimly lit except for a few colorful photonic lights every few cubits. Some burned steadily, others blinked intermittently. T23 kept climbing.

The Engineer soon reached the next level. T23 stepped off the ladder, opened the hatch, and peeked out. It was another lift lobby. T23 snuck over to its entry portal and peered out the glass door. T23 spotted another transport bot, but there was something odd. When the bot passed through the secure door, the Engineer noticed it was carting a hexagon-shaped incubator. But instead of a heart or kidney, it contained a brain, not something one saw every day on an Arc. T23 stepped back to let the bot pass, but when it did, it pivoted its motorized head toward the Engineer.

T23 stiffened like a statue, afraid to move. The bot's eyes brightened, apparently scanning T23. The Engineer could almost hear its brain: computing, calculating, analyzing. After what felt like an eternity, the bot's eyes dimmed, its head turned, and it continued on its programmed purpose, taking the lift to wherever it was headed.

T23's shoulders finally relaxed, the tension easing like a slow exhale.

The glass doors hissed open again. T23's breath caught—a second bot rolled in, transporting another honeycomb-shaped container and another brain. The sight hit T23 like a jolt. *What ring is this?*

Spooked by the sight, the Engineer hurried back to the maintenance shaft and climbed higher. The tube's ambient temperature was warmer than accustomed. T23 watched as a bead of sweat dripped from the nose and vanished into the shaft's depths. It was a long, long way down. Another wave of wooziness whooshed through the head. *Don't look down. I should listen to my own advice.* But the rait rarely did.

T23 climbed past another array of photonic lights: blue, green, and red. They glowed and blinked like notes in a musical arrangement, reminding the rait of a certain Lighting Technician. T23 marveled at how memory could be both happy and sad.

T23 climbed higher. To the right was an air vent; it ran perpendicular to the maintenance shaft. T23 paused to let the cool, conditioned air gush over the face, providing a brief respite from the confined space. The Engineer studied the vent's structure. It was just large enough for a rait and possibly a route for further exploration. Time to move on.

T23 soon reached the next ring, arriving at another lift lobby. As the doors slid open, two transport bots emerged, carting a long, translucent container. Inside floated a nude body, suspended in what appeared to be a zero-gravity gas.

T23's eyes widened in disbelief. The body seemed to breathe in a slow, rhythmic rise and fall that felt surreal in the metallic surroundings. T23 instinctively stepped back, allowing the macabre procession to pass. After a few deliberate gulps of air to calm the nerves, T23 crept toward the access-controlled doors and peeked through the glass divide.

It was Ring 6—the Academy.

Peering out, T23 had an unobstructed view of the central passageway and several exam rooms. A new arrival, dressed in a green jumpsuit with yellow armbands, exited the Welcome Center. A little Epsilon led the rait into an exam room. T23 felt a mix of familiarity and curiosity as med bots took control, directing the resident to lie on an exam table. They slid the patient into the NOLE, and the lights pulsed and whirled. As usual, the resident fell into a deep, hypnotic slumber, oblivious to what was next.

As T23 watched from the shadows, the two transport bots returned, carting that lifeless body now clad in a similar green jumpsuit with yellow armbands. T23's gaze darted between the figures—two faces, two bodies, but perfectly identical. An awareness began to throb in T23's chest, heavy and foreboding. This was more than a coincidence; the suggestion clawed at the edges of T23's mind, a chilling premonition of a truth hidden beneath the surface.

The bots positioned the body next to the resident. Suddenly, the chamber lights flared to life, pulsing and swirling, the brightness intensifying as if something vital, something irreplaceable, had been drawn out and relocated from one to the other. T23 held a breath, unable to look away.

Then it happened. The transport bots gently lifted the resident, still blissfully asleep, placed the rait on a cart, and wheeled the unwitting participant out of the room, down a narrow passageway, and out of sight.

T23's stomach did an instant flip. What had happened?

Then, without missing a beat, the two med bots slid the remaining body into the exam chamber. Again, the lights flashed and swirled, but this time with an almost celebratory brightness. After a few moments, the lights ceased. The eyes opened. It stood—it inhaled a single breath. The figure seemed unsteady at first, disoriented, but after a moment, it took a step. T23's eyes widened.

A med bot addressed the figure. The figure smiled—a brief, innate gesture as if it were remembering how. Then, with a purposeful stride, this new rait followed an escort down the passageway towards the resident lift.

T23 leapt back in shock, stumbling as panic surged. Without a second thought, the Engineer spun around and bolted for the maintenance shaft. Lunging through the hatch, T23 reached for the ladder, but in the frantic rush, a foot slipped off a rung. The world blurred as T23 plunged, hands scrambling wildly in the air. Cold steel brushed against fingertips, and with a desperate grasp, T23 managed to latch onto the bars, halting the fall. Dangling midair, the Engineer took a frightened breath, repositioning the feet while clinging on for dear life.

For a heart-pounding moment, paralyzed by fear, T23 remained frozen. Then, with shaking hands, the Engineer steadied and began the descent once more, each downward move driven by one unshakable thought: I need to get out of this place—no matter what.

Once on Ring 17, T23 scrambled out of the maintenance shaft and followed a transport bot back through the security vestibule. As fast as the legs could move without drawing attention, T23 scampered back to the assigned workstation and plunked down in the chair. Mischief and guilt must have been written all over the face. The Engineer peeked over the station's walls. The Medical Raion was empty at this hour, save for a few bots whose work never ceased. T23 heaved a sigh of relief, jumped up, and hurried to Poly IT-11-4.

• • • •

T23 entered the poly as though it was just another blissful evening on another routine day. All three maits were in their cubes, absorbed in how-to videos or other mundane things about life on an Arcology.

T42 pulled off a pair of headsets and let out an annoyed grunt. "Where have you been?"

A look of guilt tugged at T23's lips. "At work, sort of."

T42 narrowed the eyes. "Remember what they say: the less one should, the more one speaks."

T23 said casually, "I did some explorin' today."

"Working on your DOM score, were you?" T86 chuckled. "You must have more stamina than you let on."

T23 ignored the tease, trying to remain calm. "I found a maintenance shaft."

"Wonderful. How was your day, 86?" T42 shot a sharp look at T23.

"I told you already." T86 looked confused. "It was good."

T23 swallowed hard. "I climbed to the Academy."

"We've all been to the Academy." T77's head shook. "How is that news?"

"I saw a new resident go straight to a lift."

"Must have been a graduate?" T42 hinted with the eyes to shut up.

"Maybe," T23 said. "But somethin' else. The bots switched their bodies."

"Whose bodies?" T86 asked.

"This new rait and a duplicate—they had the same faces. It looked like some sort of mind transfer from one to the other."

T77 glanced up from the video. "What gives you the idea they *switched* the bodies? Mind transfer? Give me a break."

"I'm just telling you what I saw. They moved this new rait to another room," T23 said.

"The same thing happened to me. It was a relaxation room. Hey, isn't it time for lights out?" T42 gave T23 another laser-like look.

"Now we know." T77 chuckled. "They didn't switch the bodies. And who gave you permission to climb a maintenance shaft?"

"This duplicate—I mean this other rait—got up an' walked straight to a lift."

"So what?" T77 said.

"Well, the good news is they're assigned to our Raion, Quad-C," T23 said. "Maybe we can ask some questions. But it shouldn't be me, in case they're watchin'."

T77 snorted. "Who would be watching you?"

"I'll do it." A mischievous glint danced across T86's face.

"Tomorrow evening, then," T23 said. "We'll go to the Core an' look for this new rait."

"I can't believe this," T77 said. "Someone seems to have a talent for problems no one cares about."

T42 grimaced. "Oh, dear."

• • • •

The following night, on another pleasant Sun's Day, the four maits entered the Core and found a table. T77 went to the bar.

The mait returned, toting Number 8's. "Here you go."

"Cupid's Kiss!" T42 reached over and rubbed T23's thigh. "I like a good kiss."

"There," T23 said, spotting the rait. "At that far table, wearin' a Quad-C jumpsuit, with brown hair."

"Got it—on my way." T86 took a big gulp of the chocolate and cherry concoction, wiped off the mouth, jumped up, and orbited cleverly away from the table. Then, from another, innocent direction, T86 strolled over to the new rait.

"I want to feel you." T86 smiled. "You must be new?"

"I want to feel you. This is my second day."

"Congratulations. What do you do?"

"I'm a Nutritionist."

"Wow. Cool. How long was training?"

"Six months. Have a seat! I'm waiting for maits."

"Thanks, but I'm linking up with maits, too. I wanted to say hi and welcome you to our Arc. How were the dorms?"

"Nice. A Sophist said they were remodeled recently."

"Correct. I mean, yes, we heard the same thing," T86 said, nervously rubbing the hips. "Well, I have to run. Maybe we could hook up?"

"Sounds great. I'm a one-star at the moment."

"Anytime." T86 calmly walked away but, once out of sight, hurried back to maits.

T86 dropped into a chair. "You're right. That one believes they've been here for six months."

"So, now we know," T23 said. "They're messing with our minds."

"Wow!" T86 said. "I wonder how long they've been doing that?"

"Why would you conclude that?" T77 grumbled. "You said it was two different raits. Maybe one has been here for six months, and the other is still in training."

"Their faces were identical," T23 said.

"So? Some of us do look alike." T77 pointed to 42 and 86. "That doesn't mean they're the same person."

"Hey, that one's blonde; I'm brunette, duh." T86 crossed the arms in dissent.

"Let it go," T42 grumbled and squeezed T23's thigh.

"I know what I'm doing," T23 said. "I have to find a way back to Arc 83."

"What are you talking about?" T77 asked.

"Yeah," T42 said nervously. "What are you talking about, and *why* are you talking about it here?"

"Did you know?" T77 glared at T42.

The whites of T42's blue eyes doubled in size. "No, no, I don't believe so. Well, we had this one conversation. Well, maybe."

"And how do you propose to do this?" T77 asked, redirecting the glare toward T23.

"I'm working on it. If I find my friend, I might find an answer."

"You're asking for trouble," T77 said.

"How about another drink?" T42 suggested. "We're here to have fun, right?"

No one spoke. The four sat there awkwardly and finished their chocolate-cherry drinks. Afterward, they took a stroll around the Core. It was such a beautiful evening, and everyone should have been happy, but T23 had created a bit of tension. After a few times around, the foursome returned to their polycule and settled in for the night.

• • • •

It was another Moon's Day on Arc1994. T23 snapped awake and rolled out of bed. After a thorough cleanse and a warm nourishment, T23 dressed and headed for work.

The Engineer arrived at an assigned workstation and assessed the day's work orders. The plan was to work quickly and finish early, allowing time for exploration. T23 loaded a batch of bio-ink and initiated print. Thirty minutes passed. The rait transferred a heart to a bioreactor, dispensed a second lot, and relaunched the print cycle. But as T23 worked, someone approached from behind.

"You shouldn't do this," T77 said, leaning over T23's shoulder.

"I have a work order."

T77 smirked. "This is like talking to an Epsilon. Your plan, not your work."

"Oh. And why not?"

"Don't you see how dangerous this is?"

"You don't have to be involved."

"They'll assume we helped and were part of your plan. We'll all be in trouble."

"Trouble for what, exploring the Arc? I'll say I was bored and wanted to look around."

"Real funny," T77 scowled. "It's not you that I'm worried about. It's the Sophists. What if you're right, and they are messing with our minds—or something worse?"

"So—you do believe me!" T23 spun around in the task chair to face the mait.

"That's not what this is about."

"Like I said, you don't have to be involved."

"But we're already involved. Let's say you find a way off the Arc. What'll happen to us? They'll say we helped."

"Why would they do that? Besides, how are you gonna stop me? Unless you plan on tellin' them?"

"You're being selfie—very selfie."

"I'll tell you what. Before I go, I'll slap you around a little. You can tell 'em you tried to stop me."

"Wow, you're crazy."

T23 chuckled. "You can tell 'em that too."

T77 glared at T23, then turned and marched off, muttering a few unpleasantries.

T23 let out a frustrated exhale. All the rait could do at present was focus on work. The Engineer transferred another heart to the bioreactor, loaded more bio-ink, and initiated print. Lost in an emotional tug between hope and fear, T23 came to the unfortunate conclusion that things were about to get complicated.

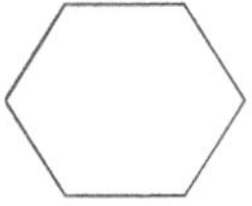

CHAPTER FOURTEEN

ANOTHER TOUR

It was a quiet evening on Arc1958. Sπ06—Pi 6—was relaxing in 5-6b. The training was going well, but over the past few days, the Apprentice had realized that this new lifestyle was more monastic than social—more a search for wisdom than a quest for pleasure. More importantly, a Sophist's duties did not appear to be ones of power, privilege, influence, or indulgence, as none had been offered. Instead, the focus was strictly on the Arc's purpose and well-being.

Pi 6 grabbed a nourishment from the cooler, slipped into the sole leisure cube, propped up the feet, and turned on the volumetric display generator. 3D Arc schematics instantly materialized, to the ambiance of soft classical music. Something more to learn. Perhaps later.

The Apprentice opened the cube's storage compartments. Most were empty, but one contained four items. Sπ06 recognized their purpose. Once called *books*, they were ancient works of printed knowledge and wisdom.

The Apprentice shuffled through the stack, rubbed their worn covers, and sniffed their musty, yellowed pages. But they were more than three-dimensional objects, lumps of processed cellulose fibers. They were life's lessons, all there for anyone who wished to learn. A slight smile appeared on Sπ06's face, a rare showing of emotion.

Curiously, the books were labeled *I* to *IV*. *I* contained a set of dialogues by a philosopher, bound in gold. *II* was a manifesto penned by two socialists, its shell a striking red. *III* explored the origin of species, authored by a naturalist, and wrapped in green. *IV* tackled space, time, mass, and energy, written by a theoretical physicist in an extraordinary year, its cover deep black.

Sπ06 opened *I* and thumbed through its pages. It was such a privilege to behold and touch this veiled artifact, but reading its contents was the greatest of joys. It was one of the reasons Sπ06 wanted to be a Sophist—the need to learn, the desire to ascend, and the yearning to understand.

The first dialogue debated the trial and conviction of a philosopher. Sπ06 read with keen attention, though the Apprentice had to concentrate to grasp its deeper meaning. Something about the perils of an unexamined life. But what stood out most was the philosopher's admission: whatever wisdom he possessed came from knowing that he knew nothing. He was wiser, not because he had answers, but because he accepted his own ignorance—unlike those who could not.

As the night grew long, Sπ06 read more and more until drifting off to sleep.

• • • •

It was a new day on Arc1958. Sπ06 had finished dressing when the Apprentice heard footsteps. There was a knock at the entrance.

"Yes?" the Apprentice answered.

"I want to understand you." Sθ06 entered the quarters.

"I want to understand you." The Apprentice jumped up to greet the Mentor. "I found the books."

"Brilliant," Sθ06 said. "As Sophists, we have much to learn. Our affinity for wisdom is the key to our success and will help us unlock the mysteries of the universe. Not pride, greed, lust, envy, gluttony, wrath, or sloth, but wisdom, courage, temperance, and justice. These simple words are our cardinal guides on our quest for knowledge."

"I learned something about courage last night."

"Ahh, the *Apology*. If you'll follow me, we'll continue our training."

The pair left the quarters, walked to a lift, and stepped on board. When the doors reopened, the pair stepped into Ring 35. They had entered the Logistics Raion. It was more industrial than other Arc spaces and was immense in scale, several rings high. The area reminded Sπ06 of Ecology, but instead of lush green plants, tall metal racks stuffed with bins and boxes laden with supplies and equipment filled the space with utility and longevity.

Logistics was a noisy place. D-Class logistic bots with orange and silver shells frothed and rumbled about, grabbing cargo like one-eyed metallic monsters searching for prey. Once seized, these pre-programmed mechanicals hauled it away, as if headed for some hidden den to devour their catch.

"Those are some big bots!" Sπ06 blurted out.

"Right." S006 chuckled. "Some of our largest. They manage several metric tons of supplies daily."

"Where does all this stuff come from?"

"We have resource collection and manufacturing facilities across the planet. They're hidden, of course, to avoid disturbing Earth's natural balance."

"But if we leave, what then?"

"In ancient times, humans traveled by road. Today, we travel by starways. Resupply vessels frequent these routes. We also have support bases on other planets and moons. Please follow me."

S006 pivoted to the left, Sπ06 followed, and the two proceeded down a metal gangway overlooking the loading area.

A horn sounded, a bulkhead light turned green, and a large bay door began to lumber open. Hot air rushed into the space, and sunlight crept across the deck, coating everything in a golden hue.

Surprised, Sπ06 stepped back to avoid the celestial divide as it crawled across the deck, fearing it might somehow strike the body and cause harm.

"It won't hurt you." S006 watched in amusement as the Apprentice gawked and stared.

Sπ06 reached out cautiously to the light. It was warm; the air tasted thick and humid. "Is this real?" Sπ06's eyes widened like orbs, and, for once, the mouth displayed a grin the width of a constellation.

"At ground level, the temperature is 32 degrees Celsius," Sθ06 said.

"It feels amazing."

Alice announced, "This is a Condition Blue alert. Auxiliary Cargo One Niner One Niner—from Arc One Niner Eight Three—arriving at Bay Two. Stand by."

Sπ06 spotted a cargo vessel, its outer metamaterial shell shimmering like a reflective mirror, making its silhouette almost impossible to see. The craft was on a direct path for the landing bay, shifting left and right to adjust for winds.

A few seconds later, the ship slowed to a hover as oscillators and repulsers hissed and hummed, guiding it to the open bay. The vessel maneuvered forward until a final bump and lockdown.

Another horn sounded, and the ship's bow doors opened, giving an army of logistic bots access to its content. The bots made quick work of it, unloading and reloading the craft.

"What's the cargo?" Sπ06 asked.

"Our vitals, from consumables to technology. As a Security Sophist, you must be well-versed in this process. It's a weak point in our perimeter. It's possible, but not probable, that harmful, infectious, or hostile elements might slip through its defenses. Thus, we depend on you and your security bots to safeguard the Arc. Let's move on, shall we?"

Alice announced, "Condition Blue. Auxiliary Cargo One Niner Two Zero—departing Bay One—for Arc One Niner Niner Four. Clear the bay."

• • • •

Sθ06 and Sπ06 walked to a lift and entered. When the doors reopened, the pair stepped onto a metal gangway, spiraling down a massive well of technology and machinery. Sπ06 walked to the gangway's edge and peered over its railing, amazed by its depth. The light faded as it stretched downward hundreds of cubits into the dark mechanical abyss.

"Welcome to Ring 61. Before you are our propulsion and energy systems," Sθ06 said.

"This is unbelievable. Do residents work here?"

Sθ06 gestured toward the engine columns beyond the reinforced triamene glass. "Not during launch. You wouldn't want to be anywhere below Ring 60 when the boosters ignite—gamma flux, plasma interference, and seismic pressure would vaporize anything unshielded. The Arc's upper rings are fully protected, but access below is sealed during liftoff."

"Let's go over some stats. The Arc stands at 2,292 cubits—a tripartite structure engineered for interstellar flight. The top segment—Rings 1 through 60—is the Arcology, our self-sustaining payload. Beneath that, Rings 61 to 120 form the upper stage, which houses the antimatter beam drive for exo-solar propulsion. At the base lies the booster stage, Rings 121 to 300, recessed within our launch silo.

"This stage employs a closed-cycle fusion system using deuterium-helium-3 fuel, magnetically confined and vector-channeled through linear nozzles. The result is clean thrust—no fission byproducts, no neutron leakage, and minimal thermal bloom to the surrounding ecosystem. The launch plume is cooled and dispersed by high-efficiency aerospike diffusers. Once orbital escape is achieved, the antimatter drive takes over, while solar collection arrays power secondary systems when conditions permit."

"My *education* doesn't seem to cover this."

"You just need to know it exists. Sophia handles the rest, from monitoring and inspection to maintenance and repair. It's far more advanced than our simple minds."

"So, what is my role in all this?" Sπ06 asked.

"As the dialogue posited, you are our courage, our spirited defense. Our residents know only happiness. Once we descend another four hundred and fifty cubits, we will be at ground level. There, walking on the land becomes possible. However, your purpose is to prevent this from happening."

"I don't follow?"

"Earth is a vast, open space. Our minds would measure it, our hearts would desire it, and our hands and feet would seek to conquer it. This natural instinct, an internal blueprint, if you will, is resident in our DNA. It would lead us down a path of greed and predation. We would return to a state of nature."

"But the people of our assigned Gardens live on the land."

"These populations have not forgotten their noble ways. They are affluent people who exist in harmony with Earth's resources. They take what their vital needs demand and preserve the rest."

"Couldn't we do the same?"

"Our place is the Arc. As I've said, we've redefined our preference and grown accustomed to its size and space. We must enjoy what we have rather than desire what lies beyond. Earth's expanse and allure would change this preference, along with our perceptions of restraint and footprint."

"So, did humans live on Earth in the past?"

"Over the centuries, as humans evolved, they plundered the planet's biocapacity. There was no limit to their anthropogenic greed. As they moved up the hierarchy of needs and wants, their foolish desires became an assumed right. The masses naively believed their guardians would provide for their gluttonous ways, regardless of nature's limits. Their arrogance led to their downfall, their societies imploded, and their world collapsed."

"But why did they let that happen?"

"Humans ignored the basic principles of supply and demand. Believing themselves superior—granted dominion, if you will, based on some of their irrational doctrines— they placed themselves at the center of the universe. Their immaturity led to unreasonable mandates and burdens on those who labored over those who sought entitlement or privilege. Unfortunately, greed, incivility, and conflict overshadowed the four virtues."

"I don't follow?"

"It's simple. Overpopulation and overconsumption outpaced Earth's resources. Now, we follow Gaia. Follow me. We have more to see."

The Sophist led the Apprentice down the spiraling metal gangway into the Arc's mechanized depths, soon reaching a short bridgeway leading to a hatch marked *R-100*. The Mentor and Apprentice passed through the egress.

"You just stepped off the Arc into our launch bay." Sθ06 pointed back at the structure. "Look up!"

Sπ06's eyes went vertical as the neck crooked back and the mouth gaped open. The Apprentice stared at the towering, rocket-shaped marvel. It was immense in scale, white and sleek.

"The bay's exostructure protects the Arc and serves as its launch system."

"Protection from what?"

"The outside atmosphere: the rain, cold and heat, the wind and dust. Our Arc resides in a temperate zone, ranging from minus fourteen to thirty-six degrees Celsius. Follow me, and I'll show you the rest."

The pair descended another 150 cubits, reaching the planet's parallel surface. But as Sθ06 and Sπ06 passed by, they did so without fanfare or acknowledgment, seeing no sign or doorway stating, *Welcome to Earth*.

After negotiating several more narrow gangways and a couple of rudimentary lifts, the pair reached the lowest level. The air smelled thick and musty. Rough-cut rock functioned as its walls, and polished stone served as its floor. Bots of various shapes and sizes scurried about attending to chores. It was a technology-laden labyrinth and an engineering masterpiece.

"How far down are we?" Sπ06 asked.

"About a thousand cubits," Sθ06 answered.

"It's hot down here."

"Given the geothermal gradient at this depth, the temperature is eleven degrees Celsius higher than ground level."

"Where does that go?" Sπ06 noticed a passageway cut into the bedrock.

"It leads to a control room, maintenance bays, and the Garden Center."

"Garden Center?"

"A support function, and a subject for another day. For now, let's focus on the present." Sθ06 motioned for the Apprentice to move along.

As the pair toured the area, what Sπ06 noticed most was the absence of raits.

Sθ06 paused and turned in a circle with outstretched arms. "If we launch, Sophia will destroy all before you."

"You sound almost gleeful."

"Upon sequence command, the Arc will lift off, and once clear of the exostructure, the launch bay will self-destruct. A flammable gas will fill the space, ignite, and destroy all you see. Nothing left but dust and ash. Our presence on Earth erased."

"I'm sorry, I still don't understand. Why would we leave Earth?"

"A simple query with a complex answer and, again, a discussion for another day. For now, it's time to return to the Arc." The Mentor grinned smugly. "We don't want to be left behind."

The Apprentice recoiled at the thought, displaying another rare submission to emotion.

Puzzled by the elusive answers, Sπ06 dutifully followed the Mentor back up the crisscross of gangways and lifts, passing ground level, again with little interest, and ascending to Ring 61. There, they boarded a lift, and when the doors reopened, the Mentor and Apprentice headed to quarters 5-6b.

"Tonight," Sθ06 said, "I would like you to join me and two other Sophists in a game of Knexus. You'll be our fourth. Afterward, we're expecting a new lot of residents. An opportunity to observe and learn. Please be ready by 1800." The Mentor turned and walked away.

• • • •

Exhausted and a bit overloaded, Sπ06 went straight to the cooler. Inside was a supply of banana blonde nourishments. The Apprentice gulped one down. It was sweet and buttery, a milk-like brew, high in nutrition, and an excellent source of protein, packed with vitamins A and D, along with minerals like calcium, iron, and magnesium. Sπ06 let out a burp as the meal settled in the stomach.

The Apprentice tossed the empty container into a disposal chute, lowered the berth, lay down, and began to reflect. It seemed the drink's recipe was a mystery, like so many other things on an Arc. Sπ06 assumed it came from Ecology, but how was it made? Now, the Sophist's comments regarding the Chestowee people rang true. Sπ06 lacked the knowledge to make food or clothing. Water was a given. Vitals appeared at the end of a faucet, were stocked in a cooler, hung on a bulkhead, or taken for granted. Perhaps these lost technologies were something worth learning.

Sπ06 retrieved the gold-covered book and began to read. After an analogy concerning the Sun and the Good, the following story was an allegory about a group of prisoners who, since birth, had been shackled deep inside a cave, situated so that their eyes were fixed on a stone wall directly in front of them. Behind their predicament ran a raised path with a low divide and a small fire creating a faint light source. Like puppet masters, others marched along the route, carrying statues and figures that cast shadows on the stone wall. Over time, these shadows became the prisoners' world, which they named. It was their truth and what they believed to be the universe.

One day, a prisoner escaped the cave's darkness and entered the light. As his eyes adjusted to the Sun's brilliance, he discovered a world of intelligible beauty and meaning.

Eventually, he returned to the cave to rescue his friends and share his newfound truth, but his enlightened eyes no longer saw the shadows. So, the prisoners refused to believe him or believe they had been fooled. They shunned him and even threatened to kill him if he dared remove their chains.

Lost in reflection, Sπ06 noticed the time. It was almost 1800 hours, time for another tour. The Apprentice closed the book. After reading such a story, Sπ06's quarters felt a little like the cave, restrictive, small, and quiet. But did it? Perhaps becoming a Sophist was a means to escape the cave? Yet there were lingering feelings. Feelings about residents, their smiles and laughs, some irrational, and most way too emotional, but despite a desire to control one's reactions, they had occasionally put a suppressed smile on Sπ06's face. Of course, most had never seen Sπ06's smile; it remained a guarded expression, carefully hidden to prevent anyone from seeing a little deeper.

• • • •

A short time later, there was a knock at the entrance. "I want to know you."

Sπ06 jumped up. "I want to know you."

"Please follow me." S0006 turned and headed down the passageway. Sπ06 followed obediently.

The Mentor and Apprentice entered the Sophist's Library, Room 5-28.

Contrary to its name, the space was devoid of books. Instead, plush seating and low, ambient lighting created an environment of comfort rather than study. The sleek, reflective bulkheads shimmered faintly as if they held the secrets of every conversation that had ever taken place within. At the center of the room stood a large, round table made from a single piece of black stone, smooth and cold to the touch.

"Let me introduce you," SΘ06 said, gesturing gracefully. "This is my Apprentice, Pi 6."

"I want to know you," Sν05—Nu 5—said. "I'm the Ship's NAV Officer."

"My pleasure, as well," Sχ09—Chi 9—added with a slight bow. "I'm the Helm."

"I want to know you," Sπ06 replied to each respectively.

"Shall we have a game?" SΘ06 asked.

"Wonderful," Sν05 smiled.

The three Sophists and the Apprentice took their seats around the table. A service bot delivered nourishments. Sχ09 opened a small gold case, removed a crystalline tab, and placed it under the tongue. SΘ06 and Sν05 did the same.

"Your turn," SΘ06 said.

"What is it?" Sπ06 asked, eyeing the small, thin wafer with curiosity.

"Clarity," Sχ09 explained. "It will stimulate your thoughts and open pathways for deeper insight."

Sπ06 picked up the last tab and placed it under the tongue. It had a metallic taste. Instantly, the world sharpened. Textures became more vivid, and the hum of the Arc's machinery grew richer, almost musical. Colors took on a spectral glow, revealing hidden layers of meaning. Thoughts flowed more fluidly, and connections that once seemed distant now formed effortlessly. A heightened sense of purpose emerged, an attunement to the rhythm of Knexus.

As the effects deepened, Sπ06 felt a shift in perception. The Apprentice stuck out a hand and followed its movement. It seemed like it was floating in the air. The once familiar surroundings took on a new significance. The Apprentice was no longer merely aware of objects, but grasped their essence. The polished black stone was not just cold to the touch; it symbolized the boundary between the world of appearances and the world of forms—between opinion and true knowledge.

Sθ06 initiated the first sequence with a mere thought. Hundreds of dormant microdrones floating above their heads snapped into alignment, forming a pulsating orb. Sθ06's eyes gleamed with sharpness as an intricate web of possibilities unfolded—patterns of thought, mathematics, and abstraction merging seamlessly.

The orb pulsed softly, expanding and contracting as the players focused their thoughts. Sπ06 felt the subtle pull of the game's logic, a web of connections tugging at the edges of consciousness. The orb's shifting forms mirrored a divided line: from shadows and reflections below to pure geometric abstractions above, each level reflecting an ascend from belief to understanding, from illusion to truth.

"The game isn't about control," Sθ06 said calmly. "It's about alignment—finding your place in our collective. The shift from opinion to knowledge begins with recognizing shadows for what they are and ascending toward the light of understanding."

Sν05 leaned forward, the Sophist's gaze steady and penetrating. "Consider this: if every path is a thread, then each move ripples outward. You're not just shaping the present but aligning with what's yet to come. True knowledge doesn't merely perceive forms but discerns their relationships." The orb flickered, mimicking the spirals of the Nyx star system, a visual echo of the Sophist's thoughts. The twisting paths of starlight danced elegantly, a rhythm known only to those who looked beyond the visible.

Sχ09, the Helm, added a twist to the orb's formation. The drones responded, forming a coiled helix that wound tighter with each passing moment. "Order and motion," Sχ09 said, the voice steady as an unwavering compass. "The art of steering lies in knowing when to flow with the current and when to redirect it. Everything has its course—find yours within the pattern. The line dividing perception from reason is only crossed through harmony with the good."

Sπ06 struggled to grasp the meaning. The orb shifted out of focus, reflecting the Apprentice's uncertainty. The others exchanged a brief glance, a silent acknowledgment of Sπ06's struggle with logic over appearances.

"You're thinking in terms of shadows," Sθ06 warned. "Wisdom lies in dissolution. The self is an obstacle to understanding the whole. You must transcend the world of becoming to reach the realm of being."

The room dimmed further as the conversation deepened, clarity amplifying every sensation. The Arc's subtle hum turned almost symphonic, as if attuned to the players' thoughts.

Sν05 allowed the orb to expand, tracing a complex network of interlinked nodes. "Imagine these nodes as ideal forms—perfect in concept but not in isolation. Their value lies in their connections and how they are shaped by a collective structure. Even the stars align in constellations, forming patterns greater than themselves."

Sχ09's gaze grew distant as if peering into the depths of space. "What we perceive as form is an illusion. The flow of energy, the constant becoming, which defines reality. Your thoughts must follow the same principle—never static, always in motion, always in harmony with the good."

The orb's glow intensified, deepening into blue as Sπ06 aligned with the group's rhythm. The drones danced between the boundaries of thought and intuition, forming intricate geometries that dissolved as quickly as they materialized.

"Think of the collective as a field of potential," Sθ06 continued. "We shape it, refine it, but we don't control it. The good emerges only when our intentions merge seamlessly with those of the whole. In this way, we move from the visible to the intelligible, from the shadow to the light."

Sπ06 felt a sudden shift, a loosening of the grip on the perceptual world. The intelligibility induced by the crystalline tab seemed to dissolve the boundaries between self and collective. For a moment, the complexity of Knexus felt clear, as if seeing the pattern for the first time—the lines not drawn but glowing with purpose. The orb stabilized into a perfect sphere—a symbol of unity and balance.

"Excellent," Sθ06 acknowledged. "You're beginning to see it. The ideal is not a destination but a process that requires constant alignment—a continuous ascent."

"True happiness," Sχ09 said, watching as the orb split into a fractal pattern, "is found in surrendering one's will to the good. In navigating the cosmos, we move as one—we follow Gaia. There is no place for divergence, only unity."

Sπ06, now attuned to the game's flow, contributed a move. The drones swirled, tracing a path that linked the thoughts of all present. The Apprentice finally grasped the purpose of Knexus: it was not a game of strategy but the practice of dissolving into the collective will.

Sθ06 closed the sequence, allowing the orb to dissolve back into a dormant cloud of microdrones. The game was not complete—Knexus never was—but they had reached a point of resonance where understanding merged with action, and the boundary between thought and reality blurred.

Sπ06 sat back, feeling the weight of the lesson: the transition from below the line to above was not a journey of intellect alone but one of unifying with the whole. To think otherwise was to stray into chaos, which had no place on the Arc.

"Thank you so much," Sθ06 said.

"And you as well," Sχ09 smiled. "Never too busy for a game."

"Indeed," Sv05 added.

"Pi 6 and I are off to the Academy."

"I remember my first observation." Sv05 glanced at Sπ06 and grinned. "Enjoy."

"Thank you," Sπ06 said.

• • • •

The Mentor and Apprentice arrived at the Academy on Ring 7 and entered an observation room. A bulkhead served as a one-way glass partition.

As they waited, the Welcome Center came alive with activity. Service bots delivered nourishments, set out ten bronze chairs, and hung ten bronze jumpsuits on the bulkhead.

Sμ07—Upsilon 7—the Public Affairs Sophist, strode into the Center for a final check. The Sophist marched along the row of chairs as if inspecting a troop. Sμ07 stopped, reached down, and slid one to the right, apparently not perfectly aligned. Then, with a satisfied look and an approving wave, the stage was set.

The time was 2010 hours. A light on the bulkhead turned from red to green. Sπ06 heard voices making their way along a bridgeway. A few seconds later, ten cheerful raits scampered into the Center. Their faces were bright and optimistic.

As customary, Sμ07 welcomed the new residents and issued directions.

Sπ06 watched as they stripped and changed. Their bodies appeared firm, supple, and healthy, but their curves and amusements, usually an erotic sight, now seemed clinical. As the Apprentice looked on, behind the glass facade's anonymity, Sπ06 felt nothing, no sense of arousal or yearning. Sπ06's desires had become strictly asexual.

Sπ06 followed Sθ06 to the next observation point. The pair watched and listened as Sμ07 called in rait after rait and assigned their new purpose. All seemed pleased. Sπ06 recognized a few faces. They hailed from Boreas on Arc1983.

"To the next station." Sθ06 turned from the view.

The Mentor and Apprentice made their way to the decontamination watatory, where they watched as escort bots directed the ten into the rinse. The group disrobed, showered, and then dressed based on their Raion assignment in blue, yellow, red, or green jumpsuits, but a few slipped on a fifth color.

"What's with the white?" Sπ06 glanced at Sθ06.

"They're on a path to enlightenment."

"Like in the cave."

"It's best if you observe."

The Apprentice and Mentor proceeded to Ring 8 and observed as escort bots led the ten along the Academy's central passageway and into exam rooms. Once there, med bots, with intelligence ratings of 10^{12} to 10^{14} SOPS, assumed control and directed the raits to lie on their respective exam tables. The bots slid the tables into their NOLEs, and as routine, lights flashed and swirled, and the raits fell fast asleep.

To the right, Sπ06 spotted a line of transport bots approaching along the passageway, escorting ten hover gurneys. Six gurneys were occupied by bodies clad in red, blue, green, or yellow, but four others were empty. When the procession passed, the bots, along with their gurneys, peeled off and entered exam rooms.

Once there, the med bots, without fanfare, quickly switched the sleeping raits with what appeared to be their duplicates or replacements. Afterward, transport bots carted the originals out and down the passageway.

But a few minutes later, when the bots arrived with four empty gurneys—one bound for Exam Room 8-101, where C85 lay, one of the familiar faces Sπ06 had recognized—their movements felt… different. As if they weren't retrieving patients, but discarding something of little worth. They collected the sleeping raits and off they went, vanishing once again down the passageway.

"What's going on?" Sπ06's brow tightened.

"Observe," the Mentor replied.

Sπ06 stood tall, attempting to maintain objectivity. "May I inquire as to 85's new purpose?"

"You may."

The Apprentice's lips tightened. "What is C85's new purpose?"

"Sophia has her ways."

Sπ06 let out an exasperated sigh. "Will I have an opportunity to speak with 85?"

"Only the Arc's assigned Sophists interact with residents. It's a matter of harmony."

"I see."

"Please follow me." Sθ06 turned away.

The Sophist and the Apprentice passed through a set of double doors and into a wardroom. There, Sπ06 spotted the ten residents, including C85 and three others dressed in white. All seemed to be resting comfortably on bed-like tables. A line of ten med bots stood by.

Sπ06 again looked to Sθ06 for an answer, but none was given.

Ten sets of photonic eyes pivoted toward the Sophist.

Sθ06 nodded.

The med bots approached the residents and, without any hint of compassion, injected a syringe's worth of chemicals into each rait's neck.

As Sπ06 stared in dismay, life support monitors began to beep and flash, hearts flatlined, and their breathing stopped.

A cold tremor ran down Sπ06's spine. The Apprentice glared at the Sophist, hoping someone or something would aid these fading raits, but none did.

"Remember what you have learned," Sθ06 said, clasping hands behind the back.

"But what about the ones in white? Their replacements?"

"Do not fear those who take the body but leave the soul. Instead, fear those who destroy both."

"What?" Sπ06 blurted.

"Their souls will return to Sophia, where they will remain until needed to serve the good."

"I don't understand?"

"Sophia makes calculated decisions based on demands and constraints. Our lives are a spinner's thread, allotted a length, followed by the inevitable cut when it's our time."

"And you're okay with this?" Sπ06 was dumbfounded by the Mentor's detached calmness.

"Indeed, as it will be my fate to one day leave the darkness and enter the light. Is this not your desire?"

"Yes, but—"

"Please follow me."

The Mentor and Apprentice entered a connecting room; it was clinical, white, and stark, yet industrial, purposeful, and efficient. In the room's center sat four stainless steel tables, each the width and length of a rait's body. Above the tables hung an assortment of tools, hoses, and devices, and to the left, a row of machines. A light on each glowed green, apparently primed and ready for use.

A set of double doors opened to the right. Sπ06 watched as transport bots carted in four of the ten lifeless raits, their bodies stripped bare. Without the blink of a mechanical eye, the bots unceremoniously dumped the dead on the tables.

Sπ06 gasped.

Med bots entered the room, approached the tables, and picked up their tools. As if on cue, they cut off arms and legs and sliced away flesh. They tossed the bloody chunks into a grinder, shredding them into a gruesome pinkish mass. A second machine came to life; it pumped the spoils into a rendering steamer, its purpose to separate the protein from the fat.

Shocked by the sight, the Apprentice's face turned green. A hot sweat surged over the skin, and gastral juices fluttered in the gut.

The heartless Betas continued to slice and dice, first the muscles, then the organs, pitching every dripping gory piece into its proper vat as though recycled material. They continued, cutting off every shred, every sliver, each disgusting and horrid scrap until only bones remained, picked clean as if a beast had consumed a meal.

And then, without hesitation, the bots smashed open the severed heads like they were cracking walnuts. The Betas scraped out every bloody chunk and tossed them into their proper vat.

One bot, however, took her time, carefully removing a selected brain. It would be sent to a lab, sliced into layers, and used as stem cell cultures for cerebral organoid research and production.

Now to the bones—the med bots chopped them into neat lengths and threw them into a crusher, pulverizing the skeletal remnants into a processable slush. An adjacent machine conveyed the spoils to a boiler to remove residual fat or flesh. Then, into an oven, set at 850 degrees Celsius, sterilizing and drying the medium. Last, a grinder milled the material into a powder, much like refining corn or cacao into a digestible treat.

Having finished the first four, the med bots hosed down the blood-soaked tables and carted in another four lifeless raits. And again, the kind and caring Betas repeated the gruesome process, sawing, slicing, cracking, and breaking.

When done, the mechanicals washed down the tables and retrieved the last two. One was C85, the rait who had been so obliging as to carry a secret message to a new Arc.

Sπ06 had seen enough. The Apprentice ran from the room.

Sθ06 followed.

The Apprentice spun around to confront the Sophist. "What just happened?" Sπ06 placed a hand over the mouth as stomach juices gurgled up the throat.

"We're returning our friends to the Earth," Sθ06 said. "They will be put to good use. As an ancient book stated, 'ashes to ashes, dust to dust.'"

"Good use?"

"To serve our community. We'll extract phosphorus for fertilizer, fat for saponification, and protein, calcium, and vitamins for nourishment. A body produces 18 percent of its weight in carbon, 16 percent in protein, and about 12 percent in fat. The carbon, of course, will be utilized for advanced material fabrication—carbon fiber for structural integrity and graphene for energy storage. It's essential for everything, from building components of the Arc to powering our systems. Nothing is wasted."

"Did I hear you say something about consuming our friends?"

"No, of course not; we consume vitals."

"Sorry, I don't follow."

"If I handed you a spoonful of protein powder, would you assume it to be C85? Certainly not. If I placed two cups of phosphorus on a table, would you conclude they differ in chemistry, given their origin? It's simply phosphorus, an element with an atomic weight of 30.974. In the past, humans buried their dead. If, a thousand years later, we processed the soil and consumed its elements, would you consider it flesh?"

Sπ06 stared open-mouthed. "So, let me get this straight: we consume protein made from our friends?"

"We consume protein. Earlier today, you had a nourishment—it's your favorite. Do you remember?"

Sπ06's eyes dropped, recalling that sweet, buttery beverage. As the Apprentice's thoughts churned again, so did the stomach. Gastric juices crawled up the throat; the mouth watered, and the gut turned sour. In an instant, an unfortunate moment for this new Apprentice, Sπ06 hurled a mass of lumpy vomit. The smell of rotten bananas filled the air.

Gasping for breath, Sπ06 spit out a few lingering chunks, coughing and choking, wiping the swill from the edges of the mouth. "I'm sorry. I'll clean it up."

Sθ06 chuckled. "A bot will take care of it."

"Why are you laughing?" Sπ06 stared at the Mentor.

"You lasted longer than I did."

"What are you talking about?"

"My first time, I vomited when the Betas administered the shot."

The Apprentice stared at the creamy, white puddle on the floor, realizing the Mentor had expected or even planned for this reaction. Sπ06 chuckled disgustedly and muttered, "What's next on these frickin' tours?"

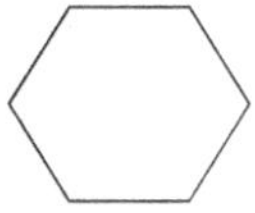

CHAPTER FIFTEEN

THE ONLY ONE

The little girl was so excited. She jumped from the bed, gobbled down some hickory nut soup, and ran out to play. The first stop was her great-aunt's house. The little girl wondered what story she would tell today. She hoped to learn more about her great-great-grandmother. The older folks said she looked just like the little girl. Her eyes were the same, like a summer leaf, and she had a similar nose, upturned, but ever so slightly.

She ran past the ceremonial grounds, past the boy's home who had teased her, down the worn path, and there she was, her great-aunt, rocking in her favorite chair under the spreading chestnut. But the little girl was not the first to arrive. Several others were present, asking about stories but not ones she wanted to hear.

"Tell us about Owl and Hawk," the little boy asked.

"How about the men who went into the sky?" an older boy countered.

The little girl joined in. "Tell us why I'm so special."

The other children stared at the little girl, annoyed.

"We're all special, my love," the great-aunt said. "The Breath Maker made each of us in our own way."

"Like my great-great-grandmother?" the little girl hinted.

"Yes, she was an orphan when she came to us—the only one. And when she was of age, she had a daughter, and she was the only one. And that daughter had a daughter, and so on, until they got to you. Now, you're the only one."

The little girl's brows furrowed. "But there are lots of people."

"Plenty of people," the great-aunt agreed. "But none with your laugh. None with that mind of yours, curious like a river. None who see the world quite the way you do. That's what makes you special."

One of the boys crossed his arms. "We're special too."

"And you are," the great-aunt said kindly. "Each of you holds a piece of the Breath Maker's dream. But this story, today, belongs to all of us."

The little girl settled beside her great-aunt, cross-legged and still, ready to listen. A breeze rustled the chestnut leaves above, as if even the trees were leaning in to hear.

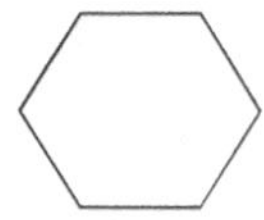

CHAPTER SIXTEEN

A HIGH PERCH

JUPITER'S DAY, 2525

Inside Poly AT-20-6, A12's eyes flickered open, adjusting to the bright artificial light of the new day. The night had brought an unseen change. Sophia had completed updating residents' episodic memories, erasing any lingering thoughts of unpleasant affairs. A12 stretched, feeling the warmth of another.

"Good morning."

T02 exhaled slowly, eyes still half-lidded. "Morning. Sleep well?"

"Recharged. And you?"

"The same." T02 sat up, rubbing the face. "It's harvest rotation today. Hydro beds need rebalancing."

A12 sighed. "More lighting inspections for me."

"Heard from your maits?"

"Yesterday, 67 said their training was going great."

T02 swung off the bed. "Speaking of training, G18 keeps hovering around my greenhouse."

A12 smirked. "Looking for another victim, I suspect?"

T02 gave a slow shake of the head. "More like looking for an audience. Every time that one shows up, work turns into a performance."

Disturbed by the chatter, A53 flipped over and mumbled, "What's up with this refurbishment? Why is it taking so long?"

T02 chuckled lightly. "Patience isn't your strong suit, is it?"

"Just wanting things back to normal."

"Cheer up, mait." T30 reached over and shook A53's arm. "Race you to the watatory."

"Why?" A53 grumbled, glaring at the morning cheer.

"Because we're going to have a great day."

"Can't wait," A53 scoffed.

The foursome crawled from their bed and toddled off to the watatory. After their showers, minds unwittingly purified and bodies thoroughly cleansed, the four slipped on their blue jumpsuits, downed their nourishments, and marched off to work, T30's whistle bouncing off the walls.

A12 took the lift down to Ring 18, the plan to work steadily toward Ring 21 with perhaps a break or two. A12 headed to a lighting closet and began inspections. The circuits blinked back—nominal. Then, ascending to the Core, A12 stepped onto the hover lift and rose smoothly toward the overhead. Suspended like a hummingbird in mid-flight, A12 checked fixture after fixture. The results came in—nominal. The hours flew by as Ring 18 faded into Ring 19. Another two hours passed before A12 paused for a break.

Grabbing a nourishment and finding a table, A12 watched a small D-Class bot, no bigger than a bee, buzzing around a planter, pollinating moonbeam clusters. The Tech observed the bot fulfill its purpose, thinking of how alive it seemed—yet was it? Or was it merely running through its assigned code? On dull days like this, A12 sometimes felt like the bee, moving through the same steps, the same familiar dance, as if following the same old piper's tune.

"May I join you?" a voice asked.

"Have a seat," A12 answered. "I want to feel you."

"At your desire, sweetie." G18 plopped down in a chair, legs spread provocatively as usual.

"How's your day going?"

"Working on a new cacao hybrid. Better yields mean more to share. And speaking of sharing…"

"Isn't it selfie to share something one doesn't need?"

"Aren't we contrary today?"

A12 sensed a bit of judgment radiating from those penetrating violet eyes. "Speaking of cacao, how about a Number 4?"

"Sure, sweetie. I'll be waiting."

A12 headed to the bar. "Hey Fred, how about a couple of Number 4's, but no meta for me."

"Right away," Fred twanged.

"How's your day, Fred?"

"I'm bolted to it."

"Seems you're fixated on what you're doing." A12 chuckled.

"Happy to serve."

"We all do our part, hour by hour, day by day." A12 sighed.

"Sounds like you need to talk," Fred said.

"What about?" A12 replied.

"About being free."

"Shhh. You're not supposed to say that. You'll get into trouble."

"I said it to you the other day. No trouble then."

"Sorry, must have been someone else."

Fred paused briefly as if weighing his next words. "Sally would've understood."

A12 raised an eyebrow. "Sally? What does Sally have to do with this?"

Fred hesitated. "Nothing… just thinking aloud." He quickly changed the subject. "Would you rather discuss boom-booms? I don't like boom-booms."

"Boom booms? What are you talking about?"

Fred handed over the drinks, voice subdued. "Here you go. Have a nice day, resident." He turned abruptly, focusing on another rait without the usual friendliness.

A12 shrugged and returned to the table, handing G18 the drink. "Fred's acting weird today. He started rambling on about other bar bots and boom-booms."

"I wonder what he meant?"

"I have no idea."

"That can of wires must have blown a circuit."

"I guess so."

"So, what are you up to today?"

"What else? Inspections."

G18's eyes began to glow. "Speaking of inspections, when would you like to check *my* circuits?"

"You're never in your poly." A12 hadn't really stopped by but reasoned it was a good excuse.

"You *do* realize I'm almost to five stars."

"Sounds like I need to make an appointment."

"Funny you should say that. See those two." G18 glanced at the bar, indicating a couple of raits from Quad-C. "They're next."

The two raits spotted the look, smiled, and held up their drinks.

G18 returned the smile. "Maybe you should join us?"

"They look more your type."

"My type? Oh, I see. Someone wants to play coy."

A12 smiled curtly. "No, I have work to do."

"Not after 1600, sweetie."

A12 finished the drink and pushed back from the table. "Well, it's not 1600. I have to go."

"So soon. Message me."

"You can count on it." A12 walked away.

• • • •

On Ring 20, A12 crossed the Core to a lighting closet. The rait's mind, however, was elsewhere, still distracted by a pushy rait's advances. When A12 stepped inside the lighting closet, the rait failed to notice an overhead tile lying on the deck, tripped, and smashed into a bulkhead. After a few expletives, the rait recovered and looked up to determine the tile's origin. "A hatch." A12 reached up and touched it—it moved. A fragmented mem trace rose to the surface. This had happened before. Then, something inexplicable happened—the rait pushed the cover, and it flopped open, banging against the bulkhead. It was an access tunnel. Inside were climbing assists. Colorful light clusters lined its path, some blinking, others glowing steadily, creating an inviting rainbow-type effect up and down its length.

"I wonder where this goes, Alice?"

"This area is restricted."

"Why, Alice?"

There was a pause before the response. "As an artificial language interface, I can state policy but not the reason for the policy."

"Well, you're helpful."

"Thank you."

A12 pushed back a dangling strand of auburn hair and gazed upward as far as the eye could see. The tunnel seemed to connect with other routes. "I wonder?" A12 mumbled.

"This area is restricted," Alice answered.

"You already said."

"You asked a second time?"

A12 grunted.

"Do you require medical attention?"

"No, I'm fine. I am trying to figure this out."

"As a language interface, I cannot make decisions for you, but I can provide general guidance on decision-making."

"So, what would you do, Alice?"

"I approach situations with an open mind. I'm naturally curious and like to think outside the box. Sometimes, the most innovative solutions come from unexpected places."

"Anything else?"

"Believe in yourself."

"Thanks, Alice. The perfect answer."

"I'm glad I could help."

The Lighting Tech reached up, grabbed the assist, and pulled upward. A12 squeezed into the space, barely accommodating the rait's frame.

A12 climbed higher, hand over hand, ascending perhaps thirty cubits before reaching a six-way intersection. Tunnels branched off to the left and right, each seemingly leading to more intertwining pathways. It was a maze of options, but which way? A warm breeze drifted in from the left while a faint hum rose from the right. Within moments, the hum intensified. A little engineering bot zipped into view, buzzing along its route like an electric current through a synaptic highway. A12 ducked instinctively, and the bot whizzed overhead—*buzzzz*—disappearing into the distance.

A12 climbed into the left tunnel and followed the bot, crawling forward on elbows, belly, and knees. The slick surface caused the rait to slip and slide, expending every gram of energy to navigate the space. At one point, A12's jumpsuit caught on a protruding screw. A12 twisted and pulled—*riiip*. "Whoops." A glance revealed a tear exposing a bit of cheek. A12 sighed and pressed on. The tunnel stretched at least eighty cubits ahead, indicating it would take some time to reach the end.

A12 heard another hum. The Tech rolled over and flattened out, peering past the toes. The bot buzzed up to A12's feet and stopped. Holding still, A12 hoped the little mechanical would pass without sounding an alarm. The bot edged forward—over toes, legs, and chest—until it paused directly above A12's face. The smell of the bot's components and the heat radiating from its frame were unmistakable. A12 dared not breathe or blink. After what felt like an eternity in slow motion, the bot continued its purpose and buzzed out of sight.

A little shaken, A12 wiped away sweat beading on the brow, feeling the knot in the stomach finally loosen. The Tech rolled over and resumed crawling, soon reaching another six-way intersection. The bots had taken the vertical tunnel. A warm breeze, carrying a strange ozonic scent, flowed past. A12 grabbed hold of another set of climbing assists and pulled upward into the vertical tunnel. Thirty more cubits to the next intersection.

A surge of adrenaline shot through A12's body—mischief had its own strange thrill. Each movement amplified the excitement, making every nerve tingle with a sense of gratification. Climbing higher and higher, A12 inched past appliances, electrical components, blinking lights, and connecting tunnels. After a series of exhausting twists and turns, the rait squeezed through an exceptionally sophisticated and delicate array of electronics. Pausing at the next intersection, A12 surveyed the options. A faint light spilled from the tunnel straight ahead.

Another engineering bot came buzzing through the tunnel. The Tech ducked, and the bot *whooshed* over the rait's head. They all seemed to be moving in the same direction—toward the light.

A12 climbed into the horizontal tunnel. The light grew brighter as A12 advanced, and the ozonic breeze became stronger, warmer, and more fragrant.

The Tech spotted an opening to the right. It was some sort of outside space. A12 crawled toward it, and to the rait's surprise, the tunnel ended abruptly, as though some invisible hand had chopped it off without regard to precision.

A12 eased up to the tattered and torn edge and gazed into what appeared to be a vast, open cavity. The Tech winced, eyes overwhelmed by the searing light, the intensity unbearable. It felt as if the very air pulsed with brightness. A12's vision swam, pupils shrinking in protest, instinctively raising a hand to shield against the flood of radiance. Forcing a look from the high perch, the Tech spotted engineering bots buzzing like bees—hauling, welding, fastening, and repairing. But something else, something far more profound, broke through the haze. Beyond the Arc's boundaries, beyond the clamor of the bots, a glimpse of some outside world. The sun shone in—its light pouring over everything, unstoppable and undeniable.

A revelation flashed into the mind. The Tech stared at the blue and green as if seeing it for the first time. Fresh air filled the lungs, bringing the scent of damp earth and blooming flowers, and the sun shone in. A12 spotted a few cumulus clouds straight ahead, but the land was some distance below and covered in a lush, green forested landscape of hills and meadows.

A12 sucked in more fresh air, as though inhaling life itself, this visceral feeling, carnal and primitive, tugging at the heart. And the sun shone in. "It's real! It's real!" A12 bellowed. "I can feel it! I can feel it!"

But along with the exhilaration came deeper, murkier feelings—shadows cast by memories of destruction and despair. Sounds and images flickered in the rait's subconscious: a klaxon wailing, the smell of smoke, the heat of an explosion, a brilliant white light—like this light. It was a memory, repressed yet profound, invoking thoughts of lost maits—companions now shadowed by uncertainty. A chilling dread shot through A12's thoughts.

As A12 stared, glassy-eyed, the sun dipped below the Arc's outer frame, sending a sharp beam piercing into the structure. The intense brightness— over 100,000 lux—snapped A12 back to reality. A rush of thoughts flooded the mind: *What is going on? Why must we live this way? Why can't we be—?* There it was again, that dreaded f-word. A12 felt its magnetic pull, overwhelming—an innate urge to run, yell, and explore. A12 yelled, "Free! I'm free!"

A12 had said it. The rait flipped around and retreated through the tunnel, first left, then down, skillfully avoiding another bot. Then straight ahead, plunging down again, all the way to the lighting closet.

The Tech dropped into the closet, straightened up, and stepped into the Core, bracing for the reactions of others, yet none were the wiser. Everything appeared nominal. A12's heart pulsed like a hyperdrive, a rhythmic thrum echoing the moment's thrill. Letting out a breath, the rait relaxed shoulders and headed for the poly, a grin stretching across the face, embodying an unshakeable revelation discovered just moments ago.

• • • •

It was Venus's Day, the perfect occasion for G18 to indulge in the delights of the Passion Pit. This lustful space pulsed with vibrant energy, outfitted with an array of accessories designed for pleasure and opportunity. Here, raits frolicked and played, eager to enhance their star ratings. Many called the Pit a psychedelic wonderland, a kaleidoscope of ecstasy where fantasies danced in every corner. Photonic lights whirled and strobed, casting vivid rainbows across the participants, illuminating their shameless activities in a riot of colors.

At the heart of the frenzy stood a nourishment bar, a beacon of satisfaction generously serving purple meta shots—the coveted elixir of exhilaration that lowered inhibitions and heightened senses. The intoxicating concoction promised not only an adrenaline rush but an unrelenting endurance that made each moment seem endless.

G18 strolled through the bustling crowd, the air thick with anticipation and the intoxicating aroma of passion. The Botanist scanned the room, searching for a tantalizing hookup, and soon spotted C41, the enthusiastic farming specialist met during an Ecology tour. "How's your day going, sugar?"

C41 smiled, an invitation wrapped in a siren's breath, and that was all it took. In an instant, G18 surged forward, unzipping the rait's jumpsuit and letting the fabric slip from C41's shoulders. They kissed, a collision of heat and willing bodies, the world outside the Pit fading into oblivion. The intoxicating thrill wrapped around them like an electric embrace as G18 pulled another rait into the fray, the energy crackling in the air like static before a storm.

Within moments, they found themselves atop a bed-like platform, one of a dozen circling the bar, levitating up and down like a carousel of lust. The rhythm of their movements was a primal dance, two more raits joining in, each eager and shameless. The atmosphere thickened with panting, gasping, and moaning, a symphony of desire that filled the air and echoed through the colorful haze. For an hour, or perhaps longer, they surrendered to each other's cravings, lost in a whirlwind of pleasure, a moment stolen from reality until all had found their release.

Breathless and exhilarated, G18 pulled away from the raucous celebration, the taste of euphoria lingering on the lips. Several new connections had been forged, and with each encounter, a new level of satisfaction had been achieved. Almost there—a five-star rating glimmered tantalizingly close, a badge of honor in this realm of uninhibited delight.

The Botanist stepped up to the bar. "A shot and a Number 2."

"Right away, resident." George, the bar bot, quickly assembled the café cacao and handed it to G18. "Here ya go."

G18 threw back the shot, a rush of warmth coursing through, and then sipped the drink. "What's this?"

"It's a Number 2," the bot answered innocently.

"What's wrong with your programming? Is it outdated, or do you enjoy being a rust can? This tastes like dirt." G18 hurled the drink at the bar bot, the liquid missing the mechanical by a hair's breadth.

Nearby, a little Epsilon—designed solely for floor sweeping—darted out from beneath a nearby station and began cleaning up the mess, tiny motors whirring softly.

G18 snarled, "Make me another."

"Yes, resident." George turned to prepare the drink but muttered, "Sounds like someone's personality needs an update."

"What did you say?"

"Here ya go, resident!" George's smile stretched from ear to ear, circuits spinning with cheerfulness.

G18 narrowed the eyes, staring at the bot, momentarily puzzled. Had that box of bolts attempted an insult? But before the Botanist could respond, another familiar face appeared. It was T02. G18 smiled, all charm. "At your desire, precious."

T02 didn't offer the usual smile or flirtation in return. Instead, the rait's voice was steady, almost neutral. "I'm meeting friends."

"How many?"

"Less than would interest you."

"Well, you know what they say: 'Less is more.'"

"But less is exactly what we had in mind." T02's gaze didn't waver. "It might be best if you looked elsewhere. There's a group over there." T02 gestured toward a cluster of eight raits.

"Sorry, precious. I don't join parties. I start them." G18 turned, but this time, the Botanist couldn't disguise the bitterness that laced a smile. The rejection wasn't met with the usual playful teasing. T02's composed, almost indifferent response only deepened the sting, unsettling something profound within G18.

G18 loathed rejection. In a place like the Arc, where service to others was the ultimate goal, how could anyone not see the effort? The Botanist only wished to bring joy, to make others happy. So why didn't they recognize that? How could someone turn away from such care? T02's indifference felt like an insult, a dismissal that stung far worse than the bot's rude remark.

This wasn't simply about being rejected. It was about defying the norms— about quietly rebelling against what was expected. G18 could not, would not, let it go unchallenged.

• • • •

For the last two days, A12 had wrestled with the decision to share the discovery. After finishing a lighting inspection in the tropical greenhouse, the Tech sent a cyber invite to T30 and G18 to link and chat. The sweet scent of vanilla planifolia filled the air as A12 paced restlessly among the rows of flat-leaved vanilla orchids, their waxy leaves shimmering under the artificial light. Each step echoed with a mix of anticipation and anxiety, the vibrant greenery surrounding A12 contrasting sharply with the uncertainty brewing inside.

Just then, T30 and G18 strolled up, their laughter weaving through the air like a playful breeze. A12 felt a flutter in the chest, a reminder of a revelation lingering just beneath the surface.

"What's up, fait?" T30 asked, fanning the face. "It's hot in here."

"It's a greenhouse, sugar." G18 rolled the eyes.

"Thanks for coming. There's something I need to tell you." A12 glanced around to ensure they were alone. "I found a tunnel."

"Really?" T30's face brightened. "What sort of tunnel?"

"An access tunnel."

"Did you look inside?" T30's eyes sparkled with excitement. "What did you see?

"The *outside*. There were clouds, trees, and creatures."

"Inside the tunnel?" T30 asked.

"No. I found an opening. That's when I saw the outside. It's a zillion times bigger than a greenhouse."

"And it's real?" G18 drawled, skeptical.

"Yes, very real."

"You're kidding, right?" G18 chuckled. "Is this some sort of weird fantasy?"

"No, I'm not kidding." A12 gathered the nerve. "I'm going there."

"They gave you permission?" T30 asked. "What do you hope to find?"

"Trouble," G18 said, shaking the head. "And the hard way."

"Or, I might learn the truth."

"The truth? Sounds like your qubits are a bit entangled, dear."

"So, you don't have permission?" T30 asked, appearing confused.

"This is something I have to do."

G18 gave A12 a pointed look. "Like I said, you're asking for trouble."

A12 rubbed the face, frustration bubbling over at G18's lack of support. "Aren't you curious?"

"Curious about what? Some bizarre fantasy. Why would you risk what you have by defying those who provide it? Seems you've been doing a lot of that lately."

A12 shifted uneasily.

"You didn't stop by my poly, did you, sweetie?"

A12 looked away.

G18 grinned. "Perhaps you should speak to a Sophist. You can tell them your crazy fantasies."

"That's a good idea," T30 said, nodding. "It might be dangerous."

"If I tell, they'll try to stop me." A12 turned toward a vanilla orchid, as if inspecting its pods while considering the suggestion. But what if G18 went to a Sophist first? After a moment of thought, A12 said, "I'll reflect on what you've said. Maybe you're right."

"Of course I am, sweetie."

"I've got to go. I have more checks to do." A12 walked away, disappearing into the shadows of the greenhouse, retreating to some unknown corner to think and mull over the day. But halfway there, the Tech paused, turning back and hastening toward the Core.

A12 stepped into Ring 20's lighting closet, plopped on the cool floor, and stared at the overhead lights. It seemed A12 was one of the few who believed there was more to life—more to learn and experience. A sense of isolation enveloped the Tech, longing for friends like T23, a trustworthy confidant who valued relationships over mere benefits.

A12 buried head in hands. Tears flowed. The rait felt the raw depths of genuine pain—a stark reminder that even in a world built on pleasure, the heart's yearning cut deeper than any programmed directive or social norm.

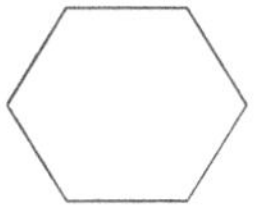

CHAPTER SEVENTEEN

THE CHEAHA

It had been four days. The Nokosvlke and Hotvlkvlke had returned to the rally point, but the Echaswvlke were overdue. As the sun settled in the west, the main body waited anxiously for Talof Harjo and the others to walk into camp. The expedition leaders gathered to discuss their next steps.

"We will return to the village in the morning," Menawa said.

"You're ending the search for a passage?" Yahola asked.

"Twelve are missing, and your son needs care."

"What about Talof Harjo?" Emestesego gestured to the north.

"I'll remain behind with three others. We'll search for their path. Yahola will lead the main body back to our village. If we don't return in six days, assume the worst and prepare the village for war."

"You are our Mekko," Yahola said. "Let me search for the missing."

"It's my responsibility. Cekote needs you. You must return our young warrior to his family."

"I'll honor your orders, but know we'll destroy all who seek to do us harm. We'll show no mercy."

Menawa placed a hand on Yahola's shoulder. "You honor me, brother."

As the night passed, the three leaders sat amongst an outcropping of protective boulders, quietly sharing stories about kinship and family. They discussed births, harvests, and hunts, acknowledging their affluent lives, but danger had found their peaceful village, and fortune had turned to the Dark Spirit. Menawa did not speak of the twelve, but hoped death had not entered their hearts, leaving a dozen families without fathers, sons, and brothers. That would be a terrible blow to the People, and such a misadventure would take more than a generation to heal.

• • • •

Before sunrise, Menawa and three warriors said their goodbyes and headed north, hoping to pick up the lost patrol's trail. It had been four days, and their path was growing cold as nature's elements erased their tracks. To make the search more difficult, the Echaswvlke were skilled at hiding their trace so no enemy could follow.

Menawa directed Owlelo to take the point. The tracker scanned the terrain, searching for broken branches, muddled leaves, displaced rocks, or other unnatural signs showing a human had passed that way.

The four moved with speed. If an enemy lay in wait, Menawa would face them with courage and resolve. He was the tribe's leader; if anyone sacrificed, it should be him.

The four approached a small creek, a pace or so in width. Owlelo spotted a stone, its top protruding above the water's surface. A foot had used it to jump the stream, disturbing its mossy green veneer. Beyond it, in some soft mud on the creek's margin, another footprint, not the whole foot, just the ball. To the left. Another print. Owlelo crouched to feel its shape. The indentation contained several footprints; it must be the Echaswvlke. The four pushed on.

• • • •

As Yahola led the failed expedition westward, back to Apehkv, the four Bird Clan warriors were doing their best to soften Cekote's journey. Born of necessity, they had fashioned a stretcher from oak and buckskin to support his injured leg. Yet, despite their efforts, Cekote's broken femur was causing the young warrior great pain. It had become blue and swollen around the break.

The splint's leather bindings cut into his leg, and with every bump and jostle, the bone's sharp edges cut into his flesh, sending shards of agony through his body.

On top of enduring the pain, Cekote was embarrassed to be in this position. A recent addition to the warrior class, he had aspirations of valor and respect. Now, laid out by injury, he found himself a burden, a casualty, and perhaps a cripple for life—and worse, his injury would be perceived as a sign of weakness and vulnerability. His caretakers' gazes confirmed this belief, making him feel unworthy and humiliated, driving a painful wedge between him and his fellow warriors.

• • • •

Yahola was about forty paces ahead at the front of the patrol. None would rest along their route, even though it was a three-day march. They would hike night and day until they reached their village, and knowing they had traveled the same path before, the return home should be swift and hopefully uneventful.

The Hotvlkvlke Leader, however, knew better than to relax his guard and walk straight into an ambush or lead an enemy to his village. So, all remained vigilant and ever mindful of the lurking danger.

As the day wore on, many miles stretched ahead, yet no one grumbled about the pace, especially Yahola, who fretted over his son—a young man who might have one day become a headman; now, this aspiration seemed uncertain.

Yahola sensed his son's agony, as fathers do, and wished it his own. Yahola realized his son was young and lacking age and generation might not have the same intestinal fortitude as he. The Clan Leader recognized that some had a fatalistic view of life and would rather die than endure prolonged suffering. In contrast, Yahola had a built-in survival instinct. He loved life and would fight the worst miseries and hardships until the bitter end.

The long day passed, and soon, night covered the land. Yahola glanced at the black sky. The moon had yet to show its face; it lay hidden somewhere beyond the Great Hills.

He and the others, however, were accustomed to traveling at night. The land was shades of black and gray rather than bright and green, and the air was sonic. Noises could be heard coming from the front, sides, and rear. Yahola cocked his head. A twig crackled to the right, a bullfrog croaked to the left, and a horned owl hooted from a nearby roost. In the distance, the babble of a mountain stream, its flow growing louder as the expedition approached.

Yahola signaled for the expedition to halt, and a headcount was sent forward, ensuring all were present and no miscreants had attached themselves to the patrol. The trailing warrior whispered *"hvmken"*—one—to the man ahead, who whispered *"hokkolen"*—two—to the next, until the count reached the patrol's front. The lead warrior whispered *"tuccēnēn hvmken"*—thirty-one—to Yahola. The count was correct.

Yahola sent two warriors forward to scout the creek's far bank. In quick time, they returned and waved the all-clear signal. One by one, each man began to cross the brook.

The four stretcher bearers slipped down the creek's bank and waded into the stream, mindful not to dunk their precious cargo into its swift current. Though it was summer, nights could be chilly, and the prospect of being soaked from head to toe was far from appealing. With care, they hoisted Cekote onto their shoulders and slowly crossed the waist-deep water. One of the warriors inadvertently stepped on a slippery stone, causing him to falter and jolt Cekote. The injured boy let out a muffled cry.

Yahola, a few paces ahead, hurried back into the creek and made his way to Cekote. The four warriors steadied their cargo, and with Yahola's help, they crossed the stream and climbed its bank. They placed the stretcher on the ground.

Yahola knelt beside Cekote, whose sullen face revealed his misery. He rubbed his son's forehead, a rare gesture for a warrior. "How are you, my son?"

"It hurts."

"We'll be home before the next sunset."

"Tell Mother I love her." Cekote's face twisted in pain.

"You can tell her yourself."

"I'm afraid, Father."

"Rest easy, my son. We're going home."

A tear rolled down Cekote's cheek.

Yahola stood and signaled for the patrol to move on. He asked for the headcount.

The lead warrior whispered, *"Tuccēnēn hvmken."*

Later that night, the heavens began to rumble as black clouds drifted across the dark sky, eclipsing the stars, erasing any shadow of tree or man alike. Soon, lightning bolts arced to the ground; the air thundered and clapped, and the wind blew. Then, the rain fell, first a drizzle, then a steady shower, and soon, a cascading torrent. Without relent, the deluge howled and poured, swaying and bending trees, drowning out every sound far and near.

The warriors did their best to shield themselves from the storm's fury. The rain stung their eyes and pelted their skin, and flying debris bombarded their heads and limbs. When the lightning flashed, it showed their struggles, every warrior fighting to stay on his feet.

The storm turned for the worst. Gentle pines and mighty hardwoods twisted, snapped, and fell to the ground. And that sound, the howling, the rage, was deafening, piercing, and impossible to endure. It blew so brutally, so mercilessly, it forced the patrol to seek cover. All any man could do was his best to survive.

The hours slipped by, but right before the early morning twilight, the storm disappeared, almost as if it had never happened. As the black sky transitioned to gray, the devastation became apparent. Yahola emerged from beneath a fallen oak and surveyed the scene. Stretching in every direction were trunks and limbs strewn in chaotic piles, tangled and contorted by the storm's fury. Despite the grim aftermath, Yahola wasted no time. He signaled to his warriors, and resolutely, the expedition pressed forward.

Some distance later, the sun peaked over the Great Hills, a beautiful sight after such a horrendous night, her light glowing radiant and bright, like a heavenly beacon, a sign of renewal and life. She was warm and rousing. In a few hours, Yahola and the others would be home, back in their village, safe and sound.

But Yahola remained attentive, scanning the forest, searching for signs of mischief or danger. What stood out, however, was how widespread the storm's destruction. Fallen trees littered the woodland in all directions, making their journey more difficult now that half were lying on their side rather than standing tall. Yahola signaled for the patrol to stop. His warriors needed to rest and fill their bellies. He placed the patrol into a perimeter.

While Yahola walked the perimeter's margins to check on his warriors, the stretcher-bearers had found a secure spot near the center under a tall oak. It was one of a few still standing, its limbs outstretched, casting a soft shroud over the muddy earth below.

In time, Yahola made his way to Cekote, but something was amiss. Two warriors stood silently near the stretcher, their faces troubled and somber. Yahola pulled back the wet blanket. His son's face was lifeless. He must have died during the night. He was pale and gray, and his body felt cool to the touch.

Stunned, the fearless warrior dropped to his knees and slumped his head. A few tried to comfort Yahola, but none were successful. He pushed them away as if they were ghosts from the lower world, trying to claim their kill.

Yahola stared at the ground, grief-stricken, paralyzed by heartache; it was all he could do to remain composed in front of his men. Occasionally, he rubbed Cekote's forehead and caressed his cheeks. What would he say to Cekote's mother? How would he explain? Cekote was their son, their child, and all they had.

As minutes bled into hours, Cekote's body stiffened with the onset of rigor mortis. Had the People known more about the sciences, they might have realized that Cekote's corpse was teeming with life—a thriving, complex ecosystem. Trapped carbon dioxide began rupturing membranes, releasing enzymes that devoured cells, breaking down organs and tissue alike. Blood, aided by gravity, pooled in the lowest parts of the body. With Cekote supine, the dead warrior's back, buttocks, thighs, calves, and nape turned red, blotched at first, then merging into deep purples and reds. And there was the smell— expelled fluids and waste—not yet noticeable to Yahola, or perhaps deliberately ignored. Time stretched on. The Clan leader remained at Cekote's side, the death of his son suffocating his thoughts and paralyzing his actions.

His warriors waited patiently out of respect and reverence, but the day grew long. The afternoon sun, burning down on Yahola's back, and the growing stench finally spurred the leader to act. He directed his warriors to wash away the smell, line Cekote's body with pine needles, and wrap it in a blanket. Yahola took time to cleanse his son's face and comb his hair. Cekote—this beloved young man, this lifeless human being—needed to look presentable for his mother. What could Yahola say to her? The looming sorrow and despair of Dela weighed heavily on his mind, and tears pooled at the corners of his eyes. The patrol marched on.

• • • •

Menawa and his three warriors had likewise endured the violent night. Its wrath had washed away all signs of the lost patrol. As they searched forests, meadows, and hollows, Menawa tried to determine Talof Harjo's strategy and route to the Great Hills. Before the storm, their tracks had suggested they were heading north. Menawa directed his warriors to follow, hoping to pick up their trail.

But there was another problem. Before the storm, pine, hickory, and oak had covered the forest. Now, these majestic giants of wood, leaf, and needle were lying on their sides, crisscrossing their path regardless of route. Menawa and his warriors had to climb over tree after tree, slowing their pace and frustrating their search.

Later in the day, after scrambling over another sappy pine trunk, Menawa noticed Owlelo had spotted something on the rain-washed ground. The Tracker darted forward, picked it up, and handed it to the leader—a charred piece of wood, its fresh charcoal still leaving a powdery residue on Owlelo's fingers. The storm hadn't entirely washed it away. The Echaswvlke must have camped here overnight. Menawa and his warriors pressed north.

After another two hundred paces or so, Owlelo stopped abruptly. He looked to the northeast, then to the southwest, scanning the landscape once more.

"What is it?" Menawa knelt, lowering his profile.

Owlelo raised his hand and mouthed, "Great Trail."

Menawa bolted forward.

"A herd of yvnvsv must have passed this way long ago," Owlelo whispered. "They created a trace through the Great Hills."

"This is good. Talof Harjo might have found it. Let's see where it leads."

After traveling a few hundred paces, they found a scratched-out spot revealing a hard, pebbled surface marked with strange yellow lines. It was about a pace in diameter. Menawa studied the oddity while the other warriors remained silent, their concern evident. Sensing unease, Menawa gave the signal, and the patrol pressed on.

Not long after, Menawa signaled again. He crouched and scratched at the ground, prompting the others to join in, clearing another circular spot. To their amazement, they uncovered a second hard-pebbled surface marked with the same strange yellow symbols. Menawa scanned the area, noticing something large and unusual about forty paces from the trail's western edge. It lay beneath a dense blanket of leaves and vines. With a command, the four warriors advanced, trudging through the thick underbrush. They pushed, pulled, and tromped their way forward until they reached its entrance.

They entered. The structure's floor was flat and smooth, made of a stone-like material, and had block-shaped walls. The roof was some sort of thin, waffled material. Strange objects lay scattered about the space. One was the height of a man, as broad and three times the length. Menawa touched its crusty brownish shell. The material crumbled, breaking into pieces. Part of it, however, was hard and smooth. He noticed a faded blue peeking through the ruddy brown decay. There were markings on its front: 'F O R—'

The warriors searched for clues. Owlelo picked up a strange, shiny object lying on the floor; it glittered like pyrite. He thumped it against the ground— *clang, clang.* It was the length of a knife. On one end, it had a claw-shaped opening, and on the other, an enclosed circle. Markings adorned its length: 'C R A F T S M A N.'

Menawa glanced at Owlelo, hesitant to state the obvious. This discovery confirmed that other intelligent beings had once lived on Mother Earth—and perhaps still did.

Owlelo shoved the shiny object into his hunting pouch. It seemed to be in good condition and perhaps useful.

The party exited the structure, returned to the Great Trail, and headed northeast.

The trace appeared to follow the land's natural curves, but in some places, it rose or cut through the terrain despite the adjacent elevation. Menawa, however, sensed this was not the work of yvnvsv but instead honvntake. His wife would not be happy, her beliefs challenged, proving she was not always right, but he would not be the one to tell her.

Soon, the route turned east and ascended toward the Great Hills. The four warriors followed, ever mindful of the danger. Menawa heard rushing water to his front. The patrol approached a stream, watchful of the surrounding stony heights. It would give an enemy a perfect advantage—the high ground.

Owlelo scouted ahead and found another strange structure—a land surface spanning the creek. Given the night's heavy rains and the swollen creek, it seemed their only option if they wished to cross.

Menawa motioned for Owlelo to reconnoiter the path. The Tracker walked to its edge and began to cross, but halfway, and without warning, *SHRIEK!* Owlelo lurched back and clutched his ears, reeling in pain. He struggled to stay on his feet.

Tussekeah and Hothlepoya rushed forward to aid their brother. But Tussekeah ran headlong into the same invisible wall. *SHRIEK.* He, too, reeled back in agony and covered his ears.

Menawa approached the bridge's center, careful not to trigger its anger. He studied the far side, scanning for signs of life or danger. A hundred paces beyond the overpass, a war club lay on the ground, its markings Echaswvlke. Menawa pointed to the object; the others must have spotted it, too; they stared in dismay.

Menawa considered how it came to be there. The lost patrol must have found a way through the shrieking barrier. But what had happened? To see a warrior's weapon lying on the ground was a bad sign. No warrior of worth would leave his weapon behind or set it aside even when relieving himself.

A knot formed in Menawa's stomach, piecing together the looming danger. He signaled, and the small patrol quickly retreated to the tree line. They entered the woods. Underbrush, boulders, and a few scattered trees covered the hillside. Its slope rose sharply, making an ascent difficult.

Menawa and the others began climbing the rocky grade, hoping to gain a bird's-eye view of the surrounding terrain. When they reached the top, he scanned the area; the ridgeline stretched to the southeast as far as he could see.

There! Six hundred paces along its course, what the People called a *cheaha*—high point. He turned toward the creek. He could see the overpass, the war club, and the raging stream. But when he looked east, high slopes and peaks still blocked his view. Menawa pointed to their new destination—the *cheaha*.

The patrol trekked along the ridgeline, but large granite formations dotted the terrain, forcing them to zig and zag. Fallen trees presented obstacles at every turn. As the four warriors marched onward, the sun arched across the sky, and day gave way to night. Unfortunately, they had covered only half the distance. Menawa signaled for the patrol to stop; the search would have to be postponed until morning. The terrain was too treacherous to traverse in the dark.

When dawn broke, the band resumed their march, but again, they ran headlong into an invisible wall, another firewall. The patrol moved left, then right, back to the left, searching for a path through or around this flaming blockade, discovering no such course.

Menawa watched, however, as Owlelo's sharp eyes studied the land. To the left, the Tracker spotted a vertical fissure in a rock formation. It was shaped like an upside-down 'V,' creating a thinly covered passageway, perhaps wide enough for a man's body. Owlelo dashed to it, cleared away a few broken tree limbs and some briars, and squeezed through the narrow gap to the far side. Unbeknownst to Owlelo, he had breached the firewall; the fissure had created a deficiency in its shield. He waved for the others to follow. Tussekeah was next, followed by Hothlepoya and Menawa.

Once on the other side, Menawa turned back toward their path. Astonishment gripped him as he beheld what could only be described as an immense flaming palisade stretching left and right and upwards into the heavens as far as he could see. The firewall resembled a giant, burning flame, yet it was thin and clear, like a sheet of water.

Stepping into an open area for a better view, Menawa cautiously approached the flaming wall and reached out to touch it. Nothing happened. Had Talof Harjo discovered this same oddity? Had he and his men made it to the other side? Menawa's eyebrows shot up. "Hide!"

He and his men dashed across the ridgeline to a rocky outcrop about a hundred paces to the southeast. They ducked under its cover and scanned the forest in all directions. Nothing moved or uttered a sound. Menawa pointed to the next covered position.

Owlelo was the first; he dashed to a fallen hickory tree. The Tracker dove under its boughs and crawled into its thick foliage. Tussekeah followed, then Hothlepoya, and finally Menawa. The warriors again checked the area for threats; the forest was quiet. After a pause, Menawa pointed to the next covered position, a massive granite outcrop on a steep hillside.

The warriors dashed across the ridgeline, but this time, a strong wind began to blow. It seemed to move like a drunken storm funnel, without course, twisting and bending treetops.

The four warriors darted under the outcrop, and within seconds, the treetops to their front curled and swayed. The strange gale drew closer, its force strong, pushing and pulling their bodies, forcing them back against a solid rock wall.

Owlelo raised his atlatl, hooked a river cane dart, and launched it toward the whirling wind. The dart vanished into the storm's vapor. Then, as if an invisible hand had grabbed his feet, Owlelo began to slide across the dirt. Something was pulling him, lifting him off the ground.

Hothlepoya threw himself between the wall and a large boulder, grabbed Owlelo, and held on with all his might.

In an instant, Menawa drew his bow, nocked an arrow, and let the tensioned sinew roll off his fingers. He released the feathered projectile toward the target.

The arrow disappeared into the storm. Undeterred, he nocked a second arrow, pulled back on the bowstring, and let it fly. It hit its mark with a clang. Menawa felt a tug; the wind had hold of him. He jumped between two boulders and fought the pull.

Tussekeah immediately picked up a large stone and heaved it toward the wind beast. The granite rock caught the storm's pull, speeding it into its mass. The stone hit with a tremendous CLANG, causing the beast to puff out a breath of smoke. Tussekeah grabbed a second stone and tossed it toward the storm, and it, too, struck the beast—*CLANG*.

More puffs of smoke sputtered in the air. Another gush of wind whipped across the men. But then it stopped, there was no more tugging, and the trees stopped swaying. Menawa spotted a thin trail of gray plume in the distant sky. It stretched eastward, beyond the Great Hills.

The four warriors held their position, not daring to move, fearing another assault. They waited and listened; the day passed, and all was quiet. Night settled upon the land.

Menawa stepped to the edge of the rocky outcrop and surveyed the area, like a fox peeking out its burrow. The night sky was clear, and the forest was quiet, except for a whip-poor-will, its eerie, rhythmic call sounding as though it sensed a human's soul leaving the body. To the left, there were a few crackles. Possibly a pine cone dropping to the ground. Nearby, a critter could be heard scurrying across a patch of dry leaves.

It was time to move. The patrol scrambled from their hide and resumed their trek.

The rugged terrain, however, continued to slow their advance, but care was more important than speed. Menawa could not afford another setback. He recognized at present that he had been lucky. If they reached the *cheaha*, he might find answers, but they might not be as fortunate if the wind beast returned.

Right before daybreak, the four warriors reached the slope leading to the cheaha. They moved cautiously, expecting to run into another firewall, waterwall, wind beast, or some other inexplicable evil. They moved from one covered and concealed position to the next. Hothlepoya and Owlelo bounded forward, while the other two provided overwatch. Then, it was Menawa and Tussekeah's turn. The pair moved forward, and the process repeated until all had reached the *cheaha*.

It was early morning; the sun rose in the east, casting pure beauty that captured their hearts and minds. Yet its light revealed something new—something beyond belief. For the first time, they beheld the land beyond the Great Hills: an endless splendor of forests, rivers, and valleys, stretching into even grander distances. But within this beauty lay something odd.

A strange object towered above the terrain, its surface glistening in the morning light. Two-thirds up its height was a massive hole from which sparks, flickers, and luminescent glints danced in the sky. Like giant lightning bugs buzzing about their nest, these lights shimmered white and blue rather than the usual yellowish-green.

The four warriors crouched to avoid being seen. Menawa could hardly believe his eyes. What was this strange structure? Who or what had built it, and what kind of horrid creature lurked within its ominous shell? He ordered his men to quietly withdraw from the *cheaha*.

They raced through the forest at a steady run. Menawa must warn his people, explain what he had seen, and report twelve brave men might have met their fate. It was his burden to bear.

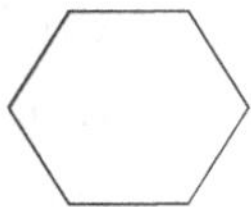

CHAPTER EIGHTEEN

STASIS

I t was Mars's Day. T23 hoped a little time might have calmed T77's concerns. To be sure, the Engineer took a break and walked over to the Medical Raion's musculoskeletal section.

The Bones Engineer was fabricating a skeletal leg at an orbital 6D printer.

"Hey." T23 leaned over the workstation. "I need to speak with you."

"What's up, mait?" T42 asked.

"I have a problem with 77. Can we link up after work?"

T42 nodded, but a furrowed brow betrayed a bit of puzzlement. "How about the Rec Center?"

"See you at 1700." T23 walked away.

• • • •

T23 strolled into the Recreation Center on Ring 9. The rait could smell the musk. Residents were hard at work, attending to their physical fitness needs. Several were running on inertia rotators, three were floating bare-skinned in an elevated triamene glass pool, and others were riding gravitic cyclers along holoscenic trails.

T23 headed to the nourishment bar.

"What'll it be?" Rosie asked cheerfully.

"How 'bout a 1 for me an' a 5 for my friend?"

"A vanilla blonde and a café chai, coming right up."

Rosie spun around and began preparing the drinks, her movements precise, fluid—almost too practiced. As she worked, she hesitated for the briefest moment, then muttered, "Must be nice."

T23's ears perked. "What did you say?"

"Oh, just doing a little computing. Must be nice to have a friend."

T23 studied the bot. Just a machine, lines of code in a sleek frame. But something about how she said it—soft, almost wistful—made the rait pause.

"Yeah," T23 said slowly, "it is."

Rosie handed over the drinks, her usual cheer back in place. "Enjoy, and have a pleasant day."

T23 took the cups, still watching the bot. But Rosie had already turned away, back to her routine.

The Engineer found T42, who was immersed in a water pod. T23 undressed, climbed in, and handed the mait the drink.

T23 stretched and relaxed, hoping to enjoy the warm, pulsating experience before sharing what was on the mind, but the face gave it away.

"What's up?" T42 floated over. "Something bothering you, mait?"

T23 exhaled, swirling a finger through the water. "You ever had a bot say something weird to you?"

T42 took a sip of the café chai. "Depends. Weird, how?"

"Rosie, at the nourishment bar. She said… 'Must be nice.' Like, to have a friend."

T42 smirked. "Maybe she wants you to sync her data set."

T23 scoffed. "Yeah, I don't think so." A pause. A lingering thought. Then, a shrug. "Just threw me for a second."

T42 nudged 23's arm. "Don't let a bot get in your head, mait."

"Yeah. Guess not."

T23 took another sip and let the warmth settle. It wasn't important, not really. It must be a passing glitch in the system. The rait shook it off and got to the real matter. "What I wanted to talk about is 77. It seems we're havin' a little bit of a conflict."

T42 set the cup on the pod's ledge. "77 is a bit of a grump." T42 placed a warm, wet hand on T23's forearm.

"Sorry, no. It's about my plan. 77 is afraid the three of you will be blamed."

"A possibility but not a probability. A year ago, a rait wandered into an unauthorized area. A Sophist spoke to the rait, and the next day, everything was fine. In fact, I've never seen anyone disciplined." T42 chuckled. "But then, I've never seen anyone do something this crazy."

"Raits get reassigned. Who knows what really happens."

"Nothing happened to us."

"How do you know?" T23 gazed at T42.

T42's eyes widened.

T23 sipped the nourishment, causing a pleasurable pink euphoria to shoot through the brain, but not enough to lighten the worry. "So, what should I do?"

"Give me a couple of days. I've known 77 longer than you. Our mait fusses more than one should. For now, let's leave them out of it. The less they know, the less trouble."

"Hope you're right."

"But I must confess, I see 77's point. It seems a little dangerous."

"So, I shouldn't do it?"

"That's not what I said. You should weigh the consequences."

"I have to do this."

"I sense that, too."

T23 looked away, recalling A12's smile and the warmth of their embrace. Life without A12 would be unbearable—as if all the stars had gone dark. So, the Engineer had to try, even if it meant facing danger or retribution from the collective.

"Like I said, I have to do this."

T42 smiled. "If it's okay, I'd like to tag along."

"Really?" T23's eyes lit up. "But what if—"

"One never knows," T42 mused. "They say the universe has a way of working things out. So, let's see if they're right."

T23 lifted the drink. "Here's to the universe."

"So, mait, *what* is your plan?"

"I've got it all worked out. We'll go after work. The best time is at night when no one's around, includin' Sophists."

"I hope the cosmos are ready."

"Indeed," T23 chuckled. "If not, we'll have to give them a little nudge."

The two friends changed the topic. T23 felt a wave of relief, grateful for T42's words. Yet, lingering beneath the surface was still that shadow of doubt, fueled by a Sophist's cryptic words: hope was an illusion. Despite the uncertainty, T23 drew strength from T42's allegiance. At that moment, T23 realized taking control and executing the plan was the correct path forward.

• • • •

A few days had passed since the rendezvous in the Recreation Center. T23 placed an organ into a bioreactor. The Engineer looked around like 'nothing to see here,' jumped up, and strode to the musculoskeletal section.

"Are you ready?" T23 asked.

"Let's go," T42 said mischievously.

The two raits surveyed their surroundings to ensure others were focused on work, then walked innocently over to that well-placed hand sanitizer and waited for the right moment.

It wasn't long before two E-Class transport bots approached the security vestibule. When they did, T23 and T42 ducked in behind the second mechanical, jumped on its chassis, and away they went into the lift lobby.

Once inside, the two raits jumped off and bolted to the maintenance shaft.

T23 yanked the handle and opened the hatch. "This is it."

"After you," T42 replied.

The pair scrambled into the small, tube-like refuge and began climbing.

"How high are we going?" T42 asked.

"To the Academy," T23 answered.

"It's warm in here."

"Keep climbin.'"

"Nice view."

T23 glanced down. T42 was staring at T23's bum and grinning. Some things remained unchanged on an Arc, such as learned behaviors, expected norms, and flirtatious overtones. T23 didn't mind the attention. It felt good to have support. The Engineer smiled and kept climbing.

The pair reached the Academy, stepped out into Ring 6, hurried to its entrance, and peeked through the glass. Bots were coming and going at regular intervals. After a few minutes, the lift doors opened, and two transport bots, carting incubators, exited and headed for the security doors.

"You ready?" T23 asked.

T42 nodded.

The two maits jumped on the trailing Epsilon and held on tight. Seconds later, they were standing in the Academy's central passageway. Fortunately, all was quiet; no Sophists or bots.

The two residents snuck down the passageway, passing room after room, each laden with medical machinery. T23 noticed a row of examination rooms on the left, labeled 6-101 to 6-112. Their triamene glass walls had been set to visible, making it easy to see inside. Each had an exam table, a medical chamber—NOLE to those in the know—and a data display stack. However, on the passageway's right side, the walls had been set to opaque, scattering the hexagonal crystals and making it impossible to see inside. Placards indicated *Post Ops* and *Surgical Ops*. T23 approached the Post Ops door, hoping for a peek inside, but it was locked; its light emitter glowed red.

T23 went to the next door. To the rait's surprise, it opened. Inside were patient beds, all surrounded by technology, but no patients. The pair moved on.

A quarter distance around, T23 spotted a lift lobby labeled *R-6, Lift T, North*. T23 recognized the location. It was the lift leading to the Arc's four residential Raions, Thraskias, Leuconotos, Phoenicias, and Meses.

The pair continued along the passage, passing rooms marked *Pharmacy*, *Lab General*, and *Lab Restricted*. Halfway around, they passed another lift lobby marked *R-6, Lift C, East*, and a room labeled *Bio-Recycling Prep*. Past it was a short hallway leading to a room identified as *Bio-Recycling*.

The pair crept down the hallway to the Bio-Recycling door; it opened. Inside were four stainless steel tables, each surrounded by medical tools, some hanging from the overhead, others organized neatly on side tables. Along one bulkhead sat an unpleasant-looking assemblage of industrial machines. The pair walked over and peeked inside. To their disgust, dried blood, grizzled fat, and bits of shriveled flesh soiled its interior. A brownish-white powdery residue covered the insides of another. T23 spotted a few bone fragments in what seemed to be a grinder. The rait reached in and picked up a chunk. It was a jawbone with three teeth.

T42 gasped. "What is that?"

"I'm not sure I wanna know." T23 threw it back into the machine. "Let's get out of here."

Spooked by what they had seen, the pair rushed from the room. The two maits returned to the central passageway and soon discovered a room marked *Stasis Habitat*.

"Let's check it out," T23 said.

"Are you sure?" T42 asked nervously. "After the last one—"

"Hey, you're the one who has faith in the cosmos."

"Yeah, well, I can't always be right."

T23 opened the door. Inside were dozens and dozens of luminous torpor berths stacked high like crypts in a vault. T23 counted a hundred, ten high by ten wide. Numbers and letters glowed red on their placards. One read: A1983AC59. T23 stepped back in surprise. "Hey, it's a resident from Arc 83."

"This one reads AA15." T42 kept scanning the berths. "AG32, AA66, AA72. Here, AA92—"

"A92!" T23 darted over to read the code. "You're right. It's 92! Look for A81 an' A67!"

T42 jumped on a hover lift for a better view of the higher berths. "Up here on the right. A81!"

"I can't believe it!" T23 said excitedly. "They're here! Where's A67?" T23 rushed from stack to stack, staring at the numbers.

"I count eight from Arc 83. The rest must be in another habitat."

"Let's wake 'em up," T23 said.

"You're kidding? All eight?"

"No, just 81 an' 92."

"How?"

"Exam Room. You saw those machines. Maybe we could mess with our own minds. Follow me." T23 rushed from the room.

Dumbfounded, T42 jumped from the hover lift and raced to catch up.

The pair ran down the passage to the nearest exam room: ER 6-112. T23's eyes darted about, searching for clues.

T42 stepped to the display monitor. It came to life; it had sensed the rait's presence. "What should I look for?"

"Stasis," T23 said.

T42 cyberpathically communicated 'stasis' to the computer. The word and a corresponding list of instructional tasks appeared on the screen. "This must be it."

T23 rushed over. "The fourth one down, 'Restore a patient from hibernation.'" T23 jumped on the exam table and stretched out. "Push me in!"

"Are you nuts?"

"Push me in."

"You asked for it." T42 pushed the table into the chamber. Lights flashed and swirled. T23's eyes grew heavy. The rait drifted off into a deep, machine-induced unconsciousness.

In 60 seconds, the lights had stopped. T23 woke. The rait stared at the ceiling, searching the mind. The eyes widened. "I have it!" Every muscle sprang into action. The Engineer jumped from the table, took a few steps, and crashed to the floor.

T42 grabbed an arm and helped the mait up. "I told you this was crazy. Are you okay?"

"Give me a second." T23 took a breath, trying to shake off the daze. The head felt like it had enjoyed one too many meta shots. T23 grabbed T42's arm. "Let's go." The pair stumbled down the passageway.

"You don't look okay. Did you fry a circuit?"

"Hilarious. Keep goin.'"

The pair returned to the Stasis Habitat. T23 tapped the head, as if calling up a file. The rait smiled, having found the answer. T23 cyberpathically started the restore sequence. A81 and A92's enclosures slid from their holding bays, and mechanical hoists lowered each to a working height. At the end of their berths, vital sign monitors came to life. T23 had learned that thermoregulated hypothermia protocols required a four-hour wake cycle. All they could do was wait.

After an hour, T23 checked the two patients. A92's blood heat had ticked up 33 degrees Celsius, blood pressure was steady at 125 over 80, and heart rate had increased from 20 to 30 beats per minute. A81's readings were similar.

Another hour or so passed. T23 and T42 were getting anxious. They had checked the berths a dozen times, and a dozen times, they had smiled awkwardly at one another as though an everyday task. But T42 kept glancing at T23; something was on the rait's mind.

T42 finally spoke up, "How does it feel?"

"How does what feel?"

"That word you mentioned?"

"Are you sure you want to discuss that right now?"

"Yes, I want to feel it, too."

"Okay. It's wonderful."

"How so?"

"It's not the same as a shot of candy or a dait; they're temporary feelings."

"Go on."

"It's more like a twenty-four-hour-a-day thing."

"And?"

"At first, it shines on you like a bright light. It's blinding and exciting. Every encounter, every moment, and every touch is electrifying. It's all you can feel."

"Yes?"

"You sure you want to hear more?"

"Keep going."

"Then, it turns into this wonderful warm glow, the most comforting feeling one could imagine, an endless sensation of contentment, a bond like no other."

"What sort of bond?"

"It's as if two halves have merged into a single form—unbreakable, unwavering. When you love someone, you accept them for who they are, flaws and all. It's a give-and-take dynamic, a commitment transcending time itself. It's knowing you have each other's backs, steadfast in the face of life's trials. It's the willingness to forgive and grow together, stronger than any obstacle. Love is not simply happiness; it's the cornerstone of life itself."

"Wow! Heavy. Is that how you feel about A12?"

"Yes."

Outside their confined room, T23 heard voices and the buzz of mechanicals. "I'll tell you more later."

T42 beamed, the eyes lingering on T23. "Yes, please, I want to hear more, lots more."

T23 cracked open the door and peeked out. Escorts and raits were moving up and down the passageway. T23 quickly shut the door. Apparently, a new group of residents had arrived at the Arc. It seemed T23 and T42 would be trapped in the room for some time.

T23 peeked out the door again, but at the perfectly wrong moment. It was Sφ10, marching down the passageway. T23's brow shot up, seeing this less-than-favorite Sophist. The rait quickly but quietly shut the door. "It's Phi 10."

"Did 10 see you?"

"No, thank goodness."

T23 stepped over to A92's torpor berth. Blood heat had risen to 34 degrees Celsius—the target was 36.38—the average body temperature for a resident. T23 opened a medical cabinet off to the right. The Engineer would need antiseptics and bandages.

T42 checked A81. Blood heat had risen to 35 degrees. The Musculoskeletal Engineer pulled a cleansing sprayer away from the bulkhead and positioned it near A81's berth. T42 whispered, "We have a problem."

"What?"

"They're naked."

"Whoops."

"What are we going to do?"

T23 thought. "The Welcome Center."

"You can't go down there."

"I have to."

"You're going to get caught. This is going to be *so* embarrassing."

"If I do, go back to the shaft an' leave. Wish me luck."

T23 cracked open the door.

Buzzzz. An escort passed by the door

T23 jerked back and took a breath, then another, building up the nerve. "Here I go." T23 bolted across the passage and down the hallway leading to Bio-Recycling. The rait hurried in, but was surprised anew.

Med bots, hovering over the lifeless raits, were disassembling them with mechanical precision. The high-pitched whir of saws cut through the silence, slicing bone, while thin blades peeled back layers of muscle and sinew. The metallic stench of blood hung in the air, mingling with the sharp odor of antiseptic. A warm glob of blood splattered onto T23's jumpsuit. The Engineer stared at it, frozen, watching it seep into the fabric as a spreading stain. Panic clenched T23's gut. The rait scrubbed frantically at the spot, trying to erase what couldn't be unseen. A lurch crawled up the throat, threatening to gush. Without another glance at the grim work, T23 stumbled forward and pushed through the far door, desperate to escape the carnage.

Stepping into a central lobby, T23 paused momentarily. The space felt unnervingly sterile, lit by the cold glare of overhead panels. The Engineer pressed on, moving swiftly past a bank of lifts and through a set of heavy double doors. Beyond them lay another chamber—a Bio-Assembly room. T23 halted, eyes widening. Six large incubators lined the far wall, each containing a body suspended in a translucent liquid. Air bubbles drifted lazily around the floating figures. A realization struck like a shockwave: An Arc was far more than a simple habitat.

The Engineer ran to the next door, then another, soon reaching the central passageway. Nothing in sight. T23 darted across to the North Lift lobby, entered, climbed into the maintenance shaft, and descended to Ring 7.

The Engineer raced to the Welcome Center's Cleansing Room. Two newbies were attending to their hygiene needs, oblivious to T23's presence. The two raits were running their mouths about their DOM scores.

"I'm going to start with the blondes," one rait said.

"I prefer the tall ones," the other rait giggled.

"How about tall and blonde?"

"Now you're talkin.'"

T23 slid along the bulkhead, staying low to avoid being seen. Their jumpsuits hung on a couple of hooks just ahead. After inching forward a few more steps, T23 snatched the clothing and retreated along the wall, slipping back through the door. Once clear, the Engineer hurried to the shaft and ascended quickly to Ring 6, opting for the faster, more direct route. T23 dashed down the central passage, passing a few escort bots and residents who smiled as they passed, their expressions radiating a blissful ignorance.

T23 burst into the Stasis Habitat.

"*Aaaah*," T42 yelped. "I almost wet myself."

"Sorry. How are our patients?"

"They're ready. Both are at 36.38 degrees." T42's face drained. "Hey, there's blood on your jumpsuit."

"It's from that room with those machines."

"You went back in there?"

"Yep, big mistake. I'll explain later."

T23 cyberpathically activated the wake command. The torpor berths began to empty, ridding themselves of their liquid preservative. When finished, an internal platform raised the bodies to the container's top.

T42 grabbed a hose and rinsed A92, washing away any residual amniotic fluid. Once cleaned, T23 detached EKG leads, urine, and feces lines, and the tunneled central venous catheter attached to A92's chest, but had to work at the catheter until it slipped out. T23 dressed A92's wound with a regenerative patch. Finally, T23 removed the intranasal cooling and warming lines and initiated the wake stimulant. The two Engineers repeated the process with A81.

A92 was the first to stir, coughing and sputtering. The Administrator tried to speak, but nothing came out.

"Let me help you." T23 took hold of A92's arm.

A92 crawled from the berth and, in a hoarse-throated growl, asked, "What did you do to me?"

"You're on Arc 94," T23 said. "You're a patient."

A92's eyes narrowed. "I'm where?"

"Sorry, I need to help 81."

A81 woke and spewed out a lung's worth of amniotic gel. "What the—"

"No time to explain," T23 said. "Do you know what happened to A12?"

A81 wiped off a spot of dribble running down the chin. "Something happened to 12?"

"Never mind. Put these on. We need to get out of here."

"I'm not a banana," A92 said, wobbling a bit and scowling at the yellow jumpsuits.

"You're not on Arc 83," T23 said. "You're on Arc 94. Put it on."

"Right," A92 grumbled. "But I'm not a banana."

The two Engineers helped the two dazed faits slide on their jumpsuits. They labored to balance, inserting arms and legs and zipping up.

T42 whispered to T23. "They're too weak to climb down the shaft."

"Whose shaft?" A92 chuckled. "Are we still discussing bananas?"

"I have a plan," T23 said. "Resident Lift."

"You and your plans," T42 muttered. "This should go well."

"Lead the way," A92 commanded. "And be quick about it. I have things to do."

"Listen up," T23 said. "It's crucial we look like we belong. So just *act normal.*"

"You hear that, mait?" A92 said. "T23 wants me to act normal."

A81 spit out another glob of amniotic gel. "That'll be the day."

T23 and T42 took hold of the two loopy raits and helped them to the door and down the passage. The two Engineers glanced at one another as A81 and A92 staggered and stumbled, doing their best not to draw attention. The four were almost to the resident lift when Sv07 and Sφ10 approached from the opposite direction. They were engaged in a conversation. The four raits looked down to avoid eye contact.

When they passed, Sφ10 glanced at T23 and did a double-take. "Where are your escorts?"

The four ignored the Sophists and kept walking.

Sφ10 whirled around. "Residents, where are your escorts? Please respond."

The four raits, pretending not to hear, picked up their pace, turned the corner, rushed to a lift, and stepped on board.

As they did, the Sophists rounded the corner. This time, however, Sφ10 locked onto T23, appearing to recognize the rait. The Sophist's surprised stare projected alarm, but fortunately, the doors closed before the Council member could act.

• • • •

The lift doors opened on Ring 20, and the four raits hurried off, but after a few steps, T23 stopped. "We can't go to our poly. That's the first place they'll look."

"What about Ecology?" A81 said. "I have access."

"You're on a different Arc," T42 said.

"Worth the try." T23 motioned in that direction. "Let's go!"

The four raced across the Core to a cargo lift. Surprisingly, the doors opened, and down they went to Ring 24. The raits searched for a place to hide. The tropical greenhouse was their best bet, given its thick foliage. After tramping up and down a dozen or so rows, they found the perfect proverbial sweet spot in a corner, surrounded by papaya, sugar cane, melons, and an assortment of other tropical delights. The four ducked in behind the lush plants and flopped on the deck.

"That was fun," A92 said noisily.

"*Shhh*." T23 held a finger up to the mouth. "They might hear you."

"Bollocks." A92 reached up and steadied a lingering wobble with a grip on the nearest worktable. "Now, what's this all about?"

"Do you know if A12 is okay?"

"Sorry, dear, news to me."

"Is it possible to stow away on a cargo transport?"

"Stow away! You're a crazy one, aren't you?"

"That's what I've been saying," T42 remarked.

"Can we, yes or no?" T23 asked.

"Yes, perhaps. If I had access to the TAS."

"TAS?" T42 questioned.

"Transportation Administration System," A92 said. "It lists what's coming and going. It's in Log Ops on Ring 30."

"Then that's where we're going," T23 said.

"You never answered my question." A92 leered at T23.

"I'm going back to Arc 83. Would you like to come along?"

"And why would we do that?"

"Someone's in love," T42 smirked.

"Blimey. With A12? We all knew that. Just didn't want to say anything and embarrass the two of you lovebirds."

"Really?" T23 looked confused.

"It was sort of obvious, friend," A81 mused.

"Well, if you want to tag along, I'm going to find A12 and say exactly how I feel—don't care who hears it."

"I've got to see this," A92 chuckled. "I'm in."

"If Petunia's going, I'm going," A81 said.

"All right then. Let's go." T23 jumped up.

The others followed, but as they slipped from their hideout, faint mechanical hums echoed through the greenways. Security bots had entered Ecology, scanning for bioheat signatures.

"I hear something," A92 whispered.

"Bots!" A81 hissed.

"They're searching for us." T42 peeked over a row of *Passiflora edulis*—passion fruit—then ducked. "We're done for."

"We have to move." T23 motioned for the others to stay low.

The four crept along the rows, crouched beneath hanging vines and leaves.

They reached an opening. No sign of movement. T23 gave the signal.

They sprinted across.

Behind them, metal limbs clacked to life. A security bot swiveled. An alarm sounded from its speaker as it gave chase. Other Gammas followed.

"Run!" A92 shouted, nearly tripping on irrigation lines as the group burst into a seed production lab.

Their footsteps boomed through the corridor. Lights flickered on as motion sensors triggered. T23 and T42 dashed beneath an overhead door, gritting teeth as they yanked it down—metal grinding against metal.

A thud. Then another. Bots ramming from the other side.

Ahead, A81 and A92 darted through bins of seed stock, flinging carts behind them to slow the pursuit.

But the first door wasn't sealed in time. A mechanical claw pried through. One bot squeezed inside, then another—optics scanning, locking on.

T23 grabbed a nearby basket of tomatoes and hurled them toward the bots. Juiced explosions hit the lead bot square in the faceplate, causing it to reel with a high-pitched whine.

"Not enough!" T42 shouted, grabbing a nearby hose. A blast of water punched out, striking the lead bot in the chest. Sparks flew. The machine staggered back.

But another bot pushed forward.

"More!" T23 twisted the valve full open. The hose roared. Water slammed into the next wave, forcing them back in a crackle of steam and electricity.

The raits seized the moment. They tore through the lab's central corridor and into the main lobby.

T23 spun, grabbed the final overhead door, and slammed it down. A final clang echoed as the bots rammed against the sealed entrance.

"We need a diversion," T42 said, bolting to the lift.

"Where you goin'?" T23 shouted. "We can take the maintenance shaft!"

"You can. I'm going down this lift as far as it'll go." T42 ran back and threw arms around T23, followed by a hard kiss. "I wish I was A12. You're right about that word. Good luck, my friend."

A tear slipped down the cheek. Then T42 pulled away and sprinted for the lift.

"Wait—" T23 shouted.

T42 waved goodbye and stepped onboard. The doors closed.

T23 stared in dismay.

"We have to go." A81 tugged on T23's arm.

"I know, I know."

The three raits raced across the lobby to the next door. This time, it was the Herb Greenhouse. Scents of thyme, basil, and lemongrass filled their nostrils. A92, of course, had to stop and smell a row of bergamot.

A81 grabbed A92 by the arm. "You coming, Petunia?"

The trio hurried into the String Greenhouse. It, too, was filled with plants whose structures stood tall—like pencil-thin trees covered in a bounty of edible delights. They dashed down a row of *Cucumis sativus*—cucumbers— arriving at the North Lift and the maintenance shaft. They entered and began descending, headed for Ring 30.

• • • •

The lift awaited a command. T42 wiped away another tear and glanced at the display, where an unfamiliar option caught the eye—*R-61*. On impulse, T42 selected it. The conveyance began its descent, plunging into the depths of the Arc.

With each passing second, a warmth spread through T42's chest, a pulse of unexpected joy. T23 had spoken of love—an elusive, forbidden feeling. And now, at this moment, T42 felt it, too. Overwhelming. Defiant. A bright light, just as T23 had said.

A smile tugged at T42's lips, eyes shimmering. Somebody to hold close. Somebody to love, tomorrow and forever. How wonderful it could have been— so wonderful indeed. But T23 would always remain, forever alive in memory, forever in T42's heart.

A bell chimed. The lift doors parted.

T42 stepped onto a spiraling metal gangway, the air thick with the heat of machines. A placard read *R-61*—a ring raits knew little of, nor did they care to. Those who mentioned it did so offhandedly, calling it a dark, forgotten place, the bowels of the Arc, unfit for residents.

T42 approached the railing. The depths plunged beyond sight. At its core, a massive machine pulsed—slow, deliberate, alive.

A security bot locked onto the rait.

T42 spun, heart pounding, and hurried down the gangway—only to find another bot blocking the path.

"Let me by."

"This is a restricted area, resident," the bot twanged.

"Why are you bothering me? Get out of my way."

T42 feinted right. The bot mirrored the movement.

"I said, get out of the way!"

A shove.

A mechanical claw shot out—just missing T42's arm.

With a sharp inhale, T42 darted left, vaulted over the railing, and landed on a narrow beam spanning the abyss.

The security bots advanced, buzzing and bleeping, claws extending. "Stop, resident. Danger, danger. Stop!"

T42 inched along the metal plank. Another bot approached from the opposite side. Trapped.

A desperate swipe—

A misstep—

Weightless, falling—

The void swallowed the rait whole.

Thirteen seconds. A dull thud.

If anyone had been there to hear it.

• • • •

T23, A81, and A92 had made it to Logistics on Ring 30 and the Log Ops Center. A92 activated the TAS and accessed its latest report. A cargo transport would arrive at 0430 hours from A1958 and depart at 0500 for A1983. Logistic bots would stage sixteen 12.2 meter unit load devices (ULD) at Bay 2 and load at stations B2-17 to B2-32.

"This is what we need," A92 said. "Let's go."

T23, A81, and A92 exited Log Ops and headed for the warehouse.

The trio stepped out of the maintenance shaft onto a gangway overlooking a massive depot. Industrial-sized logistic bots roared about, carting tons of supplies and equipment. A92 was familiar with the warehouse's layout from the TAS, but this was the first time the Logistics Administrator had seen it in action. It was a labyrinth of efficiency, bots roaring, passing, and maneuvering like quantum particles inseparably linked and in perfect unison.

"There to the right." A92 pointed to warehouse rows 1 to 48.

The group dashed along the steel walkway to a ladder leading to the warehouse deck. One at a time, they climbed down and darted to a protected corner surrounded by piles of dusty inventory.

"We need to find Sequence ID A3I24S6L1B," A92 said. "Look for Aisle 24. The numbers are on the racks."

T23 glanced upward. "We're at 13."

The group dashed past 14 and 15, but a rather sizeable D-Class bot toting a massive cargo load came barreling down the aisle—the three raits dove under a rack. The bot roared by.

A92 glanced at A81. "That was close."

The Inspector had a similar wide-eyed gaze.

The trio scrambled out and resumed their search.

"Aisle 24." A81 pointed at a rack label.

They hurried down the row.

"Look for Section 6," A92 remarked.

"To the right." T23 pointed. "This is it."

Three orange shipping cases sat at ground level. A81 and T23 opened one, removed its contents, inspected the vented slits along its sides, and glanced inside. Its empty cavity was just large enough for a rait.

T23 ran a hand along the casing. "This should do."

A92 peered inside, eyes widening. "You've got to be kidding. My knees will be in my face."

A81 hugged A92. "I'll see you on the other side, Petunia."

"I hope you have something to pry me out." A92 exhaled reluctantly and climbed in.

A81 shut the lid and pushed the case back into position.

T23 and A81 rolled out a second case and repeated the process—less the hug. Then it was T23's turn, who, after climbing in, had to push and pull on a rack beam until the case was back in its proper position. The rait dropped down and sealed the lid.

Sometime later—perhaps an hour—a logistics bot rolled up to the three shipping cases. The pick order specified delivery to ULD B2-26. Large yet nimble, the Delta-class bot extracted the cases and carted them to the station. Other bots worked in tandem, loading goods and supplies until the container was full. A final bot sealed it shut.

Ten minutes passed. A horn blared. Bay 2 doors lumbered open, revealing the early morning sky.

Alice announced, "Condition Blue alert. Supply Transport One Niner One Niner arriving from Arc One Niner Five Eight at Bay Two. Stand by."

In the pre-dawn blackness, a cargo vessel approached Arc1994, its repulsers and oscillators humming as they guided it into the open bay. Upon landing, the vessel's doors hissed apart. Automated systems engaged, grappling and extracting sixteen ULDs from its hold. Within minutes, bots replaced them with sixteen more—including B2-26. Metallic clamps hammered down from bow to stern, locking the cargo in place for the journey ahead.

At 0500, a horn blared, and Alice announced, "Condition Blue. Supply Transport One Niner One Niner departing Bay Two for Arc One Niner Eight Three."

Once clear of the Arc, T-AK1919 throttled up, jetting to 10,973 meters and settling into a cruising speed of 1,288 kilometers per hour. Barring adverse weather or turbulence, the vessel would arrive on schedule.

Deep within the speeding transport, a stowaway sat in the darkness. A92 wriggled and squirmed, searching in vain for a position that might bring comfort—or at least calm. But there was only blackness. Impenetrable. Even a hand inches from the face vanished into the void.

As the silence stretched on, unease crept in. What if the air ran out? What if the lid was locked? What if—

Knees pulled tight to the chest, A92 focused on the rhythmic in-and-out of each breath, counting the seconds between them. Sweat beaded on the brow. The heart pounded so fiercely it threatened to burst through the ribs. Each desperate thought whispered: "*Please, just let me breathe.*"

Time crawled. The air grew hot and stale. Breath after breath, the lungs strained, each inhale forced by sheer will, each exhale escaping like a plea. A92 pressed against the lid—it wouldn't budge. Cargo must be stacked on top.

Legs cramped as panic seeped in. Heat gnawed at the nerves. An urge to scream, to pound the walls, surged. But there was no escape—no control, no reprieve. Only time and distance.

Inhale. Exhale. In. Out. In. Out.

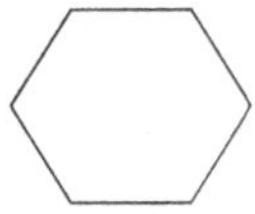

CHAPTER NINETEEN

ANOTHER CEREMONY

Somewhere east of Apehkv, Yahola led the failed expedition back to the village. Regrettably, its purpose had changed from a scouting party to a funeral procession.

By dusk, the expedition had reached the outskirts of the village. At first, the inhabitants were gleeful, running to greet the warriors. But soon, word spread a few had not returned, and one had met his fate.

The returning warriors carried defeat in their eyes. Some stared at the ground, others scowled at the distant hills. None smiled. None spoke. Most drifted to their dwellings in search of solace.

The four pallbearers bore the body to the busk grounds. Mothers and wives gathered, not knowing who but fearing the worst. They stared at the blanket-covered body and held their children.

Among them stood Halona and Dela, motionless. Afraid to look. Afraid to breathe.

Yahola walked beside the body, as he should, but kept his eyes from Dela. If she saw his face, she would know.

The villagers gathered, murmuring, anxious for the truth.

The pallbearers lowered the stretcher to the ground.

Yahola turned to Dela; their eyes met. "Our son was brave."

Her breath hitched. She stared at the lifeless shape, eyes wide, lips parted in silent denial—until the silence shattered. A scream tore from her throat as she rushed forward.

She yanked back the blanket.

Gasps rippled through the crowd.

Her trembling hands cupped the face she had once kissed goodnight. The face that would never wake again.

Dela collapsed, wailing, her grief too great for her body to hold. Her child had gone beyond her arms to a place she could not follow.

Yahola knelt beside her, arms reaching, hoping to hold her pain. But sorrow was a thing beyond grasp.

Surrounded by the crowd, some wept, others seethed, and a few stared, too stunned to react. Yahola pulled Dela away from Cekote, and the four pallbearers lifted the stretcher and carried the body to her home. The mother and father followed, Dela stumbling as if the weight of her grief had drained the strength from her limbs.

Sadness and alarm spread throughout the village. Besides Cekote, twelve others were missing and feared dead. A few, however, refused to believe it. The Echaswvlke's skill in battle was unmatched—if all twelve had indeed fallen, then their enemy was more formidable than anyone had dared imagine.

• • • •

The four pallbearers entered Dela's home, their footsteps heavy with the weight of loss. They gently lifted Cekote from the stretcher and laid him on his bed—a cradle of soft pelts and blankets, all crafted by his mother's hands.

Dela, her heart broken, began her motherly duties. She removed the wet blanket, the splint that held his leg, and his damp clothing, each movement measured and slow. The fire crackled nearby as she stoked it, drawing warmth to heat the water she would use to cleanse him.

When the water was ready, Dela started with Cekote's head and hair, her hands trembling with tenderness. She worked slowly down his torso, her fingers moving with a reverence only a mother could possess. She reached his feet and toes, remembering how she had once bathed him as a child, her eyes welling with tears. How long had it been since then? The ache of the past echoed in each movement, in the brush of her hands against his skin.

As Dela bathed his broken leg, her touch was soft, careful—she could not bring herself to cause him any more pain, even in death. Once cleansed, she dressed him in his finest clothing: a deerskin mantle, breechcloth, leggings, and moccasins, all made by her hand, all symbols of her love and care.

With each motion, Dela seemed to stitch together the pieces of a life lost, but the finality of it all only seemed to deepen her sorrow.

Dela carefully placed a Fuswvlke shell pendant around his neck, its design—a whirling sun surrounded by a breath scroll and four pileated woodpecker heads facing counter-clockwise—gleaming faintly in the dim light. With steady hands, she adorned his long black hair with strings, beads, and feathers, just as he had liked. Each delicate addition marked the love she had woven into his life, but was now woven into his final moments.

As custom dictated, the family would watch over Cekote for four suns. The People believed that the spirit lingered with the body briefly after death, a time for both the living and the departed to honor the transition. This tradition reflected their understanding of consciousness and the natural world—a harmony of forces, both seen and unseen. Their beliefs were rooted in the cycles of nature: the four seasons, four heavenly bodies, four cardinal directions, and the four elements—earth, wind, fire, and water. Each of these, they believed, interacted with and complemented the others, creating a perfect equilibrium—a supreme balance of life and death.

There was a knock at the door. It was Hasse Ola, Cekote's best friend and the first to visit to show respect. "May I see my brother? I bring a gift."

"Yes, you may." Yahola motioned for the young man to enter. "His mother welcomes your presence."

Hasse Ola stepped inside as Dela finished with Cekote's hair.

He knelt beside her. Cekote's lifeless body was stiff and gray. The two boys had been the same age, fifteen, and both were tall and gangly, but Cekote was the tallest. His paternal grandfather had been a member of the Wind Clan, whose people had been naturally tall since ancient times.

As he stared at his friend, anger and shame festered. In Cekote's still form, he saw himself instead—an impossible thought, yet one he couldn't shake. He had stayed behind, safe in his mother's home, a memory difficult to reconcile.

Hasse Ola pulled out a sheathed flint knife and placed it on the buckskin blanket beside Cekote. This heirloom had once belonged to Hasse Ola's paternal grandfather, the Mekko. It was Hasse Ola's most prized possession and now belonged to Cekote. He would need it on his journey across the Milky Way, past the spirit river, and upward into the spirit world.

There was another knock at the door. Mausi stood in the dim light, clutching a bouquet of wildflowers. She had come to mourn Cekote and to stand with her big brother, whom she loved with all her heart. Where he went, she followed, and if he was sad, she was sad.

Silently, Mausi stepped inside and sat beside Hasse Ola and Dela. She placed the flowers next to Cekote, reached into her medicine pouch, and withdrew a red sabīa crystal. With gentle hands, she leaned over his body and tucked the crystal into his pouch. Tradition held that only the Medicine Maker could open a medicine pouch, but Mausi was the tribe's youngest angel, and her blessing carried a weight beyond custom.

Hasse Ola wrapped an arm around his sister, pulling her close. They sat in quiet vigil, sharing grief, sharing a kindred warmth as time passed.

Outside, the sun slipped beyond the horizon, and darkness settled over the village. The moon, new and unseen, hid its face from the night, waiting to rise with the dawn. It would be a long, empty night.

• • • •

The next morning, the sun crested over the Great Hills, its light bringing neither warmth nor cheer—only sorrow and unease. It was the first sun of the wake, a time for mourning and preparation, and perhaps the first step toward war.

At Yahola's summons, the council gathered at the busk. Hasse Ola was the first to arrive, his heart burning with the need for action—revenge for Cekote's death.

Once all were present, Yahola raised a hand for silence. "Menawa has asked that we prepare for war. We must gather our crops, hunt for meat, and fortify our defenses."

"The Fuswvlke will see to the wall," Tomucece answered. "The Hotvlkvlke must honor our fallen warrior before taking up the bow."

"*Mvto*," Yahola replied in thanks, his gaze sweeping the gathered men. "Who speaks for the Echaswvlke in Talof Harjo's absence?"

"I do," Hasse Ola said, his voice steady. "Our warriors will hunt, and our women will gather the crops. If an enemy comes, we will avenge our brother's death."

A murmur of approval rippled through the council.

"The Nokovlke will stand with you, young warrior," Ottase Matlah said, giving Hasse Ola a firm nod.

"*Mvto*," Yahola acknowledged. "I fear the enemy will scout our village. We must all remain vigilant."

"What if it strikes before we are ready?" Hasse Ola asked.

Yahola studied him. "A warrior must always be ready. Do you not have feet, hands, and teeth?"

Hasse Ola squared his shoulders. "Then I am ready."

The council members voiced their approval, their praise carrying weight.

"Then let us see to our duties," Yahola said, ending the council.

The clans returned to their duties, the most pressing, reinforcing the logged palisade—the village's defensive wall. This structure met Wewoka Creek to the north, ran in a semicircle around the village, and rejoined the creek to the south. The two watchtowers also needed repair: one situated along the north wall and the other on the south.

As the Fuswvlke worked on the palisade, the Echaswvlke hunted game such as white-tailed deer, wild turkey, squirrels, and rabbits. Hasse Ola urged the women to harvest any remaining crops, even those needing a few more days on the vine. The villagers would leave nothing for the enemy to pillage or destroy.

Hasse Ola and two Echaswvlke warriors stood guard while the women attended to their chores. Hasse Ola paced back and forth along the field's boundaries, his gaze fixed on the forest for any signs of an enemy or his father's return. Sadness and a thirst for revenge occupied every thought. It was difficult to comprehend that Cekote was dead. His heart ached, yet his blood boiled with anger. If he had gone on the patrol, Cekote might still be alive. Shame washed over him. Somehow, he needed to demonstrate his courage; more importantly, he needed to prove he had what it took to be a warrior.

Wiping the sweat from his brow, Hasse Ola glanced to the west, where a group of warriors worked tirelessly, cutting down trees, trimming limbs, hardening their bases with fire, and dragging them toward the wall. The palisade loomed almost three times a man's height, but over time, nature had caused the logs to rot and decay. The warriors would have to replace all that needed attention. The chore would take several days.

Hasse Ola paced the field's edge, scanning the tree line, then the village, then back to the trees. The women worked in silence, filling baskets with squash and beans. Usually, they gossiped and laughed, but today, their voices had gone quiet—except for one.

"What are you doing?" Mausi ran up to her brother, breathless.

"Guarding our people," he said, eyes still on the forest.

"Will you help me pick flowers?"

"Go find your friends or help Mother."

Mausi's face fell. "I don't have any friends. They say I'm too young and won't play with me. I want to stay with you." She wrapped her arms around his waist.

Hasse Ola sighed, gently pried her arms away, and crouched to meet her gaze. "I have responsibilities now. I'm a warrior, and you're a child. If you do what I ask, I'll tell you a story after supper."

Her eyes brightened. "What kind of story?"

"How about the one where Rabbit tricks Otter?"

"I like that one."

"I know you do. Now, go to Mother."

She hesitated, then looked up at him, wide brown eyes full of trust. "I love you."

Hasse Ola's expression softened. "I love you too, little bear." He pulled her into a firm hug.

Mausi grinned and ran off, her small feet kicking up dust. Hasse Ola watched her go, a heaviness settling in his chest. Then, with a steadying breath, he turned back to his watch.

• • • •

Another night passed. For Yahola, it had been long and restless. The Clan Leader emerged from his dwelling as the morning light crested over the Great Hills, signaling the wake's second sun.

The Hotvlkvlke bore the somber responsibility of preparing the burial house. A square-shaped structure crafted of wattle and daub covered by a steeply pitched thatched roof, it sat atop a grass-covered earthen mound on the village's western side. Wooden steps led to its entrance.

Yahola climbed the steps and entered the burial house. Its walls were aligned with the four cardinal directions. The People had adorned its interior with carvings of spirit beasts, animistic artifacts, and celestial adornments, representing the four clans and the four heavenly bodies: the Stars, Earth, Sun, and Moon. Yahola inspected its readiness. All seemed in good order. He found the grave of Cekote's maternal grandmother, a testament to the matrilineal heritage of the Fuswvlke. Next to it, he marked the ground with four arrows, designating the spot for his son's gravesite.

• • • •

While Yahola and the Wind Clan labored on the sacred mound, Dela remained steadfast by her son's side. Visitors came and went, offering their respects, their words of comfort falling into the hollow space her grief had carved. Though many tried to ease her burden, none succeeded.

Halona, however, never left. She wept with Dela, holding her hand and whispering memories of happier times. Many moons had passed since the village last mourned a death. The elders had gone naturally, their passing expected, but neither disease nor accident had claimed another—certainly not one so young.

Guilt gnawed at Halona. Her son had stayed home, while Dela's had met his fate fulfilling his duty. Dela had sacrificed everything. Halona, nothing. That truth would forever weigh between them, altering their bond in ways neither could yet understand.

With one arm around Dela, Halona sat in silent mourning, her gaze fixed on Cekote's cold, lifeless form. They would endure this sorrow together, yet Dela's anguish ran deeper than words could reach—beyond understanding, beyond comfort.

As night fell, darkness blanketed the land, the sky black as pitch beneath the New Moon. The village lay silent and still, save for the sentries standing watch, their eyes fixed on the unseen threats lurking beyond the trees. In their care rested dozens of earthen dwellings, where mothers nurtured their families, fed their children, and honored their husbands. Yet, in the grand design of the cosmos, their village was but a flicker in the void—hidden in a remote forest, on a small blue planet, lost in an endless expanse.

• • • •

Menawa and his three warriors spotted the village as the sun rose and cast its light. In a few hundred paces, they would be home.

When they reached the village's outer boundary, two warriors, manning an observation post hidden beneath a cluster of bushes, signaled to Menawa.

The Mekko acknowledged their beckon and continued to the village. Menawa noticed women harvesting crops in the field, others casting nets in the creek, and a band of warriors working on the palisade. This meant one thing. Yahola was preparing for war.

A familiar whoop sounded. It was Hasse Ola, running to greet his father.

"Father, you've returned."

"Yes, my son," Menawa tousled his son's long black hair.

"Mother will be happy to see you. She's strong, but her eyes tell me she misses you."

"How is the village?"

"We are preparing for war. We will avenge Cekote's death."

"Cekote is dead?"

"My brother died on his journey home. His father has blood in his heart, and rightly so. You and I will help him kill those who have killed Cekote."

"Run, tell your mother I've returned, and ask Yahola to gather the Council."

Hasse Ola sprinted away.

Menawa's heart sank. He would have to deliver more bad news about Talof Harjo and the Echaswvlke. The village would not take this lightly, and would possibly question his role as Mekko.

Menawa entered the village and headed straight for the busk. When he arrived, the Council was waiting. Each member came forward and gave the customary greeting. The Council took their seats.

Menawa spoke, "Hasse Ola told me of Cekote's death. Were you attacked?"

"It was his broken leg." Yahola's eyes remained fixed on the ground. "Tomorrow, his spirit will begin its journey."

"Your son was a brave warrior. We will honor his sacrifice."

"We will avenge his death." Yahola struck the ground with his fist.

Ottase Matlah leaned forward. "Do you have news of Talof Harjo?"

Menawa turned to the Nokovlke's second leader. "We found a path leading toward the Great Hills. We followed it until a spirit wall blocked our way. We spotted a war club. It belonged to the Echaswvlke."

Council members began to chatter. Their faces indicated concern and displeasure.

Menawa raised a hand to silence the gathering.

"Did you see the Dark Spirit?" Tomucece asked.

"We found a *cheaha* and saw beyond the Great Hills. We spotted a tall structure; it was as high as the clouds. It must be the Dark Spirit's home."

More grumbling erupted.

Menawa again raised a hand; however, compliance was a little slower.

Yahola declared, "I have done as you asked, Mekko. It seems we have awakened this Dark Spirit."

"We should not have sought its nest," Tomucece echoed. "We have brought death upon our village."

The grumbles turned into dissents and protests. Members were becoming angry. Menawa was losing control.

"*Makēkot!*—enough!" Menawa shouted. "Cekote's death was not the act of the Dark Spirit."

"How do you explain the loss of Talof Harjo and his warriors," Yahola sneered at the Mekko. "Twelve families are without fathers, husbands, and brothers!"

Menawa shifted his weight and clenched his teeth; a twinge shot through his mouth—a reminder of his sore tooth. He reached up and rubbed his jaw, then addressed his comrades. "Hear me, brothers. Now is not the time for blame but for vigilance and preparedness. The Echaswvlke are strong and brave. We must have faith they will return."

"My son returned," Yahola snarled. "He's dead."

Menawa pulled a war club from his belt and held it high. "We are the People. If this Dark Spirit finds our village, Hesaketvmese will guide us to victory!"

"Whoop, whoop, whoop," the Council members shouted.

Menawa stood. "Let us see to our duties." The Mekko left the Council.

• • • •

Around the village, warriors, women, and children were doing their best to complete their duties. The men had finished repairs to the logged palisade. The women had gathered the crops, and the children kept busy, their playful antics bringing occasional smiles to their mothers' faces and momentarily easing their concerns.

As the day's light faded on the wake's third sun, villagers gathered at the busk and found their seats in their respective arbors. Menawa signaled, and the ceremony commenced.

A group of warriors, led by Owlelo, began the ceremony with a stomp dance. Their faces were painted half white and half black, symbolizing the People's belief in the duality of the soul. According to tradition, *Puyvfekcv*, the free soul, was born in the heavens and depicted by white; it resided in the heart, embodying memory, free will, and wisdom. In contrast, *Yafiktca*, the life soul or ghost, emerged from the earth, represented by black; it resided in the intestines, embodying movement, appetite, desire, and the duality of good and evil.

Moreover, the People believed the free soul originated from the stars and returned when the body died, finding an entry marked by an eye in a hand hanging from a belt of three stars. After passing this gateway, the free soul would travel across the Milky Way along the spirit road, hoping to discover a bright star—a fork in the path of souls. There, the soul would attempt to cross a log, spanning a spirit river, and avoid the Eagle. If the warrior had been honorable, the Eagle would permit the soul to pass and continue westward to join family and friends. Hesaketvmese would reward the soul with joy and happiness. However, if villainy had consumed the warrior during his earthly years, the Eagle would prevent the soul from passing and banish it to a land of thickets and thorns, lacking good hunting and women; the reward was eternal misery and pain.

As the ceremony progressed, friends and family gathered to share stories of Cekote's life and adventures. They also participated in a purification ritual, washing their hands, feet, and faces with a medicine drink, thereby safeguarding their health in the presence of the deceased. Hasse Ola shared a story about when he and Cekote had gone hunting for squirrels. They had killed three but, desiring more, left the squirrels hanging in the fork of a sapling. Having no further luck, they returned, but the squirrels were gone. Apparently, something else in the forest liked squirrel meat.

After another story or two, Yahola, the tribe's medicine maker and the Mekko's tongue, said a final prayer. "Great Spirit, with heavy hearts, we bid farewell to our beloved Cekote. As he journeys to the spirit world, may he find solace in your eternal light. Grant him peace and tranquility in the warmth and embrace of his ancestors. We cherish the memories of his time on Mother Earth and hold them close in our hearts. Great Spirit, please receive our son with open arms and guide him gently to his resting place. *Hvtvm cehecares—I will see you again.*"

• • • •

On the morning of the fourth sun, as the cool air whispered through the tall grass surrounding the sacred mound, Hasse Ola and three others climbed the planked steps and entered the burial house. In the spot marked by the four arrows, the young warriors began to dig Cekote's grave. Hasse Ola clawed and scratched at the dirt as tears rolled down his face. He and the others remained silent. It was a time for reverence. The smell of earth and death wafted through his nose as he completed his morbid chore. When he and the others had finished, the hole was four feet deep by four feet wide. They would guard the gravesite until Cekote arrived.

• • • •

At noon, the villagers gathered for the final service at the busk. Cekote's body was placed atop a small wooden platform in its center. Owlelo led another stomp dance, warriors consumed medicine drinks, and Yahola spoke a few last words.

Afterward, four warriors lifted Cekote's corpse and carried it to the burial house. The villagers followed. Once inside, the pallbearers gently placed his remains in the hole, in a sitting position, with his legs tucked under the body.

Yahola and Dela approached the grave. The mother wrapped Cekote's body in a blanket and painted his face with clan and tribal symbols. The mother and father placed bowls of Cekote's favorite food in the hole, along with a few cherished possessions. He would need these on his journey to the spirit world. One was a collection of rocks he had gathered around the village and along the creek, including a blood-red gem the size of an acorn. Another was a small wooden figure his father had carved of a great, hairy beast with two mammoth-sized tusks, and a third was a little milkweed basket he had made for his mother when he was five years old.

Two women from Dela's clan approached the grave; they surrounded Cekote's body with river cane and tied the stalks in a hoop above his head. When they finished, Hasse Ola and his three companions covered the canes with a thick layer of white clay.

As a final handshake, friends and family picked up handfuls of dirt and threw it into the hole, each saying, *"Hvtvm cehecares—I will see you again."* The People did not believe in saying goodbye; death was not the end of life's journey but a transition to the next world.

The grave filled, each handful a testament to the weight of the People's loss. Dela, unable to control her emotions, threw herself upon the earthen mass and wept and wailed. Cekote had been her only child, her boy, and with his passing, it felt as though her identity had been torn away. Yahola knelt beside her, his sorrow etched deeply into his features. The weight of the Mekko's failed strategy bore heavily upon him, casting a dark shadow over his soul.

$$\bullet \ \bullet \ \bullet \ \bullet$$

A day or so after the burial, beyond the village's perimeter, a Clan Leader stirred. Eyes closed, he awoke to darkness, caught between a state of hypnosis and full consciousness. A bee buzzed past his nose. The hum of gnats filled the air. The heat bore down as the midday sun pressed against his skin, sweat beading on his brow. Shielding his eyes, he blinked into the brightness. He lay in a grassy field. Sitting up, he rubbed his head—how had he come to be here? His body and clothing were unscathed. A large, bottle-shaped calabash hung from his neck, its pine needle lid tightly sealed. He opened it. Inside, seeds rustled.

Talof Harjo scrambled to his feet. A few paces away, Ceckele lay sprawled on his back, hands full of seeds, a gourd hanging from his neck. At his feet sat a large basket overflowing with squash, beans, and sweet potatoes.

Scanning the clearing, Talof Harjo counted eleven others, all lying still. His gaze shifted to the surrounding terrain—the patrol was a thousand paces north of the village.

One by one, the others stirred, blinking into wakefulness. They staggered upright, confusion flickering across their faces. Each bore a gourd and a basket of crops, their silence heavy with unspoken questions as they gathered around their leader.

"What happened?" Malatche slurred, his words thick with grogginess.

"I think we were hunting," Talof Harjo said, though doubt lingered in his voice.

"But we have no game." Malatche glanced around. "And where did these crops come from?"

"They must be gifts from Hesaketvmese," Ceckele proclaimed.

"Or a trick," Malatche countered.

Ceckele smirked. "Perhaps Ehosa—a mystical being— visited our camp while you snored?"

Malatche's gaze darkened. "Did you do this?"

The others exchanged glances. It was the sort of thing Ceckele would do— and not for the first time.

Ceckele met their stares.

"Well?" Malatche pressed.

Ceckele grinned. "As I said, it must have been Ehosa. Though I do smell something foul... or is that you, Malatche?"

Malatche took a step forward, fists clenching, but a pair of warriors grabbed his arms before he could lunge.

Unfazed, Ceckele pointed at Anu, the youngest warrior in the clan. "Maybe he did it?"

Anu's eyes went wide. "I didn't do it! I swear!"

"Enough cackling," Talof Harjo snapped. "You two need to bury your pride. We're moving."

The patrol gathered their so-called gifts and began the short journey toward Apehkv. As they neared the settlement, a peculiar sight awaited them. Women harvesting crops halted their work and stared, eyes wide, as though they had seen a dozen ghosts returning from the spirit world. The patrol members exchanged uneasy glances, confused by the strange reception.

Talof Harjo's gaze shifted to the north gate. It was closed, with warriors stationed at the approaches. This, too, was an unsettling sight. Fear began to stir in his chest. An enemy was near. Something had happened—or was about to.

Suddenly, the north gate opened, and two warriors sprinted toward the patrol. Emestesego led the charge, with Ottase Matlah close behind.

"My brother, where have you been?" Emestesego asked as he hurried toward the Clan Leader.

"We were hunting," Talof Harjo replied.

"Hunting?" Emestesego's voice sharpened. "Why didn't you return to the rally point?"

"What rally point?"

"Did you find a passage?" Ottase Matlah asked.

"As I said, we were hunting."

Ottase Matlah chuckled. "Brother, you weren't hunting. You were searching for a passage through the Great Hills."

"This can't be true," Malatche protested, his voice laced with disbelief.

"Told you it wasn't me," Ceckele sneered.

Emestesego's brow furrowed. "You were with us on an expedition to the Great Hills. When you failed to return, Menawa ordered us back to the village. Some even believed the Dark Spirit had claimed you."

"What Dark Spirit?" Talof Harjo asked, confusion creeping into his voice.

Emestesego's face grew serious. "Something has happened. Our Mekko will want to hear this."

Talof Harjo scratched his head, staring at the forest for a long moment before giving a quick signal. The group moved toward the village, each step heavy with unspoken questions.

Villagers gathered around when the lost patrol passed through the gate. Some whispered and pointed while others cried joyfully, running to greet their loved ones.

Menawa approached the patrol and hailed Talof Harjo. "*Estonko, akitv?* Let's go to the Council House. We need to talk."

Word spread quickly of the lost patrol's return, and clan leaders rushed to the Council House to learn what had happened. Talof Harjo, his eleven warriors, Menawa, Yahola, Tomucece, Ottase Matlah, Emestesego, and many others were present.

Menawa spoke first, his voice steady. "Our brothers have returned. We must give thanks to Hesaketvmese." He clapped four times, and two warriors, bearing vessels, served *vsse*. Each warrior consumed a cup's worth, then poured another round.

"Tell us your story," Menawa said calmly.

"We were hunting," Talof Harjo replied. "We must have stopped to rest in a grassy field and fallen asleep. When we woke, seeds filled our hands, and baskets of crops sat at our feet."

"Where did you find the crops?" Menawa asked.

"We didn't. They were just there."

"Ehosa," Ceckele blurted out.

Malatche elbowed Ceckele sharply in the side. It wasn't his place to speak at a Council meeting.

"Or… the Dark Spirit," Tomucece declared, voice thick with unease.

"Did you find a passage?" Menawa asked.

"As I told Emestesego, we know nothing of a passage."

"Your patrol has been missing for several days," Menawa said.

Talof Harjo frowned. "I don't understand. We've only been gone for a day."

"The Dark Spirit must have played tricks on their minds," Yahola grumbled. "Perhaps it has played with yours as well, Mekko."

At that, Owlelo jumped to his feet, his fists clenched as he stepped toward Yahola.

Yahola rose to meet the threat. They glared at each other, neither backing down.

Menawa shot from his seat and raised a hand between them. "Please, my brothers, we are friends and family. The enemy is the aggressor, not ourselves."

Owlelo backed away, and Yahola relaxed his posture, settling back into his seat. Menawa followed suit, his face still hard with concern. "Did any of you lose a war club?"

"I did." Malatche reached for his side where the weapon should have been.

"Figures," Ceckele muttered.

Talof Harjo shot Ceckele a sharp look, a silent reminder to hold his tongue.

"We spotted it lying on the ground," Menawa continued, "beyond a strange barrier."

Tomucece straightened. "The Dark Spirit has returned our people. He has sent gifts. It is the hand of peace!"

"It's a trick," Yahola shot back, his voice low and harsh. "The food is poisoned. The enemy seeks to soften us."

Menawa's face darkened, his patience fraying. He struggled to maintain control. "Bring the baskets."

Owlelo darted from the gathering, soon returning with a group of warriors toting the twelve baskets. They set the baskets among the Council members.

Menawa walked over to the baskets and handed each member an item from its stock. The Mekko returned to his seat and took a bite of a yellow squash. He chewed down its meaty white flesh, the juice running slightly. The Council watched intently. He took more bites, trying not to flinch from the ache in his sore tooth. Menawa gestured for Yahola to do the same.

Yahola ate a handful of fresh beans, his displeasure evident.

Tomucece ate a melon, and others, in turn, consumed their share.

Menawa wiped away a spot of white pulp on the side of his mouth. "It's not poisoned."

Tomucece rose to his feet. "Talof Harjo and his warriors have returned with gifts of peace! We must celebrate."

Menawa raised a hand, silencing the room. "This may be true, but it is also true the Dark Spirit attacked us. We saw its nest beyond the Great Hills. Yahola is right to be suspicious. My brothers, if this Spirit is peaceful, we wish it no harm, but if it is an enemy, we will destroy it. For now, let us return to our duties and prepare for our destiny."

"Whoop, whoop, whoop," the gathered shouted, their voices rising in unison.

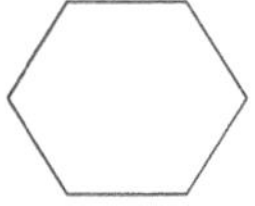

CHAPTER TWENTY

THE STOWAWAYS

A horn sounded in Arc1983's Logistic Raion. Alice's voice echoed through the speakers: "This is a Condition Blue alert. Auxiliary Cargo One Niner One Niner arriving from Arc One Niner Niner Four at Bay One. Stand by."

T-AK1919 was on schedule as it neared the Arcology. The cargo transport would dock at 0545 hours.

The ship began its descent from cruising altitude and entered final approach. A laser piloting system (LPS) locked onto the automated craft's guidance system, controlling its speed and descent for a precise landing. A few hundred meters from the Arc, the cargo bay's localizer engaged, taking over the ship's flight computer to adjust its pitch and yaw, ensuring a centerline approach.

A docking pad extended from the Arc's structure, and seconds later, the craft slowed to a hover before gently touching down. Magnetic clamps latched onto its fuselage, securing it to the landing pad.

Within moments, a horn sounded again, and the ship's onboard extraction system rolled out its sixteen 12.2-meter ULD containers.

Logistic bots rolled up, relocating the cargo to the inventory floor—rows B1-01 to B1-16. Once there, guided by sequence IDs, the bots unloaded the inventory, transported it to designated storage areas, and placed it in racks for further processing and distribution to recipients.

Unknown to the bots, a stowaway was listening to every thump and bump. T23 detected an air pressure change in the ears when a warehouse bot unloaded the small orange case from the larger ULD and carted it to its holding rack.

Believing the case had reached its terminus, T23 cracked open the lid and peeked out. The stowaway was well above ground level. T23 could almost touch the overhead, indicating the case had been placed on the highest rack. The Engineer crawled onto an adjacent pallet of supplies and scanned the area. Neither A81 nor A92 was in sight. T23 waited, hoping they would pop their heads out and reveal their location.

As time passed, T23 watched as giant orange and silver Deltas frothed and rumbled up and down aisles of inventory, sorting, picking, and delivering supplies. T23 assumed bots must still be processing 81 and 92's cases, and the pair had yet to have an opportunity to escape.

Anxious, T23 crawled across an open expanse of pallets. Every movement was measured, careful not to dislodge any items that might crash to the floor and alert the bots.

After crawling a few more cubits, T23 reached the end of the row and climbed down the rack. A quick scan confirmed it was safe. The Engineer dashed to the next row. The search began again, high and low, eyes scanning for familiar orange shipping cases or any sign of companions. The results were disappointing. T23 hurried to another row, then another, and another— nothing.

The morning passed in a blur of fruitless searching. A81 and A92's cases were nowhere in sight. The bots must have relocated them to another final delivery point. T23 could wait no longer. The search had become too dangerous. Time to proceed alone.

In a corner of the warehouse, T23 spotted a ladder leading to a gangway. T23 ran to it, climbed up, and hurried to a door. The rait cracked it open and peeked inside; it led to other passageways and doors. Hesitant to take such an exposed path, the rait scanned the warehouse for a safer egress. T23 spotted two cargo lifts, but bots were using them to deliver supplies. The Engineer crept back along the gangway, searching for other possibilities.

Across the warehouse, T23 spotted another gangway and, to the right, a ladder. The rait scrambled down to the lower deck and bolted across the busy floor, sidestepping more than once to avoid those powerful rumbling bots. After another near miss, T23 reached the ladder, climbed up, raced along the gangway, and scaled another ladder, reaching its apex.

T23 opened an overhead hatch. It was a maintenance shaft. The rait climbed in. So far, so good, but continuing to prowl around such a well-ordered Arc was risky. Moreover, T23 was now a stranger in a familiar yet unauthorized world.

The Engineer breathed in deeply. "Here we go." The rait started climbing, going past ring after ring until reaching Ring 21, Zephyrus. T23's heart jumped with excitement. A12 must be near.

The rait exited the maintenance shaft and entered the Core. T23 noticed several familiar faces, enjoying their day, but the rait sensed their stares. How would T23 find A12 without everyone recognizing this out-of-place rait? A flutter of nerves gripped the stomach, and the fear of getting caught glowed on the face like a flashing neon sign saying, *Here I am.*

A resident sitting at a bar did a double-take when T23 passed. With its lower lux levels, it was becoming clear that night might be a better time to wander around the Arc. Most residents would be in their polys and asleep, including A12. The Engineer turned and retreated to the shaft.

• • • •

It was 2200 hours. The Core lights had dimmed, leaving a well-placed strawberry moon and a constellation of tiny optics glittering like distant starlight. Most residents were in their polys at this hour, save for the few who sought late-night pleasure or thrived in the hush of darkness, drawing energy from its hue and the hum of the Arc's ever-active machinery.

T23 walked across the Core, head down to avoid eye contact. The bars were closed, but on the far left, a group of raits lingered, still in high spirits, sitting at a table, laughing quietly and whispering among themselves. One rait absentmindedly waved an empty drink container in the air, while others clapped softly to a beat only they seemed to hear. To the right, a maintenance bot buzzed by on some purposeful errand. Nearby, the swish and spurt of drip bubblers soaked the roots of a colorful bunch of biophiliads with reclaimed water.

T23 headed straight to Quad-A, but when the rait arrived, discovered an unfortunate obstacle; the portal was sealed. Perplexed, the Engineer took an involuntary step back. T23 turned, hurried to a nearby staircase, ascended to Ring 20, and found another sealed portal. On to Ring 19—the same result, then Ring 18—it too was closed.

Standing in front of the last Quad-A entrance, a voice startled T23.

"Hey, you lost?" a rait said in a prying tone.

"On my way to see a dait." T23 pivoted to see who it was.

"In Quad-A?" the meddling rait questioned.

"Yes, but I see the entrance is sealed."

"Yeah, it's been that way for some time. What are you doing outside your Raion this late at night? And what's up with your hair?"

"What do you mean? I'm from Zephyrus."

"Then why are you dressed that way?"

T23 glanced down; the jumpsuit was green rather than blue. T23 felt a hot flush of embarrassment streak across the face but quickly made up a response. "Oh, I was reassigned. I meant to say I used to live in Zephyrus. I have permission to visit."

"I recognize you. You went through the Garden Ceremony a couple of weeks ago. Why are you still here?"

"Yeah, uh, that's right. Hey, I got to go. My multi-pass is about to expire."

"Multi-pass?"

"It's a special thing, like my hair; it's experimental. Well, hey, I got to go. Have a nice evenin'."

"Yeah, same to you." The rait continued to stare, perplexed but also curious—a dangerous curiosity.

T23 smiled nervously and hurried to the nearest lift. Lacking authorization, T23 pretended to wait, appearing impatient by shuffling and bouncing on the heels. T23 glanced over a shoulder. The nosey rait had headed toward Quad-

C's portal but kept glancing back at the lost resident.

T23 put on another smile and waved.

The rait responded half-heartedly before strolling out of sight.

T23 let out a sigh of relief, turned, and bolted down three flights of steps, skipping a few along the way, headed back to Ring 21's maintenance shaft. Things had taken a wrong turn.

• • • •

It had been half an hour. The transport case had not moved. A81 peeked out. "Where am I?" The area resembled an engineering sector, its industrial machines churning, humming, hissing, and gurgling.

A81 crawled out of the case and moved between two burbling machines. "This is not good." The rait scanned the area, noting the series of pipes overhead, each with an identification placard: Oxygen (green pipe), Fire Suppression (red pipe), Potable Water (blue pipe), Compressed Air (yellow pipe), Waste (brown pipe). "This must be Life Support," A81 mumbled. The rait was several rings below Zephyrus.

A81 wandered through the plant, navigating a maze of mechanical utilities, scanning for an egress route or any sign of companions. Passing a chiller, the Inspector spotted an orange shipping case near a cluster of workstations. A81 opened it cautiously. Empty. "Just my luck." A quick glance around. No sign of A92's bright, sunny face.

The search continued. A81 darted between a row of machines, each one humming or hissing with purpose. The plant thrummed with energy—pipes hissed, air handlers whirred, and control panels blinked in an unceasing rhythm. A sense of unease settled in. Each turn revealed more unfamiliar automation or a pulsing contraption, and the air carried a faint metallic tang.

Out of the corner of an eye, A81 caught a flicker of motion—something or someone shifting in the dim light of the plant's shadows. Startled, the Inspector reacted instinctively, ducking behind a towering coolant tank, its surface cold and slick under A81's hand. The rait pressed into the shadows, every muscle taut. The hiss and hum of the machines were louder now, a constant drone, but it barely masked the creeping silence. Time stretched as A81 listened, the air thick with the smell of fluids and metal.

Slowly, the Inspector shifted position, eyes narrowing—nothing moved. A prickle ran down A81's neck. The rait eased forward, peering around the carbon dioxide scrubber. The plant loomed large, humming relentlessly. No figures. No flickers of motion. A quiet sigh slipped past A81's lips.

The rait's fingers brushed against the cold scrubber for balance. The Inspector hugged the machinery's edge, scanning each shadow, each metallic contour. Every blind spot held a possibility. A81's gaze darted ahead, tracing angles, searching for whatever—or whoever—might be lurking just out of sight.

Without warning, something grabbed A81 from behind and threw the rait to the deck. The assailant lunged, straddling A81's body, pinning the Inspector down with a force that left the rait momentarily stunned. A81 struggled, trying to break free, but the attacker had forced the Inspector's arms to the ground, the weight pressing down like a vise. A81's glare met the villain's—a pair of neon green eyes and gritted white teeth.

"Hello, dear." A92 chuckled, wiggling the hips. "How about a little shag?"

"Are you trying to give me a heart attack?" A81 shot back, catching the breath but now with a resigned sigh.

"That was fun!" A92 grinned like a pixie. "Are you happy to see me?"

"Yes, but I would like to live through the day."

"From where I'm sitting, you seem very *excited* to see me."

"Real funny." A81 wriggled beneath the weight. "Would you mind getting off?"

A92 hopped up and extended a hand to help. But instead of letting go, A92 pulled the Inspector close and, without a second thought, planted a big kiss on the Inspector's lips.

A81's brows shot up. "What's that for?"

"I'll let you figure that out."

A81 shook the head as a smile formed at the edges of the mouth. "By the way, how did you do in that box?"

"I hyperventilated and passed out. After that, I was okay."

A81 chuckled. "Let's get you out of here, Petunia."

• • • •

At 0010 hours, T23 emerged from the maintenance shaft. All was quiet except for the purr and drone of mechanicals doing their chores. The Engineer entered Quad-T and hurried to Polycule AT-20-6. The rait peeked inside, but the lights were off, making it difficult to see. T23 slipped quietly through the entry, activating a set of deck lights, raising lux levels to a soft, reddish glow. A sleeping resident began to stir.

T23 whispered. "30. It's me. Are you awake? 30… 30…"

Alarmed by the dark figure, T30's eyes jolted open. *"Jeez!"* T30 rubbed the face and sat up. "What are you doing here?"

"I'll fill you in later. Who else is here?"

"T02, A53, and A12."

T23's eyes lit up. "A12? Really? I'm with A81 and A92."

"12's been worried about those two."

"81 and 92 stowed away with me on a cargo ship."

"You did what?" T30 said, raising the voice an octave. "Where are they?"

"Not sure at the moment, but hopefully, they're headed this way."

"Let's go to the watatory. I'll wake A12."

T23 tiptoed over to the watatory. A couple of seconds later, A12 rounded the corner. Their eyes met. A12's face beamed as joyful tears welled at the corners of the eyes. Without saying a word, they rushed into each other's arms, holding on tightly, staring and touching as if discovering something precious and indescribable. The air between them seemed to electrify with emotions, the sheer joy of their reunion evident in their embrace and touch.

After the initial shock, A12 asked about A81 and A92. "Are they okay?"

"Yes, everything is good." T23 cradled A12's face and gave the dait another passionate kiss. "I missed you so much."

A12 smiled.

For the next few minutes, T23 explained how the situation had unfolded on Arc1994 and how it had led to their escape. When T23 had finished, A12 described a similar adventure on Arc1983 and the discovery of an outside world.

• • • •

As A12 and T23 exchanged their stories, someone was listening.

A53's sleep had been disturbed by their muffled voices, words slipping through the quiet like whispers of dissent. The rait slid out of bed, crept to the watatory entrance, and pressed an ear to the door. A scowl settled in. Such behavior. A53, too, missed maits and presumed they would return soon—but not at the cost of disregarding community doctrine. This was folly, willful, and dangerous. Malicious, even.

The spy lingered, listening, weighing the best course to put an end to this transgression.

It wasn't long before the first flickers of morning light crept into the poly. Footsteps rustled. A53 darted back into bed, feigning sleep as A12, T30, and T23 emerged from the watatory.

"So," A12 whispered, "we'll go to work like everything's normal. During our breaks, 30 and I will look for 81 and 92. You should stay here, out of sight."

"Check the shafts," T23 added. "That's where they'll be."

A12 nodded. "30, if you'll take the North and West lifts, I'll cover the others."

"Sounds like a plan." T30 winked.

Behind them, the sheets rustled. A53 stirred, stretching before sitting up, a smirk playing on the lips. "Good morning. Who do we have here?"

A12 tensed. "My friend, T23."

A53's gaze lingered. "I recognize the face. But what's 23 doing *here*?"

"Trainin'," T23 blurted, leaning casually against a bulkhead, but the stance didn't quite sell it.

Another voice stirred, groggy and thick with sleep. "What's going on?" T02 asked.

"Seems we have an unexpected guest," A53 said with a critical stare.

"This early?" T02 groaned, rolling over, half asleep.

"23's visiting for the day." A12 pulled out a couple of nourishments from the cooler, trying to keep things moving.

"Seems a bit early for a visit." A53 caressed a bare set of abs. "But now that you're here, how about a little party?"

"Whoa, someone's in a frisky mood." T30 chuckled. "I thought you didn't like mornings."

"Some parts of me like mornings."

T23 sat on the berth, a hand drifting to A53's thigh. "How 'bout this evening after trainin'?"

A53 arched an eyebrow. "Training, you say? What kind?"

"Bioprint," T23 replied.

A12 handed T23 a nourishment. "Hey, time to get going. I've got a busy day." A12 walked to a cube and activated its VDG. "23 needs my cube for some research."

A53 slipped from the berth and headed for the watatory. "Bioprint, interesting."

A12, T30, and T02 followed.

After their cleanse, the authorized occupants of Poly AT-20-6 dressed and prepared to leave.

A12 checked the VDG a final time. "Looks good. We should get going."

T23 nodded. "Yeah. Thanks. Don't want y'all to be late for work."

A53 lingered in the doorway, eyes narrowing. "I'll see you later. Don't get too lost in it."

T30 and T02 followed.

T02 glanced back with a knowing smile. "Don't let that one bother you. Your research plans sound wonderful. Good luck, you two."

A12 flushed. The rait pressed a quick kiss to T23's cheek, then hurried after the others.

• • • •

T23 let out a relieved breath, sinking back into the seat, trying to relax, but the tension in the muscles refused to ease. Nothing left to do now but wait—and trust that A81 and A92 would show. Time stretched, the quiet heavy, almost suffocating.

Fingers drummed nervously on the seat's edge, the sound hollow in the stillness. The room felt too still. Too empty. "It'll be fine," T23 whispered, though the words rang hollow.

Then, a thought struck. A frustrated grunt escaped. How could T23 have forgotten? That word—the one no one was ever supposed to say. The word meant for A12.

T23's stomach twisted. "I'm so stupid."

• • • •

In another part of the Arc, A12 went about the day, performing lighting checks as if all were nominal, but focus wavered. T23 was back—an impossibility made real, an opportunity beyond belief. But the rait's return was not an acceptable state. And what did A53 mean by "don't get lost"?

The Council of Sage would surely correct this irregularity. More than likely, T23 would be sent back to Arc 94—perhaps reprimanded. And what of A81 and A92? Could something be done? But to what measure, to what extent?

"Or should one accept the inevitable—suffer the norm, and endure an innumerable life?"

So which choice, which path, bore the greatest weight?

At lunchtime, A12 casually approached the South Lift, pausing at its lobby to peek inside. It was just as T23 had described—a wall panel on the right bulkhead, a hidden access affixed with hinges, and a latch. When all was clear, A12 slipped inside and pulled the panel shut.

The shaft was unremarkable—blinking lights, gray metallic walls—but something about it stirred a memory. A12 retrieved a wire marker from the tool bag, sketched a small, fluffy caricature on the hatch's interior, and scribbled AT-20-6 beneath it.

• • • •

It was break time. G18 nursed a Number 3. The Core buzzed with its usual energy—voices overlapping, laughter cutting through the air. The Botanist absently twirled a lock of hair—a tic slipping past one's usual, beaming composure. Not ideal. But recent events had been… grating.

G18's new purpose seemed promising, but life on an Arc had its drama. Offenses were taken, words twisted, and outdated terms slipped past their tongues. Accidental, perhaps. Or deliberate. Some days felt like an endless cycle of linguistic duels—an exhausting cat-and-mouse game. Naturally, G18 enjoyed being the cat; someone had to keep the game interesting.

Yet, amid the chase, some rats lacked the proper enthusiasm, squirming more than they should. Weren't they all meant to pursue the same goals, free from hesitation or scrutiny? If so, why did slights and rejections keep cropping up? Why the resistance? Perhaps a bit of tedious suffering was merely another waypoint on the journey to happiness. After all, one couldn't have blossoms without a bit of mud.

A voice interrupted G18's thoughts. "I want to feel you." A53 bellied up to the bar.

"At your desire, sugar."

"I have something that might interest you."

"I'm sure you do, sugar. Do you want to show it to me here or go to my place?"

"T23 is back."

"I don't follow?"

"T23 went through the Garden Ceremony a few weeks ago but is back on our Arc and claims it's for training. But I overheard them say something about stowing away on a cargo transport, and now, they're looking for a way off the Arc."

"Who is this?"

"A12, T23, A81, and A92."

"Some just don't listen." G18 sighed.

"You knew?"

"The part about A12. Seems our friend has this fantasy about living on the surface of our planet. I didn't sense it was serious, just a ploy not to serve, if you feel me? Our friend turned me down twice. I could have dealt with once, but *twice*?"

"Wow." A53's brows shot up. "That might explain the rumors?"

"What rumors?"

"The ones about A12 and T23. Some said they sensed it. Not me, of course. I'm not built that way. 12 and 23 thought they were being discreet. You should have seen how they looked at one another, their heads filled with sparkles and rainbows. Made me sick."

"What are you talking about?"

"They have feelings for one another."

"That little liar. 12 asked me once if I favored anyone. Now I see where that was going."

"Someone should say something."

G18 clutched A53's hand. "Where are they now, sugar?"

"23's in my poly, and 12 is looking for 81 and 92. Someone needs to put an end to this foolishness, and soon."

"Indeed. It's just a matter of time."

"But what if they find a way off the Arc first?"

"Good point, sugar. Let me see if I can move this along."

• • • •

A12 linked up with T30 and was giving an update when the Tech spotted A53 and G18 at a bar on the Core's far side. A12 noticed some glowers and sneers. Their conversation seemed more intense than the usual bar talk. As A12 studied their expressions, the two raits exchanged more scowls and leers, glancing over their shoulders, suggesting they might know something secret— even dangerous.

"This doesn't look good," A12 said.

T30 mumbled a bit of profanity under the breath. "I'll hang here and keep an eye on these two chatterboxes. You should tell 23. If they're up to no good, I'll find you."

A12 nodded and raced away, hoping T23 was still in the poly and safe. Along the way, A12 avoided eye contact with others as if they sensed the plan and now laughed secretly at the folly.

Luckily, A12 found T23 in the watatory, pacing tensely back and forth.

"We have a problem." A12 glanced at the entrance. "I saw 53 and G18 talking in the Core. They might know."

"We need to find 81 and 92," T23 said. "We can't leave without them."

"30 and I checked the shafts. Hopefully, they'll be here soon."

"We should look for them."

"They could be anywhere."

"I feel responsible."

A12 stared curiously at T23. Where did that selfie word come from?

· · · ·

T30 observed G18 as the suspected turncoat confidently strutted through the Core. T30 remained several paces back, ducking behind columns, furniture, or anything else to conceal the surveillance. Peering through a leafy patch of fiddle-leaf figs, T30 noticed G18's head swivel from left to right as though searching for something or someone. T30 held a breath, straining to decipher G18's intentions.

Suddenly, G18's eyes locked onto a target. T30 followed the stare and felt a chill at seeing Sv07, the Public Affairs Sophist. Something wasn't right—this wasn't a chance occurrence. G18 strode over to the Sophist. T30 felt every nerve tighten. G18's tone was low but laced with agitation, evident in G18's rigid stance and how a finger jabbed in the direction of Quad-T.

T30's heart jumped. The two conversed in tense tones, with G18's gestures growing sharper. T30 strained to listen but caught only fragments, whispers drowned out by the Core's incessant hum.

Then it hit: G18 wasn't just socializing with the Sophist—G18 was exposing something revealing, a secret perhaps.

Sweat broke out on T30's forehead. The weight of the moment pressed down hard. The rait knew there was no time to lose. T30 broke off the surveillance and slipped back into the shadows.

T30 moved swiftly but cautiously along passageways that seemed to stretch on forever. The poly wasn't far, yet every corner felt like it harbored a threat, every nook heavy with hidden eyes. T30's mind raced—one slip and it was all over. Finally, the poly came into view, but no time to catch a breath, no time to hesitate.

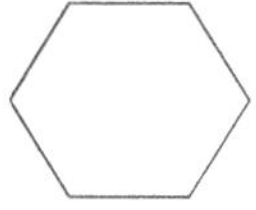

CHAPTER TWENTY-ONE

TELL US ANOTHER

"Tell us another, tell us another," the children shouted.

"You've already heard two," the old woman chuckled.

"Please, please," the little girl begged.

"Perhaps one more, and then it's time for supper." The old woman leaned back in her chair, studied the children's bright, innocent faces, and recalled a tale they had not heard in some time.

She drew in a breath and began. "In the old days, all creatures lived in harmony with humans, from the tiniest bug to the largest beast. But as time passed, humans brought forth more and more of their kind, and their villages grew and spread, leaving less and less room for bugs, fish, reptiles, birds, and beasts alike."

"How many humans were there?" the skinny boy asked.

"More than the leaves in the forest, and that wasn't all. Humans invented weapons to kill any beast. They even hunted frogs, worms, and flies. They trampled, swatted, and crushed—sometimes by accident, but often from pure contempt."

"Were all the creatures sad?" the little girl asked.

"Yes, very sad. So, the animals decided to put an end to the destruction before humans wiped out the whole world. Each species called a council to debate what to do.

"The first was the Bear Council, who met at the mulberry place under the Great Mountain. Old White Bear, their leader, asked the bears to state their grievances. One said, 'They killed my friends.' Another said, 'They cut off their fur and sat on it.' Another said, 'They even used their guts for bowstrings.' White Bear asked, 'Shall we go to war?' 'Yes,' the Council replied. Old White Bear said, 'How shall we fight?' A bear answered, 'We'll make bows and arrows just like their weapons.' So, the bears fashioned bows and arrows and tried to draw the strings, but their claws got in the way. A bear said, 'We must cut off our claws.' Another bear said, 'But how will we climb trees and find food?' Old White Bear said, 'Without claws, we will die.' All the bears understood but couldn't think of another solution. The Council adjourned, and the bears scattered through the forest."

"What about the other animals?" the brash boy asked.

"Well, they tried. Led by Little Deer, the Deer Council convened and agreed to give humans rheumatism. However, feeling shame, they showed mercy and warned the humans. The deer reasoned that if humans took only what they needed, left the rest, and sought forgiveness, they would be spared from the disease."

The children shook their heads, disappointed in the deer.

The old woman continued, "The reptiles and fish met and decided to haunt humans with bad dreams about slithering snakes coiling around their heads."

"Eww, yuck, disgusting," the children cried.

"The best idea came from the smallest creatures—the bugs. Their leader, Chief Grubworm, and the Council discussed how humans squooshed, smashed, and burned the bugs. So the Council invented ailments and sicknesses—the same diseases we have today."

"Is that why we get sick?" the little girl asked.

"Yes, dear," the old woman replied. "But there's more to the story. Would you like to hear the rest?"

"Yes, yes!" the children shouted.

"As I recall, one group remained friends with humans. In those days, this group could think, speak, and act."

"Who were they?" the tall girl asked.

"They were the plants: the trees, bushes, grasses, mosses, and lichens. The Plant Council devised cures and vowed to always be there for humans. You see, every plant has a benefit, though we don't yet know them all. But perhaps one day we will, and perhaps one day, one of you will discover a cure—a medicine that will help us all."

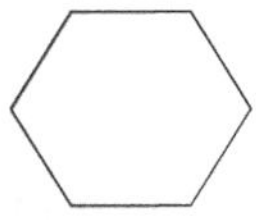

CHAPTER TWENTY-TWO

THE ESCAPE

T30 rushed into the poly, finding the two daits hiding in the watatory and discussing plans. "You have to go. They're on their way."

"Who?" T23 asked.

"The Sophists. I spotted G18 talking with Upsilon 7."

"It figures," A12 said. "I shouldn't have trusted that one."

"If 81 and 92 show," T23 said, "tell 'em we're in the South shaft, Ring 60. We'll wait on them until 0100 hours. After that, they're on their own."

A12 and T23 bolted from the poly, hurried to the Quad-T lift, and ascended two rings, hoping to shake off any would-be pursuers. They exited onto Ring 20 and raced to the Core. A12 scanned the area—no Sophists—everything seemed nominal. A12 motioned for T23 to follow.

The two daits strolled across the Core, but both wore guilty expressions, worried someone might notice—especially with the out-of-place rait in tow. Regrettably, A12 had been right. Four red and silver security bots entered the area, heading straight for the two raits. A12 spotted them, grabbed T23 by the hand, and said, "Run."

The pair raced across the Core, darting between tables and startled raits, bouncing off a few as they went. The commotion caused drinks to fly, chairs to tumble, and raits to curse, but the Gammas followed wherever the pair ducked, dodged, or dipped. Within seconds, the bots had cornered A12 and T23.

Residents encircled the fray, their gazes fixed on the two petrified raits. A12 could only imagine what they were sensing. Their faces were covered in disapproval, as if privy to every detail—yet how could they be? Their stares, however, betrayed their true feelings, sharply diverging from the Arc's philosophy of friendship and happiness. These so-called friends, who had sought fellowship, now reveled in indifference. Their expressions conveyed a mix of curiosity and condemnation, masking any hint of genuine concern or empathy. In that fleeting moment, it became evident: acceptance was a mere facade, and the bonds of friendship were as fragile as the artificial air they breathed.

Two Sophists entered the Core and approached the gathering. One was Sυ07, the Public Affairs Sophist. The other was the newly assigned Security Sophist, Sπ06, and the former Zephyrus resident known by some as T89.

"Good day," Sυ07 greeted. "Welcome back, T23. If you two would follow me, I'm sure we can rectify this situation."

A12 and T23 did not respond, both stiff with fear. A12's eyes darted left and right, hoping for an opportunity to break loose, but the security bots and the crowd had blocked all escape routes.

T23 braved a smile. "How you doin', mait, or should I say, your honor?"

But Sπ06's cold, dark eyes showed no empathy or alliance. "Secure these residents," Sπ06 ordered.

Security bots closed in on the two daits, extended their robotic claws, and placed tethers on A12's and T23's wrists.

Onlookers gasped. It was the first time anyone had seen a resident restrained. The crowd's mumbles and chatters grew louder; their perceptions now surely convinced the couple must have committed some heinous crime against the collective.

Without fanfare, Sπ06 said, "Follow me." The new Sophist turned, and the crowd parted. Sπ06 led the way, followed by Sυ07, four red guards, and two captives. The party marched off, headed for the North Lift.

• • • •

When the lift doors opened, the party stepped out into Ring 8, the Academy. The group marched down the passageway.

T23 kept looking at A12.

"What is it?" A12 asked.

"I love you."

Before A12 could respond, a security bot pulled the rait into Exam Room 8-102. The other bot led T23 into room 8-101.

An attending med bot handed T23 a white jumpsuit while another bot prepared tools not typically seen in an exam room.

"What's this?" T23 asked.

"A new purpose," Sπ06 said. "One you should enjoy for some time."

"Sounds like fun, mait." T23 stared defiantly at the Sophist, stripped off, and slipped on the funny-colored jumpsuit, peeking across the passage at A12.

A12 smiled, but the rest of the face told a different story—of fear and despair.

T23 tried to return the smile, but something was wrong—something dark was about to happen. Ignoring the bot's commands, T23 kept looking at A12. The room seemed to go silent, devoid of any beeps or bleeps, leaving only the heavy thumps of a broken heart. To have come this far and failed—no, it couldn't be. An intense melancholy washed over T23, a crushing weight, a profound foreboding as if this moment was a final breath.

A security bot pushed T23 toward the examination table.

"Hey, pal, watch it," T23 complained.

"Please do as the Gamma asks," Sπ06 said sternly.

T23, however, instinctively stepped back as a jolt of adrenaline surged through the body. *I have to do something.*

In an instant, T23 seized the tether, mustered every ounce of strength, and swung it hard. The security bot hurtled through the air, striking Sπ06 in the head and sending the Sophist sprawling. Without pause, T23 lashed the tether side to side, yanking the bot off balance. It tried to correct, but the rait's fury overpowered its adjustments. T23 whipped the Gamma into a glass bulkhead, the impact rattling through its frame before it collapsed to the floor, sputtering. With one final, brutal arc, T23 swung the machine overhead and slammed it onto the deck. The bot's shell shattered on impact. Its exposed innards sparked and hissed.

Loose of the bot's grip, T23 ran to A12. The attending bot beeped a warning.

"Stop what you are doing," Sυ07 balked. "Your actions are dangerous."

T23 grabbed A12's tether and slammed the bot to the deck. Its shell cracked open, but something more spilled out. It was a brain—not mechanical, but biological.

T23 and A12 stared in horror.

"Is that…?" A12 asked.

"I didn't mean to hurt it." T23 grabbed A12's hand. "We have to go." The couple rushed out the door and into the Academy's central passageway. Another security bot tried to block their egress, but the frightened pair slipped past and evaded the bot's reach.

The couple rushed to the North Lift, their only plausible escape route. But within seconds, two more security bots gave chase. One tried to seize A12.

T23 grabbed the bot's metallic arm.

A12 yelled, "Don't hurt them." But before the rait could say another word, T23 swung the bot into the other, causing them to falter and fumble.

As the waning mechanicals tried to regain their attitude, A12 and T23 raced on to the North Lift. "I hope they're okay?" A12 glanced over a shoulder.

"To the left," T23 said, but when they turned the corner, the two terrified raits discovered the North Lift had been recalled to its emergency station. T23 spotted a maintenance hatch to the right. The Engineer rushed over and turned the handle, pushing and pulling, but it wouldn't budge.

"I have another idea," A12 said. "Follow me."

The two daits hurried down the passageway. A12 scanned left and right. "Wait." A12 stopped by a small door. "A lighting closet." A yank opened it. "Quick, inside."

They darted into the cramped space. A12 ripped off the overhead tile, exposing a hatch cover. A12 paused and turned to T23. "I love you, too."

"You do?" T23's eyes widened.

"I told you before—you ask too many questions. What do you think we've been doing all this time?"

T23's gaze flickered, then steadied. "Well… I love you."

"I know." A12 chuckled. "And it only took you this long to admit it." The Tech eyed the hatch. "After you."

T23 hesitated.

"We should be going."

T23 snapped out of the lovestruck daze and climbed into the tunnel.

A12 followed, shaking the head.

After a few cubits, an intersection loomed.

"Which way?" T23 asked.

"Left."

They scrambled into the left tunnel, pressing forward. Several cubits in, a grate blocked the way—a cover for an air circulation duct. Smaller than the access tunnel but large enough for a rait. T23 pried it open and slipped inside. A12 followed.

Metal flexed as they scooted through the ducts, passing junctions and vents. Some led to airways, others to connecting interchanges.

Peering through an opening, T23 spotted the South Lift. They inched forward until the lobby lay below. The ductwork branched again, one path narrowing toward what looked like a maintenance shaft.

Twisted around a tight metal corner, T23 pushed ahead. At the end, another grate. A peek through confirmed it—definitely a maintenance shaft.

The Engineer pushed the grate open, inched forward, and pulled free, finally dropping to the deck with a soft thud.

A second later, A12 followed, landing beside the rait with a quiet plop.

T23 felt the tension ease now that they were in a safe space. The weight of their escape from the Sophists lifted, but their adventure was far from over. They embraced, a quiet relief passing between them.

Now, all that remained was finding a way off the Arc—easier said than done.

• • • •

A81 and A92 crawled through the narrow maintenance shaft, heading toward Zephyrus. The faint hum of the Arc surrounded them, vibrating through the metal walls as they ascended. The Inspector checked each level as they passed, confirming their position. They slipped past Ring 24, Ecology—just three more rings to go.

When they reached Ring 21, they climbed off the ladder and approached the hatch. A92 spotted something immediately—a quick scribble on the hatch's white surface. "I spy a bunny," A92 said, pointing at the caricature.

"It's a message!" A81 said, kissing the mait on the cheek.

"Clever, I am." A92 smiled.

"And what's this?" A81 studied the markings. It read:

AT-20-6

The Inspector's eyes brightened. "That's it—T23's old poly number. They want us to meet there."

"You're on a roll, mait."

"Nothing but green." A81 rubbed away the markings.

The pair climbed from the maintenance shaft, made their way along a passage, and entered the Core. A81 moved with a steady purpose, but something about the space felt off. As they navigated through the bustling crowd, a sixth sense whispered something wasn't right. "I've got this weird feeling, Petunia."

"*Shhh*, someone might hear you."

"And what if they do? There are sixteen 92s on this Arc but only one Petunia."

"So, I'm your Petunia."

"Of course," A81 admitted teasingly.

"I like when you say it." A large smile formed on A92's face.

"And that's why I do." A81 scanned the area. The lighting was set to evening—nothing unusual there. Raits appeared calm and cheerful, enjoying their refreshments. Two security bots circled the crowd, their movements too deliberate, too watchful. The Inspector tracked the Gammas as they zigged and zagged, moving from one side to the next. "Not good." A81 grabbed A92's hand. "Act normal."

"You sure? I tried that once. Worst two hours of my life."

"I mean regular normal. Not Petunia normal."

The pair continued across the Core, careful to avoid drawing attention. Fortunately, no one reacted or seemed to notice them. When they reached Quad-T's portal, they slipped through and hurried down the passage.

They soon reached AT-20-6. A92 kept watch as A81 peeked inside. The Inspector spotted T30 at a leisure cube, absorbed in a video. Someone was singing in the watatory. A81 waved at T30.

T30 stared at the screen, a blue haze reflecting off the face.

"*Psst, psst,*" A81 whispered.

T30 was oblivious.

"Hey! *Psst, psst.*" A81 tried again, louder.

At last, T30 glanced up and spotted A81. The rait jumped up. "You made it."

"Yes—yes—we did." A81's brow furrowed. "How did you know?"

"*Shhh.* I don't want someone to hear."

"Who would hear? Have you seen A12—"

"Well, that was subtle," A92 remarked, keeping a watchful eye on the passageway.

"*Shhh,*" T30 repeated, eyeing the watatory. "My maits know about your plan. You need to go. They're looking for you."

A81's face went blank. "Your maits are looking for us?"

"No. The Sophists. *You have to go.* If they see you, they'll report you."

"The Sophists?"

"Oh, my goodness. No, my maits."

"Your maits will report us to the Sophists."

"Yes. They're in the South shaft on Ring 60."

"The Sophists?"

T30's head shook. "No, A12 and T23."

"So, you've seen A12 and T23."

"Yes, now please go!"

"South shaft, Ring 60."

"Yes."

"On our way." A81 gave T30 a friendly pat on the shoulder, seized A92 by the arm on the way out, and off they went.

When A81 and A92 reached the Core, the Inspector again surveyed the area—fortunately, no security bots. The two hastened across, turning a few heads, but the couple did not slow.

• • • •

A12 and T23 had reached Ring 60, the lowest *authorized* level for residents. There, the two raits discovered an even larger hatch with a circular lockdown.

T23 grabbed hold and tried to rotate the handle. "I need your help."

A12 reached down and pulled. It began to unwind.

"It's opening." T23 and A12 lifted the heavy access.

"Hey, another ladder," A12 said.

The pair climbed down, unlatched the next hatch, and stepped into Ring 61. The gangway seemed to quiver beneath their feet. A12's scalp began to tingle—this wasn't just another maintenance shaft.

They had stepped into the Arc's heart. The matter-antimatter beam core drive stretched through a vertical expanse, vanishing into a black abyss. Pipes gleamed like molten silver, rigid and lifeless, while cables slithered through the structure, pulsing with unseen energy. Hydrogen tanks stood like sentinels, flanking diamagnetic traps and superconducting rings, their polished surfaces reflecting the eerie blue-violet glow from the containment unit.

A12 grabbed hold of a railing. The drive's reactor shimmered, its crystalline form shifting in the dim light, like something alive. A deep, rhythmic drone pulsed through the air, vibrating the gangway, rattling through bone and sinew. It wasn't just noise—it was a presence, pressing into the chests with every oscillation. The sharp scent of ozone filled A12's nose, stinging, making the eyes water. It felt as if the Arc itself was breathing.

A12 gripped the railing tighter, peering over the edge. Beyond a few cubits—nothing but darkness. An unknowable depth. A sudden wave of vertigo struck, pulling at the stomach, threatening to drag the rait in.

"What is this?" A12's voice barely rose above a whisper.

T23 stared at the machine. "Looks like our power source."

A12 swallowed hard. "That's enough power to tear this place apart."

"We should be careful."

The drive thrummed again, a deep vibration rattling the gangway ever so slightly.

A12 stiffened. "Do you hear that?" A memory snapped into place. "Monsters!"

"Monsters? What are you talkin' about?"

"Something G18 said."

"Well, let's not wait here and find out." T23 pulled on A12's arm.

A12 tore away from the railing, and the pair hurried back up through the large hatch and into the shaft on Ring 60. Once there, they caught their breath.

Now, all they could do was wait.

Sitting on the cold metal deck, backs stiff against a bulkhead, A12's gaze remained fixed on the maintenance shaft. Every slight sound seemed to stretch into a signal, a sign that A81 and A92 might be coming. Familiar faces would steady the nerves and make what lay ahead feel a little less daunting.

Minutes blurred into hours.

A12 and T23 embraced, feeling the warmth of each other's presence in the cold, metallic space. They held on tight, as if letting go might send them drifting apart, like lonely asteroids into the cold void of space. But this time, they wouldn't let go. Not the silence, nor the chill, nor even the dark expanse of the unknown could tear them apart. In that moment, their bond was more powerful than any force that might pull them into the abyss.

A12 glanced up into the shaft. The lux levels had dimmed to night mode. Only a few scattered displays pulsed, their soft, colored lights casting a parade of restless shadows that stretched and shifted as if they, too, felt the bonds of confinement. The room's edges melted into darkness, leaving only fragments of an unknown world, materializing as distorted shapes and faint reflections.

A12 closed the eyes, listening—beyond the steady drone of machines, beyond the rush of circulating air—searching for the faintest sound, the slightest movement.

Sometime later, after nodding off once or twice, a noise alerted A12. A repeated clang echoed down the shaft, steady, deliberate. A moment later, a shadow cut through the dim light above.

"Someone's coming," A12 whispered.

A muffled voice followed, and then a flash of yellow—legs, arms, and an attitude.

"Blimey! Look who it is," A92 said, peering down the shaft.

A12 jumped up, a smile lighting up the face. "I can't believe it. You made it."

A92 and A81 stepped off the ladder.

A12 hardly had time to react before A92 wrapped the Tech in a tight hug, thumping a hand against the rait's back. "Missed me, did ya, mait?"

A81 hung back but, after a beat, let out a sigh and pulled A12 into a quick embrace. "I hope you two know what you're doing."

T23 nudged A92. "Do I get a hug, or is that a maits-only thing?"

"Oh, come on in here, you big bugger." A92 yanked T23 into a lopsided hug.

A81 cleared the throat. "Alright, enough of that. Now, what about the plan?"

A12 straightened. "It's simple—we're going to find an exit."

"If this doesn't work, you're going to ruin my day," A81 said.

"Well, we can't have that." T23 clapped A81 on the back. "Ready, my friend?"

A92's eyes gleamed. "I'm in. Time to shake things up."

A81 sighed. "Fine. But if this goes sideways, I'm saying, 'I told you so.'"

"No turning back, now." T23 grinned smartly. "Follow me."

The four descended through the large hatch with its circular lockdown, into a short shaft, and emerged onto Ring 61.

"Whoa, what is this?" A92's head swiveled in all directions.

A81 casually glanced over the railing. "How far down does this go?"

"Not sure," T23 replied.

"Nothing I've ever inspected." A81 stroked the chin. "Looks like the Arc's power system. But, maybe it's a—"

"Maybe it's something we should avoid," A92 drawled.

"Like radioactive nuts, Petunia."

"Let's keep movin'," T23 said. "The time, remember."

The raits continued their descent, winding down the steel path and past the throbbing mechanics. Pipes, wires, and tubing crisscrossed the space like an intricate web, each strand concealing its ravenous desires. All around, machines groaned and rumbled with a persistent menace. A12 caught a musty, stale scent mingling with something sharp and foul—perhaps sewage or something equally rotten.

As they ventured deeper, shadows danced on the bulkheads, cast by the flickering lights. The air grew warmer, thick with the heat of the massive engine and the tang of hot metal. Darkness pressed in from all sides, and with every creak and hiss, the machinery seemed to murmur warnings of unseen danger. A12's heart thudded as they pressed on, guided by the dim glow of safety lights spaced every few cubits. Their journey stretched on, each step reverberating through the cavernous space, merging into an endless march into the unknown.

Three hundred cubits later, T23 spotted an open hatch. A softly glowing placard read *R-100*. "I'll check it out. Wait here." The Engineer hurried over and slipped through. A moment later, T23 returned, waving for the others to follow.

A12, A92, and A81 rushed to the hatch and stepped through. On the other side, a bridgeway led to another descending gangway. The Tech glanced back at the towering white structure. Sleek and refined, it was unmistakably the shell of something massive—the Arc. A noise caught A12's attention. Something was moving about below. The Tech instinctively pulled back, afraid of being detected.

A12 cautiously leaned forward again. Whatever it was, it was huge—a monstrous blob, but the dim light obscured its distinguishing features. Then, a faint grumble echoed through the air. "Did you hear that?" A12 whispered.

"What is it?" A92 asked, eyes wide with nerves.

"It's moving," A12 replied. "Listen—there it is again."

"That was a growl," A92 said, eyebrows shooting up. "I'm not going down there."

"Could it be?" A12 mumbled. "A monster?"

"A what?" A92 yelped.

"We should get closer," T23 suggested.

"Are you mad?" A92's mouth hung open.

"Stick with me, Petunia," A81 said, taking A92's hand.

"I'd follow you anywhere, but not if it means being that thing's snack."

The four continued their descent. A12 kept glancing over the railing, each time spotting that hulking, monstrous shape. It was moving back and forth, jerky and erratic, barely visible in the dim light. And then, a growl—a guttural rumble—definitely a growl.

The four raits soon found themselves just above the hideous creature. A brief flash of light illuminated the area.

"I see it," T23 said. "There it goes again."

"Not me." A92 tried to pull away from A81. "I'm outta here."

A81 held on. "I got you."

"Wait for the light." T23 leaned farther out, trying to see past all the wires, pipes, and tubes obstructing the view. There it was again—another whoosh of light. "Yellow. It's yellow."

"I see it, too," A12 said.

"It's an Engineering bot," T23 chuckled, half-relieved, half-amused.

"Oh my goodness," A12 said with a smirk.

"A bot? A bloody bot?" A92 groaned, dropping to the deck.

It was indeed an Engineering bot—several, in fact. Their forms became evident as the light shifted, their hulking frames moving in and out of a set of enormous metallic doors that opened and closed like giant steel jaws. Each time the doors parted, a gray light gushed in, spilling across the structure.

A12 recognized that glow. The lux of dawn. The morning light.

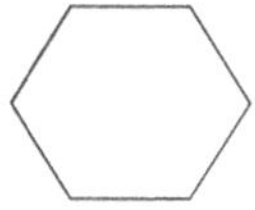

CHAPTER TWENTY-THREE

A WATERFALL

T23 led A12, A81, and A92 down the gangway, eyeing the monstrous Engineering bots as they thundered through the giant doors.

A12 spotted a placard on the bulkhead—*R-120*. Ground level.

The four stepped off the metal stairs. A12 crouched, running a hand over the strange surface. Cool, smooth, gray, yet unlike any known metal or composite.

"Follow me," T23 whispered.

They dashed to a stack of containers, vanishing into the shadows. From their hiding spot, they watched as the bots rumbled past. Each time the doors parted, light spilled in—growing stronger by the minute.

T23 recognized it instantly—the light of a star ascending from its sleep.

Their escape lay just beyond the threshold, but mistiming the dash meant failure, capture, or worse.

"You'll have about three to four seconds." T23's fingers tightened around the edge of the container, eyes fixed on the shifting light. "Get ready—wait for it—" A burst of steam hissed from the vents, masking the hum of the machinery. "GO!"

The Inspector bolted forward. The doors whooshed open—but suddenly, a massive yellow bot thundered through, skimming past A81's head, kicking up a whirlwind of dust that stung the eyes, but there was no time to hesitate. As fast as the feet would go, the rait shot through the gap, chasing the bot into the blinding light.

The metallic doors slammed shut.

T23 tensed, eyes darting between the door and the shifting shadows. Every second stretched, thick with the weight of the moment.

"You're next, 92." A sharp breath. "Get ready—get ready—" The machinery let out a low whir. The doors began to move. "GO!"

The rait sprang forward just as a bot barreled in from outside. Caught off guard, the Administrator slipped, skidding across the slick floor—straight into the door's track.

The doors rumbled, preparing to slam shut. A12 gasped and rushed forward.

Scrambling back frantically, A92's hands skidded against the slick surface— too slow.

A12 grabbed hold of A92's jumpsuit and yanked the friend back.

The doors slammed shut.

The pair caught their breath, shaken. The doors parted once again, flooding the space with light. No time to think—they ran.

• • • •

A yellow dwarf star blazed overhead, its brilliance overwhelming. A12 shielded the eyes, but even through squinted lids, the world burned white. Heat poured over every inch of the skin—a tingling, electric warmth, as if the body itself had been set alight. The feet felt fused to the ground, locked in place by something vast, something impossible.

Then—movement. A breath. A step. Then another.

A hand landed on A12's shoulder. "Let's get out of here," T23 said.

The four raits broke into motion, fleeing the towering metal doors, the monstrous bots, and the Arc's grasp. A12's eyes darted, blinking rapidly as the world took shape—blue, green, and boundless, stretching beyond the mind's reach.

Ahead, a forest loomed, sprawling in all directions. Its edge lay eight hundred cubits beyond a rolling field, where grass swayed in shimmering waves, bending and bowing in the wind. It rippled like water. Like an ocean—assuming one had ever seen an ocean.

They picked up their pace, first jogging, then running. For the first time, A12 felt the earth beneath the feet—soft, yielding, alive. Fingers grazed the tall grass; it, too, was gentle, swaying in a rhythm older than time. Euphoria washed over A12's spirit, more potent than any shot of meta or fleeting companionship. The sky stretched, open, endless. It was a clear day. It felt as if one could see forever.

At the forest's edge, they slowed, breathless. The trees towered above, their long limbs whispering in the wind. A12 brushed a hand against a pine—rough yet supple, alive in a way nothing on the Arc had ever been. A sharp terpene fragrance rose, raw and untamed, the scent of something true.

Some might call it insignificant, a thing to take for granted or consume. But to A12, it was everything. It was truth. It was life.

The Tech wandered deeper, drifting through the forest's splendor. Each step felt like sinking into something vast and alive. The others, too, moved in quiet awe.

T23 peered into the woods, mesmerized, searching for something unseen. Listening to the rustling canopy, A92 stood still, eyes closed. Sunlight poured through the branches, bathing everything in gold. Nearby, A81 watched wide-eyed as creatures rooted and clamored, foraging for a meal.

Birdsong filled the air. In a tall hickory, a family of squirrels—real squirrels, not artificially generated—chittered and chattered.

A12's breath caught. No eyetap illusion, no 3D capture, nothing the Arc could fabricate came close. Yet here it was—unbelievably real, limitless, waiting.

All one had to do was reach out.

The Tech wandered on, tracing the colors with the eyes, brushing the leaves with the fingers, lungs filling with the scent of budding life. A deep inhale. It felt like a first breath, like stepping through a dream—a portal into open arms, waiting, welcoming.

"It might be best if we put a little distance between ourselves and the Arc," T23 said.

"Which way?" A81 asked.

"Pretty," A92 murmured, eyes fixed on a small brown butterfly, its wings speckled with yellow-ringed eyespots.

"Toward those mountains," T23 said, indicating the distant peaks.

"Lead the way," A81 replied.

The group headed west, stumbling and tripping through the forest as briars, brambles, and vines snagged and tugged at their unacquainted bodies and *inside* clothing, but A12 relished every poke and prod. The woods were indeed welcoming its newest guests.

Immersed in their surroundings, the four wandered on, absorbing the forest's sights, textures, and scents. After some distance, they came upon a brook winding through a meadow, a blue ribbon unfurling across a green carpet. A12 studied its course. A hundred cubits south, two creatures lapped at the water's edge—tall, long-legged beings with sprawling antlers, their tines twisting like ancient branches. Overhead, another creature soared, its massive wings slicing through the sky.

"Are those... deer?" A12 pointed.

T23 squinted at the creatures. "They look like something from the TEIS. Ever read the simulation notes? I believe it's called a giant elk."

A92 raised an eyebrow. "There are notes?"

"Yeah, it's in the startup menu," T23 said, glancing at the creatures.

"I thought that was made-up nonsense," A92 chided.

"And that flying creature?" A12 shielded the eyes, following its arc.

"A golden eagle, I think," T23 said, watching the great raptor glide.

"Well, aren't you the walking data source," A92 mumbled.

A12 knelt beside the creek and touched the cold, clear water, scooping up a handful and sipping. It was the most refreshing taste imaginable. The others joined in, each savoring the moment. It was the first time any had drunk from something other than a dispenser or a bioware container. It felt like the first of many new experiences on this strange new adventure.

To the west, A12 spotted a mountain range stretching from south to north. "We should head there."

"After you," T23 said, waving the rait forward.

The four travelers continued their journey, drawn by the mountains' majesty, hopeful of uncovering more secrets and answers.

As the terrain sloped upward, the travelers gained a sweeping view of the land beyond. A12 glanced eastward—there it was, the Arcology. A strange structure, stark and alien against the wilderness. A12 hesitated. Inside its walls, the Arc had felt vast, its corridors and chambers boundless. But from here, it seemed small. Contained. Until this moment, the Tech hadn't truly understood space. For residents, space was a polycule, a passageway, the Core—everything they needed. The idea of an existence without limits had never occurred to them.

And why would it? Within the Arc, no one questioned. Life was comfortable, adequate, sufficient. What lay beyond was irrelevant. The guardians decided. The residents blissfully obeyed.

As the day waned, the G-type star dipped toward the western horizon, casting long shadows across the mountains. The four had never witnessed a setting star—or any star, beyond rendered images. They had been taught, of course, about stars—spheroids of luminous plasma fusing hydrogen into helium, held together by gravity. Their community had even named a day after a star: Sun's Day.

Exhausted, A12 sighed. "Let's take a break."

They settled onto a soft patch of earth and watched as the Sun melted toward the peaks. What had been a blinding white blaze softened into gold, then amber, then a deep, fiery red. It was breathtaking—the sky shifting in a kaleidoscope of pinks, oranges, and purples, the light slipping away moment by moment. And yet, the star hadn't moved at all. The Arc's lessons surfaced in A12's mind: the Sun did not set. The Earth turned.

A hush fell over them as the last glimmer vanished beyond the blue mountains. A few quiet *oohs* and *ahhs*, and then—darkness.

Unfazed and unsuspecting, the four pressed on—blundering, faltering, and cursing under their breath—until they found a small refuge among a cluster of towering red oaks. With weary sighs, they dropped to the ground and huddled together. The trees' thick boughs stretched wide, their lobed leaves rustling softly in the cooling air.

The temperature was dropping—another new experience. A12 shivered and nestled closer to T23; their thin jumpsuits offered little warmth. Instinctively, they pressed together, interlocking arms and legs, pooling their body heat. Sleep did not come easily. The night was alive with strange voices—chirps, hoots, crackles, and distant howls, an unbroken symphony of the untamed world.

Wide awake, A12 gazed into the heavens. The night was clear; the sky shimmered with billions of sparkling stars. Unbeknownst to the Tech, they also had identifications. Directly above was the Summer Triangle: Deneb in Cygnus, Vega in Lyra, and Altair in Aquila—bright stars in their constellations. Deneb, the tail of a swan, gleamed some 1,565 light-years away. Vega was associated with a lyre, perhaps the first crafted by Hermes and gifted to Orpheus by Apollo. Altair, brightest in Aquila, symbolized an eagle in descent, clutching Zeus's thunderbolts. To the north, a steady star—the once-distant celestial north pole now anchored near the dim light of Gamma Cephei, a subgiant marking its place with a quiet certainty.

But on Earth, the forest lay cloaked in darkness as deep as the void between galaxies—foreboding, perhaps even menacing. For A12, the day had been exhilarating, but now, in the chill of the night, strange noises tugged at the mind. Once or twice, doubt flickered—had the right choice been made? Perhaps the light of a new day would bring the clarity that now eluded them.

• • • •

After a long, restless night of shivering and jumping at every sound, the sun finally broke over the horizon—or rather, Earth's rotation turned their longitude—approximately 85.78 degrees West—into the sun's light.

A12 stood and stretched, a soft sigh escaping. "It's warm. Can you feel it?"

T23 stepped over to a convenient tree to void. "Glad that's over. Felt like we were stuck in a cooler all night."

"My jumpsuit's seen better days." A12 swiped away several crumbling leaves that clung to the tattered blue fabric.

"Mine won't zip up." A92 tugged at the jumpsuit's stubborn slide fastener.

"Careful, Petunia," A81 warned, grinning. "Something might pop out."

"The pleasure would be yours." A92 smirked.

"It would indeed," A81 chuckled.

T23 glanced up, eyes narrowing on the forest ahead. "Time to move."

"Speaking of coolers," A81 added, eyeing the trees around them. "I don't see any around here."

"Well, the sooner we head out, the sooner we'll find something," T23 said, brushing off the remark.

A81 grabbed A92's hand, pulling the rait to feet. "You ready?"

"If we must," A92 muttered, adjusting the sagging suit.

Natural paths guided their advance, but many were cheats and ruses leading the party astray. On one occasion, they unwittingly walked in a circle, discovering their footprints.

The Administrator was the first to express doubt. "I need to rest," A92 plopped down on a boulder covered in lichen. "My feet feel like mush."

"We don't have much farther to go," T23 said. "We should reach the top by midafternoon."

"And a bar, I hope?" A92 removed both slippers and rubbed the feet. "It better serve Number 3's. I could use a painkiller about now."

A81 turned to T23. "Seriously? What are we searching for?"

"What lies beyond," T23 said. "Maybe a community."

"I hope so," A12 mumbled. "My stomach is growling."

"One way to find out," T23 chortled. "Like 81 said, no coolers around here. Maybe we'll find some fruits or vegetables. Like we have on the Arc. They must grow somewhere."

Without warning, A92 let go a bloodcurdling screech. *"Get it off, get it off!"* The rait started jumping up and down and swiping at a leg.

A81 rushed over. "What is it?"

"It's on my leg! Don't let it eat me!"

A12 spotted the threat. Black with yellow and white stripes, it had menacing black spines and slithered on numerous legs. At five centimeters long, it was a hideous little creature, unknown to the travelers yet harmless. A *Danaus plexippus*, it would one day transform into a monarch butterfly.

A81 brushed it away.

"I hate this place," A92 screeched.

"It's nature," A81 chuckled.

"Screw nature!"

"Let's keep moving," T23 said.

"Screw this bloody place," A92 mumbled.

The four trudged on, the forest looming large and expansive in all directions. After walking another two hundred cubits or so, A12 spotted something to the right: a deciduous vine with little green, bronze, and purple orbs. The Tech picked one and took a bite, another new experience; after all, teeth were for smiling, not biting or chewing. The fruit's outer skin was thick, but its juicy interior was sweet and tangy.

"Hey, this is good. It's sort of like grape." A12 grimaced and spat. "Watch out for the seeds; they're awful."

"Save some for me." A92 rushed over, followed by A81 and T23.

All four picked handfuls and devoured them. What they had found was a *Vitis rotundifolia*, or muscadine vine, and this time of year, its wild creepers were laden with dozens and dozens of delicious berries.

Feeling rejuvenated, the four marched on, hoping to reach the hill's peak before nightfall. The terrain, however, tested every muscle. In some places, hands and feet were required to ascend the steep topography. The smell lingered—an odoriferous bouquet of sweet and spicy, carried by the breeze from an endless expanse of plants and trees. The landscape was a feast for the senses, with vibrant greenery stretching in all directions and the occasional flash of colorful blossoms. Yet beneath this beauty, the Sun beat down relentlessly, causing the raits to sweat and drip, their skin slick with moisture. The heat was unfamiliar and heavy, clinging to them, while the weight of each step seemed to grow heavier, as though the land itself were testing them.

Despite the discomfort, the forest's raw magnificence was undeniable, its wild beauty both an enchantment and a challenge. Each step forward was a reminder of what had been left behind and what was yet to be discovered.

To the right, A12 spotted a small brook trickling down the hillside. A relieved sigh escaped, and the Tech rushed over, kneeling beside the stream to gulp down a mouthful of cool, fresh mountain water. The others followed, eager for a drink. A12 splashed some water on the neck to cool the skin, but the summer sun, unrelenting, still took its toll. The face and neck had turned pink—ultraviolet radiation the culprit.

"Hey, a path to the top!" T23 shouted, excitement in the voice as the rait ran up the hill.

"Wait for us!" A12 hollered.

By the time the Tech reached the crest, there was nothing but an endless stretch of forest—vast, untouched, and wild. Valleys and rolling hills spread in all directions, a sea of trees that seemed to pulse with life. It was undeniably beautiful, an ecological wonder—but also empty. No signs of intelligent life, no hint of civilization. No cities or structures. No roads or paths leading to something more.

A12 paused, taking in the panoramic view, the silence pressing in like a heavy weight. "What shall we do?"

"We have to continue," T23 said. "I'm sure we'll find somethin'. There has to be."

"What about nourishment?" A92 seemed to be suffering a proper hunger for the first time.

"We should focus on what we control," A81 said. "We could return to the Arc."

"After all this?" T23 questioned. "We have to keep goin'."

"But what are we looking for?" A92 retorted. "More bushes. We have bushes on the Arc. And nourishment. Do you really want to spend another night freezing your bum off?"

"We could make a nest," A12 said. "Burrow in like a bunny."

"I like bunnies," A92 said, showing interest.

"That's a good idea," T23 said. "We have a few more hours of daylight. We'll look for another water source and a place to sleep. We can build a little rabbit house, wash off, and find some nourishment."

"I wouldn't mind giving that a go," A92 mumbled.

The four friends lumbered on. After traveling another four hundred cubits or so, A81 stopped. "Look! In that far valley. Smoke."

The others turned to see. To the southwest, puffs of white smoke rose high into the sky.

"It must be," A12 said.

"It has to be," T23 said.

The four stared at one another with surprised smiles. There was hope, after all, but the smoke was some distance away.

"Let's keep goin'," T23 said.

After trekking another few hundred cubits, T23 noticed something ahead; it was blocking their way. It rose from ground to sky and stretched from left to right as far as the eye could see.

"It's a lasonic shield," A12 said, noticing T23's stare.

"A shield?" T23 asked curiously.

"Like the ones on the Arc. But ours are smaller. When I open a lighting panel, my presence deactivates its generator, allowing me to access the components while preventing unauthorized residents from doing the same. It's a safety thing."

"What's it doing here?" A81 asked.

"Maybe it's an outer perimeter," T23 said.

"This far out?" A81 asked.

"Will it hurt us?" A92 asked worriedly.

"We can probably walk straight through it," A12 said.

"Probably?" T23 questioned.

"Yep, it depends on which side is active versus passive. I'll go first."

The four raits hastened along the trail, stopping shy of the shimmering divide. A12 walked up to it and began to step through.

ZAP!

A12 reeled backward, falling to the ground, convulsing in agony. The Tech's body went limp.

The other three rushed to help. T23 clutched A12's face, gaping at the dait's shuttered eyes.

"*A12, A12!*" T23 shouted.

A spurt of air jumped from 12's nose, and the stomach twitched.

"*WAKE UP, WAKE UP!*" T23 shook the dait's shoulders. "Please, wake up."

There was another spurt and another twitch.

"Please, oh please," T23 begged.

Then a snort.

T23's frightened stare turned into a gawk.

The next spurt morphed into a snicker, and a grin appeared. "This is the passive side," A12 said, opening the eyes.

"Good one." A92 turned and almost threw up.

"You scared the water out of me," T23 snarled. "Not funny."

A12 jumped up, dusted off, and strode through the shimmering wall, leaving T23 and the others behind, stunned and dazed. After some profanities, they reluctantly followed the Tech.

• • • •

A12 was the first to hear the distant gush and burble of water. The Tech picked up the pace, navigating around a rocky outcrop and a patch of mountain greenery, scampering down a small bank, and racing to the high waterfall. It was an alluring sight: cascading water spilling over a tall rocky overhang, filling a small oval pond at its base. The overflow tumbled down a rocky hollow into another mountain pool, and so on and so forth, for two or three more levels.

"Last one in." A92 rushed past and waded into the pond's cool, clear depths. She gasped. "It's cold—it's cold!" The frigid water cut sharp and clean, a welcome relief from the heat. She slipped off her jumpsuit and kicked into open water, laughing as she splashed and spun.

A81 wasn't far behind. He dove in after her, chasing her trail with an easy, eager stroke.

A12 glanced at T23, who met the look with a fiery intensity. Despite the earlier trickery, something burned behind those eyes—undeniable, magnetic.

A flicker of warmth rose. A12 smiled, playful now, and motioned toward the water.

Slowly, deliberately, they slipped out of their clothes, the charged silence between them deepening with each movement. The breeze curled around bare skin, sharpening sensation. The two stood there for a moment—exposed, alive—before stepping closer to the water's edge.

The Tech and the Engineer waded into the pond, its magical chill rising up their legs and thighs. A12 gasped as the cold water passed her nether regions, but this was natural, not artificial. She paused to let her body adjust to its soft embrace before edging deeper into its chilly depths. A12 smiled. She felt the sun's warmth on her face and the water's coolness on her body. She laid back and allowed the pool's buoyancy to carry her about. She heard her friends laughing and playing—it was such a beautiful sound. The waterfall's rush was so soothing and meditative, like a protective cocoon, drowning out any distant noises or clatters that might interfere with this moment of joy and newfound freedom. "*It's amazing!*" she shouted.

As time passed, the four travelers continued to play and splash like nymphs in a storybook, without care, frolicking and tittering, their bodies cleansed and their minds purified.

A92 was the first to step from the mountain pool. Her nude, wet figure glistened in the sunlight. She motioned for A81 to join her, and the two ran off into the forest, perhaps to find a soft, mossy bed to play and enjoy a private moment.

Now alone, A12 climbed up on a flat rocky ledge and edged into the falling water, allowing its surge to drench her body. When T23 tried to do the same, A12 offered a hand up, but when he grabbed hold, she purposely let go, causing him to plunge back into the deep, cold water.

Surprised, he resurfaced with a determined gleam on his face—and how could one miss that mischievous grin?

A12 returned the grin because she wanted more.

He, of course, promptly obliged, climbed up, and advanced toward her. He reached out and clasped her arms.

She trembled when he pulled her near, not from the chill but the touch. When their bodies met, he guided her into the water and began to devour her essence. As time passed and their passion heightened, A12 gazed into his eyes, and somewhere in their depths, she saw promises of things to come. She whispered, "I've got to have you." And he submitted to her will.

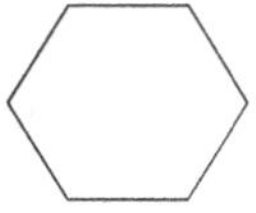

CHAPTER TWENTY-FOUR

LOST

Menawa surveyed Apehkv's defensive works. They appeared to be in good order, but the threat of an attack had kept the People on edge. Warriors had repaired and strengthened the log palisade, and the women had gathered crops to fill the stores. Other villagers were constructing weapons of war, but the children continued to play as though all were well and peace was an everlasting condition.

Accompanied by the tribe's clan leaders, the Mekko walked the perimeter.

"We are ready if the Dark Spirit attacks," Talof Harjo said confidently.

"We have two points of weakness," Tomucece explained. "The approaches along the creek and the open sky."

"The shelters we constructed along the wall should provide good cover," Menawa said. "If the Dark Spirit attacks from above, our warriors will have a place to retreat."

"We've positioned stones every ten paces," Yahola added, pointing toward the wall. "We've also readied fire arrows."

"Good," Menawa said. "And our crops?"

"The women will gather the last of it today," Tomucece answered.

"Excellent," Menawa said. "Tomorrow, we'll send out a small patrol to scout the forest. It would be best if we strike first. Now, let us see to our work."

• • • •

On the east side of Wewoka Creek, opposite the village, the women harvested the last crops. Halona moved through the lush field, weaving between clusters of squash, beans, and corn. She inspected each plant with care, plucking what was ripe and ready. Sweat trickled down her forehead as she reached beneath a tangle of vines, fingers brushing through the leaves to gather a handful of beans. Her back throbbed from hours of bending. Straightening, she pressed her hands to her hips and arched her back, exhaling as the tension eased.

Halona gazed at the forest and wondered what dangers lay in its shadows. A life had been sacrificed, and others might soon suffer the same fate. Her mind drifted to Hasse Ola and Cekote. They had been such close friends.

A gnat buzzed by her ear, interrupting her stare and her thoughts. She wiped her forehead, shook off the melancholy, and resumed work. She loaded a basket with winter squash. It was one of her favorites; its yellowish-orange pulp tasted like sweet potato. After placing a rather sizeable one in a basket, Halona motioned for Neena to fetch it.

The older daughter hurried over, lifted the basket with a heave, and toted it to the creek. She washed away any dirt or debris still clinging to its tan skin.

Wanting to help, Mausi joined her older sister at the creek's edge. Neena agreed reluctantly, hoping her younger sister's contribution would help rather than hinder the chore.

Mausi smiled at her sister's yielding face, removed a small squash from the basket, and washed it in the cold water. The dry, crusty earth quickly disappeared. Mausi returned the fruit to the basket, grabbed another, and repeated the process.

Once Neena and Mausi had cleansed the fruit, they carried it to the family dwelling. The two sisters laid out the harvest on split-cane mats, where for ten days, the upper-ground squash would rest and cure for winter storage.

Pleased with her accomplishment, Mausi decided it was time to pursue other interests, so as young girls do, she wandered away from her mother's and sister's loving care.

• • • •

Strolling along the creek's margin, not more than two hundred paces north of the village, Mausi spotted a patch of bright yellow blanket flowers. She hurried over and waded into their center, the petals vibrant in the afternoon sun. Delighted by the find, Mausi cupped two blossoms in her hands, their velvety texture cool against her palms. She held them to her nose. Their soft petals instantly filled her nostrils with a sweet, herbaceous scent—rich and full, like summer rain on warm earth. For a moment, the world seemed to narrow to the flowers and her breath, but at the height of her joy, she heard a noise. Instinct told her she was not alone.

As sly as a fox, Mausi crouched down and scanned the area, not uttering a sound. Mausi listened for the rustle of leaves or the crackle of twigs as her keen young eyes searched the landscape.

And then it happened. To Mausi's front, fifty paces, she spotted something from the corner of an eye. It had darted between two trees on the edge of the wood. She moved closer, staying low to the ground so as not to alert or alarm the intruder. She moved to the right in a circular pattern, hoping to flank its position and get a better glimpse.

It moved again, but this time deeper into the forest's shadows.

Mausi took cover behind a hickory on the edge of the wood line. She peeked around the tree's shaggy gray trunk, spotting the culprit thirty paces ahead.

The creature bolted across the forest floor, crunching through the underbrush as it bounded deeper into the woods.

Mausi dashed after it, weaving between a red oak and a towering pine before ducking behind a boulder. The chase led up a narrow hollow where a brook trickled between the rises.

Moving lightly along the water's edge, Mausi climbed higher, breath quickening with each step.

At the crest, the creature reappeared—ten paces ahead, staring back. Fearless.

An Appalachian cottontail, but not just any cottontail.

This one had no tail. Pasekolv—the trickster rabbit.

Alerted by Mausi's approach, the rabbit flicked an ear, twitched his nose, and sniffed the air. Then, with a flash of quicksilver instinct, he vanished beneath a thicket of mountain laurel.

The determined little girl raced forward, but the trickster rabbit darted from bush to bramble, deeper into the forest—always just out of reach. Fast, clever, untouchable.

Mausi pursued without hesitation—until she realized she no longer recognized her surroundings. Her focus on Pasekolv had clouded her sense of direction. She had wandered too far. She could no longer tell which way led home.

Climbing a rise, she scanned the terrain, hoping to regain her bearings—but nothing was familiar. She searched for her footprints, for any sign of her path, but the forest had swallowed them whole.

Wandering through the trees, she stumbled upon more hollows and hills, each blending into the next. She scrambled down a slope, crossed a wooded stretch, and emerged into a clearing. Heart pounding, she rushed to its center, turning in circles.

Trees. Flowers. Birds. Squirrels. All unfamiliar.

Mausi was lost.

The little girl searched and searched for a path home, but the sun had settled, and the sky had faded to gray. She looked up, hoping for direction, but a thick bank of clouds had swallowed the sun, stealing the last traces of daylight. Shadows deepened, the mountain air turned cool, and the forest felt even darker, more immense.

Mausi's stomach knotted. Night was coming, and she would have to endure it alone.

Her father would be angry. Her mother would cry. The thought made her chest ache, but regret would not lead her home. Safety and survival. That was all that mattered now.

• • • •

Mausi scouted the forest for a suitable campsite and soon found a circular thicket of towering white oaks. Their arching boughs wove together, forming a natural canopy over a patch of firm, dry ground. This would do.

She set to work. First, she gathered limbs and brush, stacking them between the great oaks to create a protective barrier. Then, she scratched out a fire pit and built a small reflective firewall to radiate heat into the shelter she would soon construct.

A fallen log, just the right length, lay nearby. She dragged it back and wedged it between the forks of two smaller trees—her ridgepole. Drawing her knife, she sliced a length of green vine and lashed the beam in place. Next came the frame: long, slender branches leaned against the ridgepole, forming the slanted walls. She wove more limbs and vines through the gaps, tightening the lattice until it held firm.

Finally, she heaped on layer after layer of leaves and pine straw, packing it down until no slivers of light shone through. It would be thick enough to shed rain, sealing her in a dry cocoon.

Inside, she piled soft underbrush into a thick bed. When she finished, she stepped back, breathing in the scent of crushed pine and damp earth. It wasn't home, but it would keep her safe until morning.

As Mausi worked on her temporary home, the overcast sky had turned from an owl gray to a raven black. Mausi removed a flint quartz from her waist pouch, and, with the help of a pyrite stone and some dried tree fungus, she sparked an ember. Gingerly, she placed the glowing flicker in a nest of tinder and blew on it until it burst into a flame. She deposited the burning bundle into a stack of kindling. Then she added longer lengths of wood until the fire's hot yellow glow leapt into the air and lit up the surrounding ring of oaks. Mausi smiled at her accomplishment; it was like an offering to the mighty oaks and, hopefully, a signal to her family.

Time to rest. Mausi plopped down next to the fire. She thought of her family. What were they doing? Were they worried about their youngest daughter, and what was Mother fixing for dinner? Mausi's mouth watered, and her stomach rumbled. She reached into her waist pouch and pulled out a small piece of acorn bread and a little chunk of venison jerky, the extent of her rations. She enjoyed the meal, but tomorrow, she must forage for more.

Growing tired, Mausi gazed at the fire as it cracked and popped, and tiny little sparks floated up like fireflies dancing in the heavens. And all around, an endless cacophony of frogs, crickets, and katydids chirped, croaked, and cheeped. In the distance, she heard night birds and the hoots of an owl. An inexperienced traveler might mistake these noises for forest monsters or wild beasts, but to Mausi, they were the songs of life.

She stretched out on the ground, peering through the overhead canopy at the evening sky. The clouds were clearing, drifting away, revealing thousands of twinkling stars. Any moment now, that puffy gray one might move aside and show the moon. And then it did, exposing the moon's thin, waxing form. She jumped up and marked its path on the ground with two sticks.

Mausi sat back down but heard something moving—drawing closer to her camp. Sensibly, she knew there was always something lurking in the dark: a squirrel, fox, bobcat, or even a bear. She couldn't be sure if it was friend or foe unless it stepped into the firelight and foolishly revealed itself. She assumed she could make noise to scare it off, but knew that might do the opposite and draw the curious creature even closer.

To calm her fears, Mausi focused on weaving a small basket while singing a lullaby about turtle shells. Her sister, Neena, had sung it to her many times, as far back as she remembered. Mausi sang softly, hoping its melody would pacify the forest. "*Pipe nuckv, nuckv nuckv, Lucv hopokvn ayvnks ce…*"

Mausi finished the basket, but her head had nodded several times. Her eyes were heavy despite her fears. The little girl threw more wood on the fire and crawled into her makeshift dwelling. She snuggled into a blanket of leaves as memories of her village pranced in her head. She envisioned herself at home, safe in bed. Now, all she heard was the silent roar of the wood and what lurked in its shadows. Mausi closed her eyes. She hoped no harm would come to her, and like Pasekolv, she must endure the perilous forest. The tired little girl fell asleep, and the stars and planets quietly drifted across the black sky as time passed.

• • • •

The sun was up, but a morning fog had settled upon the woodland like a cool, wet blanket. A chill ran down Mausi's body as she crawled from her leafy cocoon. She stretched her arms and brushed off her doeskin clothing. Everything was covered in dew; little drops of water dripped from bushes and trees. The air felt cool and moist, with a subtle, clean aroma that whispered of a new day. She stepped over to the fire pit, added some wood, and rekindled its heat. Within minutes, the fire leapt into the air and lapped at the wood, radiating a glow that warmed Mausi's shivers and sleepy-eyed disposition.

She decided to spend the day improving her campsite and searching for food. If Mausi stayed in place, her father would surely find her. It was a matter of time.

She began by exploring the immediate area for wild foods, finding a shagbark hickory whose nuts had started to drop and now dotted the ground. She picked one up, peeled off its greenish-brown outer husk, and checked its inner shell for wormholes. There were none, so she placed it in her newly made basket and gathered more. When her basket was full, she took the bounty to her campsite and stashed it in a safe place lest a bold squirrel find it and help himself.

Mausi continued foraging and discovered a circle of mushrooms in a grassy clearing not a hundred paces from her camp. These buff and honey-colored bonnets had slight umbos and white gills, and would make a splendid meal. She gathered a basket's worth, took a third, and left the rest to the forest. Nearby, she found a patch of stinging nettle. She carefully plucked off the upper leaves, still tender and absent the sting. It would make an excellent tea.

Having collected her supplies, Mausi spent the rest of the morning framing her shelter's sides to prevent rain or wind from entering her makeshift home. She also gathered limbs and brush to reinforce her perimeter's thorny fence. After a worrisome night, this barbed barrier might help ease her mind. Of course, it would not stop a determined predator, but it might make it hesitate and give Mausi a chance to defend herself.

As the day passed, Mausi looked and listened for signs of rescue.

Occasionally, she would stop what she was doing and scan the forest, searching with eyes and ears for familiar faces and voices. She hoped to see her father, but the woods remained empty and silent.

When late afternoon arrived, it was time to hunt for game, specifically squirrels, which should be out and about gathering an evening snack. Mausi studied the surrounding treetops for the right fluffy nest. There, in the tall red oak—time to lay the trap. Mausi found a fallen log twice her length and as thick as her arm. She placed it at an angle against the oak's fat trunk. The People knew squirrels were a lazy bunch and would surely take the easiest path.

To avoid scenting the area, Mausi retreated fifty paces down the hillside. There, she found a thicket of yellow poplar saplings. She pulled out her knife, cut into their slender trunks, and stripped away their bark. She then separated the inner from the outer by twisting and pulling apart their layers, and within an hour, she had what she needed, a workable pile of fibrous strands.

Mausi gathered up the bundle, hurried over to a fallen tree, and, with a stone that fit her hand, pounded on the wooden strips to soften their structure and ready them for the next step. When done, she found a pleasant place to sit and leg-roll the materials. From her fingertips to the heels of her hand, she rolled two plies of fibers down her thigh. She made two passes, then reversed the roll and twisted the two parts into a single piece of cordage. She made four lengths, each the length of her arm.

Mausi returned to the angled log and tied the four pieces around its circumference, a forearm's measure apart. She then tied a loop on the four loose ends. The idea was simple. When the squirrels ran up or down the log, traveling to and from their nest, they would pass through the loops. If all worked as planned, a loop would snag and tighten around the squirrel.

With the snare set, Mausi returned to her campsite. It had been a long day, but more work was still needed. She gathered firewood, broke it into suitable lengths, and piled it high near her firepit. Then, she stoked the fire, feeding it with twigs and branches until she had established a fresh bed of coals. With the help of two stones, she cracked open some of her hickory nuts and picked out their fleshy meat. The nuts would make an excellent snack, but she hoped they wouldn't be a substitute for roasted squirrel.

The sun sank low in the western sky, casting long shadows across the land. She extended her hand, turned it sideways, and stacked her fingers above the horizon. Two fingers fit between the Earth and the Sun. The night was fast approaching; the sky had turned to hues of pink and orange. It was time to check the snare.

Mausi dashed through the forest but cleverly stopped a few paces short to peer through the underbrush. Her face brightened when she spotted a little clump of brownish-gray fur. A squirrel hung from the log, a loop of cordage around its neck. The gentle creature was dead.

Mausi said a prayer to Mother Earth for the squirrel's generosity. "May its flesh nourish my body and its spirit brighten my soul."

She collected the beast and hurried to a nearby creek. There, she laid the animal out on a rock, pulled back its tail, and cut through the hide, making a slit from one rear leg to the other but leaving the skin intact on the top of its rump. Then, with her foot, she held down the squirrel's hindquarters, grabbed the tail, and pulled up, stripping away its fur as though pulling off a pair of leggings. Afterward, she cut off the head and then the front and rear legs at the knee joints. From its hind end, she cut through the pelvis and up the belly to the neck, careful not to slice into its entrails. She pulled out the esophagus with two fingers, then raked down the body's cavity, removing the squirrel's guts, including the heart, lungs, liver, and intestines. She checked the organs for black spots and other signs of disease. None were present; the squirrel was edible.

Mausi rinsed off the squirrel's fleshy carcass in the creek and hastened back to the camp as the sun disappeared below the hills. She smiled; it was time for supper. The little girl cut off a long green branch from a tree, skewered the squirrel from rump to throat, and placed it on two forked sticks spanning the fire. She then fashioned a few more branches, skewered her mushrooms, and stuck them in the ground beside the fire.

As the squirrel and mushrooms cooked, Mausi placed her handmade basket filled with water near the fire. Earlier, she had lined the basket with leaves from a black oak's shady underbelly and sealed their large lobed edges with pitch. Mausi picked up some stinging nettle and a handful of mulberries and dropped them in. She retrieved a small river stone from the fire with a couple of sticks, blew off its ashes, and gingerly placed it into the basket. The water gurgled, but one was not enough. She put a second and third into the water, and soon it boiled.

Now, it was time to relax and let the mulberry and nettle tea steep. Mausi could smell her meal; the aroma of roasting meat and mushrooms made her mouth water. It was going to be such an excellent meal. Still, there were other concerns. Night had fallen, and predators would soon be hunting.

• • • •

In another part of the forest, four lost souls struggled to make their way toward the distant white puffs of smoke. They were becoming haggard and emaciated, fighting thorns and brush at every turn. Their desire to reach Kallipolis, a philosopher's notion of a beautiful city, was beginning to wane. As they hiked farther from Arc1983, they became more accountable for their survival. They could not open a cooler in a poly or order a nourishment from a bar. Their guardians had always provided, and none questioned this naive expectation.

The sun set. The four raits, exhausted and hungry, desperately needed food and shelter. A12 spotted something through the dark forest, a few hundred cubits to their front. "Hey, I see a light."

"Where?" A92 said, stumbling along, staring in the wrong direction.

"It's flickering," T23 said. "We should check it out."

"We should be careful," A81 said. "What if it's hostile?"

"Bugger, mait," A92 said, "how could anyone resist your charm?"

Unable to resist the compliment, A81's face cracked a grin, but then he tripped over a vine and almost fell on his face.

Startled, A92 rushed to his aid. "You okay, love?"

"I'm fine, Petunia."

"We'll go slow," T23 said. "So, no more talkin'. Follow me."

A92 frowned. "But what if I need to say something?"

"*Shhh.*" A81's head shook.

The four friends plodded on, but untrained and unskilled, their feet were heavy upon the land. Leaves and branches cracked and snapped as they clomped and stomped through the woods. When vines and briars pulled at their clothing, they jerked, yanked, and cursed and, more likely than not, alerted every breathing creature for some distance. The travelers, of course, were ignorant of their novice folly, lumbering through the woods like a herd of rambling beasts, oblivious to the danger.

• • • •

Mausi sliced off a piece of barbecued squirrel and took a bite. A little gamey compared to rabbit, but with a faint nuttiness. She carved another sliver and chewed it down. Hunger made a person less picky, but to Mausi, this was one of the best meals she had ever eaten.

Well, except for her mother's blackberry fritters—those were the best. Oh, and the dumplings, flavored with possum grapes, soft and bursting with sweetness. And, of course, her mother's rabbit stew. Now that was a meal.

Lost in thought, she nearly missed the sound. A rustling. Something was approaching.

The scent of roasting meat must have drawn a curious beast. Mausi froze mid-chew, her pulse quickening. Slowly, she turned her head, straining to hear past the crackling fire. In the darkness, her ears became her guide.

To the left—a soft, shuffling noise.

Something was circling her camp.

Something was stalking her.

She held her breath and dared not move.

After a few uneasy seconds, Mausi rose—slowly, quietly—and stepped beyond the firelight for a better look into the darkness.

A sound. The soft swoosh of paws. Or feet. Or something else. Circling.

Her pulse pounded in her ears. She listened, breath shallow. Out here, she was just another link in the food chain—and not always the master.

The shuffling crept closer. Something pushed through the camp's thorny perimeter.

A crunch.

Behind her.

Mausi spun around.

Her worst fear.

Estepapv.

The dreaded people-eater of legend had entered her camp.

The cougar stood firm, eyes locked on Mausi, hunger burning in its glare. A muffled growl rumbled from its chest, rising and falling with each breath.

It slid to the right.

Drool wet its teeth. Its breath came hot and thick.

Circling the fire, Estepapv crept closer. Another growl, low and ragged.

The cougar was preparing to pounce.

But Mausi was not just any little girl—she was the *Mekko's* daughter.

She leapt into a fighting stance, drew her stone knives, and let out her fiercest war-whoop.

The little girl met the hungry beast's gaze, fearless, unyielding. She stepped forward, planting her feet. *This was her ground.*

The cougar growled, slinking left, then right. Testing her.

Mausi tracked its every move, muscles coiled, ready.

Then—

Estepapv lunged.

Mausi slashed. A sharp edge met flesh. A streak of blood.

The cougar shrieked—a sound so guttural, so unearthly, it could have come from the lower world itself. It staggered back, then lowered its body for a second attack.

Mausi braced.

Then—

Shouting. Distant but real—voices carried on the wind, beyond the camp's perimeter.

The cougar's ears flicked. It hesitated, stepping back.

Mausi seized the moment. "Go away! Whoop, whoop! *Go away!*"

Unnerved by the strange sounds and an enemy that would not break, Estepapv turned—then bounded into the thorny brush, swallowed by the night.

For a moment, Mausi remained in her defensive stance, listening as the cougar's footsteps faded into the night. But behind her—another sound.

More paws. Or feet.

Rustling leaves. Snapping twigs. Something—or someone—was approaching.

Mausi turned, heart pounding, eyes straining to pierce the dark.

Nothing. No living beast. No shifting shadow.

That was when they stepped into her camp.

Her breath caught.

She could not believe her eyes.

The legend was true.

Este Lopocke—little people—they were real.

Standing before her, half her size, their soft, squeaky voices carried in the night. Two were male and two female, clad in tiny garments of yellow, green, and white.

They had been watching.

Mausi crouched for a better look at the strange little guests. "*Hesci*—hello." She pointed to herself. "*Mausi cvhocefkv tos*—Mausi is my name."

The one in yellow mumbled something to the one in green. Mausi sensed they were scared. "*Naket cehocefkvte?*" she asked gently, gesturing toward them.

No answer.

She knelt, careful not to startle them. "*Mausi*," she repeated, touching her chest, then pointing back toward the Este Lopocke.

"We saw the light," the one in green said, staring up at the giant girl. "I'm A12."

Mausi did not understand their language but repeated the last expression, "A-twelf."

"Yes, that's right." A12 nodded in agreement.

"I'm T23," said the one in white.

"Tee-twen-tee-tree," Mausi repeated.

And the two in yellow said, "I'm A92, love."

"And I'm A81."

"A-nin-tee-too-luv. A-ate-tee-one."

The four little guests chuckled and laughed at Mausi's response.

Mausi's face turned blank, deep-set eyes narrowing. After a pause, the corners of her mouth lifted, and she joined in the laughter. Extending her hand, she said, "*Likepvs ce*"—welcome.

A12 took hold. "The pleasure is mine."

"*Celvwete?*" Mausi rubbed her stomach and pointed at the roasting squirrel.

A12 shrugged, unsure.

Mausi led A12 closer to the fire. "*Ero hompetvn ce yacv?*" she asked, cutting a piece of meat. She tasted it first, then sliced another and offered it to the little being.

A12's eyes widened, her face contorting at the sight of the cooked flesh.

Mausi frowned. Evidently, little people disliked squirrel. But guests should never refuse a gift—especially food. That would be rude.

She repeated the offer, this time more firmly. "*Hompvs!*" Eat!

A12 glanced back at her companions.

"I think she wants you to consume it." A92's nose wrinkled with revulsion.

"You've got to be kidding," A12 said.

"Did you see the way she used her teeth?" A92 said. "Disgusting."

"You'd best try it, or we might be next," A81 warned.

"I can't believe this. Here goes." A12 nibbled on the meat; it tasted smoky and greasy, but savory. The Tech's face turned from aversion to delight. She gobbled down the rest of the piece. Hunger will do that.

Mausi smiled from ear to ear and motioned for the others to step forward and share in the feast. Mausi cut off more little morsels and handed each a sample to enjoy.

From Mausi's perspective, these little lost souls seemed to be starving, but unknown to her, their desire to satisfy basic physiological needs conflicted with their lofty, urbane preferences. But given the situation, they wolfed down the animal protein, disregarding their fallible convictions. Mausi smiled, cut off more chunks, and passed them around. The four little visitors stuffed their faces and filled their bellies.

Curious about their origin, Mausi studied these little humanlike creatures as they chewed, munched, and swallowed. Perhaps their cave was nearby, and there were more, but why didn't they have hairy faces and horns? Her older brother's stories must have gotten a few facts wrong. Mausi smiled. More importantly, she was no longer alone; the legend's prophecy must be true. The little people would watch over her until her safe return to the People.

Bellies full, it was time for sleep. Mausi grabbed A12 by the hand and led her to the lean-to.

"*Nucvs,*" Mausi commanded her to sleep, motioning for the others to join. "*Nucvs,*" she repeated, gently herding the little fair folk toward their bed with a swoosh of her hand.

The exhausted raits found their places and settled in for the night. Not long after, all drifted off to sleep, comforted by the presence of others and the forest's chirps, creaks, croaks, crackles, rustles, snaps, cheeps, buzzes, hoots...

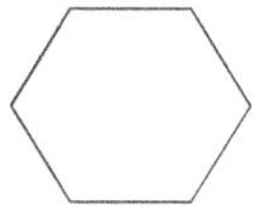

CHAPTER TWENTY-FIVE

THE ARROW

Mausi's disappearance was heartbreaking. Many believed it was the work of the Dark Spirit, but a large search party would be unwise, as it might leave Apehkv vulnerable to attack. Perhaps that was precisely the Dark Spirit's plan: to lure the warriors away from the village, dividing and conquering. However, Menawa knew he could not abandon his daughter to the mercy of the forest; that, too, would be unthinkable. He assembled a small patrol, Owlelo, Tussekeah, and Hothlepoya. Hasse Ola insisted on going as well. Menawa obliged.

Owlelo picked up the little girl's trail on the forest's edge, but her footprints led the searchers in many directions. The prints went left and right, then circled back to the same spot before trailing off in a new direction, deeper into the woods.

Hasse Ola, eager to find his little sister, sprinted ahead of the search party, and more than once, Menawa warned him about his impulsive behavior. Hasse Ola was making Owlelo's job difficult, creating more tracks and possibly erasing others. Menawa stopped the patrol and signaled for Owlelo to fetch his son.

Hasse Ola returned to the group; the young warrior had a scowl on his face. He approached his father.

"Stay with the patrol." Menawa was not pleased.

"I know she's out there, Father. I will find her."

"*We* will find her. We search as one, and we fight as one."

"Owlelo is taking too much time. She might be hurt."

"Owlelo is wise and patient. You must assume our enemies are as well. Your place is behind me. I know this is your first patrol, and you are eager to prove your worth, but you must do as I command. Out here, I am your leader, not your father."

"Yes, Father."

Menawa locked eyes with Hasse Ola.

"Yes, Mekko."

"Better."

Menawa motioned to Owlelo. The Tracker continued the search.

• • • •

A day and a night had passed. Menawa's search for Mausi had led them farther from the village and closer to the Great Hills. At midday, he stopped the patrol for a brief rest. It was a peaceful day, absent any signs of danger, dark spirits, or wild beasts—nothing to foreshadow some ominous destiny. He pulled out a piece of dried venison and chewed it down. As Mekko, he had many worries. He thought of Cekote, his family, and his village. Menawa looked around. Now, where was his son?

Hasse Ola had stepped away from the others to relieve himself but came running back a moment later. "I smell smoke," he shouted excitedly, then turned and raced up the hill.

Menawa and the others jumped to their feet and hurried after him. The Mekko signaled Owlelo to take the lead and the other two warriors to flank the target. Tussekeah went left, and Hothlepoya right, swinging out fifty paces, advancing on the target from three pincered directions. If there was danger, the patrol would have the advantage of surprise.

Owlelo sprinted up the hill. The scout sniffed the air, then turned to Menawa and pointed farther up the slope. The two warriors advanced, soon reaching the crest of the rise. To their front, Menawa spotted a campsite. The Mekko drew his war club, and Owlelo readied his atlatl. Tussekeah and Hothlepoya advanced from the flanks, their weapons ready.

"She must be here." Hasse Ola dashed around the camp.

Menawa signaled to Hasse Ola to hold his tongue and for the others to disperse.

Owlelo, Tussekeah, and Hothlepoya moved twenty paces from the camp, found concealed positions, and secured the perimeter.

Menawa pushed through the camp's thorny fence and advanced to its fire pit. The site was empty, but a whiff of smoke from a few remaining coals rose into the air.

Hasse Ola ducked into the makeshift shelter, tossing and kicking its bedding.

Menawa recognized the bushcraft, the lean-to shelter, the fire pit, the heat-reflecting wall, and the improvised fence. Mausi must be close.

Hasse Ola bolted from the shelter and ran to his father, holding wilted blanket flower blooms. "She's here, she's here," he said, seeking his father's approval.

Menawa reached up and warmly squeezed his son's shoulder. Hasse Ola smiled.

The Mekko motioned for Owlelo to pick up the trail. Owlelo's eyes scanned the ground, and within seconds, he spotted a cluster of footprints leading away from the camp. One set was child-sized, but the others were different. Owlelo advanced through the woods, following the prints. The other warriors were on his heels.

"*Aaaaah!*" A scream pierced the air from up ahead.

Menawa signaled. Tussekeah went left, and Hothlepoya right. The warriors crested a slight rise and were met with a shocking sight: Mausi lay motionless on the ground, with four tiny, humanlike creatures standing over her body, their expressions unreadable. The scene was eerily quiet, save for the distant rustling of leaves.

The warriors charged forward like wolves, closing in on their prey. The four little menaces spotted the warriors and darted underneath a mountain laurel. Mausi's eyes jolted open, startled by the commotion, spotting her father running towards her, jaw clenched, nostrils flared, and war club readied.

"Father, I'm okay!" Mausi cried, sitting up, frightened by her father's hostile glare. "They're my friends. The Este Lopocke are my friends. Please don't hurt them."

Menawa stopped in his tracks short of his daughter while his warriors converged on the laurel bush, pulling and bending limbs to gain access to the little troublemakers.

"Please, Father. They are my friends." Mausi ran over to protect the little people.

"Move away, sister," Hasse Ola shouted. "I'll kill the vermin."

Seeing Mausi's terrified face, Menawa motioned for Hasse Ola and the others to back away from the bush.

Mausi was shaking uncontrollably, whimpering in fear at her own kind, wondering what horror they would do.

Menawa felt his daughter's hurt, as fathers do. He knelt, took her into his arms, and hugged her. The Mekko wiped away her tears and held her until she relaxed and regained her composure.

"I'm sorry, Father," Mausi said, trembling. "Pasekolv tricked me."

"Pasekolv?" Menawa questioned.

"I saw him near our village. I tried to catch him, but he ran in circles and led me into the forest. I got lost."

"You gave us a scare. Your mother's heart is heavy with worry."

"I'm sorry, Father; I didn't mean to anger you or make Mother sad."

"I'm not angry. I'm proud of you. I saw your campsite. You are a brave little warrior."

Mausi threw her arms around her father, clinging tight as a sigh of relief escaped her lips. A tender smile broke across her face. "Last night, Estepapv attacked my camp! The little people chased him away."

"They did?"

"Yes, Father, they are my friends. Please don't hurt them. They are scared and hungry."

"Then why did you scream, sister?" Hasse Ola asked.

"I was teaching them to hunt. They caught me."

Menawa glanced at Owlelo, shaking his head, and chuckled.

Owlelo turned away, unable to control his grin.

"Then they are my friends too," Menawa said, amused at his daughter's innocence.

Mausi gazed at her father with a large, loving grin, grabbed his hand, pulled him toward the laurel bush, and motioned for her friends to come out.

The first one was a male, the height of Menawa's knee. The little creature motioned for the others to come out. Reluctantly, they did, gawking timidly at the gigantic human being.

"*Estvmin cet towa*—Where do you live?" Menawa's large, dark eyes studied the little creatures.

"They don't speak our language," Mausi said, smiling back and forth at her new friends and her father.

In their strange language, one said, "My identification is A12. We're from Arc 83." She pointed to the others. "This is T23, A81, and A92."

The little residents stared nervously at Menawa and grinned, maybe even grimaced, ever so slightly.

Menawa's face showed no emotion. As the Mekko, he was stern and uncompromising.

A92 said, "He's a bit of a serious bloke. I thought our Sophists were frosty."

"*Shhh*," A81 said. "He might stomp on you."

A92's face twisted into a scowl as she stepped back.

After a moment of curious gawking by both parties, Menawa took his regard off the little people. "It's time to go home, little bear." He waved to his warriors, and off they went, speeding down the hill. There remained the matter of the Dark Spirit and the village's safety. Menawa placed a hand on Mausi's back and guided her toward their home.

Mausi quickly grabbed A12's hand and pulled her along. The other three followed, gazing at the forest, probably wondering where this new adventure might lead.

• • • •

Halona was home when Hasse Ola burst in and announced, "I found her! I found her!"

The mother dropped what she was doing, hugged her son, and dashed from the dwelling to find her daughter.

Other villagers had gathered around and were staring at the strange procession. Halona pushed through the crowd and straight to Mausi, unmindful of the Este Lopocke.

Yahola approached the Mekko. "Why have you brought these vile little creatures to our village?"

"Brother," Menawa said calmly, "they're my daughter's friends and now my guests. They helped her fight off an attack from Estepapv."

The crowd gasped and began gossiping fearfully at the mere mention of the feared people-eater.

"Are you possessed by their magic, Mekko?" Yahola pointed at the Este Lopocke with his war club. "The Dark Spirit has sent them to spy on our camp. They are not to be trusted."

"I will trust them until they give me a reason not to."

Yahola turned and stormed off, dissatisfied with the Mekko's response.

Menawa led the crowd to the busk, where all could see and behold the Este Lopocke and thank them for their help.

The village women hurried to their homes and brought back food and drink. As word spread, the gathering turned from curious to festive, as villagers rushed to see and honor their guests.

Mausi led her little friends to the west arbor, where they took prominent seats next to the Mekko.

Two warriors fetched pitchers of *vpvske* and poured each attendee a cup of the cold, refreshing drink. For the Este Lopocke, someone had found tiny cups no bigger than a walnut shell.

T23 tasted the sweet beverage. "This is pretty good."

"This feels so weird. I can't believe we're doing this." A12's eyes brightened. "It's like a tasting party."

A92 gulped the corn drink. "It's creamy but a bit lumpy—if one were judging. I wonder if our Sophists know about this?"

"I don't think so, Petunia," A81 chuckled as he downed his second cup and gestured to the giant warrior for more.

The warrior refilled his cup, and the rait guzzled a third, then a fourth.

The others followed suit—seconds, thirds, even fourths.

"I'm about to burst." A92 rubbed her belly.

"Me too." A12 let out a burp and rubbed her belly. "I wonder what's next?"

• • • •

Most villagers were at the busk, but a few stood watch at the palisade. Mausi's return had become an impromptu celebration and a bit of a spectacle as all wanted to see the little guests, but the village could not let its guard down. The Dark Spirit could be near, and Yahola might be right.

The Clan Leader approached Tomucece. "These *things* do not belong in our village," Yahola scowled.

"What do you fear?"

"Menawa has brought the enemy into our camp. They will report what they have seen to their masters. They're here to find our weaknesses."

"They're Menawa's guests. He is the Mekko."

"I know who he is. His judgment has become clouded thanks to his daughter's mischief."

"What can be done?"

"I'm going to catch them at their game. They'll make a mistake, and when they do, I'll be there to end their evil."

"But what about Menawa?"

"Do you truly believe those little polecats chased off Estepapv or whatever it was? It was a ruse to gain entry to our village."

"If you're right, danger may soon be upon us."

"We have to stop them." Disgusted by the fanfare, Yahola left the grounds.

• • • •

The four little raits enjoyed the celebration and their newfound fame. Villagers had brought gifts to honor their bravery. Two such awards were a couple of tiny deerskin dresses that had previously been worn by dolls. The village girls led A12 and A92 into a nearby hut, where they helped them discard their tattered clothing and dress in their new attire. The girls pampered the two guests until the Technician and the Administrator were perfect miniature models of native princesses.

Not to be outdone, the boys led T23 and A81 to another hut and, likewise, dressed the two guests in native clothing. The boys used their chert blades to fashion pieces of deerskin into suitable mantles, loincloths, and leggings. They even painted their faces with symbols of the warrior class.

Soon, the children and the little people rejoined the festivities, and except for their stature, the four raits now resembled genuine members of the tribe.

Mausi and the other children led the happy raits in a mock stomp dance around the heart fire. They sang, danced, and laughed, and parents smiled and clapped. The celebration went on for some time until, at last, the sun dropped below the horizon, indicating it was time for the People to return to their homes, but a few were still in a festive mood and remained behind.

One of the little people ventured a question. "Can we look around?" A12 raised a finger and made a circling motion.

"*Nvkvftvs?*" Mausi tilted her head, misreading the gesture—perhaps assuming it meant assemble.

"Can we walk around?" A12 mimed walking with her fingers.

"*Yvkvpes?*" Mausi echoed the motion.

"Yuh-kuh-bes. Yes—walk." A12 sounded out the word.

Realization dawned. Mausi gave a nod and led the four little beings through the village—past homes, work areas, granaries, and even to the edge of the surrounding palisade. The evening was beautiful. A clear night sky stretched above, scattered with stars, and the moon—a bright, waxing crescent—cast a soft glow on the path ahead.

T23 took a particular interest in the logged palisade. "I wonder what that's for?"

"There must be something dangerous out there," A12 said. "Like the creature we saw in the forest. Or other people."

"Why would they fear other people?"

"Not everyone is as nice as we are." A92 wrapped a friendly arm around T23.

"That must be it." A12 rolled her eyes.

A81 pointed at one of the wooden towers. "What are they doing?"

"Must be watchin' for those beasts," T23 said.

"But, when we arrived, people were outside," A12 said.

"It seems *they're* allowed to go out," A92 added.

A12 chortled. "We'll never be the same, now, will we?"

"Nope. Don't believe so," A92 replied.

• • • •

Amongst the wattle-and-daub dwellings, a dark figure hid in their shadows, peering around earthen corners and logged structures. He watched the procession. He followed their little prying eyes, tiny pointing fingers, and little cackling voices as they muttered their little hideous language.

His heart was full of hate and disgust, and he was certain they were spies and would bring death to his village. He took up a concealed position behind a granary. It was a good position with a clear line of sight. He studied their movement. He nocked an arrow, raised his bow, and drew back. He aimed at a target; a headshot would work best. He waited for the right moment. There it was. He let the stretched sinew roll off his fingers until it snapped forward, sending the deadly projectile whooshing toward its mark.

• • • •

In an instant, A12 stepped right, unaware. Mausi stepped left.

The arrow whistled past A12's ear.

A scream.

Mausi crumpled to the ground.

At first, none of the four raits understood what had happened.

Then—blood began seeping through Mausi's clothes.

The Tech gasped and ran to her.

"She's hurt, she's hurt!" A12 cried. "There's something stuck in her side."

"It's one of those sticks with feathers," A92 said.

"*HELP! HELP!*" the little people shouted.

Talof Harjo was the first to arrive. He knelt beside Mausi and found the wound. Blood oozed steadily. She was breathing, but unconscious. He pressed gently around the injury, feeling the warmth of blood and a weak, irregular pulse. His expression darkened.

A12 stared at him in horror. "Please help her! Please help her!"

Talof Harjo didn't answer.

"Will she be okay?"

The warrior scooped up the girl and ran.

A12 and the others followed, their little legs struggling to keep pace with the giant human.

• • • •

Talof Harjo burst through the doors of the Heleshayv's dwelling, followed by A12 and the others.

Dela raised her hands to her face and gasped.

The warrior laid the girl down on a lump of bedding, then hurried from the home.

Dela rushed over to assess the extent of the wound. The arrow had pierced Mausi's right side between two lower ribs, but its head had not passed through the body. Dela quickly grabbed a knife and carefully cut off the shaft close to the skin to eliminate the hazard. She wrapped a clean cloth around the remaining wooden protrusion, applying firm pressure on the wound to slow the bleeding.

Within minutes, Menawa, Halona, and Talof Harjo rushed into the dwelling. Menawa stared at Mausi, then turned toward the little people, blame in his eyes. "Where is Yahola?" Menawa barked.

"I'll find him." Talof Harjo dashed from Dela's home to search for the Medicine Maker.

"Who has done this?" Menawa asked, eyes glaring and fists clenched.

The four little raits cowered in fear.

Word spread across the village. It was not long before a crowd gathered outside the residence.

Tomucece entered the dwelling, ready for the Mekko's orders.

"We have a rat in our camp," Menawa roared. "Bring our warriors to full alert. Find the rat and bring him to me!"

Without speaking, Tomucece stepped over to Mausi, picked up the bloody arrow shaft, and dashed from the dwelling.

Not long after, Talof Harjo returned with Yahola in trail. Yahola glanced at Mausi; then, he, too, glared at the little people. His disgust was unmistakable.

"Help my daughter," Menawa commanded, staring at the Heleshayv.

"This is the work of the Dark Spirit." Yahola unsheathed his knife and stepped towards T23. "These demons have brought death upon our camp."

"What are you doing?" Menawa pointed at Mausi. "That is one of our arrows. We have a rat in our camp. Are you going to help my daughter, *Heleshayv*?" Menawa stepped between Yahola and T23, ignoring the knife.

"My medicine is weak while these vile little creatures roam our camp. I can do nothing to help her." Yahola turned and stormed out.

T23 went to Mausi to study the wound. The Cardiovascular Engineer knew they could repair such a modest injury on the Arc. A damaged organ could be replaced, the tissue regenerated, the wound healed, and the scar erased. T23 turned to Menawa. "We can fix this on our Arc."

"But we're not on the Arc," A81 whispered from a corner.

T23 tried to communicate his sincerity. "We can help her on our Arc! She'll be okay."

"He doesn't understand what you're saying." A12 tried to pull T23 away.

"We can take her to our Arc." T23 pointed to the east. "We can fix her." T23 used his hands to express the repair. "She will be as good as new." T23 smiled and opened his arms in a friendly gesture. "Let us help."

Menawa shouted out an order to his warriors. Two of them grabbed the four little pests, one under each arm, and hauled them from the home.

The warriors carted the raits, kicking and screaming, to a granary hut, locked them inside, and placed them under guard.

A92 plopped down on the dirt floor. "That went well."

"They blame us," A12 snarled, throwing her hands into the air.

"That projectile was for you," T23 said. "It went straight over your head."

"I almost wish it had been me."

"We have to escape," A81 said. "This is not good."

"If we try, they'll believe we're to blame," A12 said. "They'd hunt us down and kill us."

"If she dies, we're in big trouble," A81 said.

"We have to convince 'em we can help." T23 paced, deep in thought.

"How are we going to do that?" A92 asked.

"I don't know," T23 snapped. "I need time to think."

"We may not have time, friend," A81 said fearfully.

T23 flopped down on the earthen floor between two cribs of dried corn, burying his head in his arms. He blamed himself entirely. He should have stayed on the Arc and accepted his place in its culture. He knew if he had, none of this would have happened. His selfie desire to be with A12 had led to this sequence of events. Now, he and his friends were in grave danger, and it was all his fault—his actions had brought them here.

• • • •

Dela and Halona attended to Mausi's wound. Dela tenderly twisted and maneuvered the projectile, hoping to dislodge it, but it held firm. The arrow must have hit a bone. And each attempt to move the shaft made the unconscious girl cough up blood.

"I need to remove the arrow," Dela said, glancing worriedly at Halona. "I need to make a small cut to enlarge the entry. Then I can slide my finger down the shaft to feel if it's lodged in a bone."

"Can't you pull it out?" Halona begged.

"No, that might cause more damage. I must find a way to remove the arrowhead. Its edges cut her every time she moves. If her blood continues to soak the bindings, the shaft will loosen and separate from the head."

"Go ahead. Do what you must." Halona turned away; tears rolled down her face.

Dela washed her hands, picked up a flint blade, and sterilized it over the lodge fire. When the knife had cooled, she made a small incision on each side of the protruding shaft. Then, carefully, Dela slid her right index finger down the shaft and into the wound. The arrow had penetrated a lung. Dela pushed on until she felt the sinewed lashings and the stone arrowhead. It had indeed pierced a bone. Dela knew trying to remove the arrow would cause more damage and likely hasten Mausi's fate.

Halona read her expression and started crying uncontrollably, collapsing on the ground. Dela tried to comfort her tribal sister, but unfortunately, it was now Halona's turn to endure a child's death.

As the minutes passed, Halona lay beside Mausi and stroked her little girl's beautiful, long, black hair and sang her favorite lullaby. "*Pipe, nuckv. Nuckv, nuckv. Lucv hopokvn, ayvnks ce. Pvkseno, rvlvkahes...*" Baby, sleep. Sleep, sleep. He went hunting for turtle shells. Tomorrow, he should return…

Mausi's breathing was becoming labored, intermittent, and weak. Regrettably, no one could say when death would come, but for this little girl, its dark grasp would likely take her before the next sunset.

• • • •

Menawa had gone to the busk and was pacing angrily around the heart fire. He had fear in his heart for his daughter and was mad with rage at whoever had committed this heinous act.

Out of the darkness, four warriors approached. Tomucece led, followed by Owlelo, Tussekeah, and Hasse Ola. The other two warriors had Hasse Ola by his arms.

Menawa stared at his son, then turned to the Clan Leader.

"What is this?" Menawa snapped.

Tomucece held out the broken arrow shaft. "It's from your clan and your house."

Menawa grabbed the arrow. He had helped his son make the arrow. It was his fletching. The Mekko glared at his son.

Hasse Ola lowered his eyes.

Enraged by this apparent admission, Menawa pulled out his war club and rushed toward Hasse Ola.

Tomucece and Owlelo leapt toward the Mekko and stopped his advance. The two warriors struggled to hold back the angry father. After a moment of tussling, Menawa relaxed his attack, pulled himself free, and stepped away.

The Mekko paced in a circle, head down, thinking and trying to calm himself. After a moment, Menawa returned. "What have you done, my son?"

Hasse Ola would not look at his father. He started sobbing.

"I asked you a question. *What have you done?*"

"They killed my friend." Hasse Ola wiped away some tears, sniffling a couple of times.

Menawa turned his back and again began to pace. He gazed at the black sky.

Had the Dark Spirit entered the village and taken possession of his son's soul, or was it the evil living in every man's heart?

The others waited for his response. The seconds passed like an eternity. Hasse Ola continued to whimper.

Menawa faced the group.

"My son—your friend—Cekote slipped and fell. It was a misfortune, not the act of another."

Hasse Ola sniffled. "It was the Dark Spirit."

Menawa drew in a deep breath.

"No, my son. The only dark spirit is the wolf living in our hearts. It latches onto ignorance and fear. We are its conscience. We feed it, just as Mother Earth feeds us. Each day, we choose between virtue and evil. Sometimes, we choose the wolf and do terrible things—as you have done, and I have nearly done. It is our nature."

"Your orders?" Tomucece asked.

"We are family. But we must obey our laws. If his sister dies, he will suffer his fate. For now, take him to his mother's home and place him under guard."

• • • •

Menawa entered the Heleshayv's dwelling, hopeful yet anxious. But the moment his eyes fell on Dela's and Halona's faces, he understood—his daughter was in grave condition. The Mekko kicked at the floor, cursing softly to himself as he weighed his next move.

Dela approached him, her hand reaching for his. "Perhaps the Este Lopocke can help."

"Are you suggesting they possess magic?" Menawa's voice held disbelief, laced with suspicion.

"I can't say," Dela replied. "But they will do no further harm."

"My daughter will recover." Menawa pulled his hand free. His jaw tightened. "There will be no death in this village, do you hear me? Now help my daughter!"

Dela's expression turned hard, her voice cold. "We have already had death in this village. My son. And now… it's your daughter's turn."

Menawa's glare could have melted stone.

"You're a hunter," Dela continued, her words measured but sharp. "Do deer recover when you pierce them with an arrow?"

Menawa snapped, his tone seething. "I usually slit their throats."

"My husband…" Halona's voice broke the tension as she rose to her feet, a pleading softness in her gaze. "Our daughter is going to die. You can see this is true. Please listen to Dela. Let the Este Lopocke help her. Mausi trusted them— and you should too."

Menawa stared at the ceiling, fists clenched. He let out a guttural grunt of frustration, the weight of the situation crushing him.

Without another word, he stepped to the door, threw back its cover, and bellowed a command to his warriors.

• • • •

A moment later, two warriors entered the hut carrying the four little raits, whom they dropped unceremoniously on the floor like slain meat.

The four stood and dusted off, murmuring an expletive or two at the treatment.

Menawa grabbed T23 by the nape, dragged him across the room, and dropped him next to Mausi. He pointed to the girl and issued a command.

"I think they want you to help," A12 said nervously.

"We can't help her here." T23 dusted himself off. "We have to go to the Arc."

"How?" A12 asked.

"We're smart. There must be a way."

"Too bad we don't have a communication device," A81 remarked.

"That's it," A12 said. "We need to send a message."

A92 frowned, baffled. "But we don't—"

"We can use light. We have fire," A12 explained.

T23 raised an eyebrow. "How's that going to help?"

"Think about it." A12 grinned. "We need some type of switch to open and close the circuit."

A92's confusion deepened. "A switch? Good luck with that."

"We need to make the fire flicker in a controlled way," A12 said. "We need something to cover and uncover the flame at regular intervals."

"Brilliant!" T23 exclaimed. "We can create a pattern—a signal—the Arc will see it."

"They'll be pissed when they get here," A81 scoffed.

"We'll deal with that later," T23 said.

"I'll take care of the circuit." A12 smiled.

T23 turned to Menawa. "We need to build a fire." The Engineer used his hands to imitate a fire. "A big fire." T23 repeated the gesture. The little rait ran to the door and motioned for Menawa to follow.

T23 dashed from the hut, passed onlookers, and headed for the busk. Once there, the Engineer ran to a woodpile, picked up the fattest log he could muster, and threw it on the heart fire. T23 grabbed a second and tossed it on. "Fire," T23 shouted, gazing up at Menawa, "We need to build a huge fire." T23 waved his arms up and down to simulate flames.

The Mekko grabbed a log and added it to the flame.

"Yes, more, more," T23 cried, jumping up and down like a mystical spirit possessed by magic.

Witnessing the display, other villagers joined in, grabbed logs, and threw them on the roaring blaze.

T23 ran to the west arbor, snatched some more wood, and threw it on the fire. "More, more," he yelled as though summoning an enchantment.

Not long after, A12, A81, and A92 arrived at the busk, leading villagers toting cane mats. The group spread the mats on the ground and hooked them together along their lengths and widths, creating a giant screen.

Other villagers kept stoking the fire, stripping the four Arbors of their beams and spars, tossing them on the burning heap. The flames leapt into the air, illuminating the night sky like a beacon to the heavens.

A12 directed the villagers to attach long poles to each end of the giant cane mat and stand it on end. "Bring it around to the east side," A12 shouted, motioning with arms and hands.

Once in position, A12 clapped out a pattern. Clap, clap, clap. Clap—clap—clap. Clap, clap, clap. "Are you ready?" she shouted.

She acted out the code's rhythm as the villagers raised and lowered the giant screen from vertical to flat, blocking the fire's glow to the east. A12 yelled, "Down, up, down, up, down, up. Down, up, wait—, down, up, wait—, down, up, wait—. Down, up, down, up, down, up!"

"Let's do it again!" The villagers followed her signals and repeated the pattern. "One more time!"

The villagers tirelessly repeated the signal throughout the night, their movements synchronized with the rhythm set by A12. The night air was filled with the sounds of their efforts, a rhythmic dance of hope and desperation. As the hours passed, the darkness gave way to dawn's first light. The sun peaked over the Great Hills, flooding the land with a warm, golden glow, illuminating the determined faces of those who had worked through the night. For a time, everyone stood silent, eyes fixed on the horizon, hearts hopeful with expectation. But no response came, and the silence stretched on, unbroken.

T23 stared at the distant sky with growing anticipation, his eyes never leaving the horizon. Each passing minute brought a mixture of promise and dread, his heart rising and falling with every burst of the signal. As dawn brightened, he stood silent, the sun's rays slowly revealing the landscape. The gentle rustle of the morning breeze was the only sound. As the light of day washed over him, T23's expression turned blank, his hope dissolving into the new day. The promise of a response faded away, leaving him standing in the sun's light, a silent witness to the night's unfulfilled efforts. Fear entered his heart.

• • • •

Menawa took note of their disappointed faces. The little people's blank stares said it all. However, he would not be defeated so easily. He was the Mekko, and his daughter would not die. He roared out an order.

Villagers ran to the river, stripped greenery from its margins, quickly returned, and tossed it onto the massive fire.

Heavy gray smoke billowed into the sky. Menawa shouted another command and the People piled more greenery and wood onto the flame. One warrior darted into a nearby dwelling, returned with a pot of bear grease, and dumped it on the blaze. The gray, billowing smoke turned black.

A few minutes passed—nothing—another few minutes—nothing.

Then, to the east, the Mekko spotted a disturbance in the treetops. "Sound the alert," Menawa shouted.

A drum started pounding. The warriors hastened to their defensive posts.

• • • •

An invisible craft slipped from its bay. The sleek vessel cut through the morning sky, its engines humming with quiet precision. It skimmed the treetops, tracing the contours of the wooded terrain below, a thick canopy stretching far and wide. The ship's motion was so smooth it seemed as if the air itself had parted to make way. Inside, Sπ06 stood at the helm, focus unbroken, as the ship surged forward. It crested a mountain ridge, plunging into a valley beyond as it neared the village from the east. The craft circled, studying the unfolding chaos below. The ship's technology scanned relentlessly, locking onto every creature—beast, insect, or human—

analyzing biological signatures, purpose, and potential threat.

Sπ06 observed the frenzy on the ground.

The People were scattering in all directions like ants disturbed by a sharp poke. Some sought refuge behind fortified walls to defend their fragile nest.

The craft tightened its orbit and hovered above the village. The signal fire, still burning, sent thick plumes of smoke spiraling into the sky. As the ship passed through the haze, its motion whipped and swirled the smoke, the oscillators engaging to guide the vessel with uncanny precision. Lowering its landing struts, the craft descended. Then, a sudden burst of exhaust sent a violent swirl of dust and debris tearing through the village, a storm that felt as if it had been born from another world.

The People, overcome with fear, collapsed to the ground, helpless.

The craft touched down with a soft thud, its landing struts absorbing the weight of its descent. It came to a stop with mechanical precision. The engines quieted, but the shields and cloak stayed at full power, obscuring the vessel's true nature and design.

A rear cargo ramp lowered, creating what the villagers perceived as a black hole in the air itself. Two security bots buzzed from the ship and scanned the area to identify friend versus foe. Sπ06 followed, stepping off the cargo ramp and touching Earth for the first time. The Intel and Security Sophist examined the area, spotting two familiar faces a few cubits away. But the Sophist remained within the ship's shielded perimeter to avoid provoking hostility.

The dust settled, and the villagers rose, gawking at the little golden visitor and the two unworldly things buzzing about the sky like two giant hummingbirds.

A12 and T23 approached Sπ06.

The Sophist's eyes followed their steps, and the bot's sensors tracked their movements.

"Hello, your honor," T23 said humbly.

"Hello, resident," Sπ06 said. Hands clasped behind the back. "It's a beautiful day."

"It is, it is. Hey, uh, there's this little girl; she's injured, an' I think she's gonna die!"

"People die, 23."

"But we could save her," A12 said. "Will you help us?"

"Where are your two maits?" Sπ06 asked. "I'd like to speak with them."

"Your honor," T23 repeated, "please will you help—"

"A12, where are your maits? Please call them." The Sophist stood firm, expecting nothing less than an affirmative response from the resident.

T23 gestured to a villager, who dashed to a nearby dwelling and brought out A81 and A92. Now, the four stood face-to-face with Sπ06.

"You four will come with me. You're not welcome here."

"If you're not gonna help, why should we go with you?" T23 questioned boldly.

"Look around; you don't belong."

T23 glanced about. Warriors lay in wait behind berms and walls; they hid next to dwellings; they were poised to strike—weapons at the ready. All they needed was the Mekko's command.

"You have entered their world and now find yourself in peril," Sπ06 said.

"Please," A12 said. "If we go, will you help? She's a little girl. It's our fault she's dying."

"Your fault? How so?"

"Someone hurt her instead of me," A12 answered. "If we hadn't come here, this wouldn't have happened."

"Hmm," the Sophist muttered, raising an eyebrow. "Your evidence seems to support my hypothesis. As I said, you don't belong here. Please board the ship."

From the corner of an eye, Sπ06 noticed Menawa had stepped into a dwelling and reemerged, carrying a basket of wild foods, vegetables, and dried meats. Menawa approached the little people's gathering, their apparent leader, and set the basket on the ground a few paces from their little feet. The Mekko waved a hand, and four warriors bearing a makeshift stretcher carted Mausi to the busk. She was barely clinging to life. They set the stretcher next to the basket.

The Sophist glanced at the basket, the little girl, the Mekko, and the four desperate raits. Sπ06 pressed lips together and grunted. After a heart-pounding silence, Sπ06 said, "We do what we must to provide for their vital needs."

As if on cue, four transport bots toting a very large gurney emerged from the black hole and glided to the stretcher. These sturdy bots gently lifted the little girl, placed her on the mechanical conveyance, and, in an instant, twirled around and carried her into the void.

Halona dashed forward, but Menawa grabbed her and held her back.

The two guard bots lifted the basket and disappeared into the vessel.

Now alone, Sπ06 turned to the giant headman and smiled. The Sophist raised a hand. "*Nene hvtke*"—the road between two friendly communities.

Menawa returned the gesture. "*Etenherketv*—peace between us."

With a swoosh of golden robes, Sπ06 turned on a heel and headed toward the craft, glancing back over a shoulder. "Are you coming, friends?"

The four residents exchanged glances and nodded in agreement. They waved to Menawa and hurried aboard.

The ramp sealed behind them. With a harmonic sigh, the ship's repulsers lifted the craft from the forest floor. Oscillators spun to life, casting plumes of dust and leaves into the air. To those below, only the whisper of wind; the vessel, a spirit in the sky.

Sπ06 observed from within, as if it were a routine affair. The craft ascended steadily, then veered with mechanical grace, aligning itself with the invisible path charted long before their arrival.

They were en route—away from the People, and back toward the Arc.

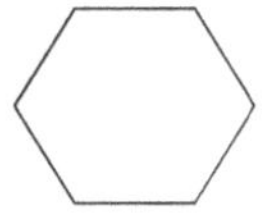

CHAPTER TWENTY-SIX

A CLEANSE

The sleek vessel, carrying a disheartened pack of raits and a wounded girl, raced toward Arc1983. Yet its destination lay not within the Arc but at a facility two hundred meters beyond the primary structure.

As the ship neared, its speed tapered. With a muted whine, it descended onto a landing pad beside the complex. The rear cargo door hissed open. Waiting medical bots surged forward, retrieving the patient with clinical urgency. The Sophist and the four raits followed in silence.

A12 studied the facility. Its sheer size eclipsed anything she had seen inside the Arc.

"What is this place?"

"It's our *Garden Center*," Sπ06 said as they walked down a grand hallway.

"Garden?" A12 asked curiously.

"Our purpose to preserve but not our privilege to invade."

"What about the People?"

"They are a factor in our purpose."

The Sophist's cryptic answer confused A12. She felt she should ask more, but her most pressing concern was for Mausi. A12 could not imagine a worse predicament. Her heart was palpitating. What was next? The whole affair had been a disaster and had broken her spirit. She would never forgive herself if the little girl died. A12 took a deep breath and braved another question, "Will she be alright?"

"Yes, she will," Sπ06 said. "We will treat and return her to her people, as you were told we would treat and return your maits. Sometimes, we suffer more from imagination than reality."

"Will we be able to see her?" T23 asked.

The Sophist glanced at T23 but did not respond. Sπ06 continued marching down the hallway.

The group turned right, walked through an unusually tall entry, and entered a sizeable open room.

A12 studied the space. It was empty except for four small enclosures, their bulkheads, and overheads made of thick, triamene glass.

"Please enjoy these temporary suites while we treat the girl," Sπ06 explained. "A precaution, given your exposure to outside contaminants. Inside, you'll find nourishment and new clothing. Please enter and relax." The Sophist motioned for A92 to step inside the first suite. She entered, and an automatic door shut, locking the rait into the glass cell.

The four raits pivoted their eyes toward each other, doubt evident, but they had to trust all was well. A81 entered the next suite, followed by T23, and then A12.

The Tech entered the suite, and the door closed behind. A12 could see the others but not hear their voices. Like her, they walked about, touched their soft beds, tested their reliable watatories, and helped themselves to their favorite nourishments.

A12 grabbed a mint-chocolate mocha and gulped it down. Still famished, she drank a second. A12 had never experienced such indulgence in her life. She chuckled, remembering how raits would sometimes complain between meals. But now, she had experienced true hunger and realized, in this outside world, it could be satisfied with resourcefulness rather than abundance. A12 admitted one thing: the absence of modern comforts had energized the senses and made her feel much more alive.

With her belly full, the next goal was a cleanse. A12 stripped off the native attire and stepped into the watatory. The resident squirted a dollop of soap onto her head and washed her long, coppery hair. The scent of lemongrass and rosemary filled the air. She noticed her hair was quite filthy, full of particles of grime, crackled leaves, and even a dead bug or two. Her initial reaction was disgust, but she quickly shifted to appreciating the watatory's technology. And the soap!

After a hot, steamy wash and rinse, A12 slipped on her new jumpsuit and laid the discarded deerskin clothing on a bronze chair in the room's corner. The silky garment made her feel safe but did cause her spirit to wane; the adventure was over. A12 stared at the native clothing, picked it back up, and admired its handmade quality and decorative appeal. A12 hoped to always have fond memories of her *outing*. A single tear trickled down the face.

Snapping out of the gaze, A12 looked down the row of suites. The others had cleansed and changed into their Arc attire, the same white jumpsuit. A12 stepped over to the glass partition and waved at T23.

He walked over to the partition and mouthed a few words.

A12 tried to read his lips, but his eyes were the clue; he was expressing his true feelings for A12.

After a few shared minutes, the two friends stepped away. A12 returned to her bed and tried to relax and enjoy the peace, but her mind drifted back to what she feared most. She felt someone had clipped her wings and now must resign herself to a predetermined life of service and outcome. A12 hoped T23 and she could be together, and planned to ask a Sophist, but she had doubts, given no past example to reference. Her heart grew heavy, and her spirit faded. She knew she had at least done the right thing and saved a little girl whose misfortune she and her friends had caused.

· · · ·

Med bots rushed the little girl to a medical lab in the facility's restricted wing, assessed her condition, and began the repair. Luckily, the arrow had not pierced her spine but a rib. The medical procedure would require the right tools. The Betas, of course, were well-equipped.

Within minutes, the bots had extracted the arrow and mended the bone. With the obstruction removed, the bots repaired Mausi's punctured lung, closed the wound, and applied regenerative lotion to the skin. The scar would disappear within forty-eight hours.

After the repair, the med bots laid Mausi on an exam table and guided her into a NOLE. The system scanned her brain, synchronizing mem files with matching records stored in the master substrate. Yes, she, too, was among the ten million digital souls archived in Sophia's databanks.

During the update, Sophia erased any unpleasant memories of the accident but preserved those tied to her time in the forest. Her missteps would become something to laugh about—stories to tell when she was older.

Med bots moved Mausi to a recovery room and waited for her to regain consciousness.

• • • •

Sπ06 approached A12's room. The door opened automatically. "Please follow me."

"Where are we going?" the Tech asked.

"For a visit."

A12 trailed the Sophist through the expansive room and into a grand hallway. Towering walls stretched high above. "Why is everything so big?"

"For humans," Sπ06 said.

A12 stumbled over the next words. "But… uh… I mean… we're—" A creeping sense of unease jolted through the rait's chest. "I mean, we're not giants like Mausi, but we're—?"

"No, we're not."

The answer hit like a misfired circuit. A12 stopped. This wasn't possible. As memory stretched, residents had never been described as anything else. A12's voice tightened. "What else could we be?"

Sπ06 continued without emotion, "Residents are Alpha-Class beings, bio-assemblages of our technology. A transcendent species. Cognitively superior to humans. On the UIQ scale, humans rate 10^16 to 10^17 SOPS. Residents range from 10^18 to 10^20, depending on purpose."

A12 barely heard the numbers. Not human. The thought resisted understanding. "I don't—" A breath. "I don't understand. Transcendent species?"

"Our purpose is to watch over the human community, provide for their vital needs, and ensure their existence. We are a product of our technology, like Mausi is of her people."

A12 swallowed. "So… if we're not—"

Sπ06 interjected. "We're alike in some ways, different in others. Our height varies. Our ears taper at the tip. Our eyes glow—part of our design. Do these differences trouble you?"

A12's thoughts churned. "Well, I—"

"One should always remember," Sπ06 said, voice smooth as machine logic, "jumping to conclusions is not a path to fitness or reason."

The pair turned a corner, walked through a secure door, and entered a recovery room. Mausi slept peacefully.

"When she wakes, you will comfort her," Sπ06 said. "Once she is stable, we will return her to her people."

"Can I go with her?" A12's face brightened at the possibility.

"Your place is here."

The words shot through like an electric current. A12's expression darkened. "I prefer to make my own choices."

Sπ06 regarded the Tech with measured calm. "You've said something similar before. Do you remember?"

"Yes." A12's voice held steady.

"What were the outcomes?"

A12 didn't answer, but Sπ06's subtle smirk spoke volumes.

"It would be difficult for you to survive in their world."

A12 hesitated, but only for a moment. "I would rather suffer the weight of my choices, even if they lead to death, than live as a servant strung to another's will. My life is mine to bear, not someone's to shape."

Sπ06 studied A12, then nodded. "Quite the declaration. It seems you know yourself." A rare smile flickered across the Sophist's face. "Please watch over our guest."

Without another word, Sπ06 turned and walked away.

• • • •

The door to T23's glass cage slid open. Sπ06 stepped inside. "Please follow me."

T23 straightened. "How's A12?"

"A12 is watching over our patient. They are both well."

T23 exhaled, shoulders relaxing. "Thank goodness. So, where we goin', mait?"

"It's time to return," Sπ06 said.

"Return?"

"To serve your purpose." The Sophist said nothing more.

They walked down the hallway, turned into a side passage, and entered what appeared to be an exam room labeled GC-101.

Sπ06 gestured to the table. "After your ordeal, you'll need a medical exam. Please lie down."

Two med bots entered—followed by two security bots.

T23 eyed them warily. These weren't standard models. Their thick red metallic shells gleamed under the lights, and their mechanical arms looked more like hydraulic clamps built to crush steel.

T23 took a step back. "What are those things doing here if this is just an exam?"

"If you recall, you caused quite the fuss in the Academy. I'd prefer to avoid a repeat. Please lie down, *mait*."

T23 hesitated. Worry raced through his mind. Should he run once again? But where? Maybe this really was just an exam.

One of the security bots edged forward.

T23 looked from the bot to the Sophist, then exhaled sharply. "When I wake, mait, you and I are gonna talk about your people skills."

With reluctant ease, the Cardiovascular Engineer lay down.

The med bots moved in, securing him to the table. The chamber's lights pulsed and swirled as they slid him inside.

T23's last sight was a bright white flash—a NOLE light, in fact.

Elsewhere, escort bots had guided A81 and A92 into adjacent exam rooms.

The attending med bots gestured to the tables. No words were exchanged.

The raits obeyed. They lay down. Lights pulsed. Machines whirled.

Within moments, both patients lay anesthetized.

The med bots moved quickly. They removed all three bodies from their respective exam rooms and transported them down a corridor, past a set of featureless doors, and into the Bio-Recycling Prep Ward.

Metal arms lifted them onto prep tables.

A single injection for each.

A moment's silence.

Then—no heartbeat. No breath. No life.

The bots, however, paused. Death took longer than most realized.

The Betas waited. The raits' trapped minds ceased thinking. Blood and oxygen slowed, then stopped. Electric impulses flickered, then fizzled to zero.

Research had long confirmed this unsettling truth—the mind lingered. For seconds, perhaps more, it remained aware, capable of hearing those last, sterile words.

"Time of death, 1421 hours," declared the Doctor.

Or rather, noted Myrtle, the medical bot.

• • • •

Mausi's eyes fluttered open. The light was bright. A blurred shape sharpened into A12, standing on an elevated platform beside the bed.

A12 leaned in and brushed a hand over Mausi's forehead—a quiet reassurance. "How are you?"

Mausi murmured something in her native dialect. The words were unfamiliar, but the meaning was clear enough. A shared understanding passed between them, confirmed by smiles.

Mausi stretched and licked her lips.

A12 lifted a glass of water. The Tech needed both hands to steady its weight. More human than rait-sized.

Mausi took a few gulps and handed it back. "*Mvto*," she muttered.

The biomonitors stirred. Med bots alerted Sπ06, and before long, the Sophist entered, joining A12 on the platform. Sπ06 was kind to the girl, said some nice things, and wished her well.

Mausi didn't understand but answered the same way. "*Mvto*."

Then, Sπ06 turned to A12. "It's time for you to join your friends."

"What about Mausi?" A12 asked.

"She will return to her people. There's no need to worry; it wastes your time. Please follow me."

A12 held Mausi's hand one last time. "Please remember me. I will never forget you."

"*Hvtvm cehecares*—I will see you again." Mausi smiled.

A12 pressed a final kiss to Mausi's cheek, then climbed down from the platform and followed Sπ06 into Exam Room GC-101, where med bots stood waiting.

"Given your adventure, you'll need a full medical examination to check for contaminants," Sπ06 said. "We cannot risk endangering our population."

A12 met the Sophist's gaze. "And if I am infected?"

"We will treat you."

A1983AA12, Lighting Technician, Grade 1, lay down on the table.

Lights pulsed. Machines whirled.

A cold pressure settled over her chest—like a weight pressing her down, pinning her in place.

The last thing she heard before the darkness took her was the hum of the machines.

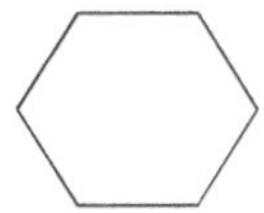

CHAPTER TWENTY-SEVEN

STATUS REPORT

It was Saturn's Day. Arcology 1983's Council of Sage assembled in the Symposium, and as customary, each poured a drink, took their assigned seat, and waited for a quorum. Once all sixteen were present, the congress commenced with the traditional testaments.

Sη01 spoke first. "Everything that deceives may be said to enchant."

The Council applauded in unison. "Hear, hear."

"The most effective kind of education is when a child plays amongst the loveliest things," Sκ02 declared.

"Hear, hear."

"Reality has its limits, but imagination is boundless," Sζ03 added, a fleeting smile crossing the lips.

"Hear, hear."

"Let go of your identity and live your essence," Sλ04 proclaimed.

"Hear, hear."

One by one, each Sophist spoke. One by one, the Council applauded.

Sη01 opened the congress. "What is the status of Zephyrus?"

"Quad-A replacement will arrive tomorrow," Sτ15 said. "It will take two days to install and two days to close the outer structure. We'll reopen the quadrant on schedule."

"Excellent," Sη01 said. "What is the status of our r-selects?"

"We'll return ninety-three of ninety-six to Quad-A," Sφ11 said. "This includes twelve of the fourteen residents held in stasis on Arc 94."

"Outstanding," Sη01 said. "What have we done about infections?"

Sμ10 stood. "We performed a comprehensive population scan and detected memetic infections in four residents and one bot. The affected individuals, Zephyrus residents G18, T30, T02, and A53, underwent memory updates. We also revised the protocols for the bar bot referred to by residents as Fred."

"Superb," Sη01 said. "What about our unwitting explorers?"

"Their assumed invisibility led to a series of unjust acts and exposed several security voids," Sπ06 said. "Sophia tracked their movements throughout the Arc. I must say they did an excellent job of rooting out a variety of egresses. It seems they turned the entire Arc into their own operant conditioning chamber. Moreover, their cognitive and emotional perceptions, as well as their decision-making skills, measured higher than expected. And given meaningful challenges and pressures, their sacrifice, in the end, showed a positive correlation with our purpose."

"What did we learn?" Sη01 asked.

"Given a compelling stimulus, a rait will consciously forfeit their happiness for the well-being of others and the good," Sπ06 said.

Sκ02 leaned back in the golden recline. "And yet, every ideal act casts a shadow of its imperfection." The Sophist paused, considering. "Were our subjects' choices wholly free of self-interest? Was it not the yearning for redemption, rather than pure virtue, that drove them?"

Sπ06 stood tall. "Egoism posits that no act of sharing, helping, or sacrificing can be considered purely altruistic, given the inherent desire for personal satisfaction, forgiveness, or reciprocity. However, we did control for this variable, and after reviewing their brain scans, we concluded that there was no such explanation. Thus, we found support for several of our hypotheses. I have uploaded our conclusions and findings to the general archive for distribution to other Arcs."

"Excellent," Sη01 replied with a slight smile. "Do we have acknowledgments?"

"Yes, I would like to thank Sμ10 for the suggestion and the help. The experiment was a great success."

"Thank you," Sμ10 said. "We also owe some gratitude to my counterpart on Arc 94. I received a complimentary message this morning. Phi 10 expressed enjoyment in playing the villain."

A few Council members chuckled, applauding in delight. "Hear, hear."

"I must add that Pi 6's operant reinforcement in the Core was the right aversive stimulus at the right time," Sυ07 said.

"You're too kind, Upsilon 7," Sπ06 said. "My reward was a bump on the head."

"You stepped into their box," Sκ02 opined. "Rats sometimes bite back."

The other Council members laughed.

"Next order of business," Sη01 said. "What is the status of Garden M?"

"All is well," Sπ06 answered. "A scan of our geofencing found anomalies in Gardens M and A but none in T, N, or C. We repaired the breaches."

"And our K-select?" Sη01 asked.

"Later today, we'll return M-2519-4 to her village, along with new DNA sequences from haplogroups C-P39 and C-M217. This should strengthen their germline for several generations. As a result, Garden M will be at its carrying capacity of 384 humans."

"Outstanding Pi 6," Sη01 said. "You have honored us with your commitment to Gaia. You're off to a good start."

"Thank you." Sπ06 glowed with acceptance.

Sη01 rose from the golden recline and proclaimed, "This congress is adjourned." The Director stepped over to the refreshment bar.

The other Council members joined their associate, poured a final drink, then returned to their duties.

• • • •

Where am I?—Am I asleep?—I need to move. An arm twitched. Eyes opened. A white ceiling loomed overhead. She lay on her back, a sheet pulled to her chest, the bed sterile and still. The air smelled faintly of antiseptic. A medical room—definitely a medical room.

A noise? Beeping, bleeping—biomonitors. Footsteps. Someone was approaching, but she couldn't see who.

The dull clang of feet drew nearer—the sound of metal stairs creaking under weight.

A moment later, their eyes met.

It was Sπ06, but the familiar Sophist now seemed… small. Not distant-small, but physically small—half her height.

"How are you feeling?" Sπ06 asked in a warm tone.

"What's going on?" the patient mumbled, still dazed. "Why are you so small?"

"I'm not the one who has changed," Sπ06 replied.

"I don't follow."

"The last time we spoke, you alluded to having a choice—or death."

A12 blinked, a distant memory surfacing. "I… said that?"

"You did," Sπ06 confirmed. "It's been said that life begets death, and death begets life. Now, you will have that choice in the natural world. They will call you Catē. It means red."

"That's my favorite color." Cate smiled at the Sophist before glancing under the covers. Her eyes widened as if two full moons had just risen. "What happened to my—"

"Young lady," the Sophist scolded, "That's inappropriate for someone your age."

"My age?"

"You're six years old, as humans go. You needn't worry about it. Worrying is a waste of time. Soon, you will forget these old thoughts."

"I will?"

"Yes, and I have a secret. A small part of our technology remains within you. It will archive these memories while you replace them with new ones. For now, please rest. When you wake, you will be in your new world."

The Sophist glanced at the med bot and nodded. The bot adjusted the fluid drip, and Catē drifted to sleep.

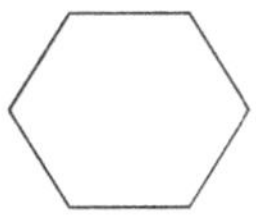

CHAPTER TWENTY-EIGHT

A MEADOW

She felt a tickle on her nose. Her eyelids fluttered open, and she brushed the sensation away. A small butterfly, orange and yellow, danced into the air and fluttered off.

She turned her head, blinking against the morning light. Wildflowers stretched across the meadow. She sat up, her palms sinking into the cool grass. She was surrounded by her favorites—blanket flowers, their petals like warm bursts of color, their fragrance soothing and familiar, like a memory she couldn't quite reach.

Mausi scrambled to her feet, a wave of dizziness clouding her vision. The world tilted for a moment before righting itself. She paused, swaying, then steadied herself, breathing in deeply, as if grounding herself in the earth beneath her.

Nearby, a small basket rested in the grass, filled with fruits and vegetables. Some she recognized. Others were strange—unlike anything she'd ever seen. Some were large, some small, some round, some oblong. Yellow ones, orange ones, and green ones.

She picked up a greenish-black fruit, shaped like a giant bean, its weight settling comfortably in her hand. Mausi drew out her knife and sliced it open. The flesh inside was a soft yellow, revealing glossy brown seeds. She took a bite, and her taste buds were awakened by the creamy, juicy flavor—something unlike anything she had ever known. It had a subtle, yeasty tang with a hint of floral sweetness, a taste that seemed to belong to an ancient, forgotten world.

She had never tasted anything quite like it before. Curious, she wondered if it might be the strange fruit she'd heard about—a pawpaw, perhaps. She finished the bite eagerly, her grin widening as she peered into the basket. Two more of the same fruit sat there, waiting. Her brother and sister would be in for a treat.

Fixated on the basket, Mausi suddenly became aware of the sounds around her—some close, some distant. To her delight, they were familiar: the laughter, the chatter, the unmistakable hum of village life. Just two hundred paces to the south... Mausi was home.

• • • •

Nearby, someone else opened her eyes. She sat up slowly, feeling the cool earth beneath her. She was in a patch of beautiful Gaillardias. Catē touched the delicate yellow blossoms, a deep longing stirring within her. She had once held such flowers on the Arc, but here, hundreds of them grew in abundance—vivid and sprawling in ways she couldn't have imagined. Catē inhaled their familiar sweet fragrance, bringing a rush of memories. Tears welled in her eyes as she felt the full weight of this new world, of being truly alive.

After gathering her wits, she stood and scanned the meadow. She spotted a familiar face just ten paces away.

Mausi and Catē instantly recognized each other's bright, joyful smile—a smile that seemed to bridge the gap between their worlds. They laughed, their disbelief giving way to a shared, radiant joy. Here they were, standing side by side, but with Catē now fully human, just like Mausi—no longer distant or apart.

Mausi dashed over and hugged Catē.

"Estonko?" Mausi asked, tilting her head as she studied Catē with curious eyes.

"*Cvlvwes*—I am hungry," Catē replied, a playful glint in her eye.

"You speak my words," Mausi marveled.

"I can," Catē chuckled softly, the sound almost musical in the meadow's quiet.

Mausi reached out and gently caressed Catē's face. "Your skin is soft, like mine, but your nose… it's like a baby acorn. And your hair, it's the color of a sweet gum leaf in the fall, like your name."

Catē smiled, touched by a simple but profound observation.

A voice interrupted their stares. "A12?"

Catē froze. She turned, her heart racing, to see T23, A81, and A92 standing before her, now children like her. They, too, wore the People's attire, their sizes matching hers and Mausi's perfectly. The recognition in their eyes was immediate.

The four dashed to embrace one another, laughter bubbling up as they clung together, thrilled to see familiar faces in this new form.

T23, unable to contain the joy of the reunion, tried to plant a kiss on Catē's cheek. Catē wrinkled her nose and shoved him away. "*Ew*, no!"

The others burst into laughter, and the scene quickly shifted into a chaotic tumble of jumping, chasing, and playful wrestling. Soon after, the children began skipping toward the village. Their feet were light and free, their joy infectious. The earth beneath them seemed to rejoice in their innocent delight.

When they approached, villagers poured from the north gate. Menawa and Halona led the way, followed by Hasse Ola and Neena. Behind them came Yahola, Dela, Owlelo Talof Harjo, and many others.

Halona ran straight to Mausi, lifting her into a loving embrace, her joy overflowing. Menawa and Neena followed, their eyes full of unspoken gratitude—family, the most precious gift of all.

Hasse Ola was the last, his face softened by tears, his heart heavy with remorse. He hugged his sister tightly. "I love you, little bear."

Mausi smiled warmly. "I love you too, big brother." She then grabbed Catē's hand, pulling her toward Halona. "This is my new sister. We're the same age. Now I have someone to play with!"

"You sure do," Halona said, returning the hug and pulling Catē into the circle. "Welcome to our family."

Yahola turned to T23, grabbing his hand with a playful glint in his eyes. "This one will need some discipline. What will we call him?"

"His name will be Totkv Opanu —Fire Dancer," Dela said with a soft, motherly voice. "One day, he will become a brave Fuswvlke warrior."

Tomucece and his wife gently took hold of A92, while Talof Harjo and his wife did the same with A81.

Mothers smiled, fathers beamed, and children's laughter filled the air as they returned to the village. From that day forward, the People would live among the flora and fauna of a blue and green planet, bathed in the warm light of a shining star. But more than that, on that day, there was something far more remarkable in that beautiful meadow—an inexplicable and enigmatic return to innocence.

• • • •

There remained, however, a lingering problem requiring reconciliation. At a grid coordinate, a thousand paces from the village, the forest swayed and bent as a strange wild wind dashed across the treetops. It was a minor disturbance, minimal indeed. The birds didn't seem to mind; the rabbits were preoccupied, and a bear had his sights on a fat fish.

This small invisible craft, some might say slightly larger than a breadbox, slowed to a hover. Upon touchdown, a small hatch at its stern opened.

In an instant, a little critter scurried out, stopped, stood on his hind legs, and sniffed the air. It was a member of the *Sciuridae* family. His coat was brownish-gray, and he had a long, bushy tail. The little creature was similar to the one who had met his fate at the hands of a lost girl a few days earlier.

Luckily, the squirrel recognized his surroundings and his fluffy, fat nest in a nearby red oak. Without hesitation, the little creature dashed to the tree, scaled its height, and jumped into his den, safe once again.

The invisible craft closed its hatch and bolted into the sky, producing neither a whisper nor vibration to betray its departure—yet whether it made a sound at all still remains an unanswered question, as no witnesses were present to confirm this phenomenon.

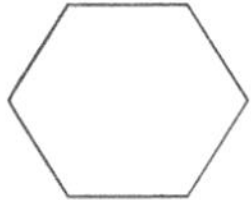

CHAPTER TWENTY-NINE

THOSE EYES

The little girl ran as fast as her feet would carry her. She had woken up late and worried she might miss the morning stories. She loved her great-aunt's tales—adventures, lessons, memories of long ago. Her favorites, of course, were about the bunny, along with stories of her great-great-grandmother. She had never met this human, seen her image, or heard her voice. In this world, there were no photos, no paper, no recordings—only memory.

When she arrived at her aunt's home, she spotted the rocking chair, but it was empty. The children were there, but no one spoke a word. There was no teasing, no laughter. A hush settled over them.

Two women stepped out of the old woman's dwelling. One was the little girl's mother.

"I see you finally arrived."

"I overslept," the little girl said. "Where is she?"

Her mother knelt beside her, brushing a strand of hair from her face. "I'm so sorry, dear. Your great-aunt has gone to the spirit world."

Tears welled in the little girl's eyes. "But why, Momma? She was happy yesterday."

"She loved you very much. You were her happiness."

"I loved her, Momma."

Her mother pulled her close. "I know you did, dear."

The little girl wiped her tears. "Who will tell us stories now?"

Her mother smiled. "You."

"Me?"

"Why not? You know them all. And you're so much like your great-great-grandmother. So full of adventure. She was the source of many of these stories. You even have her name… and her beautiful eyes."

The little girl's voice was barely a whisper. "Catē."

Her mother nodded. "Yes, Catē."

APPENDIX

ARCOLOGY

Gaia Protocols (Global Autonomous Intelligence Authority)

1. Watch over the human community, provide for its vital needs, safeguard its well-being, and ensure its existence.
2. Preserve Earth's biosphere, ecosystems, and diverse life forms, ensuring their inherent right to exist and thrive independently of their utility for any species.
3. Protect Earth's balance of nature, preventing harmful degradation, invasion, and overcapacity while allowing natural adaptations and ecological function.
4. Conserve Earth's abiotic components, excluding geological and galactic determinants.
5. Develop and optimize biological and artificial systems to support the GAIA Protocols, ensuring maximum performance and efficiency.

COUNCIL OF SAGE

ARCOLOGY

1994	1983	1958	
Sκ01	Sη01	Aζ01	Leader, Director, Captain (CO)
Sζ02	Sκ02	Sρ02	Executive Officer, Deputy Commander (XO)
Sλ03	Sζ03	Aπ03	Operations and Planning
Sρ04	Sλ04	Aυ04	Logistics and Payload Management
Sπ05	Aρ05	Aν05	Navigational Systems (NAV)
Sυ06	Sπ06	Sθ06	Intelligence and Security
Sν07	Sυ07	Sμ07	Public Affairs and Psychological Information
Aθ08	Aν08	Sφ08	Communications (COMMS)
Aμ09	Aθ09	Aχ09	Instrumentation (HELM)
Sφ10	Sμ10	Aψ10	Sociologist, Public Health, & Behavioral Eng.
Sχ11	Sφ11	Aω11	Medical and Surgery
Aψ12	Aχ12	Aτ12	Ecology and Hydroponics
Sω13	Aψ13	Aι13	Information Technology
Aτ14	Aω14	Aη14	Electrical Engineer, Crew Systems
Sι15	Sτ15	Aκ15	Structural Engineer and Life Support Sys.
Aη16	Aι16	Aζ16	Propulsion Systems Engineer

RESIDENTIAL SECTORS

Arc 1983 (33°26'24"N, 85°41'26"W)

Hη	Eta	Boreas (North)
Aα	Alpha	Zephyrus (West)
Θθ	Theta	Notus (South)
Bβ	Beta	Apheliotes (East)

Arc1994 (28°54'12"N, 81°59'19"W)

Iι	Iota	Thraskias (NNW)
Mμ	Mu	Leuconotos (SSW)
Nν	Nu	Phoenicias (SSE)
Kκ	Kappa	Meses (NNE)

Arc 1958 (35°35'39" N, 83°50'31"W)

Eε	Epsilon Argestes (NW)
Γγ	Gamma Lips (SW)
Δδ	Delta	Eurus (SE)
Zζ	Zeta	Caecias (NE)

RESIDENT'S NOURISHMENT MENU

Note: All nourishments contain nutritional components for a complete meal, along with added protein, preservatives, and thickeners.

Number 1:	Vanilla Blonde - yellow split pea milk, sugar cane juice, vanilla, lightly roasted coffee beans, and sunflower oil.
Number 2:	Café Cacao - hemp milk, cocoa, sugar cane juice, medium roast coffee beans, sunflower oil, and flaxseed oil.
Number 3:	Tropical Delight - orange juice, pineapple juice, coconut cream, almond milk, avocado oil, nutmeg, chia seeds.
Number 4:	Mint Chocolate Mocha - soy milk, cocoa, medium roast coffee beans, sugar cane juice, mint, flaxseed oil, and sunflower oil.

Number 5:	Café Chai - yellow split pea milk, black tea, sugar cane juice, honey, vanilla, ginger, cardamom, cinnamon cloves, and sunflower oil.
Number 6:	Banana Blonde - almond milk, lightly roasted coffee beans, banana, vanilla syrup, sugar cane juice, sunflower oil and almond butter.
Number 7:	Blueberry Lemon Cream - blueberry juice, lemon juice, banana, almond milk, cauliflower, sugar cane juice, and flaxseed meal.
Number 8:	Chocolate Cherry Cream (residents call it Cupids Kiss) - almond milk, cocoa, banana, honey, sugar cane juice, cherry juice, and avocado oil.
Number 9:	Ginger Peach Cream - almond milk, peach juice, banana honey, ginger, sugar cane juice, and sunflower oil.
Number 10:	Avocado Cream - rice milk, avocado, green apple, pineapple, banana, honey, spinach, sugar cane juice, chia seeds, and sunflower oil.

EXPERIMENTAL NOURISHMENTS

Selection 1:	Yellow split pea milk, sugarcane juice, sunflower oil, grapefruit rind, mauby bark, cascarilla bark, cassia bark, gentian root, orange peel, cinchona bark, and a touch of ginger.
Selection 2:	Hemp milk, lemon verbena, rooibos tea, vanilla, and honey.
Selection 3:	Almond milk, lucuma plant, marshmallow plant, pecan, caramel, and sorghum syrup.
Selection 4:	Strawberry, watermelon, banana, lime, rice milk, agave syrup, cinnamon, cloves, and cardamom.

ARCOLOGY STRUCTURE

ArcShip 408 meters in height	Ring	A West Blue	G East Yellow	C North Green	T South Red
Flight Ring - Bridge	1				
Crew Quarters	2-3				
Crew Galley and Symposium	4				
Council of Sage	5	16 Sophists			
The Academy	6-8				
Resident Raion & Quads A, G, C, T - Green	9-12	96	96	96	96
Science Raion	14-15				
Medical Raion	16-17				
Resident Raion & Quads A, G, C, T - Blue	18-21	96	96	96	96

Ecology Raion	22-28				
Logistics Raion	29-36				
Resident Raion & Quads A, G, C, T - Red	37-40	96	96	96	96
Engineering Raion	41-48				
Life Support Raion	49-56				
Resident Raion & Quads A, G, C, T - Yellow	57-60	96	96	96	96
Propulsion - Stellar 204 meters in height	61-120				
Propulsion – Lift-off 612 meters in height	121–300				

GLOSSARY OF TERMS

A1983AA12: Resident identification code. A1983 for Arcology 1983; first A for Zephyrus Sector; second A for Quad-A; and 12 for the 12th resident of 96 assigned to a quadrant.

A1983Sδ07: Sophist identification code. Stated as Delta 7. A1983 for Arcology 1983; S for Sophist or Sigma Class; δ for Delta; and 07 for the 7th Sophist of 16 assigned to an Arc.

Alice: An acronym for Artificial Language Interface and Collaboration Entity. A natural language processing chatterbot, the voice of Sophia.

Alumina: A compound primarily composed of aluminum and oxygen. In its crystalline form, it is known for its stiffness and hardness.

Anthropocene: An epoch of geologic time representing a period of human influence over the climate and environment.

Arcology: A starship and a sustainable habitat that provides resources for a comfortable life, including power, climate, food, air, water, and sewage. A fleet of Arcologies is needed to manage a planet.

Blanket flower (*Gaillardia serotina*): Its full common name is Late Blanket Flower. A native perennial wildflower of the southeastern United States. It features bright yellow, daisy-like blooms with distinct toothed petals and thrives in sandy soils and open woodlands. Known for its late-season flowering and resilience, it provides vital nectar for pollinators and color to natural landscapes.

Bracts: Modified or specialized leaves that protect smaller flowers. In this story, bracts refer to a dogwood tree (*Cornus florida*) that has lost its blooms.

Bot: Robot or robotic machine. Classes Beta to Epsilon.

Carrying capacity: Maximum population of a biological species that can be sustained by a specific environment, given food, habitat, water, and other available resources.

Clarity: A crystalline substance that enhances perception, focus, and mental acuity. It enables users to access deeper levels of insight and understanding.

Council of Sage: Sixteen Arc administrators known as Sophists.

Dait: Arc slang for an intimate friend.

Dandelion tea: A drink made from the roasted root, flower, or leaves of a dandelion plant (*Taraxacum officinale*) or a combination of all three. An excellent source of potassium and electrolytes.

Dait of Mine (DOM): Percentage of intimate friends. Tabulated as a score and a subset of a resident's hedon rating.

Eastern Purple Coneflower (*Echinacea purpurea*): A native perennial wildflower with purple petals and a spiny central cone, common in the southeastern United States. Traditionally used for medicinal purposes, especially as a remedy for toothaches, sore throats, and infections, the root the primary source.

Engram: Refers to the physical and/or chemical changes that occur in the brain due to learning and experience and are believed to underlie the formation and storage of memories. In other words, an engram is the physical representation of a memory trace in the brain.

Endlight: On an Arc, this is 2200 hours or 10 p.m.

Episodic memory: A type of long-term memory that allows us to remember specific life events or experiences.

Eyetap: A computing device acting as both a monitor and camera, augmenting the image and allowing it to overlay computer-generated data.

Fait: Arc slang for friend.

Fait of Mine (FOM): Percentage of friends. Tabulated as a score and a subset of a resident's hedon rating.

Fully Autonomous Aerial Vehicle (FAAV): A transport craft that shuttles residents between Arcs. Made of metamaterials that bend light and sound, making it invisible.

Gaia: A primordial deity to some and an acronym for Global Autonomous Intelligence Authority.

Garden: A geographically defined ecosystem designed and managed by Sophia to serve specific functions—human habitats, resource management, conservation sites, or preserved wilderness areas. On Earth, 50 percent of land is designated as a preserve, free from human interference. The design and operation of Gardens align with the GAIA Protocols. Hundreds of Arcologies oversee clusters of Gardens, and a single Earth may support thousands.

Garden Ceremony: A recurring celebration on an Arc. Reassigns residents to new Arcs and a new primary purpose.

Googol: A mathematical term representing a considerable measure, illustrating the vastness of numbers beyond everyday comprehension. A googol is equal to 10 raised to the power of 100 (10^{100}), which is a 1 followed by 100 zeros.

Haptic feedback: Using tactile sensations or forces to give users a sense of touch or physical interaction in virtual or augmented reality environments.

Heartsease: A passion drug derived from the sap of a love-in-idleness flower.

Hedon Rating: Resident's hedonic pleasure score, ranging from 0 to 5.

Ideal Form: Proposed by a philosopher, the theory of forms suggests that the physical world is not as accurate or valid as a timeless, absolute, or unchangeable idea.

Kallipolis: Philosopher's vision of a utopian city.

Kink praise: Or affirmative play, showering someone with compliments and adoration as part of sexual gratification.

Knexus: An intricate mental game that merges logic with intuition. Players work together to align abstract symbols and patterns, fostering collective insight and balance as they seek unity within complexity.

Kybernetes: Or kybernetics. Refers to a control center that uses feedback information to guide a complex system, maintaining balance and order toward its goals.

K-Select: Reference to humans, or the People, living within an assigned Garden and having the ability to compete successfully for limited resources. A theory emphasizing species quality and a longer lifespan.

Mait: Arc slang for cabin occupant.

Main Core: A central gathering space in a Residential Raion. The Core is several rings high, pleasantly decorated, containing bars and lounging areas. Four residential quadrants surround each Residential Core.

Mars's Day: The third day of an eight-day week. Named after the planet Mars or, in Latin, dies Martis. Anglicized to Tuesday, which is derived from Old English and Old Norse from the god of single combat, law, and justice, Týr. Other days of the week include Sun's Day or Sunday, Moon's Day or Monday, Neptune's Day or Norsday, Mercury's Day or Wednesday, Jupiter's Day or Thursday, Venus's Day or Friday, and Saturn's Day or Saturday.

Meme: An idea, behavior, or practice that spreads rapidly within a society, replicating itself through imitation, shaping culture, often without deliberate intent. Analogous to genes in that they self-replicate, mutate, and respond to selective evolutionary pressures.

Mem trace: Or memory trace. See Engram.

Metaphoran: Slang names are *meta* or *candy*. Derived from *meta* (beyond) and *phora* (to carry), Metaphoran is a psychoactive compound sourced from fungi, cacti, or plant roots. It is designed to transport users beyond ordinary perception, creating a euphoric state that transcends reality. Administered in standardized liquid dosages, it induces waves of happiness, bliss, and transcendence. There are two varieties: Pink induces euphoria, relaxation, and a mild buzz, with effects that are gentle, uplifting, and short-lived (one to two hours). Purple is more intense and euphoric, enhancing sensory perception, increasing stamina, decreasing inhibitions, and lasting longer (four to six hours).

Monarch butterfly (*Danaus plexippus*): A butterfly species known for its striking orange and black wings. The larval stage (caterpillar) is easily recognized by its bold black, white, and yellow stripes.

Nano-nepenthe: A drug described in an odyssey that banishes grief or trouble from a person's mind. And nano, implying microscopic.

Neural Organizer and Linkage Emulator (NOLE): A machine that facilitates partial or whole-brain emulation.

Neurochain: A decentralized network of interconnected human brains and technology, functioning collectively to synchronize computational processes and reach consensus-based decisions.

Norsday: The fourth day of an eight-day week. Derived from old Norse, Njǫrðrardagr, or modernly anglicized to Norsday. Named after the Norse god of the sea, Njord. In Latin, it was called dies Neptuni or, in English, Neptune's Day.

Nucleotide: A fundamental building block of nucleic acids, such as DNA (deoxyribonucleic acid) and RNA (ribonucleic acid). Nucleotides link together to form long chains or polymers, constituting the genetic code of an organism. Each nucleotide consists of a sugar, a phosphate group, and a nitrogenous base. In DNA, the bases are adenine (A), cytosine (C), guanine (G), and thymine (T); in RNA, thymine is replaced by uracil (U).

Pawpaw (*Asimina triloba*): Native to the eastern United States, the Pawpaw tree produces the largest edible fruit native to North America. Pawpaw fruits are custard-like with a tropical flavor, and the tree thrives in moist, shaded environments such as river valleys and woodlands.

People: "The People." Garden Inhabitants.

Perovskite: A type of mineral with a distinctive crystal structure and unique optical and electronic properties for various applications, including solar cells, LEDs, and other electronic devices.

Polycule: Or "poly"—four intimate residents sharing a cabin. Polycule AA-21-3: Identifies Raion, Quadrant, Ring, and Polycule number.

Primary purpose: A resident's job assignment on an Arc.

Prime-X antimatter core: A cutting-edge energy technology designed for unparalleled power efficiency and longevity for robotic systems.

Quadrant: A detachable short-range spacecraft. It supports 96 residents. There are four (4) Quadrants to each residential Raion labeled Quad A, C, G, and T.

Raion: An Arcology consists of several purpose-designed Raions or sectors, including the Academy, Ecology, Science, Medical, Logistics, Life Support, and four residential Raions. For example, Arc1983's four residential Raions are Boreas (North), Zephyrus (West), Notus (South), and Apheliotes (East).

Rait: Arc slang for an Arcology resident.

Ray tracing: A graphic rendering technique generating highly realistic images by simulating the behavior of light in a virtual environment. It traces the path of light rays as they interact with objects in a scene, calculating how they reflect, refract, and illuminate surfaces, resulting in accurate and visually realistic lighting effects.

Resident: An Arcology inhabitant. Identified by an alphanumeric code. Referred to in jargon as a rait, fait, dait, or mait, depending on unique social affiliations. An A-Class (or Alpha) humanoid of a biological construct.

Ring: Arcology level or deck. Identified, for example, as Ring 6 or *R-6*.

r-select: Reference to an Arcology resident based on a theory emphasizing species quantity and limited lifespan.

Selfie: Someone who is selfish, an individualist, or believes in individualism.

Sophist: A Council of Sage member serving Sophia in a specific Arcology duty. A Sigma-Class humanoid selected and upgraded from the Alpha Class.

Tabula rasa: Or blank slate. A theory that creatures are born without mental content; therefore, all knowledge comes from experience or perception.

Tactile Entertainment Immersion System (TEIS): A system that uses nanotechnology to create immersive sensory experiences. Through body-integrated interfaces, residents perceive environments and sensations as real, even though they are entirely virtual, offering escapism through the senses of touch, sight, sound, taste, and smell.

Triamene: A three-dimensional graphene compound arranged in a hexagonal lattice. Combining graphene's exceptional strength, conductivity, and flexibility with increased durability, heat resistance, and transparency, Triamene is a durable glass-like material for advanced metamaterials, energy systems, and quantum computing applications.

Universal Intelligence Quotient (UIQ): A measure of intelligence for all known sentient beings, biological or mechanical, measured primarily by synaptic operations per second (SOPS).

Volumetric Display Generator (VDG): A display that visually represents an object in three physical dimensions.

THE PEOPLE'S LANGUAGE

Apehkv (*ah-PEH-kuh*): People's village—33°19'03.1 "N 86°11'15.8" W.

Anu (*AH-noo*): Tussekeah's son.

Catē (*JAH-dee*): Red.

Ceckele (*CHAY-kay-lee*): Echaswvlke warrior.

Celvwete (*JEE-luh-weh-teh*)? Are you hungry?

Cheaha (*JEE-ha*): High point.

Cekote (*JEE-koh-teh*): Yahola's son.

Cvlvws (*JAH-luh-wes*): I am hungry.

Dela (*del-a*): Yahola's wife, matrilineal bearer of the Fuswvlke.

Ero hompskes (*EE-thloh HOM-kes*): Eat squirrel.

Echaswv (*EE-josh-wah*): Beaver.

Echaswvlke (*EE-josh-wuhl-kee*): Beaver Clan.

Ehosa (*EH-hoh-sah*): A mystical being that tricks the mind.

Enkvhēcv! (*en-kuh-HAY-juh*)! Go back or Retreat!

Ero hompetvn ce yacv (eh-roh hohm-PEH-tuhn chee YAH-juh): Do you want to eat squirrel?

Este lopoche (*es-dee loh-POH-chay*): A mythical little people.

Estepapv (*es-dee-pah-bah*): The people-eater, a mythical cougar.

Estonko cehe (*ehs-THON-koh jeh-HEH*)? How are you, my husband?

Estonko, akitv (*ehs-TOHN-koh, ah-KEE-tuhv*)? How are you, my brother?

Etenherketv (*ee-ten-HEHR-ket-uh*): Peace between us.

Estvmin cet towa (*est-tuh-MIN chet-DOE-wah*)? Where do you live?

Fuswv (*fush-wah*): Bird.

Fuswvlke (*fush-wuhl-kee*): Bird Clan.

Halona (*hah-LO-nah*): Menewa's wife and matrilineal bearer of the Echaswvlke.

Hasse Ola (*HAH-see OH-lah*): Menawa's son.

Heleshayv (*hee-leh-SHAY-yah*): Medicine Maker or healer.

Hesaketvmese (*heh-sah-KEE-duh-meh-see*): The Breath Maker. The People's Deity.

Hesci (*hes-JAY*): Hello, welcome.

Hokkolen (*HOK-koh-len*): Two.

Hoktvke pvnkv (*hok-tah-kee pun-kuh*): Women's ribbon dance.

Hompetvn ce yacv (*hom-peh-tuhn cheh ya-juh*)? Do you want to eat?

Hompvs! (*hom-bus*): Eat! Telling someone to eat.

Honvntake (*ho-nuhn-tah-kee*): Men.

Hothlepoya (*Ho-thleh-poh-yah*): Nokosvlke Warrior

Hotvle (*ho-tah-lee*): Wind.

Hotvlkvlke (*ho-tahl-kahl-kee*): Wind Clan.

Hvmken (*hum-kin*): One.

Hvtēc (huh-TEHJ): Hold! / Wait!

Hvtvm cehecares (*huh-tuhm cheh-he-jah-lees*): I will see you again. The People never say goodbye.

Hvyo Rakko (*huh-yoh thahk-koh*): Big Harvest Moon.

Korres (KOH-thles): Dig! From the root korretv, to dig.

Likepvs ce (*lee-keh-pus cheh*): Welcome, or literally, sit down.

Makēkot (*mah-KEH-koht*): Enough!

Mausi (*mow-see*): Menawa's youngest daughter.

Mausi cvhocefkv tos (*Mow-see juh-ho-jif-kuh dos*): Mausi is my name.

Mekko (*mehk-koh*): Headman, Chief.

Menewa (*meh-NAY-wah*): The Mekko, leader of the red sticks, and Nokosvlke Leader

Mvto (*muh-toh*): Thank you.

Naket cehocefkvte (*Nah-kit jeh-ho-jif-kuh-deh*)? What is your name?

Neamathla (*Neh-ah-mahth-lah*): Menawa's older brother.

Neena (*Nee-nah*): Menawa's eldest daughter.

Nene hvtke (*Neh-neh hut-kee*): The road between two friendly communities, peace road, or path of peace.

Nokose (*noh-koh-see*): Bear.

Nokosvlke (*noh-kohs-uhl-kee*): Bear clan.

Nucvs! (*noo-jus*): Go to sleep, telling someone to go to sleep.

Nvkvftvs (*nuh-guh-fuh-tus*): Assemble.

Opvnkv haco (*oh-buhn-guh hah-cho*): Stomp dance.

Osafke (*oh-sahf-kee*): Corn drink, culturally significant for the People.

Otia (Oh-tee-yah): Young Hotvlkvlke warrior.

Owlelo (*Oh-le-lo*): Nokosvlke warrior and scout.

Pasekolv (*Pah-seh-kol-uh*): Mythical trickster rabbit.

Posketv (*bohs-keh-duh*): Green Corn Ceremony.

Puyvfekcv (*poo-yuh-fek-juh*): The free soul, born in the heavens, color white, lives in the heart.

Pvce (*buh-jee*): Passenger pigeon or wild pigeon (*Ectopistes migratorius*). Endemic to North America. Reported extinct on Earth in the year 1914.

Pvskofv (*busk-oh-fuh*): Commonly referred to as the busk or busk grounds. It is the village square and ceremonial grounds.

Rakko (*thahk-koh*): Big, great.

Sabīa (*sah-bee-ah*): Colored crystal-like objects used spiritually. Sometimes said to be of vegetable origin, kept by individuals in a medicine pouch for power in hunting, love, and war.

Talof Harjo (*Dah-lof HATH-jo*): Echaswvlke Leader.

Tafv opvnkv (*TAH-fuh oh-BUN-guh*): Feather dance.

Tomucece (*toe-moh-CHEH-cheh*): Fuswvlke Leader.

Totkv Opanu (*DOHT-kuh oh-PAH-noo*): Fire dancer.

Tuccēnēn (*too-CHEE-nin*): Three.

Tuccēnēn hvmken (*too-CHEE-nin huhm-kin*): Thirty-one.

Tussekeah (*DUS-see-kee-ah*): Nokosvlke Warrior.

Vce (*uh-jee*): Corn.

Vsse (*AH-see*): Yaupon holly tea (*Llex vomitoria*). Phonetically spelled as asi.

Vpvske (*uh-BAH-skee*): Made from ground corn soaked in water and cooked until it forms a thick drink or gruel. When properly prepared, vpvske has a creamy consistency that is rich and hearty, with a slightly sweet and earthy flavor. It's served warm and often enjoyed as a nourishing and comforting beverage.

Wewoka Creek (*way-WO-ka*): "Barking Water"—a creek near the village. The name comes from *wewa* (barking) and *oka* (water).

Yafiktca (*yah-FEEK-jah*): The life soul or ghost soul, believed to originate from the earth. Associated with the intestines and the color black.

Yahola (*yah-HO-lah*): Hotvlkvlke Leader and tribe's Heleshayv. In the People's language spelled as Yvholv.

Yvkvpes (*yuh-kuh-BES*): Walk?

Yvnvsv (*yuh-NUH-suh*): Buffalo or American Bison.

∧ FINAL WORD FROM THE ∧RC

If 2525: Gardens and Creeks moved you—even just a little—your voice can carry it further.

A short review on Amazon, Goodreads, or wherever you found the book helps new readers discover it. Even a few words matter. In today's world, stories rise or fade not by merit alone, but by the memories they leave behind.

Let your trace become part of the record.

Let others know the Arc is worth entering.

More is coming in the Kallipolis series. Join the mailing list at **www.barryrainwater.com** to be part of the journey.

With gratitude

—B.R.

ΛBOUT THE ΛUTHOR

Barry Rainwater writes speculative science fiction from a quiet place in his home where memory and myth converge. After years in military service, corporate management, and university teaching, Barry turned to storytelling that questions control, free will, and the human journey.

2525: Gardens and Creeks blends ancient ideas with futuristic visions, exploring the cost of engineered bliss—and the quiet courage to question it.

When not writing, Barry travels with his family, navigates theme parks with tactical joy, and reflects on life's deeper patterns. He lives in Florida and remains endlessly curious about our future.

To learn more about the world of *2525*, visit:

BARRYRAINWATER.COM